The Best
AMERICAN
SHORT
STORIES
1985

The Best
AMERICAN
SHORT
STORIES
1985

Selected from
U.S. and Canadian Magazines
by Gail Godwin
with Shannon Ravenel

With an Introduction by Gail Godwin

 1985

Houghton Mifflin Company Boston

Shannon Ravenel is grateful to Margaret Doyle and Tina Brawn, who gave valuable consultation on science fiction and science fantasy.

ISSN 0067-6233
ISBN 0-395-36450-7
ISBN 0-395-39058-3 (pbk.)

Printed in the United States of America

V 10 9 8 7 6 5 4 3 2 1

Contents

Publisher's Note

The *Best American Short Stories* series was started in 1915 under the editorship of Edward J. O'Brien. Its title reflects the optimism of a time when people assumed that an objective "best" could be identified, even in fields not measurable in physical terms.

Martha Foley took over as editor of the series in 1942 when Mr. O'Brien was killed in World War II. With her husband, Whit Burnett, she had edited *Story* magazine since 1931, and in later years she taught creative writing at Columbia School of Journalism. When Miss Foley died in 1977, at the age of eighty, she was at work on what would have been her thirty-seventh volume of *The Best American Short Stories*.

Beginning with the 1978 edition, Houghton Mifflin introduced a new editorial arrangement for the anthology. Inviting a different writer or critic to edit each new annual volume would provide a variety of viewpoints to enliven the series and broaden its scope. *Best American Short Stories* has thus become a series of informed but differing opinions that gains credibility from its very diversity.

Also beginning with the 1978 volume, the guest editors have worked with the annual editor, Shannon Ravenel, who during each calendar year reads as many qualifying short stories as she can get hold of, makes a preliminary selection of 120 stories for the guest editor's consideration, and selects the "100 Other Distinguished Short Stories of the Year," a listing that has always been an important feature of these volumes.

The stories chosen for this year's anthology were originally published in magazines issued between January 1984 and January 1985. The qualifications for selection are: (1) original publication in nationally distributed American or Canadian periodicals; (2) publication in English by writers who are American or Canadian; and (3) publication *as* short stories (novel excerpts are not knowingly considered by the editors). A list of the magazines consulted by Ms. Ravenel appears at the back of this volume. Other publications wishing to make sure that their contributors are considered for the series should include Ms. Ravenel on their subscription list (P.O. Box 3176, University City, Missouri 63130).

Introduction

Our perceptions are sharpest when we're estranged. We can see the shape of things.
— E. L. Doctorow, "The Leather Man"

He was amazed to note the range of emotion in the cluck of a chicken. Fear and anxiety soon gave way to a soft, throaty warbling for reassurance. Huggins responded.
— Wright Morris, "Fellow-Creatures"

I'm still the man in this story, and Sarah is still the woman, but I'm telling it this way because what I have to tell you now confuses me, embarrasses me, and makes me sad, and consequently, I'm likely to tell it falsely.
— Russell Banks, "Sarah Cole: A Type of Love Story"

"We gave it all the surfaces of fantasy — dark walnut, wind instruments, candlelight, chimes. For you, conscious fantasy is enthralling. For images, on the other hand, it is the blackest despair. All the acts we might have carried out we knew in advance to be artifice. So we sat in that quiet, horrible room, unable to speak or raise our heads or even cry."
— Bev Jafek, "You've Come a Long Way, Mickey Mouse"

THE ABOVE IS MEANT to serve as a little overture to the selections that follow. Though the main criterion for my choices could be expressed by the simple *Sic enim mihi placuit*, because such is my pleasure, the motto of this collection might well be: "Tell me something I need to know — about art, about the world, about human behavior, about myself."

Any assemblage put together by an individual and labeled "the best of" is bound to be a reflection of that person's tastes

and values, as well as a revealing showcase of her pet subjects
and idiosyncrasies; but it has been a treat for me, in these times
when personal judgment is frequently eroded and diluted by
committee meetings and group consensuses, to exercise the au-
tocrat's refreshing freedom of choice. The twenty stories in this
volume are here because I thought they were the best of the 120
sent to me by Shannon Ravenel (122, actually: we had to dis-
qualify two of my favorites at the beginning, Robb Forman
Dew's "Silverfish" and Louise Erdrich's "Sainte Marie," because
they were parts of novels; then, at the last minute, Mark Hel-
prin's "Palais de Justice," which I admired, had to be bumped
because it had been originally published in an earlier year) and
the best of the stories I had read in magazines during 1984. I
chose sixteen of the stories from Shannon's batch; the other
four, Margaret Edwards's "Roses," Starkey Flythe's "Walking,
Walking," Joyce Carol Oates's "Raven's Wing," and Joy Williams's "The Skater" were from my personal file.

The good news this year is that there were more stories than
ever to choose from, which led us to the corollary that more
stories were *being published* than ever before. Shannon Ravenel
culled her favorites from a total of 1,663 in 555 issues of 154
different U.S. and Canadian periodicals. "On looking back over
past records," she wrote from St. Louis, "I see that the number
of magazines has remained fairly consistent while the number
of eligible stories has risen. This is the largest number of stories
I've ever covered, by about 200."

In one of our phone conversations, I tried to worm out of her
what her pet subjects were, and she did go so far as to admit a
predilection for stories about children. I in turn admitted to a
weakness for stories about fathers. But ultimately, we agreed,
our preferences were for the stories we remembered vividly
regardless of subject matter, those stories that left us with the
impression that they had demanded to be written. In fact, there
are only two stories that can be described as being "about" children, H. E. Francis's "The Sudden Trees" and Joy Williams's
"The Skater," but these stories are also "about" death, so there
goes that neat category. As for father stories, this year's crop
was a vintage harvest. Though I finally chose only one, Deborah
Seabrooke's "Secrets," I could have compiled an anthology. I

particularly liked Mary Morris's "Conquering Space," William Maxwell's "My Father's Friends," Joan Givner's "The Lost Sheep," Max Apple's "Bridging," Norma E. Depledge's "Except I Shall See in His Hands the Print of the Nails," and Stephen Dixon's "Wheels."

How did I go about choosing the stories you find here? Well, a registered packet would arrive from Shannon in St. Louis (there were four thick ones between July and February), and I would sit down on the sofa with a pile of stapled tearsheets, or I would carry off a stack to bed, and then I would simply shuffle through, inviting a first sentence or paragraph to snare me. Of course I found that many an arresting opening leads to a slackening middle or end, but when you are in the grip of a good story, you experience elation. As desire (for something to happen, for something to be revealed) takes on a definite shape, you begin to count on the story to fulfill the expectations it is arousing in you. As trust grows, there may even be a feeling of being in partnership with the author. If this trust lasts to the conclusion, the story attains the status of inevitability in your memory. You see it as always having moved toward this ending; it couldn't have been as satisfactory any other way, given the trail of events and images that followed that first sentence or paragraph.

Three of the stories in this volume caught me up in their opening lines and proved steadfast to the end. I was immediately attracted to the narrator's voice in Russell Banks's "Sarah Cole: A Type of Love Story." Even the title expresses Ron's dogged intention not to let himself off easy, his determination to get to the bottom of something that cannot be comfortably classified. This narrator is prepared to risk embarrassment and artlessness in order to *understand.* That this artlessness — the refusal to let narrative flow or consistent point of view lead him away from his quest — *becomes* the art is the story's own reward. Banks also helped me clarify something about the nature of innovative fiction. Truly experimental writing is forced from the pressures of the material, not imposed on it by the writer's whim or wish to be "original."

John L'Heureux's "Clothing" and Marjorie Sandor's "The

Gittel" also won me over with their first lines. I like stories about people who live intense and scrutinized inner lives, and when a writer as proven in that sort of fiction as L'Heureux begins with, "Conor had been a Jesuit for sixteen years now," I can take it on faith that this is my kind of story. (This one exceeded my hopes in its masterful stripping away of some of the kinds of illusions in which we clothe our deepest decisions.) "The Gittel," through the rhythm and language at the beginning, promised a tale of traditional dimensions but with modern implications — and Sandor delivered, with powerful resonances attained as much by the method of the telling as by the awful reality into which the innocent dreamer walks.

So choosing those first three was easy. I put them into my "Priority" folder, where, over the months, they successfully sat out their contenders.

Then there were the stories I kept passing by because I was wary of how they began. I was afraid they would turn out to be the kinds of stories I like least. I'm talking about the ones where you know from the start that the writer is posing, or holding back, or trying to project a voiceprint rather than risk speaking in a real voice. Or the story that is choked from its outset by trendiness or condescension. I have learned to recoil at openings like (I'm making these up): "Sondra, fiddling with the strap of her Gucci watch, waits in the Express Checkout line to pay for her blueberry yogurt and arugula leaves." Or: "Noreen is catching the leaks from the ceiling of their single-wide mobile home in her husband's GM cap." I don't believe in Sondra and Noreen. I rather suspect their authors of doing market research into ordinariness so that I will conclude that "the Sondras" and "the Noreens" are capable of only a limited response to life. Why they should want me to conclude this I haven't yet figured out.

So gun-shy of this type of opening have I become that I at first mistook Sharon Sheehe Stark's fine story for a "Noreen." Was I ever wrong. "The Johnstown Polka" is a *rebuttal* of the notion that people are easily judged, or that you can predict anyone's actions on the basis of exterior trappings. But I would have missed the point had I not felt duty bound to persist beyond the opening sentence.

I include this small confession of antipathies to give you a back room glimpse of the selection process, which, I believe, is as individual as the vagaries and the passions and the prejudices of each judge. I learned a lot about myself as a choosing creature as I scanned these piles of stories, heading for the most promising ones as a bug homes in on the brightest lights. After I had exhausted that "first impression method," I adopted other approaches equally impulsive or idiosyncratic. I had no organized program. I didn't go in for any sort of equalizations. At one point, I looked down at my list of "chosens" and saw that I had eight stories, so far, by men and only one by a woman. Oh God, I thought, this will never do. But I was determined to keep faith with my first choices and leave statistics to the sociologists. Fate, however, was kind, and I ended up with a ten-to-ten ratio without having to compromise.

The Doctorow and the Oates and the Wright Morris and the Joy Williams choices were initiated by my "trusted author bias" method. I have become familiar with and admired these writers' sensibilities, and so, when I spotted their names, I stopped and read their stories. There were three by Oates, and Shannon Ravenel wondered why I hadn't found *her* favorite irresistible (she liked the weird one, "Harrow Street at Linden," about a repressed couple living vicariously off their more sensual neighbors' marriage). I admitted that I had read this with a writhing attentiveness, but that "Raven's Wing," about the pickpocket and the wondrously healing horse, wound itself around my mind, as the wife in the story winds that twist of stiff black tail hair around her wrist at the end. There were two excellent stories by Wright Morris, who always has something to say, and I believed, right up until the time I was writing this introduction, that I had chosen "Going Into Exile," because it explained to me, in that oblique way only art can, something about how the South has changed. But at the last minute "Fellow-Creatures" displaced it: I remembered those cows, with their craggy, primitive masks of faces, congregating on the deck of a house "like guests at a cocktail party." And like Colonel Huggins, U.S. Army, retired, who is "amazed to note the range of emotion in the cluck of a chicken," I underwent a change.

You see what I mean? Vagaries.

But a connecting thread does run through these Top Twenty despite my slippery *modus operandi*. Every story I have chosen is a skillfully rendered, compassionate foray into a unique combination of individual experiences, whether it is a retired colonel's visionary relationship with an undersized pullet named Lucy or a handsome man's nagging memory of his obsessive love affair with an ugly woman — or Mickey Mouse's own account of how we have made him suffer! The paradox I have discovered, in writing and in reading the writing of others, is that the more you respect and focus on the singular and the strange, the more you become aware of the universal and the infinite. Michael Bishop's "Dogs' Lives" is a felicitous illustration of how this paradox operates: Look at what can be made, through imagination, memory, and the ability to *connect*, out of a particular black Great Dane stalking into a freshman classroom and releasing his "power and aloofness." Or watch the ripple effect in the consciousness of one sixty-nine-year-old astronomy teacher as a result of his confrontation with a coarse neighbor who is determined to cut down his venerable elm, in Ethan Canin's "Emperor of the Air."

The seemingly endless combinations of individual experiences of human evil have provoked the storyteller's imagination since ancient times. Take just a single branch of evil — exploitation — and see how many variations of subject matter and artistic treatment you get in five stories. Angela, in Bharati Mukherjee's story of the Bangladesh girl adopted by an Iowa family, has built a new life on sheer gratitude for having survived a savage and mutilating physical exploitation. But can her New World spirit survive the "kind" and persistent courtship of Dr. Menezies, who comes from "the same subcontinent of hunger and misery"? Lily, Jane Smiley's lovely spinster-poet, invites two married friends to visit her, hoping they can help her discover why, despite all her prizes and fan letters, no one wants to love her. The couple bring their turbulent, dying marriage to her, use her to stir up its embers, and leave her frightened of her own accomplished and organized life. In "Raven's Wing," we experience the exploiter through his own (sympathetic) consciousness. So far inside his skin are we that we aren't really aware of what he has been *doing* until the end. We see him as he sees himself: a guy who's had some rotten luck and so can treasure the good omen of a spirited racehorse who survives a shattered leg. Peter Meinke's piano tuner *is* Exploitation, a huge, hairy symbol-made-flesh who is allowed by the passive narrator to wreck his home. As the story unfolds with all the inevitability of a bad dream, we become uneasily aware that there is collusion between the "civilized" capitulator and the violent intruder. It is a very modern parable. "Walking, Walking," by Starkey Flythe, takes a surprising tack, turning a crooked funeral director's outrageous gypping of an old woman into a bizarre opportunity for grace. Rosa is utterly believable in her individuality: from the "light-skinned friend" she invents to keep her company after her son's death to her "virtue in letting go," which baffles the law enforcement officers who fully expected her to force them to bring the undertaker to justice.

Looking over my list, I see that I have picked three stories about seduction. Margaret Edwards's "Roses," though the story of an emancipated woman's one night stand, is notable for its freshness, its refusal to take a jaded view.

It is May, and roses are blooming in carefully groomed plots. She is still experiencing the wonderment of disorientation. Her mind is putting down rudimentary paths in what is otherwise a blank acreage of the unfamiliar. Directly in her line of sight sits a handsome man.

Whereas Norman Rush's seducer in "Instruments of Seduction" is a more sinister character. Her *method* has become her rapture. This is a cold *frisson* of a story, which had for me the attraction of an elegant weapon lying in wait on a bed of silk.

Beth Nugent's "City of Boys" shocked me into including it. It is streetwise and raw, and the "lady" who resides somewhere inside me kept protesting, "You don't want to put *this* in your book, surely." But I read on, and the story stayed with me, and I did. Shocking the "lady" may be what this story's all about.

What makes Deborah Seabrooke's "Secrets" art, rather than just a fascinating description of a family of resolute individualists and of all the havoc caused by their independent pursuits, is the narrator's ability to pull the whole thing together with an illuminating counterbalance in nature, the school of big brown bass in the hatchery at home, "swimming in perfect synchronization along the slippery walls of their tanks."

> "I'm going to go upstairs to change," he said, "then try to pull the day together at the lab." Pull the day together. That was what you did. When the water's surface broke and gave you glimpses of the harmony below, of how we could all have gently swum together like a school of fish, it only made you realize such beauty wasn't in you.

Joy Williams's "The Skater" and H. E. Francis's "The Sudden Trees" are both concerned with the death of children. Williams's laconic style, with its spare vocabulary and short sentences, corresponds exactly with the manner in which a bereaved family parcels out to itself as much memory as it can bear of a dead daughter while interviewing potential boarding schools for the surviving daughter. "The Sudden Trees" is a testament of how far compassion can reach when someone (in this case, a lonely teacher who adopts a dying girl) decides to immerse himself in the experience of another. It exerts an uncanny power through its close-range focus, its "hold back nothing" account of one person's journey into another's death.

Bev Jafek's "You've Come a Long Way, Mickey Mouse" and E. L. Doctorow's "The Leather Man" each in its original way offers thought-provoking insights into our culture. Jafek offers a playful but profound indictment of our insatiable need for images. Not the least of the pleasures I got from this story was imagining how the figure of Mickey had grown (to six feet four, no less), in the writer's mind, into the tall and velvety talk show guest, "eyes shining like wet coal and wet diamonds, dressed fit to kill, and every bit of fur combed and glowing," who explains why he doesn't see Minnie anymore. What came first, I wondered, the conception of an incarnated Mickey as an embodiment of our swollen needs, or the recognition of certain ironies shimmering behind a cigarette ad? And how did the two coalesce into a story that demanded to be written? (That is the kind of thing writers are always wondering about the stories of other writers they admire.)

As for Doctorow's, well, I can't fathom all the reasons for its lasting effect on me.

"Who is this Slater, do you think?" I asked Shannon Ravenel one Sunday in February, when I had phoned her long distance to inquire about the eligibility of a story I wanted to include. Then we got around to discussing some of the other stories, which brought us to "The Leather Man."

"I'm not sure," said Shannon, who speaks with those soft consonants that make me nostalgic for my Southern childhood. "But I think he and the other man are sort of combination policemen and psychologists."

We kept the wires humming between Woodstock and St. Louis a little longer, mulling over why this story had illuminated some problematic corner of existence for us and made us meditate on our condition as solitary souls living tenuously on a crowded earth, but inveterately curious about one another.

"Well, anyway," Shannon concluded, "I really like that story."

I still don't know who Slater is, but I really like it, too.

GAIL GODWIN

RUSSELL BANKS

Sarah Cole: A Type of Love Story

(FROM THE MISSOURI REVIEW)

TO BEGIN, THEN, here is a scene in which I am the man and my friend Sarah Cole is the woman. I don't mind describing it now, because I'm a decade older and don't look the same now as I did then, and Sarah is dead. That is to say, on hearing this story you might think me vain if I looked the same now as I did then, because I must tell you that I was extremely handsome then. And if Sarah were not dead, you'd think I was cruel, for I must tell you that Sarah was very homely. In fact, she was the homeliest woman I have ever known. Personally, I mean. I've *seen* a few women who were more unattractive than Sarah, but they were clearly freaks of nature or had been badly injured or had been victimized by some grotesque, disfiguring disease. Sarah, however, was quite normal, and I knew her well, because for three and a half months we were lovers.

Here is the scene. You can put it in the present, even though it took place ten years ago, because nothing that matters to the story depends on when it took place, and you can put it in Concord, New Hampshire, even though that is indeed where it took place, because it doesn't matter where it took place, so it might as well be Concord, New Hampshire, a place I happen to know well and can therefore describe with sufficient detail to make the story believable. Around six o'clock on a Wednesday evening in late May a man enters a bar. The place, a cocktail lounge at street level with a restaurant upstairs, is decorated with hanging plants and unfinished wood paneling, butcher-block tables and captain's chairs, with a half dozen darkened, thickly upholstered booths along one wall. Three or four men between the ages of twenty-five and thirty-five are drinking at the bar, and they, like the man who has just entered, wear three-piece suits and loosened neckties. They are probably lawyers, young, unmarried lawyers gossiping with their brethren over martinis so as to postpone arriving home alone at their white-washed townhouse apartments, where they will fix their evening meals in Radaranges and, afterwards, while their TVs chuckle quietly in front of them, sit on their couches and do a little extra work for tomorrow. They are, for the most part, honorable, educated, hard-working, shallow, and moderately unhappy young men. Our man, call him Ronald, Ron, in most ways is like these men, except that he is unusually good-looking, and that makes him a little less unhappy than they. Ron is effortlessly attractive, a genetic wonder, tall, slender, symmetrical, and clean. His flaws, a small mole on the left corner of his square but not-too-prominent chin, a slight excess of blond hair on the tops of his tanned hands, and somewhat underdeveloped buttocks, insofar as they keep him from resembling too closely a men's store mannequin, only contribute to his beauty, for he is beautiful, the way we usually think of a woman as being beautiful. And he is nice, too, the consequence, perhaps, of his seeming not to know how beautiful he is, to men as well as women, to young people, even children, as well as old, to attractive people, who realize immediately that he is so much more attractive than they as not to be competitive with them, as well as unattractive people, who see him and gain thereby a comforting perspective on those they have heretofore envied for their good looks.

Ron takes a seat at the bar, unfolds the evening paper in front of him, and before he can start reading, the bartender asks to help him, calling him "Sir," even though Ron has come into this bar numerous times at this time of day, especially since his divorce last fall. Ron got divorced because, after three years of marriage, his wife had chosen to pursue the career that his had interrupted, that of a fashion designer, which meant that she had to live in New York City while he had to continue to live in New Hampshire, where his career had got its start. They agreed to live apart until he could continue his career near New York

City, but after a few months, between conjugal visits, he started
sleeping with other women, and she started sleeping with other
men, and that was that. "No big deal," he explained to friends,
who liked both Ron and his wife, even though he was slightly
more beautiful than she. "We really were too young when we
got married, college sweethearts. But we're still best friends," he
assured them. They understood. Most of Ron's friends were
divorced by then too.

Ron orders a scotch and soda, with a twist, and goes back to
reading his paper. When his drink comes, before he takes a sip
of it, he first carefully finishes reading an article about the recent re-appearance of coyotes in northern New Hampshire and
Vermont. He lights a cigarette. He goes on reading. He takes a
second sip of his drink. Everyone in the room, the three or four
men scattered along the bar, the tall, thin bartender, and several
people in the booths at the back, watches him do these ordinary
things.

He has got to the classified section, is perhaps searching for
someone willing to come in once a week and clean his apartment, when the woman who will turn out to be Sarah Cole leaves
a booth in the back and approaches him. She comes up from
the side and sits next to him. She's wearing heavy, tan cowboy
boots and a dark brown, suede cowboy hat, lumpy jeans and a
yellow tee shirt that clings to her arms, breasts, and round belly
like the skin of a sausage. Though he will later learn that she is
thirty-eight years old, she looks older by about ten years, which
makes her look about twenty years older than he actually is. (It's
difficult to guess accurately how old Ron is; he looks anywhere
from a mature twenty-five to a youthful forty, so his actual age
doesn't seem to matter.)

"It's not bad here at the bar," she says, looking around. "More
light, anyhow. Whatcha readin'?" she asks brightly, planting
both elbows on the bar.

Ron looks up from his paper with a slight smile on his lips,
sees the face of a woman homelier than any he has ever seen or
imagined before, and goes on smiling lightly. He feels himself
falling into her tiny, slightly crossed, dark brown eyes, pulls
himself back, and studies for a few seconds her mottled, pocked
complexion, bulbous nose, loose mouth, twisted and gapped

teeth, and heavy but receding chin. He casts a glance over her thatch of dun-colored hair and along her neck and throat, where acne burns against gray skin, and returns to her eyes, and again feels himself falling into her.

"What did you say?" he asks.

She knocks a mentholated cigarette from her pack, and Ron swiftly lights it. Blowing smoke from her large, wing-shaped nostrils, she speaks again. Her voice is thick and nasal, a chocolate-colored voice. "I asked you whatcha readin', but I can see now." She belts out a single, loud laugh. "The paper!"

Ron laughs, too. "The paper! *The Concord Monitor!*" He is not hallucinating, he clearly sees what is before him and admits — no, he asserts — to himself that he is speaking to the most unattractive woman he has ever seen, a fact which fascinates him, as if instead he were speaking to the most beautiful woman he has ever seen or perhaps ever will see, so he treasures the moment, attempts to hold it as if it were a golden ball, a disproportionately heavy object which — if he doesn't hold it lightly yet with precision and firmness — will slip from his hand and roll across the lawn to the lip of the well and down, down to the bottom of the well, lost to him forever. It will be merely a memory, something to speak of wistfully and with wonder as over the years the image fades and comes in the end to exist only in the telling. His mind and body waken from their sleepy self-absorption, and all his attention focuses on the woman, Sarah Cole, her ugly face, like a wart hog's, her thick, rapid voice, her dumpy, off-center wreck of a body, and to keep this moment here before him, he begins to ask questions of her, he buys her a drink, he smiles, until soon it seems, even to him, that he is taking her and her life, its vicissitudes and woe, quite seriously.

He learns her name, of course, and she volunteers the information that she spoke to him on a dare from one of the two women still sitting in the booth behind her. She turns on her stool and smiles brazenly, triumphantly, at her friends, two women, also homely (though nowhere as homely as she) and dressed, like her, in cowboy boots, hats and jeans. One of the women, a blonde with an underslung jaw and wearing heavy eye makeup, flips a little wave at her, and as if embarrassed, she and the other woman at the booth turn back to their drinks and sip fiercely at straws.

Sarah returns to Ron and goes on telling him what he wants to know, about her job at the Rumford Press, about her divorced husband who was a bastard and stupid and "sick," she says, as if filling suddenly with sympathy for the man. She tells Ron about her three children, the youngest, a girl, in junior high school and boy-crazy, the other two, boys, in high school and almost never at home anymore. She speaks of her children with genuine tenderness and concern, and Ron is touched. He can see with what pleasure and pain she speaks of her children; he watches her tiny eyes light up and water over when he asks their names.

"You're a nice woman," he informs her.

She smiles, looks at her empty glass. "No. No, I'm not. But you're a nice man, to tell me that."

Ron, with a gesture, asks the bartender to refill Sarah's glass. She is drinking white Russians. Perhaps she has been drinking them for an hour or two, for she seems very relaxed, more relaxed than women usually do when they come up and without introduction or invitation speak to him.

She asks him about himself, his job, his divorce, how long he has lived in Concord, but he finds that he is not at all interested in telling her about himself. He wants to know about her, even though what she has to tell him about herself is predictable and ordinary and the way she tells it unadorned and clichéd. He wonders about her husband. What kind of man would fall in love with Sarah Cole?

II

That scene, at Osgood's Lounge in Concord, ended with Ron's departure, alone, after having bought Sarah's second drink, and Sarah's return to her friends in the booth. I don't know what she told them, but it's not hard to imagine. The three women were not close friends, merely fellow workers at Rumford Press, where they stood at the end of a long conveyor belt day after day packing *TV Guides* into cartons. They all hated their jobs, and frequently after work, when they worked the day shift, they would put on their cowboy hats and boots, which they kept all day in their lockers, and stop for a drink or two on their way home. This had been their first visit to Osgood's, a place that, prior to this, they had avoided out of a sneering belief that no one went there but lawyers and insurance men. It had been Sarah who had asked the others why that should keep them away, and when they had no answer for her, the three had decided to stop at Osgood's. Ron was right, they had been there over an hour when he came in, and Sarah was a little drunk. "We'll hafta come in here again," she said to her friends, her voice rising slightly.

Which they did, that Friday, and once again Ron appeared with his evening newspaper. He put his briefcase down next to his stool and ordered a drink and proceeded to read the front page, slowly, deliberately, clearly a weary, unhurried, solitary man. He did not notice the three women in cowboy hats and boots in the booth in back, but they saw him, and after a few minutes Sarah was once again at his side.

"Hi."

He turned, saw her, and instantly regained the moment he had lost when, the previous night, once outside the bar, he had forgotten about the ugliest woman he had ever seen. She seemed even more grotesque to him now than before, which made the moment all the more precious to him, and so once again he held the moment as if in his hands and began to speak with her, to ask questions, to offer his opinions and solicit hers.

I said earlier that I am the man in this story and my friend Sarah Cole, now dead, is the woman. I think back to that night, the second time I had seen Sarah, and I tremble, not with fear but in shame. My concern then, when I was first becoming involved with Sarah, was merely with the moment, holding on to it, grasping it wholly as if its beginning did not grow out of some other prior moment in her life and my life separately and at the same time did not lead into future moments in our separate lives. She talked more easily than she had the night before, and I listened as eagerly and carefully as I had before, again, with the same motives, to keep her in front of me, to draw her forward from the context of her life and place her, as if she were an object, into the context of mine. I did not know how cruel this was. When you have never done a thing before and that thing is not simply and clearly right or wrong, you frequently do not know if it is a cruel thing, you just go ahead and do it, and maybe later you'll be able to determine whether you acted cruelly. That way you'll know if it was right or wrong of you to have done it in the first place.

While we drank, Sarah told me that she hated her ex-husband because of the way he treated the children. "It's not so much the money," she said, nervously wagging her booted feet from her perch on the high barstool. "I mean, I get by, barely, but I get them fed and clothed on my own okay. It's because he won't even write them a letter or anything. He won't call them on the phone, all he calls for is to bitch at me because I'm trying to get the state to take him to court so I can get some of the money he's s'posed to be paying for child support. And he won't even think to talk to the kids when he calls. Won't even ask about them."

"He sounds like a bastard," I said.

"He is, he is," she said. "I don't know why I married him. Or stayed married. Fourteen years, for Christ's sake. He put a spell over me or something, I don't know," she said with a note of wistfulness in her voice. "He wasn't what you'd call good-looking."

After her second drink, she decided she had to leave. Her children were at home, it was Friday night and she liked to make sure she ate supper with them and knew where they were going and who they were with when they went out on their dates. "No dates on schoolnights," she said to me. "I mean, you gotta have rules, you know."

I agreed, and we left together, everyone in the place following us with his or her gaze. I was aware of that, I knew what they were thinking, and I didn't care, because I was simply walking her to her car.

It was a cool evening, dusk settling onto the lot like a gray blanket. Her car, a huge, dark green Buick sedan at least ten years old, was battered, scratched, and almost beyond use. She reached for the door handle on the driver's side and yanked. Nothing. The door wouldn't open. She tried again. Then I tried. Still nothing.

Then I saw it, a V-shaped dent in the left front fender creasing the fender where the door joined it, binding the metal of the door against the metal of the fender in a large crimp that held the door fast. "Someone must've backed into you while you were inside," I said to her.

She came forward and studied the crimp for a few seconds, and when she looked back at me, she was weeping. "Jesus, Jesus, Jesus!" she wailed, her large, frog-like mouth wide open and wet with spit, her red tongue flopping loosely over gapped teeth. "I can't pay for this! I *can't!*" Her face was red, and even in the dusky light I could see it puff out with weeping, her tiny eyes seeming almost to disappear behind wet cheeks. Her shoulders slumped, and her hands fell limply to her sides.

Placing my briefcase on the ground, I reached out to her and put my arms around her body and held her close to me, while she cried wetly into my shoulder. After a few seconds, she started pulling herself back together and her weeping got reduced to sniffling. Her cowboy hat had been pushed back and now clung to her head at a precarious, absurdly jaunty angle. She took a step away from me and said, "Ill get in the other side."

"Okay," I said almost in a whisper. "That's fine."

Slowly, she walked around the front of the huge, ugly vehicle and opened the door on the passenger's side and slid awkwardly across the seat until she had positioned herself behind the steering wheel. Then she started the motor, which came to life with a roar. The muffler was shot. Without saying another word to me, or even waving, she dropped the car into reverse gear and backed it loudly out of the parking space and headed out the lot to the street.

I turned and started for my car, when I happened to glance toward the door of the bar, and there, staring after me, were the bartender, the two women who had come in with Sarah, and two of the men who had been sitting at the bar. They were lawyers, and I knew them slightly. They were grinning at me. I grinned back and got into my car, and then, without looking at them again, I left the place and drove straight to my apartment.

III

One night several weeks later, Ron meets Sarah at Osgood's, and after buying her three white Russians and drinking three

scotches himself, he takes her back to his apartment in his car
— a Datsun fastback coupe that she says she admires — for the
sole purpose of making love to her.

I'm still the man in this story, and Sarah is still the woman,
but I'm telling it this way because what I have to tell you now
confuses me, embarrasses me, and makes me sad, and consequently, I'm likely to tell it falsely. I'm likely to cover the truth
by making Sarah a better woman than she actually was, while
making myself appear worse than I actually was or am; or else
I'll do the opposite, make Sarah worse than she was and me
better. The truth is, I was pretty, extremely so, and she was not,
extremely so, and I knew it and she knew it. She walked out the
door of Osgood's determined to make love to a man much pret-
tier than any she had seen up close before, and I walked out
determined to make love to a woman much homelier than any
I had made love to before. We were, in a sense, equals.

No, that's not exactly true. (You see? This is why I have to tell
the story the way I'm telling it.) I'm not at all sure she feels as
Ron does. That is to say, perhaps she genuinely likes the man,
in spite of his being the most physically attractive man she has
ever known. Perhaps she is more aware of her homeliness than
of his beauty, just as he is more aware of her homeliness than
of his beauty, for Ron, despite what I may have implied, does
not think of himself as especially beautiful. He merely knows
that other people think of him that way. As I said before, he is
a nice man.

Ron unlocks the door to his apartment, walks in ahead of her,
and flicks on the lamp beside the couch. It's a small, single
bedroom, modern apartment, one of thirty identical apartments
in a large brick building on the heights just east of downtown
Concord. Sarah stands nervously at the door, peering in.

"Come in, come in," he says.

She steps timidly in and closes the door behind her. She removes her cowboy hat, then quickly puts it back on, crosses the
livingroom, and plops down in a blond easychair, seeming to
shrink in its hug out of sight to safety. Ron, behind her, at the
entry to the kitchen, places one hand on her shoulder, and she
stiffens. He removes his hand.

"Would you like a drink?"

"No . . . I guess not," she says, staring straight ahead at the wall opposite where a large framed photograph of a bicyclist advertises in French the Tour de France. Around a corner, in an alcove off the living room, a silver-gray ten-speed bicycle leans casually against the wall, glistening and poised, slender as a thoroughbred racehorse.

"I don't know," she says. Ron is in the kitchen now, making himself a drink. "I don't know . . . I don't know."

"What? Change your mind? I can make a white Russian for you. Vodka, cream, Kahlúa, and ice, right?"

Sarah tries to cross her legs, but she is sitting too low in the chair and her legs are too thick at the thigh, so she ends, after a struggle, with one leg in the air and the other twisted on its side. She looks as if she has fallen from a great height.

Ron steps out from the kitchen, peers over the back of the chair, and watches her untangle herself, then ducks back into the kitchen. After a few seconds, he returns. "Seriously. Want me to fix you a white Russian?"

"No."

Ron, again from behind, places one hand on Sarah's shoulder, and this time she does not stiffen, though she does not exactly relax, either. She sits there, a block of wood, staring straight ahead.

"Are you scared?" he asked gently. Then he adds, "*I* am."

"Well, no, I'm not scared." She remains silent for a moment. "You're scared? Of what?" She turns to face him but avoids his eyes.

"Well . . . I don't do this all the time, you know. Bring home a woman I . . . ," he trails off.

"Picked up in a bar."

"No. I mean, I like you, Sarah, I really do. And I didn't just pick you up in a bar, you know that. We've gotten to be friends, you and me."

"You want to sleep with me?" she asks, still not meeting his steady gaze.

"Yes." He seems to mean it. He does not take a gulp or even a sip from his drink. He just says, "Yes," straight out, and cleanly, not too quickly, either, and not after a hesitant delay. A simple statement of a simple fact. The man wants to make love to the woman. She asked him, and he told her. What could be simpler?

"Do you want to sleep with *me*?" he asks.

She turns around in the chair, faces the wall again, and says in a low voice, "Sure I do, but . . . it's hard to explain."

"What? But what?" Placing his glass down on the table between the chair and the sofa, he puts both hands on her shoulders and lightly kneads them. He knows he can be discouraged from pursuing this, but he is not sure how easily. Having got this far without bumping against obstacles (except the ones he has placed in his way himself), he is not sure what it will take to turn him back. He does not know, therefore, how assertive or how seductive he should be with her. He suspects that he can be stopped very easily, so he is reluctant to give her a chance to try. He goes on kneading her doughy shoulders.

"You and me . . . we're real different." She glances at the bicycle in the corner.

"A man . . . and a woman," he says.

"No, not that. I mean, different. That's all. Real different. More than you . . . you're nice, but you don't know what I mean, and that's one of the things that makes you so nice. But we're different. Listen," she says, "I gotta go. I gotta leave now."

The man removes his hands and retrieves his glass, takes a sip, and watches her over the rim of the glass, as, not without difficulty, she rises from the chair and moves swiftly toward the door. She stops at the door, squares her hat on her head, and glances back at him.

"We can be friends. Okay?"

"Okay. Friends."

"I'll see you again down at Osgood's, right?"

"Oh, yeah, sure."

"Good. See you," she says, opening the door.

The door closes. The man walks around the sofa, snaps on the television set, and sits down in front of it. He picks up a *TV Guide* from the coffee table and flips through it, stops, runs a finger down the listings, stops, puts down the magazine and changes the channel. He does not once connect the magazine in his hand to the woman who has just left his apartment, even though he knows she spends her days packing *TV Guide*s into cartons that get shipped to warehouses in distant parts of New England. He'll think of the connection some other night; but by then the connection will be merely sentimental. It'll be too late for him to understand what she meant by "different."

IV

But that's not the point of my story. Certainly it's an aspect of the story, the political aspect, if you want, but it's not the reason I'm trying to tell the story in the first place. I'm trying to tell the story so that I can understand what happened between me and Sarah Cole that summer and early autumn ten years ago. To say we were lovers says very little about what happened; to say we were friends says even less. No, if I'm to understand the whole thing, I have to say the whole thing, for, in the end, what I need to know is whether what happened between me and Sarah Cole was right or wrong. Character is fate, which suggests that if a man can know and then to some degree control his character, he can know and to that same degree control his fate.

But let me go on with my story. The next time Sarah and I were together we were at her apartment in the south end of Concord, a second-floor flat in a tenement building on Perley Street. I had stayed away from Osgood's for several weeks, deliberately trying to avoid running into Sarah there, though I never quite put it that way to myself. I found excuses and generated interests in and reasons for going elsewhere after work. Yet I was obsessed with Sarah by then, obsessed with the idea of making love to her, which, because it was not an actual *desire* to make love to her, was an unusually complex obsession. Passion without desire, if it gets expressed, may in fact be a kind of rape, and perhaps I sensed the danger that lay behind my obsession and for that reason went out of my way to avoid meeting Sarah again.

Yet I did meet her, inadvertently, of course. After picking up shirts at the cleaner's on South Main and Perley Streets, I'd gone down Perley on my way to South State and the post office. It was a Saturday morning, and this trip on my bicycle was part of my regular Saturday routine. I did not remember that Sarah lived on Perley Street, although she had told me several times

in a complaining way — it's a rough neighborhood, packed dirt
yards, shabby apartment buildings, the carcasses of old, half-
stripped cars on cinderblocks in the driveways, broken red and
yellow plastic tricycles on the cracked sidewalks — but as soon
as I saw her, I remembered. It was too late to avoid meeting
her, I was riding my bike, wearing shorts and tee shirt, the
package containing my folded and starched shirts hooked to
the carrier behind me, and she was walking toward me along
the sidewalk, lugging two large bags of groceries. She saw me,
and I stopped. We talked, and I offered to carry her groceries
for her. I took the bags while she led the bike, handling it
carefully as if she were afraid she might break it.

At the stoop we came to a halt. The wooden steps were cluttered with half-opened garbage bags spilling eggshells, coffee
grounds, and old food wrappers to the walkway. "I can't get the
people downstairs to take care of their garbage," she explained.
She leaned the bike against the banister and reached for her
groceries.

"I'll carry them up for you," I said. I directed her to loop the
chain lock from the bike to the banister rail and snap it shut and
told her to bring my shirts up with her.

"Maybe you'd like a beer?" she said as she opened the door to
the darkened hallway. Narrow stairs disappeared in front of me
into heavy, damp darkness, and the air smelled like old newspapers.

"Sure," I said and followed her up.

"Sorry there's no light. I can't get them to fix it."

"No matter. I can see you and follow along," I said, and even
in the dim light of the hall I could see the large, dark blue veins
that cascaded thickly down the backs of her legs. She wore tight,
white-duck bermuda shorts, rubber shower sandals, and a pink
sleeveless sweater. I pictured her in the cashier's line at the
supermarket. I would have been behind her, a stranger, and on
seeing her, I would have turned away and studied the covers of
the magazines, *TV Guide, People, The National Enquirer,* for there
was nothing of interest in her appearance that in the hard light
of day would not have slightly embarrassed me. Yet here I was
inviting myself into her home, eagerly staring at the backs of
her ravaged legs, her sad, tasteless clothing, her poverty. I was

not detached, however, was not staring at her with scientific curiosity, and because of my passion, did not feel or believe that what I was doing was perverse. I felt warmed by her presence and was flirtatious and bold, a little pushy, even.

Picture this. The man, tanned, limber, wearing red jogging shorts, Italian leather sandals, a clinging net tee shirt of Scandinavian design and manufacture, enters the apartment behind the woman, whose dough colored skin, thick, short body, and homely, uncomfortable face all try, but fail, to hide themselves. She waves him toward the table in the kitchen, where he sets down the bags and looks good-naturedly around the room. "What about the beer you bribed me with?" he asks. The apartment is dark and cluttered with old, oversized furniture, yard sale and second-hand stuff bought originally for a large house in the country or a spacious apartment on a boulevard forty or fifty years ago, passed down from antique dealer to used furniture store to yard sale to thrift shop, where it finally gets purchased by Sarah Cole and gets lugged over to Perley Street and shoved up the narrow stairs, she and her children grunting and sweating in the darkness of the hallway — overstuffed armchairs and couch, huge, ungainly dressers, upholstered rocking chairs, and in the kitchen, an old maple desk for a table, a half dozen heavy oak diningroom chairs, a high, glass-fronted cabinet, all peeling, stained, chipped and squatting heavily on a dark green linoleum floor.

The place is neat and arranged in a more or less orderly way, however, and the man seems comfortable there. He strolls from the kitchen to the livingroom and peeks into the three small bedrooms that branch off a hallway behind the livingroom. "Nice place!" he calls to the woman. He is studying the framed pictures of her three children arranged like an altar atop the buffet. "Nice looking kids!" he calls out. They are. Blond, round-faced, clean, and utterly ordinary-looking, their pleasant faces glance, as instructed, slightly off camera and down to the right, as if they are trying to remember the name of the capital of Montana.

When he returns to the kitchen, the woman is putting away her groceries, her back to him. "Where's that beer you bribed me with?" he asks again. He takes a position against the doorframe, his weight on one hip, like a dancer resting. "You sure are quiet today, Sarah," he says in a low voice. "Everything okay?"

Silently, she turns away from the grocery bags, crosses the room to the man, reaches up to him, and holding him by the head, kisses his mouth, rolls her torso against his, drops her hands to his hips and yanks him tightly to her, and goes on kissing him, eyes closed, working her face furiously against his. The man places his hands on her shoulders and pulls away, and they face each other, wide-eyed, as if amazed and frightened. The man drops his hands, and the woman lets go of his hips. Then, after a few seconds, the man silently turns, goes to the door, and leaves. The last thing he sees as he closes the door behind him is the woman standing in the kitchen doorframe, her face looking down and slightly to one side, wearing the same pleasant expression on her face as her children in their photographs, trying to remember the capital of Montana.

v

Sarah appeared at my apartment door the following morning, a Sunday, cool and rainy. She had brought me the package of freshly laundered shirts I'd left in her kitchen, and when I opened the door to her, she simply held the package out to me as if it were a penitent's gift. She wore a yellow rain slicker and cap and looked more like a disconsolate schoolgirl facing an angry teacher than a grown woman dropping a package off at a friend's apartment. After all, she had nothing to be ashamed of.

I invited her inside, and she accepted my invitation. I had been reading the Sunday *New York Times* on the couch and drinking coffee, lounging through the gray morning in bathrobe and pajamas. I told her to take off her wet raincoat and hat and hang them in the closet by the door and started for the kitchen to get her a cup of coffee, when I stopped, turned, and looked at her. She closed the closet door on her yellow raincoat and hat, turned around, and faced me.

What else can I do? I must describe it. I remember that moment of ten years ago as if it occurred ten minutes ago, the package of shirts on the table behind her, the newspapers scattered over the couch and floor, the sound of windblown rain washing the sides of the building outside, and the silence of the room, as we stood across from one another and watched, while we each simultaneously removed our own clothing, my robe, her blouse and skirt, my pajama top, her slip and bra, my pajama bottom, her underpants, until we were both standing naked in the harsh, gray light, two naked members of the same species, a male and a female, the male somewhat younger and less scarred than the female, the female somewhat less delicately constructed than the male, both individuals pale-skinned with dark thatches of hair in the area of their genitals, both individuals standing slackly, as if a great, protracted tension between them had at last been released.

VI

We made love that morning in my bed for long hours that drifted easily into afternoon. And we talked, as people usually do when they spend half a day or half a night in bed together. I told her of my past, named and described the people I had loved and had loved me, my ex-wife in New York, my brother in the Air Force, my father and mother in their condominium in Florida, and I told her of my ambitions and dreams and even confessed some of my fears. She listened patiently and intelligently throughout and talked much less than I. She had already told me many of these things about herself, and perhaps whatever she had to say to me now lay on the next inner circle of intimacy or else could not be spoken of at all.

During the next few weeks we met and made love often and always at my apartment. On arriving home from work, I would phone her, or if not, she would phone me, and after a few feints and dodges, one would suggest to the other that we get together tonight, and a half hour later she'd be at my door. Our lovemaking was passionate, skillful, kindly, and deeply satisfying. We didn't often speak of it to one another or brag about it, the way some couples do when they are surprised by the ease with which they have become contented lovers. We did occasionally joke and tease each other, however, playfully acknowledging that the only thing we did together was make love but that we did it so frequently there was no time for anything else.

Then one hot night, a Saturday in August, we were lying in bed atop the tangled sheets, smoking cigarettes and chatting idly, and Sarah suggested that we go out for a drink.

"Now?"

"Sure. It's early. What time is it?"

I scanned the digital clock next to the bed. "Nine-forty-nine."

"There. See?"

"That's not so early. You usually go home by eleven, you know. It's almost ten."

"No, it's only a little after nine. Depends on how you look at things. Besides, Ron, it's Saturday night. Don't you want to go out and dance or something? Or is this the only thing you know how to do?" she teased and poked me in the ribs. "You know how to dance? You like to dance?"

"Yeah, sure . . . sure, but not tonight. It's too hot. And I'm tired."

But she persisted, happily pointing out that an air-conditioned bar would be cooler than my apartment, and we didn't have to go to a dance bar, we could go to Osgood's. "As a compromise," she said.

I suggested a place called the El Rancho, a restaurant with a large, dark cocktail lounge and dance bar located several miles from town on the old Portsmouth highway. Around nine the restaurant closed and the bar became something of a roadhouse, with a small country-western houseband and a clientele drawn from the four or five villages that adjoined Concord on the north and east. I had eaten at the restaurant once but had never gone to the bar, and I didn't know anyone who had.

Sarah was silent for a moment. Then she lit a cigarette and drew the sheet over her naked body. "You don't want anybody to know about us, do you? Do you?"

"That's not it . . . I just don't like gossip, and I work with a lot of people who show up sometimes at Osgood's. On a Saturday night especially."

"No," she said firmly. "You're ashamed of being seen with me. You'll sleep with me, but you won't go out in public with me."

"That's not true, Sarah."

She was silent again. Relieved, I reached across her to the bedtable and got my cigarettes and lighter.

"You owe me, Ron," she said suddenly, as I passed over her. "You owe me."

"What?" I lay back, lit a cigarette, and covered my body with the sheet.

"I said, 'You owe me.' "

"I don't know what you're talking about, Sarah. I just don't like a lot of gossip going around, that's all. I like keeping my private life private, that's all. I don't *owe* you anything."

"Friendship you owe me. And respect. Friendship and respect. A person can't do what you've done with me without owing them friendship and respect."

"Sarah, I really don't know what you're talking about," I said. "I am your friend, you know that. And I respect you. I really do."

"You really think so, don't you?"

"Yes."

She said nothing for several long moments. Then she sighed and in a low, almost inaudible voice said, "Then you'll have to go out in public with me. I don't care about Osgood's or the people you work with, we don't have to go there or see any of them," she said. "But you're gonna have to go to places like the El Rancho with me, and a few other places I know, too, where there's people *I* work with, people *I* know, and maybe we'll even go to a couple of parties, because *I* get invited to parties sometimes, you know. I have friends, and I have some family, too, and you're gonna have to meet my family. My kids think I'm just going around bar-hopping when I'm over here with you, and I don't like that, so you're gonna have to meet them so I can tell them where I am when I'm not at home nights. And sometimes you're gonna come over and spend the evening at my place!" Her voice had risen as she heard her demands and felt their rightness, until now she was almost shouting at me. "You *owe* that to me. Or else you're a bad man. It's that simple."

It was.

VII

The handsome man is over-dressed. He is wearing a navy blue blazer, taupe shirt open at the throat, white slacks, white loafers. Everyone else, including the homely woman with the handsome man, is dressed appropriately, dressed, that is, like everyone else — jeans and cowboy boots, blouses or cowboy shirts or tee shirts with catchy sayings printed across the front, and many of the women are wearing cowboy hats pushed back and tied under their chins. The man doesn't know anyone at the bar or, if they're at a party, in the room, but the woman knows most of the people there, and she gladly introduces him. The men grin and shake his hand, slap him on his jacketed shoulder, ask him where he works, what's his line, after which they lapse into silence. The women flirt briefly with their faces, but they lapse into silence even before the men do. The woman with the man in the blazer does most of the talking for everyone. She talks for the man in the blazer, for the men standing around the refrigerator, or if they're at a bar, for the other men at the table, and for the other women, too. She chats and rambles aimlessly through loud monologues, laughs uproariously at trivial jokes, and drinks too much, until soon she is drunk, thick-tongued, clumsy, and the man has to say her goodbyes and ease her out the door to his car and drive her home to her apartment on Perley Street.

This happens twice in one week, and then three times the next — at the El Rancho, at the Ox Bow in Northwood, at Rita's and Jimmy's apartment on Thorndike Street, out in Warner at Betsy Beeler's new house, and, the last time, at a cottage on Lake Sunapee rented by some kids in shipping at Rumford Press. Ron no longer calls Sarah when he gets home from work; he waits for her call, and sometimes, when he knows it's she, he doesn't answer the phone. Usually, he lets it ring five or six times, and then he reaches down and picks up the receiver. He has taken his jacket and vest off and loosened his tie and is about to put supper, frozen manicotti, into the Radarange.

"Hello?"

"Hi."

"How're you doing?"

"Okay, I guess. A little tired."

"Still hung over?"

"No. Not really. Just tired. I hate Mondays."

"You have fun last night?"

"Well, yeah, sorta. It's nice out there, at the lake. Listen," she says, brightening. *"Whyn't you come over here tonight? The kids're all*

going out later, but if you come over before eight, you can meet them. They really want to meet you."

"You told them about me?"

"Sure. Long time ago. I'm not supposed to tell my own kids?"

Ron is silent.

"You don't want to come over here tonight. You don't want to meet my kids. No, you don't want my kids to meet you, that's it."

"No, no, it's just . . . I've got a lot of work to do . . ."

"We should talk," she announces in a flat voice.

"Yes," he says, "we should talk."

They agree that she will meet him at his apartment, and they'll talk, and they say goodbye and hang up.

While Ron is heating his supper and then eating alone at his kitchen table and Sarah is feeding her children, perhaps I should admit, since we are nearing the end of my story, that I don't actually know that Sarah Cole is dead. A few years ago I happened to run into one of her friends from the press, a blond woman with an underslung jaw. Her name, she reminded me, was Glenda; she had seen me at Osgood's a couple of times, and we had met at the El Rancho once when I had gone there with Sarah. I was amazed that she could remember me and a little embarrassed that I did not recognize her at all, and she laughed at that and said, "You haven't changed much, mister!" I pretended to recognize her, but I think she knew she was a stranger to me. We were standing outside the Sears store on South Main Street, where I had gone to buy paint. I had recently remarried, and my wife and I were redecorating my apartment.

"Whatever happened to Sarah?" I asked Glenda. "Is she still down at the press?"

"Jeez, no! She left a long time ago. Way back. I heard she went back with her ex-husband. I can't remember his name. Something Cole."

I asked her if she was sure of that, and she said no, she had only heard it around the bars and down at the press, but she had assumed it was true. People said Sarah had moved back with her ex-husband and was living in a trailer in a park near Hooksett, and the whole family had moved down to Florida that winter because he was out of work. He was a carpenter, she said.

"I thought he was mean to her. I thought he beat her up and everything. I thought she hated him," I said.

"Oh, well, yeah, he was a bastard, all right. I met him a couple of times, and I didn't like him. Short, ugly, and mean when he got drunk. But you know what they say."

"What do they say?"

"Oh, you know, about water seeking its own level."

"Sarah wasn't mean when she was drunk."

The woman laughed. "Naw, but she sure was short and ugly!" I said nothing.

"Hey, don't get me wrong, I liked Sarah. But you and her . . . well, you sure made a funny-looking couple. She probably didn't feel so self-conscious and all with her husband," the woman said seriously. "I mean, with you . . . all tall and blond, and poor old Sarah . . . I mean, the way them kids in the press room used to kid her about her looks, it was embarrassing just to hear it."

"Well . . . I loved her," I said.

The woman raised her plucked eyebrows in disbelief. She smiled. "Sure, you did, honey," she said, and she patted me on the arm. "Sure, you did." Then she let the smile drift off her face, turned and walked away.

When someone you have loved dies, you accept the fact of his or her death, but then the person goes on living in your memory, dreams and reveries. You have imaginary conversations with him or her, you see something striking and remind yourself to tell your loved one about it and then get brought up short by the knowledge of the fact of his or her death, and at night, in your sleep, the dead person visits you. With Sarah, none of that happened. When she was gone from my life, she was gone absolutely, as if she had never existed in the first place. It was only later, when I could think of her as dead and could come out and say it, my friend Sarah Cole is dead, that I was able to tell this story, for that is when she began to enter my memories, my dreams, and my reveries. In that way I learned that I truly did love her, and now I have begun to grieve over her death, to wish her alive again, so that I can say to her the things I could not know or say when she was alive, when I did not know that I loved her.

VIII

The woman arrives at Ron's apartment around eight. He hears her car, because of the broken muffler, blat and rumble into the parking lot below, and he crosses quickly from the kitchen and peers out the livingroom window and, as if through a telescope, watches her shove herself across the seat to the passenger's side to get out of the car, then walk slowly in the dusky light toward the apartment building. It's a warm evening, and she's wearing her white bermuda shorts, pink sleeveless sweater, and shower sandals. Ron hates those clothes. He hates the way the shorts cut into her flesh at the crotch and thigh, hates the large, dark caves below her arms that get exposed by the sweater, hates the flapping noise made by the sandals.

Shortly, there is a soft knock at his door. He opens it, turns away and crosses to the kitchen, where he turns back, lights a cigarette, and watches her. She closes the door. He offers her a drink, which she declines, and somewhat formally, he invites her to sit down. She sits carefully on the sofa, in the middle, with her feet close together on the floor, as if she were being interviewed for a job. Then he comes around and sits in the easy chair, relaxed, one leg slung over the other at the knee, as if he were interviewing her for the job.

"Well," he says, "you wanted to talk."

"Yes. But now you're mad at me. I can see that. I didn't do anything, Ron."

"I'm not mad at you."

They are silent for a moment. Ron goes on smoking his cigarette.

Finally, she sighs and says, "You don't want to see me anymore, do you?"

He waits a few seconds and answers, "Yes. That's right." Getting up from the chair, he walks to the silver-gray bicycle and stands before it, running a fingertip along the slender cross-bar from the saddle to the chrome plated handlebars.

"You're a son of a bitch," she says in a low voice. "You're worse than my ex-husband." Then she smiles meanly, almost sneers, and soon he realizes that she is telling him that she won't leave. He's stuck with her, she informs him with cold precision. "You think I'm just so much meat, and all you got to do is call

up the butcher shop and cancel your order. Well, now you're
going to find out different. You *can't* cancel your order. I'm not
meat, I'm not one of your pretty little girlfriends who come
running when you want them and go away when you get tired
of them. I'm *different*. I got nothing to lose, Ron. Nothing.
You're stuck with me, Ron."

He continues stroking his bicycle. "No, I'm not."

She sits back in the couch and crosses her legs at the ankles.
"I think I *will* have that drink you offered."

"Look, Sarah, it would be better if you go now."

"No," she says flatly. "You offered me a drink when I came
in. Nothing's changed since I've been here. Not for me, and not
for you. I'd like that drink you offered," she says haughtily.

Ron turns away from the bicycle and takes a step toward her.
His face has stiffened into a mask. "Enough is enough," he says
through clenched teeth. "I've given you enough."

"Fix me a drink, will you, honey?" she says with a phony smile.

Ron orders her to leave.

She refuses.

He grabs her by the arm and yanks her to her feet.

She starts crying lightly. She stands there and looks up
into his face and weeps, but she does not move toward the
door, so he pushes her. She regains her balance and goes on
weeping.

He stands back and places his fists on his hips and looks at
her. "Go on and leave, you ugly bitch," he says to her, and as he
says the words, as one by one they leave his mouth, she's transformed into the most beautiful woman he has ever seen. He
says the words again, almost tenderly. "Leave, you ugly bitch."
Her hair is golden, her brown eyes deep and sad, her mouth
full and affectionate, her tears the tears of love and loss, and
her pleading, outstretched arms, her entire body, the arms and
body of a devoted woman's cruelly rejected love. A third time
he says the words. "Leave me, you disgusting, ugly bitch." She
is wrapped in an envelope of golden light, a warm, dense haze
that she seems to have stepped into, as into a carriage. And then
she is gone, and he is alone again.

He looks around the room, as if searching for her. Sitting
down in the easy chair, he places his face in his hands. It's not
as if she has died; it's as if he has killed her.

MICHAEL BISHOP

Dogs' Lives

(FROM THE MISSOURI REVIEW)

> All knowledge, the totality of all questions and all answers, is contained in the dog.
> — Franz Kafka, "Investigations of a Dog"

I AM TWENTY-SEVEN: Three weeks ago a black Great Dane stalked into my classroom as I was passing out theme topics. My students turned about to look. One of the freshman wits made an inane remark, which I immediately topped: "That may be the biggest dog I've ever seen." Memorable retort. Two of my students sniggered.

I ushered the Great Dane into the hall. As I held its collar and maneuvered it out of English 102 (surely it was looking for the foreign language department), the dog's power and aloofness somehow coursed up my arm. Nevertheless, it permitted me to release it onto the north campus. Sinews, flanks, head. What a magnificent animal. It loped up the winter hillock outside Park Hall without looking back. Thinking on its beauty and self-possession, I returned to my classroom.

And closed the door.

TWENTY-SEVEN, AND HOLDING: All of this is true. The incident of the Great Dane has not been out of my thoughts since it happened. There is no door in my mind to close on the image of that enigmatic animal. It stalks into and out of my head whenever it wishes.

As a result, I have begun to remember some painful things about dogs and my relationships with them. The memories are accompanied by premonitions. In fact, sometimes *I* — my secret self — go inside the Great Dane's head and look through its eyes at tomorrow, or yesterday. Every bit of what I remember, every bit of what I foresee, throws light on my ties with both humankind and dogdom.

Along with my wife, my fifteen-month-old son, and a ragged miniature poodle, I live in Athens, Georgia, in a rented house that was built before World War I. We have lived here seven months. In the summer we had bats. Twice I knocked the invaders out of the air with a broom and bludgeoned them to death against the dining room floor. Now that it is winter the bats hibernate in the eaves, warmer than we are in our beds. The furnace runs all day and all night because, I suppose, no one had heard of insulation in 1910 and our fireplaces are all blocked up to keep out the bats.

At night I dream about flying into the center of the sun on the back of a winged Great Dane.

I AM EIGHT: Van Luna, Kansas. It is winter. At four o'clock in the morning a hand leads me down the cold concrete steps in the darkness of our garage. Against the wall, between a stack of automobile tires and a dismantled Ping-Pong table, a pallet of rags on which the new puppies lie. Everything smells of dog-flesh and gasoline. Outside the wind whips about frenetically, rattling the garage door.

In robe and slippers I bend down to look at the furred-over lumps that huddle against one another on their rag pile. Frisky, their mother, regards me with suspicion. Adult hands have pulled her aside. Adult hands hold her back.

"Pick one up," a disembodied adult voice commands me.

I comply.

The puppy, almost shapeless, shivers in my hands, threatens to slide out of them onto the concrete. I press my cheek against the lump of fur and let its warm, faintly fecal odor slip into my memory. I have smelled this smell before.

"Where are its eyes?"

"Don't worry, punkin," the adult voice says. "It has eyes. They just haven't opened yet."

The voice belongs to my mother. My parents have been divorced for three years.

I AM FIVE: Our ship docks while it is snowing. We live in Tokyo, Japan: Mommy, Daddy, and I.

Daddy comes home in a uniform that scratches my face when I grab his trouser leg. Government housing is where we live. On the lawn in the big yard between the houses I grab Daddy and ride his leg up to our front door. I am wearing a cowboy hat and empty holsters that go *flap flap flap* when I jump down and run inside.

Christmas presents: I am a cowboy.

The inside of the house gathers itself around me. A Japanese maid named Peanuts. (Such a funny name.) Mommy there, too. We have a radio. My pistols are in the toy box. Later, not for Christmas, they give me my first puppy. It is never in the stuffy house, only on the porch. When Daddy and I go inside from playing with it the radio is singing "How Much Is That Doggy in the Window?" Everybody in Tokyo likes that song.

The cowboy hat has a string with a bead to pull tight under my chin. I lose my hat anyway. Blackie runs off with the big dogs from the city. The pistols stay shiny in my toy box.

On the radio, always singing, is Patti Page.

DOGS I HAVE KNOWN: Blackie, Frisky, Wiggles, Seagull, Mike, Pat, Marc, Boo Boo, Susie, Mandy, Heathcliff, Pepper, Sam, Trixie, Andy, Taffy, Tristram, Squeak, Christy, Fritz, Blue, Tammi, Napoleon, Nickie, B.J., Viking, Tau, and Canicula, whom I sometimes call Threasie (or 3C, short, you see, for Cybernetic Canine Construct).

"Sorry. There are no more class cards for this section of 102."

How the spurned dogs bark, how they howl.

I AM FOURTEEN: Cheyenne Canyon, Colorado. It is August. My father and I are driving up the narrow canyon road toward Helen Hunt Falls. Dad's Labrador retriever Nick — too conspicuously my namesake — rides with us. The dog balances with his hind legs on the back seat and lolls his massive head out the driver's window, his dark mouth open to catch the wind. Smart, gentle, trained for the keen competition of field trials, Nick is an animal that I can scarcely believe belongs to us — even if he is partially mine only three months out of the year, when I visit my father during the summer.

The radio, turned up loud, tells us that the Russians have brought back to Earth from an historic mission the passengers of Sputnik V, the first two animals to be recovered safely from orbit.

They, of course, are dogs. Their names are Belka and Strelka, the latter of whom will eventually have six puppies as proof of her power to defy time as well as space.

"How 'bout that, Nick?" my father says. "How'd you like to go free-fallin' around the globe with a pretty little bitch?"

Dad is talking to the retriever, not to me. He calls me Nicholas. Nick, however, is not listening. His eyes are half shut against the wind, his ears flowing silkenly in the slipstream behind his aristocratic head.

I laugh in delight. Although puberty has not yet completely caught up with me, my father treats me like an equal. Sometimes on Saturday, when we're watching Dizzy Dean on *The Game of the Week,* he gives me my own can of beer.

We park and climb the stone steps that lead to a little bridge above the falls. Nick runs on ahead of us. Very few tourists are about. Helen Hunt Falls is more picturesque than imposing; the bridge hangs only a few feet over the mountain stream roaring and plunging beneath it. Hardly a Niagara. Nick looks down without fear, and Dad says, "Come on, Nicholas. There's a better view on up the mountain."

We cross the bridge and struggle up the hillside above the tourist shop, until the pine trunks, which we pull ourselves up by, have finally obscured the shop and the winding canyon road. Nick still scrambles ahead of us, causing small avalanches of sand and loose soil.

Higher up, a path. We can look across the intervening blueness at a series of falls that drop down five or six tiers of sloping granite and disappear in a mist of trees. In only a moment, it seems, we have walked to the highest tier.

My father sits me down with an admonition to stay put. "I'm

going down to the next slope, Nicholas, to see if I can see how
many falls there are to the bottom. Look out through the trees
there. I'll bet you can see Kansas."

"Be careful," I urge him.

The water sliding over the rocks beside me is probably not
even an inch deep, but I can easily tell that below the next
sloping of granite the entire world falls away into a canyon of
blue-green.

Dad goes down the slope. I notice that Nick, as always, is
preceding him. On the margin of granite below, the dog stops
and waits. My father joins Nick, puts his hands on his hips,
bends at the waist, and looks down into an abyss altogether
invisible to me. How far down it drops I cannot tell, but the
echo of falling water suggests no inconsequential distance.

Nick wades into the silver flashing from the white rocks. Before I can shout warning, he lowers his head to drink. The
current is not strong, these falls are not torrents — but wet stone
provides no traction and the Lab's feet go slickly out from under
him. His body twists about, and he begins to slide inexorably
through the slow silver.

"Dad! Dad!" I am standing.

My father belatedly sees what is happening. He reaches out
to grab at his dog. He nearly topples. He loses his red golf cap.

And then Nick's body drops, his straining head and forepaws
are pulled after. The red golf cap follows him down, an ironic
afterthought.

I am weeping. My father stands upright and throws his arms
above his head. "Oh my dear God!" he cries. "Oh my dear God!"
The canyon echoes these words, and suddenly the universe has
changed.

Time stops.

Then begins again.

Miraculously, even anticlimatically, Nick comes limping up to
us from the hell to which we had both consigned him. He comes
limping up through the pines. His legs and flanks tremble vio-
lently. His coat is matted and wet, like a newborn puppy's.
When he reaches us he seems not even to notice that we are
there to care for him, to take him back down the mountain into
Colorado Springs.

"He fell at least a hundred yards, Nicholas," my father says. "At least that — onto solid rock."

On the bridge above Helen Hunt Falls we meet a woman with a Dalmatian. Nick growls at the Dalmatian, his hackles in an aggressive fan. But in the car he stretches out on the back seat and ignores my attempts to console him. My father and I do not talk. We are certain that there must be internal injuries. We drive the regal Lab — AKC designation, "Black Prince Nicholas" — almost twenty miles to the veterinarian's at the Air Force Academy.

Like Belka and Strelka, he survives.

SNAPSHOT: Black Prince Nicholas returning to my father through the slate-grey verge of a Wyoming lake, a wounded mallard clutched tenderly in his jaws. The photograph is grainy, but the huge Labrador resembles a panther coming out of creation's first light: he is the purest distillation of power.

ROLL CALL FOR SPRING QUARTER: I walk into the classroom with my new roll sheets and the same well-thumbed textbook. As usual, my new students regard me with a mixture of curiosity and dispassionate calculation. But there is something funny about them this quarter.

Something *not right.*

Uneasily I begin calling the alphabetized list of their names: "Andy . . . B.J. . . . Blackie . . . Blue . . . Boo Boo . . . Canicula . . . Christy . . . Frisky . . ."

Each student responds with an inarticulate yelp rather than a healthy "Here!" As I proceed down the roll, the remainder of the class dispenses with even this courtesy. I have a surly bunch on my hands. A few have actually begun to snarl.

". . . Pepper . . . Sam . . . Seagull . . . Squeak . . ."

They do not let me finish. From the front row a collie leaps out of his seat and crashes against my lectern. I am borne to the floor by his hurtling body. Desperately I try to protect my throat.

The small classroom shakes with the thunder of my students' barking, and I can tell that all the animals on my roll have fallen upon me with the urgency of their own peculiar bloodlusts.

The fur flies. Me, they viciously devour.

Before the lights go out completely, I tell myself that it is going to be a very difficult quarter. A very difficult quarter indeed.

I AM FORTY-SIX: Old for an athlete, young for a president, maybe optimum for an astronaut. I am learning new tricks.

The year is 1992, and it has been a long time since I have taught freshman English or tried my hand at spinning monstrously improbable tales. (With the exception, of course, of this one.) I have been too busy.

After suffering a ruptured aneurysm while delivering a lecture in the spring of 1973, I underwent surgery and resigned from the English department faculty. My recovery took eight or nine months.

Outfitted with several vascular prostheses and wired for the utmost mobility, I returned to the university campus to pursue simultaneous majors in molecular biology and astrophysics. The G.I. Bill and my wife and my parents footed the largest part of our expenses — at the beginning, at least. Later, when I volunteered for a government program involving cybernetic experimentation with human beings (reasoning that the tubes in my brain were a good start on becoming a cyborg, anyway), money ceased to be a problem.

This confidential program changed me. In addition to the synthetic blood vessels in my brain, I picked up three artificial internal organs, a transparent skull cap, an incomplete auxiliary skeletal system consisting of resilient inert plastics, and a pair of removable visual adaptors that plug into a plate behind my brow and so permit me to see expertly in the dark. I can even eat wood if I have to. I can learn the most abstruse technical matters without even blinking my adaptors. I can jump off a three-story building without even jarring my kneecaps. These skills, as you may imagine, come in handy.

With a toupee, a pair of dark glasses, and a little cosmetic surgery, I could leave the government hospitals where I had undergone these changes and take up a seat in any classroom in any university in the nation. I was frequently given leave to do so. Entrance requirements were automatically waived, I never

saw a fee card, and not once did my name fail to appear on the
rolls of any of the classes I sat in on.

I studied everything. I made A pluses in everything. I could
read a textbook from cover to cover in thirty minutes and recall
even the footnotes verbatim. I awed professors who had worked
for thirty-forty years in chemistry, physics, biology, astronomy.
It was the ultimate wish-fulfillment fantasy come true, and not
all of it can be attributed to the implanted electrodes, the en-
zyme inoculations, and the brain meddlings of the government
cyberneticists. No, I have always had a talent for doing things
thoroughly.

My family suffered.

We moved many, many times, and for days on end I was away
from whatever home we had newly made.

My son and daughter were not particularly aware of the physical changes that I had undergone — at least not at first — but
Katherine, my wife, had to confront them each time we were
alone. Stoically, heroically, she accepted the passion that drove
me to alter myself toward the machine, even as she admitted
that she did not understand it. She never recoiled from me
because of my strangeness, and I was grateful for that. I have
always believed that human beings discover a major part of the
meaning in their lives from, in Pound's phrase, "the quality of
the affections," and Katherine could see through the mechani-
cal artifice surrounding and buttressing Nicholas Parsons to the
man himself. And I was grateful for that, too, enormously grateful.

Still, we all have doubts. "Why are you doing this?" Katherine
asked me one night. "Why are you letting them change you?"

"*Tempus fugit.* Time's winged chariot. I've got to do everything
I can before there's none left. And I'm doing it for all of us —
for you, for Peter, for Erin. It'll pay off. I know it will."

"But what started all this? Before the aneurysm —"

"Before the aneurysm I'd begun to wake up at night with a
strange new sense of power. I could go inside the heads of dogs
and read what their lives were like. I could time-travel in their
minds."

"You had insomnia, Nick. You couldn't sleep."

"No, no, it wasn't just that. I was learning about time by riding around inside the head of that Great Dane that came into my classroom. We went everywhere, everywhen. The aneurysm had given me the ability to do that — when it ruptured, my telepathic skill went too."

Katherine smiled. "Do you regret that you can't read dogs' minds anymore?"

"Yes. A little. But this compensates, what I'm doing now. If you can stand it a few more years, if you can tolerate the physical changes in me, it'll pay off. I know it will."

And we talked for a long time that night, in a tiny bedroom in a tiny apartment in a big Texas city many miles from Van Luna, Kansas, or Cheyenne, Wyoming, or Colorado Springs, or Athens, Georgia.

Tonight, nearly seventeen years after that thoughtful conversation, I am free-falling in orbit with my trace-mate Canicula, whom I sometimes call Threasie (or 3C, you see, short for Cybernetic Canine Construct). We have beeen up here a month now, in preparation for our flight to the star system Sirius eight months hence.

Katherine has found this latest absence of mine particularly hard to bear. Peter is a troubled young man of twenty, and Erin is a restless teen-ager with many questions about her absent father. Further, Katherine knows that shortly the *Black Retriever* will fling me into the interstellar void with eight other trace-teams. Recent advances in laser-fusion technology, along with the implementation of the Livermore-Parsons Drive, will no doubt get us out to Sirius in no time flat (i.e., less than four years for those of you who remain Earthbound, a mere fraction of that for us aboard the *Black Retriever*), but Katherine does not find this news at all cheering.

"*Tempus fugit,*" she told me somewhat mockingly during a recent laser transmission. "And unless I move to Argentina, God forbid, I won't even be able to see the star you're traveling toward."

In Earth orbit, however, both Canicula and I find that time drags. We are ready to be off to the small Spartan world that no doubt circles our starfall destination in Canis Major. My own minute studies of the "wobble" in Sirius' proper motion have proved that such a planet exists; only once before has anyone else in the scientific community detected a dark companion with a mass less than that of Jupiter, but no one doubts that I know what I am doing.

Hence this expedition.

Hence this rigorous though wearying training period in Earth orbit. I do not exempt even myself, but dear God how time drags.

Canicula is my own dark companion. He rescues me from doubt, ennui, and orbital funk. He used to be a Great Dane. Even now you can see that beneath his streamlined cybernetic exterior a magnificent animal breathes. Besides that, Canicula has wit.

"Tempus fugit," he says during an agonizingly slow period. He rolls his eyes and then permits his body to follow his eyes' motion: an impudent, free-fall somersault.

"Stop that nonsense, Threasie," I command him with mock severity. "See to your duties."

"If you'll remember," he says, "one of my most important ones is, uh, hounding you."

I am forty-six. Canicula-Threasie is seven.

And we're both learning new tricks.

I AM THIRTY-EIGHT: Somewhere, perhaps, Nicholas Parsons is a bona fide astronaut-in-training, but in this tributary of history — the one containing me now — I am nothing but a writer projecting himself into that grandiose wish-fulfillment role. I am an astronaut in the same dubious way that John Glenn or Neil Armstrong is a writer. For nearly eleven years my vision has been on hold. What success I have achieved in this tributary I have fought for with the sometimes despairing tenacity of my talent and a good deal of help from my friends. Still, I cannot keep from wondering how I am to overcome the arrogance of an enemy for whom I am only a name, not a person, and how dangerous any visionary can be with a gag in the mouth to thwart any intelligible recitation of the dream.

Where in my affliction is encouragement or comfort? Well, I can always talk to my dog. Nickie is dead, of course, and so is Pepper, and not too long ago a big yellow school bus struck down the kindly mongrel who succeeded them in our hearts.

Now we have B.J., a furrow-browed beagle. To some extent he has taken up the slack. I talk to him while Katherine works and Peter and Erin attend their respective schools. B.J. understands very little of what I tell him — his expression always seems a mixture of dread and sheepishness — but he is a good listener for as long as I care to impose upon him; and maybe when his hind leg thumps in his sleep, he is dreaming not of rabbit hunts but of canine heroics aboard a vessel bound for Sirius. In my capacity as dreamer I can certainly pretend that he is doing so. . . .

A SUMMER'S READING, 1959: *The Call of the Wild* and *White Fang* by Jack London. *Bob, Son of Battle* by Alfred Ollivant. Eric Knight's *Lassie Come Home. Silver Chief, Dog of the North* by someone whose name I cannot recall. *Beautiful Joe* by Marshall Saunders. *Lad, a Dog* and its various sequels by Albert Payson Terhune. And several others.

All of these books are on the upper shelf of a closet in the home of my mother and step-father in Wichita, Kansas. The books have been collecting dust there since 1964. Before that they had been in my own little grey bookcase in Tulsa, Oklahoma.

From the perspective of my thirty-eighth or forty-sixth year I suppose that it is too late to try to fetch them home for Peter and Erin. They are already too old for such stories. Or maybe not. I am unable to keep track of their ages because I am unable to keep track of mine.

In any event, if Peter and Erin are less than fourteen, there is one book that I do not want either of them to have just yet. It is a collection of Stephen Crane's short stories. The same summer that I was blithely reading London and Terhune, I read Crane's story "A Small Brown Dog." I simply did not know what I was doing. The title lured me irresistibly onward. The other books had contained ruthless men and incidents of meaningless cruelty, yes, but all had concluded well: either virtue or romanticism had ultimately triumphed, and I was made glad to have followed Buck, Lassie, and Lad through their doggy odysseys.

The Crane story cut me up. I was not ready for it. I wept openly and could not sleep that night.

And if my children are still small, dear God I do not want them even to *see* the title "A Small Brown Dog," much less read the text that accompanies it.

"All in good time," I tell myself. "All in good time."

I AM TWELVE: Tulsa, Oklahoma. Coming home from school, I find my grown-and-married step-sister's collie lying against the curbing in front of a neighbor's house. It is almost four in the afternoon, and hot. The neighbor woman comes down her porch when she sees me.

"You're the first one home, Nicholas. It happened only a little while ago. It was a cement truck. It didn't even stop."

I look down the hill toward the grassless building sites where twenty or thirty new houses are going up. Piles of lumber, Sheetrock, and tar paper clutter the cracked, sun-baked yards. But no cement trucks. I do not see a single cement truck.

"I didn't know what to do, Nicholas. I didn't want to leave him —"

We have been in Tulsa a year. We brought the collie with us from Van Luna, Kansas. Rhonda, whose dog he originally was, lives in Wichita now with her new husband.

I look down at the dead collie, remembering the time when Rhonda and I drove to a farm outside Van Luna to pick him out of a litter of six.

"His name will be Marc," Rhonda said, holding him up. "With a *c* instead of a *k*. That's classier." Maybe it was, maybe it wasn't. At the time, though, we both sincerely believed that Marc deserved the best. Because he was not a registered collie, Rhonda got him for almost nothing.

Now I see him lying dead in the street. The huge tires of a cement truck have crushed his head. The detail that hypnotizes me, however, is the pool of gaudy crimson blood in which Marc lies. And then I understand that I am looking at Marc's life splattered on the concrete.

At supper that evening I break down crying in the middle of the meal, and my mother has to tell my step-father what has happened. Earlier she had asked me to withhold the news until my father has had a little time to relax. I am sorry that my promise is broken, I am sorry that Marc is dead.

In a week, though, I have nearly forgotten. It is very seldom that I remember the pool of blood in which the collie's body lay on that hot spring afternoon. Only at night do I remember its hypnotizing crimson.

175 YEARS AGO IN RUSSIA: One night before the beginning of spring I go time-traveling — spirit-faring, if you like — in the mind of the Great Dane who once stalked into my classroom.

I alter his body into that of a hunting hound and drop him into the kennels on the estate of a retired Russian officer. Hundreds of my kind surround me. We bay all night, knowing that in the morning we will be turned loose on an eight-year-old serf boy who yesterday struck the general's favorite hound with a rock.

I jump against the fence of our kennel and outbark dogs even larger than I am. The cold is invigorating. My flanks shudder with expectation, and I know that insomnia is a sickness that afflicts only introspective university instructors and failed astronaut candidates.

In the morning they bring the boy forth. The general orders him stripped naked in front of his mother, and the dog-boys who tend us make the child run. An entire hunting party in full regalia is on hand for the festivities. At last the dog-boys turn us out of the kennels, and we surge across the estate after our prey.

Hundreds of us in pursuit, and I in the lead.

I am the first to sink my teeth into his flesh. I tear away half of one of his emaciated buttocks with a single ripping motion of my jaws. Then we bear the child to the ground and overwhelm his cries with our brutal baying. Feeble prey, this; incredibly feeble. We are done with him in fifteen minutes.

When the dog-boys return us slavering to our kennels, I release my grip on the Great Dane's mind and let him go foraging in the trashcans of Athens, Georgia.

Still shuddering, I lie in my bed and wonder how it must feel to be run down by a pack of predatory animals. I cannot sleep.

APPROACHING SIRIUS: We eight men are physical extensions of the astrogation and life-support components of the *Black Retriever*. We feed on the ship's energy; no one must eat

to stay alive, though, of course, we do have delicious food sur-
rogates aboard for the pleasure of our palates. All our five
senses have been technologically enhanced so that we see, hear,
touch, smell, and taste more vitally than do you, our brethren,
back on Earth.

Do not let it be said that a cybernetic organism sacrifices its
humanity for a sterile and meaningless immortality. Yes, yes, I
know. That's the popular view, but one promulgated by pessi-
mists, cynics, and prophets of doom.

Would that the nay-sayers could wear our synthetic skins for
only fifteen minutes. Would that they could look out with new
eyes on the fierce cornucopian emptiness of interstellar space.
There is beauty here, and we of the *Black Retriever* are a part of
it.

Canicula-Threasie and the other Cybernetic Canine Con-
structs demonstrate daily their devotion to us. It is not a slavish
devotion, however. Often they converse for hours among themselves about the likelihood of finding intelligent life on the
planet that circles Sirius.

Some of their speculation has proved extremely interesting,
and I have begun to work their suggestions into our tentative
Advance Stratagem for First Contact. As Threasie himself de-
lights in telling us, "It's good to be ready for any contingency.
Do you want the tail to wag the dog or the dog to wag the tail?"
Not the finest example of his wit, but he invariably chuckles.
His own proposal is that a single trace-team confront the aliens
without weapons and offer them our lives. A gamble, he
says, but the only way of establishing our credibility from the
start.

Late at night — as we judge it by the shipboard clocks — the
entire crew gathers around the eerily glowing shield of the Livermore-Parsons Drive Unit, and the dogs tell us stories out of
their racial subconscious. Canicula usually takes the lead in
these sessions, and my favorite account is his narrative of how
dog and man first joined forces against the indifferent arrogance of a bestial environment. That story seems to make the
drive shield burn almost incandescently, and man and dog alike
— woman and dog alike — can feel their skins humming, prickling, with an unknown but immemorial power.

Not much longer now. Sirius beckons, and the long night of this journey will undoubtedly die in the blaze of our planetfall.

I AM FIFTEEN: When I return to Colorado Springs to visit my father the year after Nick's fall from the rocks, I find the great Labrador strangely changed.

There is a hairless saddle on Nick's back, a dark grey area of scar tissue at least a foot wide. Moreover, he has grown fat. When he greets me, he cannot leap upon me as he has done in past years. In nine months he has dwindled from a panther into a kind of heartbreaking and outsized lap dog.

As we drive home from the airport my father tries to explain:

"We had him castrated, Nicholas. We couldn't keep him in the house — not with the doors locked, not with the windows closed, not with rope, not with anything we tried. There's always a female in heat in our neighborhood and he kept getting out. Twice I had to drive to the pound and ransom him. Five bucks a shot.

"Finally some old biddy who had a cocker spaniel or something caught him — you know how gentle he is with people — and tied him to her clothesline. Then she poured a pan of boiling water over his back. That's why he looks like he does now. It's a shame, Nicholas, it really is. A goddamn shame."

The summer lasts an eternity.

TWENTY-SEVEN, AND HOLDING: Behind our house on Virginia Avenue there is a small self-contained apartment that our landlord rents to a young woman who is practice-teaching. This young woman owns a mongrel bitch named Tammi.

For three weeks over the Christmas holidays Tammi was chained to her dog house in temperatures that occasionally plunged into the teens. Katherine and I had not volunteered to take care of her because we knew that we would be away ourselves for at least a week, and because we hoped that Tammi's owner would make more humane arrrangements for the dog's care. She did not. She asked a little girl across the street to feed Tammi once a day and to give her water.

This, of course, meant that Katherine and I took care of the animal for the two weeks that we were home. I went out several times a day to untangle Tammi's chain from the bushes and clothesline poles in the vicinity of her doghouse. Sometimes I fed her, sometimes played with her, sometimes tried to make her stay in her house.

Some days it rained, others it sleeted. And for the second time in her life Tammi came into heat.

One night I awoke to hear her yelping as if in pain. I struggled out of bed, put on a pair of blue jeans and my shoes, and let myself quietly out the back door.

A monstrous silver-black dog — *was it a Great Dane?* — had mounted Tammi. It was raining, but I could see the male's pistoning silhouette in the residual glow of the falling raindrops themselves. Or so it seemed to me. Outraged by the male's brutality, I gathered a handful of stones and approached the two dogs.

Then I threw.

I struck the male in the flank. He lurched away from Tammi and rushed blindly to a fenced-in corner of the yard. I continued to throw, missing every time. The male saw his mistake and came charging out of the cul-de-sac toward me. His feet churned in the gravel as he skidded by me. Then he loped like a jungle cat out our open gate and was gone. I threw eight or nine futile stones into the dark street after him. And stood there barechested in the chill December rain.

For a week this went on. New dogs appeared on some nights, familiar ones returned on others. And each time, like a knight fighting for his lady's chastity, I struggled out of bed to fling stones at Tammi's bestial wooers.

Today is March the fifth, and this morning Katherine took our little boy out to see Tammi's three-week-old puppies. They have a warm, faintly fecal odor, but their eyes are open and Peter played with them as if they were stuffed stockings come to life. He had never seen anything quite like them before, and Katherine says that he cried when she brought him in.

I AM AGELESS: A beautiful, kind-cruel planet revolves about Sirius. I have given this world the name Elsinore because the name is noble, and because the rugged fairness of her seascapes and islands calls up the image of a more heroic era than any we have known on Earth of late.

Three standard days ago, seven of our trace-teams descended into the atmosphere of Elsinore. One trace-team remains

aboard the *Black Retriever* to speed our evangelical message to
you, our brethren, back home. Shortly, we hope to retrieve
many of you to this brave new world in Canis Major.

Thanks to the flight capabilities of our cybernetic dogs, we
have explored nearly all of Elsinore in three days' time. We
divided the planet into hemispheres and the hemispheres into
quadrants, and each trace-team flew cartographic and explora-
tory missions over its assigned area. Canicula and I took upon
ourselves the responsibility of charting two of the quadrants,
since only seven teams were available for this work, and as a
result he and I first spotted and made contact with the indige-
nous Elsinorians.

As we skimmed over a group of breaktakingly stark islands in
a northern sea, the heat-detecting unit in Canicula's belly gave
warning of this life. Incredulous, we made several passes over
the islands.

Each time we plummeted, the sea shimmered beneath us like
windblown silk. As we searched the islands' coasts and heart-
lands, up-jutting rocks flashed by us on every side. And each
time we plummeted, our heat sensors told us that sentient
beings did indeed dwell in this archipelago.

At last we pinpointed their location.

Canicula hovered for a time. "You ready to be wagged?" he
asked me.

"Wag away," I replied.

We dropped five hundred meters straight down and then
settled gently into the aliens' midst: a natural senate of stone,
open to the sky, in which the Elsinorians carry on the simple
affairs of their simple state.

The Elsinorians are dogs. Dogs very like Canicula-Threasie.
They lack, of course, the instrumentation that so greatly intensifies the experience of the cyborg. They are creatures
of nature who have subdued themselves to reason and who
have lived out their apparently immortal lives in a spirit of rational expectation. For millennia they have waited, patiently
waited.

Upon catching sight of me, every noble animal in their open-
air senate began wagging his or her close-cropped tail. All eyes
were upon me.

By himself Canicula sought out the Elsinorians' leader and immediately began conversing with him (no doubt implementing our Advance Stratagem for First Contact). You see, Canicula did not require the assistance of our instantaneous translator; he and the alien dog shared a heritage more fundamental than language.

I stood to one side and waited for their conference to conclude.

"His name translates as Prince," Canicula said upon returning to me, "even though their society is democratic. He wishes to address us before all of the assembled senators of his people. Let's take up a seat among them. You can plug into the translator. The Elsinorians, Nicholas, recognize the full historical impact of this occasion, and Prince may have a surprise or two for you, dear Master."

Having said this, 3C grinned. Damned irritating.

We nevertheless took up our seats among the Elsinorian dogs, and Prince strolled with great dignity onto the senate floor. The I.T. System rendered his remarks as several lines of nearly impeccable blank verse. English blank verse, of course

PRINCE: Fragmented by the lack of any object
        Beyond ourselves to beat for, our sundered hearts
        Thud in a vacuum not of our making.
        We are piecemeal beasts, supple enough
        To look upon, illusorily whole;
        But all this heartsore time, down the aeons
        Illimitable of our incompleteness,
        We have awaited this, your arrival,
        Men and Dogs of Earth.
              And you, Canicula,
        We especially thank for bringing to us
        The honeyed prospect of Man's companionship.
        Tell your Master that we hereby invite
        His kinspeople to our stern but unspoiled world
        To be the medicine which heals the lesions
        In our shambled hearts.
              Together we shall share
        Eternity, deathless on Elsinore!

And so he concluded. The senators, their natural reticence overcome, barked, bayed, and bellowed their approval.

That was earlier this afternoon. Canicula-Threasie and I told the Elsinorians that we would carry their message to the other trace-teams and, eventually, to the people of Earth. Then we rose above their beautifully barbaric island and flew into the eye of Sirius, a ball of sinking fire on the windy sea's westernmost rim.

Tonight we are encamped on the peak of a great mountain on one of the islands of the archipelago. The air is brisk, but not cold. To breathe here is to ingest energy.

Peter, Erin, Katherine — I call you to this place. No one dies on Elsinore, no one suffers more than he can bear, no one suffocates in the pettiness of day-to-day existence. That is what I had hoped for. That is why I came here. That is why I sacrificed, on the altar of this dream, so much of what I was before my aneurysm ruptured. And now the dream has come true, and I call you to Elsinore.

Canicula and I make our beds on a lofty slab of granite above a series of waterfalls tumbling to the sea. The mist from these waterfalls boils up beneath us. We stretch out to sleep.

"No more suffering," I say.

"No more wasted potential," Canicula says

"No more famine, disease, or death," I say, looking at the cold stars and trying to find the cruel one upon which my beloved family even yet depends.

Canicula then says, *"Tempus?"*

"Yes?" I reply.

"Fug it!" he barks.

And we both go to sleep with laughter on our lips.

TWENTY-SEVEN, AND COUNTING: I have renewed my contract for the coming year. You have to put food on the table. I am three weeks into spring quarter already, and my students are students like other students. I like some of them, dislike others.

I will enjoy teaching them *Othello* once we get to it. Thank God our literature text does not contain *Hamlet:* I would find myself making hideous analogies between the ghost of Hamlet's father and the Great Dane who haunted my thoughts all winter quarter.

I am over that now. Dealing with the jealous Moor again will be, in the terminology of our astronauts, "a piece of cake."

Katherine's pregnancy is in its fourth month now, and Peter has begun to talk a little more fluently. Sort of. The words he knows how to say include *Dada, juice,* and *dog. Dog,* in fact, is the first word that he ever clearly spoke. Appropriate.

In fifteen years — or eleven, or seventeen — I probably will not be able to remember a time when Peter could not talk. Or Erin, either, for that matter, even though she has not been born yet. For now all a father can do is live his life and, loving them, let his children — born and unborn — live their own.

"Dog!" my son emphatically cries. "Dog!"

ETHAN CANIN

Emperor of the Air

(FROM THE ATLANTIC MONTHLY)

LET ME TELL YOU who I am. I'm sixty-nine years old, live in the same house I was raised in, and have been the high school biology and astronomy teacher in this town so long that I have taught the grandson of one of my former students. I wear my father's wristwatch, which tells me it is past four-thirty in the morning, and though I have thought otherwise, I now think hope is the essence of all good men.

My wife, Vera, and I have no children, and this has enabled us to do a great many things in our lives: we have stood on the Great Wall of China, toured the Pyramid of Cheops, sunned in Lapland at midnight. Vera, who is near my age, is off on the Appalachian Trail. She has been gone two weeks and expects to be gone one more, on a trip on which a group of men and women, some of them half her age, are walking all the way through three states. Age, it seems, has left my wife alone. She ice-skates and hikes and will swim nude in a mountain lake. She does these things without me, however, for now my life has slowed. Last fall, as I pushed a lawnmower around our yard, I felt a squeezing in my chest and a burst of pain in my shoulder, and I spent a week in a semi-private hospital room. A heart attack. Myocardial infarction, minor. I will no longer run for a train, and in my shirt pocket I keep a small vial of nitroglycerine pills. In slow supermarket lines or traffic snarls I tell myself that impatience is not worth dying over, and last week, as I stood at the window and watched my neighbor, Mr. Pike, cross the yard toward our front door carrying a chain saw, I told myself that he was nothing but a doomed and hopeless man.

I had found the insects in my elm a couple of days before, the slim red line running from the ground up the long trunk and vanishing into the lower boughs. I brought out a magnifying glass to examine them — their shiny arthroderms, torsos elongated like drops of red liquid; their tiny legs, jointed and wiry, climbing the fissured bark. The morning I found them, Mr. Pike came over from next door and stood on our porch. "There's vermin in your elm," he said.

"I know," I said. "Come in."

"It's a shame, but I'll be frank: there's other trees on this block. I've got my own three elms to think of."

Mr. Pike is a builder, a thick and unpleasant man with whom I have rarely spoken. Though I had seen him at high school athletic events, the judgmental tilt to his jaw always suggested to me that he was merely watching for the players' mistakes. He is short, with thick arms and a thick neck and a son, Kurt, in whose bellicose shouts I can already begin to hear the thickness of his father. Mr. Pike owns or partly owns a construction company that erected a line of low prefabricated houses on the outskirts of town, on a plot I remember from my youth as having been razed by fire. Once, a plumber who was working on our basement pipes told me that Mr. Pike was a poor craftsman, a man who valued money over quality. The plumber, a man my age who kept his tools in a wooden chest, shook his head when he told me that Mr. Pike used plastic pipes in the houses he had built. "They'll last ten years," the plumber told me. "Then the seams will go and the walls and ceilings will start to fill with water." I myself had had little to do with Mr. Pike until he told me he wanted my elm cut down to protect the three saplings in his yard. Our houses are separated by a tall stand of rhododendron and ivy, so we don't see each other's private lives as most neighbors do. When we talked on the street, we spoke only about a football score or the incessant rain, and I had not been on his property since shortly after he moved in, when I had gone over to introduce myself and he had shown me the spot where, underneath his rolling back lawn, he planned to build a bomb shelter.

Last week he stood on my porch with the chain saw in his hands. "I've got young elms," he said. "I can't let them be infested."

"My tree is over two hundred years old."

"It's a shame," he said, showing me the saw, "but I'll be frank. I just wanted you to know I could have it cut down as soon as you gave the word."

All week I had a hard time sleeping. I read Dickens in bed, heated cups of milk, but nothing worked. The elm was dying. Vera was gone, and I lay in bed thinking of the insects, of their miniature jaws carrying away heartwood. It was late summer, the nights were still warm, and sometimes I went outside in my nightclothes and looked up at the sky. I teach astronomy, as I have said, and though sometimes I try to see the stars as milky dots or pearls, they are forever arranged in my eye according to the astronomic charts. I stood by the elm and looked up at Ursa Minor and Lyra, at Cygnus and Corona Borealis. I went back inside, read, peeled an orange. I sat at the window and thought about the insects, and every morning at five a boy who had once taken my astronomy class rode by on his bicycle, whistling the national anthem, and threw the newspaper onto our porch.

Sometimes I heard them, chewing the heart of my splendid elm.

The day after I first found the insects I called a man at the tree nursery. He described them for me, the bodies like red droplets, the wiry legs; he told me their genus and species.

"Will they kill the tree?"

"They could."

"We can poison them, can't we?"

"Probably not," he said. He told me that once they were visible outside the bark they had already invaded the tree too thoroughly for pesticide. "To kill them," he said, "we would end up killing the tree."

"Does that mean the tree is dead?"

"No," he said. "It depends on the colony of insects. Sometimes they invade a tree but don't kill it, don't even weaken it. They eat the wood, but sometimes they eat it so slowly that the tree can replace it."

When Mr. Pike came over the next day, I told him this. "You're asking me to kill a two-hundred-and-fifty-year-old tree that otherwise wouldn't die for a long time."

"The tree's over eighty feet tall," he said.

"So?"

"It stands fifty-two feet from my house."

"Mr. Pike, it's older than the Liberty Bell."

"I don't want to be unpleasant," he said, "but a storm could blow twenty-eight feet of that tree though the wall of my house."

"How long have you lived in that house?"

He looked at me, picked at his tooth. "You know."

"Four years," I said. "I was living here when a czar ruled Russia. An elm grows one quarter inch in width each year, when it's still growing. That tree is four feet thick, and it has yet to chip the paint on either your house or mine."

"It's sick," he said. "It's a sick tree. It could fall."

"Could," I said. "It *could* fall."

"It very well *might* fall."

We looked at each other for a moment. Then he averted his eyes, and with his right hand adjusted something on his watch. I looked at his wrist. The watch had a shiny metal band, with the hours, minutes, seconds, blinking in the display.

The next day he was back on my porch.

"We can plant another one," he said.

"What?"

"We can plant another tree. After we cut the elm, we can plant a new one."

"Do you have any idea how long it would take to grow a tree like that one?"

"You can buy trees half-grown. They bring them in on a truck and replant them."

"Even a half-grown tree would take a century to reach the size of the elm. A century."

He looked at me. Then he shrugged, turned around, and went back down the steps. I sat down in the open doorway. A century. What would be left of the earth in a century? I didn't think I was a sentimental man, and I don't weep at plays or movies, but certain moments have always been peculiarly moving for me, and the mention of a century was one. There have been others. Standing out of the way on a fall evening, as couples and families converge on the concert hall from the radiating footpaths, has always filled me with a longing, though I don't know for what. I have taught the life of the simple hydra that is drawn, for no reasons it could ever understand, toward the bright surface of the water, and the spectacle of a thousand human beings organizing themselves into a single room to hear the quartets of Beethoven is as moving to me as.birth or death. I feel the same way during the passage in an automobile across a cantilever span above the Mississippi, mother of rivers. These moments overwhelm me, and sitting on the porch that day as Mr. Pike retreated up the footpath, paused at the elm, and then went back into his house, I felt my life open up and present itself to me.

When he had gone back into his house I went out to the elm and studied the insects, which emerged from a spot in the grass and disappeared above my sight, in the lowest branches. Their line was dense and unbroken. I went inside and found yesterday's newspaper, which I rolled up and brought back out. With it I slapped up and down the trunk until the line was in chaos. I slapped until the newspaper was wet and tearing; with my fingernails I squashed stragglers between the narrow crags of bark. I stamped the sod where they emerged, dug my shoe tip into their underground tunnels. When my breathing became painful, I stopped and sat on the ground. I closed my eyes until the pulse in my neck was calm, and I sat there, mildly triumphant, master at last. After a while I looked up again at the tree and found the line perfectly restored.

That afternoon I mixed a strong insect poison, which I brought outside and painted around the bottom of the trunk. Mr. Pike came out onto his steps to watch. He walked down, stood on the sidewalk behind me, made little chuckling noises. "There's no poison that'll work," he whispered.

But that evening, when I came outside, the insects were gone. The trunk was bare. I ran my finger around the circumference. I rang Mr. Pike's doorbell and we went out and stood by the tree together. He felt in the notches of the bark, scratched bits of earth from the base. "I'll be damned," he said.

When I was a boy in this town, the summers were hot and the forest to the north and east often dried to the point where the undergrowth, not fit to compete with the deciduous trees for groundwater, turned crackling brown. The shrubbery became as fragile as straw, and the summer I was sixteen the forest ignited. A sheet of flame raced and bellowed day and night as loud as a fleet of propeller planes. Whole families gathered in the street and evacuation plans were made, street routes drawn out beneath the night sky, which, despite the ten miles' distance to the fire, shone with orange light. My father had a wireless with which he communicated to the fire lines. He stayed up all night and promised that he would wake the neighbors if the wind changed or the fire otherwise turned toward town. That night the wind held, and by morning a firebreak the width of a street had been cut. My father took me down to see it the next day, a ribbon of cleared land as bare as if it had been drawn with a razor. Trees had been felled, the underbrush sickled down and removed. We stood at the edge of the cleared land, the town behind us, and watched the fire. Then we got into my father's Plymouth and drove as close as we were allowed. A fireman near the flames had been asphyxiated, someone said, when the cone of fire had turned abruptly and sucked up all the oxygen in the air. My father explained to me how a flame breathed oxygen like a man. We got out of the car. The heat curled the hair on our arms and turned the ends of our eyelashes white.

My father was a pharmacist and had taken me to the fire out of curiosity. Anything scientific interested him. He kept tide tables, and collected the details of nature — butterflies and moths, seeds, wildflowers — and stored them in glass-fronted cases, which he leaned against the stone wall of our cellar. One summer he taught me the constellations of the Northern Hemisphere. We went outside at night, and as the summer progressed he showed me how to find Perseus and Arcturus and Andromeda, how some of the brightest stars illuminated Lyra and Aquila, how, though the constellations proceed with the seasons, Polaris remains most fixed and is thus the set point of a mariner's navigation. He taught me the night sky, and I find now that this is rare knowledge. Later, when I taught astronomy, my students rarely cared about the silicon or iron on the sun, but when I spoke of Cepheus or Lacerta, they were silent

and attended my words. At a party now I can always find a
drinking husband who will come outside with me and sip cognac
while I point out the stars and say their names.

That day, as I stood and watched the fire, I thought the flames
were as loud and powerful as the sea, and that evening, when
we were home, I went out to the front yard and climbed the elm
to watch the forest burn. Climbing the elm was forbidden me,
because the lowest limbs even then were well above my reach
and because my father believed that anybody lucky enough to
make it up into the lower boughs would almost certainly fall on
the way down. But I knew how to climb it anyway. I had done it
before, when my parents were gone. I had never made it as far
as the first limbs, but I had learned the knobs and handholds
on which, with balance and strength, I could climb to within a
single jump of the boughs. The jump frightened me, however,
and I had never attempted it. To reach the boughs one had to
gather strength and leap upward into the air, propelled only by
the purchase of feet and hands on the small juttings of bark. It
was a terrible risk. I could no more imagine myself making this
leap than I could imagine diving headlong from a coastal cliff
into the sea. I was an adventurous youth, as I was later an
adventurous man, but all my adventures had a quality about
them of safety and planned success. This is still true. In Ethiopia
I have photographed a lioness with her cubs; along the Barrier
Reef I have dived among barracuda and scorpion fish — but
these things have never frightened me. In my life I have done
few things that have frightened me.

That night, though, I made the leap into the lower boughs of
the elm. My parents were inside the house, and I made my way
upward until I crawled out of the leaves onto a narrow top
branch and looked around me at a world that on two sides was
entirely red and orange with flame. After a time I came back
down and went inside to sleep, but that night the wind changed.
My father woke us, and we gathered outside on the street with
all the other families on our block. People carried blankets filled
with the treasures of their lives. One woman wore a fur coat,
though the air was suffused with ash and was as warm as an
afternoon. My father stood on the hood of a car and spoke. He
had heard through the radio that the fire had leaped the break,
that a house on the eastern edge of town was in full flame, and,

as we all could feel, that the wind was strong and blowing straight west. He told the families to finish loading their cars and leave as soon as possible. Though the fire was still across town, he said, the air was filling with smoke so rapidly that breathing would soon be difficult. He got down off the car and we went inside to gather things together. We had an RCA radio in our living room and a set of Swiss china in my mother's cupboard, but my father instead loaded a box with the *Encyclopaedia Britannica* and carried up from the basement the heavy glass cases that contained his species chart of the North American butterflies. We carried these things outside to the Plymouth. When we returned, my mother was standing in the doorway.

"This is my home," she said.

"We're in a hurry," my father said.

"This is my home, this is my children's home. I'm not leaving."

My father stood on the porch looking at her. "Stay here," he said to me. Then he took my mother's arm and they went into the house. I stood on the steps outside, and when my father came out again in a few minutes, he was alone, just as when we drove west that night and slept with the rest of our neighborhood on Army cots in the high school gym in the next town, we were alone. My mother had stayed behind.

Nothing important came of this. That night the wind calmed and the burning house was extinguished; the next day a heavy rain wet the fire and it was put out. Everybody came home, and the settled ash was swept from the houses and walkways into black piles in the street. I mention the incident now only because it points out, I think, what I have always lacked: I inherited none of my mother's moral stubbornness. In spite of my age, still, arriving on foot at a crosswalk where the light is red but no cars are in sight, I'm thrown into confusion. My decisions never seem to engage the certainty that I had hoped to enjoy late in my life. But I was adamant and angry when Mr. Pike came to my door. The elm was ancient and exquisite: we could not let it die.

Now, though, the tree was safe. I examined it in the morning, in the afternoon, in the evening, and with a lantern at night. The bark was clear. I slept.

•

The next morning Mr. Pike was at my door.

"Good morning, neighbor," I said.

"They're back."

"They can't be."

"They are. Look," he said, and walked out to the tree. He pointed up to the first bough.

"You probably can't see them," he said, "but I can. They're up there, a whole line of them."

"They couldn't be."

"They sure are. Listen," he said, "I don't want to be unpleasant, but I'll be frank."

That evening he left a note in our mail slot. It said that he had contacted the authorities, who had agreed to enforce the cutting of the tree if I didn't do it myself. I read the note in the kitchen. Vera had been cooking some Indian chicken before she left for the Appalachian Trail, and on the counter was a big jar filled with flour and spices that she shook pieces of chicken in. I read Mr. Pike's note again. Then I got a fishing knife and a flashlight from the closet, emptied Vera's jar, and went outside with these things to the elm. The street was quiet. I made a few calculations, and then with the knife cut the bark. Nothing. I had to do it only a couple more times, however, before I hit the mark and, sure enough, the tree sprouted insects. Tiny red bugs shot crazily from the slit in the bark. I touched my finger there and they spread in an instant all over my hand and up my arm. I had to shake them off. Then I opened the jar, laid the fishing knife out from the opening like a bridge, and touched the blade to the slit in the tree. They scrambled up the knife and began to fill the jar as fast as a trickling spring. After a few minutes I pulled out the knife, closed the lid, and went back into the house.

Mr. Pike is my neighbor, and so I felt a certain remorse. What I contemplated, however, was not going to kill the elms. It was going to save them. If Mr. Pike's trees were infested, they would still more than likely live, and he would no longer want mine chopped down. This is the nature of the world. In the dark house, feeling half like a criminal and half like a man of mercy, my heart arrhythmic in anticipation, I went upstairs to prepare. I put on black pants and a black shirt. I dabbed shoe polish on my cheeks, my neck, my wrists, the backs of my hands. Over my white hair I stretched a tight black cap. Then I walked downstairs. I picked up the jar and the flashlight and went outside into the night.

I have always enjoyed gestures — never failing to bow, for example, when I finished dancing with a woman — but one attribute I have acquired with age is the ability to predict when I am about to act foolishly. As I slid calmly into the shadowy cavern behind our side-yard rhododendron and paused to catch my breath, I thought that perhaps I had better go back inside and get into my bed. But then I decided to go through with it. As I stood there in the shadow of the swaying rhododendron, waiting to pass into the back yard of my neighbor, I thought of Hannibal and Napoleon and MacArthur. I tested my flashlight and shook the jar, which made a soft colliding sound as if it were filled with rice. A light was on in the Pikes' living room, but the alley between our houses was dark. I passed through.

The Pikes' yard is large, larger than ours, and slopes twice within its length, so that the lawn that night seemed like a dark, furrowed flag stretching back to the three elms. I paused at the border of the driveway, where the grass began, and looked out at the young trees outlined by the lighted houses behind them. In what strange ways, I thought, do our lives turn. Then I got down on my hands and knees. Staying along the fence that separates our yards, I crawled toward the back of the Pikes' lawn. In my life I have not crawled a lot. With Vera I have gone spelunking in the limestone caves of southern Minnesota, but there the crawling was obligate, and as we made our way along the narrow, wet channel into the heart of the rock, I felt a strange grace in my knees and elbows. The channel was hideously narrow, and my life depended on the sureness of my limbs. Now, in the Pikes' yard, my knees felt arthritic and torn. I made my way along the driveway toward the young elms against the back fence. The grass was wet and the water dampened my trousers. I was hurrying as best I could across the open lawn, the insect-filled jar in my hand, the flashlight in my pocket, when I put my palm on something cement. I stopped and looked down. In the dim light I saw what looked like the hatch door on a submarine. Round, the size of a manhole, marked with a fluorescent cross — oh, Mr. Pike, I didn't think you'd do it. I put down the jar and felt for the handle in the dark, and when I found it I braced myself and turned. I certainly didn't expect it to give, but it did, circling once, twice, around in my grasp and loosening like the lid of a bottle. I pulled the hatch and up it came. Then I picked up the insects, felt with my feet for the ladder inside, and went down, closing the hatch behind me.

I still planned to deposit the insects on his trees, but something about crime is contagious. I knew that what I was doing was foolish and that it increased the risk of being caught, but as I descended the ladder into Mr. Pike's bomb shelter, I could barely distinguish fear from elation. At the bottom of the ladder I switched on the flashlight. The room was round, the ceiling and floor were concrete, and against the wall stood a cabinet of metal shelves filled with canned foods. On one shelf were a dictionary and some magazines. Oh, Mr. Pike. I thought of his sapling elms, of the roots making their steady, blind way through the earth; I thought of his houses ten years from now, when the pipes cracked and the ceilings began to pool with water. What a hopeless man he seemed to me then, how small and afraid.

I stood thinking about him, and after a moment I heard a door close in the house. I climbed the ladder and peeked out under the hatch. There on the porch stood Kurt and Mr. Pike. As I watched, they came down off the steps and walked over and stood on the grass near me. I could see the watch blinking on Mr. Pike's wrist. I lowered my head. They were silent, and I wondered what Mr. Pike would do if he found me in his bomb shelter. He was thickly built, as I have said, but I didn't think he was a violent man. One afternoon I had watched as Kurt slammed the front door of their house and ran down the steps onto the lawn, where he stopped and threw an object — an ashtray, I think it was — right through the front window of the house. When the glass shattered, he ran, and Mr. Pike soon appeared on the front steps. The reason I say that he is not a violent man is that I saw something beyond anger, perhaps a certain doom, in his posture as he went back inside that afternoon and began cleaning up the glass with a broom. I watched him through the broken front window of their house.

How would I explain to him, though, the bottle of mad insects I now held? I could have run then, I suppose, made a break up and out of the shelter while their backs were turned. I could have been out the driveway and across the street without their recognizing me. But there was, of course, my heart. I moved back down the ladder. As I descended and began to think about a place to hide my insects, I heard Mr. Pike speak. I climbed back up the ladder. When I looked out under the hatch, I saw the two of them, backs toward me, pointing at the sky. Mr. Pike was sighting something with his finger, and Kurt followed. Then I realized that he was pointing out the constellations, but that he didn't know what they were and was making up their names as he spoke. His voice was not fanciful. It was direct and scientific, and he was lying to his son about what he knew. "These," he said, "these are the Mermaid's Tail, and south you can see the three peaks of Mount Olympus, and then the sword that belongs to the Emperor of the Air." I looked where he was pointing. It was late summer, near midnight, and what he had described was actually Cygnus's bright tail and the outstretched neck of Pegasus.

Presently he ceased speaking, and after a time they walked back across the lawn and went into the house. The light in the kitchen went on, then off. I stepped from my hiding place. I suppose I could have continued with my mission, but the air was calm, it was a perfect and still night, and my plan, I felt, had been interrupted. In my hand the jar felt large and dangerous. I crept back across the lawn, staying in the shadows of the ivy and rhododendron along the fence, until I was in the driveway between our two houses. In the side window of the Pikes' house a light was on. I paused at a point where the angle allowed me a view through the glass, down the hallway, and through an open door into the living room. Mr. Pike and Kurt were sitting together on a brown couch against the far wall of the room, watching television. I came up close to the window and peered through. Though I knew this was foolish, that any neighbor, any man walking his dog at night, would have thought me a burglar in my black clothing, I stayed and watched. The light was on inside, it was dark around me, and I knew I could look in without being seen. Mr. Pike had his hand on Kurt's shoulder. Every so often when they laughed at something on the screen, he moved his hand up and tousled Kurt's hair. The sight of this suddenly made me feel the way I do on the bridge across the Mississippi River. When he put his hand on Kurt's hair again, I moved out of the shadows and went back to my own house.

I wanted to run, or kick a ball, or shout a soliloquy into the night. I could have stepped up on a car hood then and lured the Pikes, the paper boy, all the neighbors, out into the night. I could have spoken about the laboratory of a biology teacher, about the rows of specimen jars. How could one not hope here? At three weeks the human embryo has gill arches on its neck, like a fish; at six weeks, amphibians' webs still connect its blunt fingers. Miracles. This is true everywhere in nature. The evolution of 500 million years is mimicked in each gestation: birds that in the egg look like fish; fish that emerge like their spineless, leaflike ancestors. What it is to study life! Anybody who had seen a cell divide could have invented religion.

I sat down on the porch steps and looked at the elm. After a while I stood up and went inside. With turpentine I cleaned the shoe polish from my face, and then I went upstairs. I got into bed. For an hour or two I lay there, sleepless, hot, my thoughts racing, before I gave up and went to the bedroom window. The jar, which I had brought up with me, stood on the sill, and I saw that the insects were either asleep or dead. I opened the window then and emptied them down onto the lawn, and at that moment, as they rained away into the night, glinting and cascading, I thought of asking Vera for a child. I knew it was not possible, but I considered it anyway. Standing there at the window, I thought of Vera, ageless, in forest boots and shorts, perspiring through a flannel blouse as she dipped drinking water from an Appalachian stream. What had we, she and I? The night was calm, dark. Above me Polaris blinked.

I tried going to sleep again. I lay in bed for a time, and then gave up and went downstairs. I ate some crackers. I drank two glasses of bourbon. I sat at the window and looked out at the front yard. Then I got up and went outside and looked up at the stars, and I tried to see them for their beauty and mystery. I thought of billions of tons of exploding gases, hydrogen and helium, red giants, supernovas. In places they were as dense as

clouds. I thought of magnesium and silicon and iron. I tried to
see them out of their constellatory order, but it was like trying
to look at a word without reading it, and I stood there in the
night unable to scramble the patterns. Some clouds had blown
in and begun to cover Auriga and Taurus. I was watching them
begin to spread and refract moonlight when I heard the paper
boy whistling the national anthem. When he reached me, I was
standing by the elm, still in my nightclothes, unshaven, a little
drunk.

"I want you to do something for me," I said.

"Sir?"

"I'm an old man and I want you to do something for me. Put
down your bicycle," I said. "Put down your bicycle and look up
at the stars."

E. L. DOCTOROW

The Leather Man

(FROM THE PARIS REVIEW)

THEY'RE NOTHING NEW, you can read about the Leather Man for instance, a hundred years ago making his circuit through Westchester, Connecticut, into the Berkshires in the summer, seen sitting on the roadside, glimpsed in the woods, he had these regular stops, caves, abandoned barns, riverbanks under the iron bridges in mill towns, the Leather Man, a hulk, colossally dressed, in layers of coats and shawls and pants, all topped with a stiff handfashioned leather outer armor, like a knight's, and a homemade pointed hat of leather, he was ten feet tall, an apparition. Of course it's the essence of these people that they're shy, they scurry at the sign of confrontation, never hurt a soul. But it was said of this fellow that when cornered he would engage in quite rational conversation, unlearned of course, with no reference to current events, and perhaps with a singular line of association that might strike one at times as not sequential, not really reasonably sequential on first audit, but genial nonetheless, with transitions made by smile or the sincere struggle for words, even the act of talking one assumes is something you can lose the knack of. So there is a history. And though the country of western New England, or the farmlands in the north Midwest will still find one asleep in the plains, a patch of wheat flattened in his contours, say, and although they're common enough in the big cities, living in doorways, wiping your windshields with a dirty rag for a quarter, men, or the baggers, smoking butts from the gutters, women, or the communities of them, living each in a private alcove underground between subway stations, in the nests of the walls alongside tracks, or down under the tracks in the hollows and nooks of the electric cable conduits, what is new is the connection they're making with each other, some kind of spontaneous communication has flashed them into awareness of each other, and hell they may as well have applied to the National Endowment as a living art form, there is someone running them but I don't know who.

I don't know who and I don't know why. Conceivably it's a harmless social phenomenon, like all the other forms of suffering, that is to say not planned for a purpose but merely a natural function of everything else going, and maybe it is heartless to look askance at suffering, to be suspicious of it, southern church blacks, welfare recipients, jobless kids around the pool halls and so on, but that's the job, that's our role, I don't think I have to justify it. We know how danger grows, or for that matter large intangible events, spiritual events, there were five six hundred thousand, yes? at that farmer's field twenty years ago, and fifty of them were us, you remember, one part per ten thousand, like the legal chemistry for a preservative, one part per ten thousand to keep the thing from turning bad. I was there myself and enjoyed the music. My favorite was Joan C. Baez, the most conservative of musicians, ultra-liberal pacifist peacenik, remember peaceniks? That was a coining we did ourselves and gave it to some columnist in Denver I think it was, spread like wildfire. But she sang nice, early in the game, everyone stoned on sun, chemical toilets still operative . . .

We found a girl there, incidentally, who was doing these strange spastic pantomimes that drew a real crowd. Beginning with her arms over her head. Brought her elbows down over the boobs, seemed to push the elbows out, pushing at something, and then one arm went around the back of the neck, and then all these gyrations of the head, it was the weirdest thing as if she was caught in something, a web, a net, so intense, so concentrated, the crowd, the music disappeared, and then she went down on her knees and knelt through her arms like they were some kind of jump rope, and then when her arms were behind her that was not right, she tried to get out that way, get out, she was getting out of something, enacting the attempt face all twisted and red to get out, you see. So we took some pictures, and then we diagrammed the action and what we came up with was very interesting, it was someone in a straitjacket, it was the classic terror enacted of someone straitjacketed and trying to break free. Now who can you think of, the person who in fact could do that, the person who could get out of straitjackets, who was that, he said.

Houdini.

That's right, Houdini, the escape artist, it was one of his routines, getting out of the kind of straitjacket that breaks the heart.

To do hermitage, the preference for one's own company. Picture yourself in such solitude, in natural surroundings, say, the classical version. Build a hut in the woods, split your own logs, grow things, ritualize daily subsistence, listen to the wind sing, watch the treetops dance, feel the weather, feel yourself in touch with the way things are. You remember your Thoreau. There's a definite poetical component to avoiding all other human beings and taking on the coloration of your surroundings, invisible as the toad on the log. Whatever the spiritual content, it is the action of hiding out, you see, these guys hide out. So the question is why? It may be a normal life directed by powerful paranoidal impulses, or it may be a paranoid life that makes sense given the particular individual's background. But something has happened. If he is hiding I want to know why.

But supposing on the other hand we all seek to impose the order we can manage, the more public the order the better we are known. Politicians are known. Artists are known. They impose public order. But say you are some hapless fellow, you can't keep a job, your wife nags, the children are vicious, the neighbors snigger. Down in your basement though you make nice things of wood. You make a bookshelf, you make a cabinet, sawing and planing, sanding, fitting, glueing, and you construct something very fine, you impose that order, that is the realm of your control. You make a bigger cabinet. You make a cabinet you can walk into. You build it where nobody will watch you. When it is done you walk inside and lock the door.

Before we break for lunch let me propose this idea. You have them walking into their boxes and locking the door behind them. Fine. But two people do that and you have a community. You see what I'm saying? You can make a revolution with people who have nothing to do with each other at the same time. There is a theory for instance that the universe oscillates. It is not a steady beaming thing, nor did it start with a bang. It expands and contracts, inhales and exhales, it is either growing larger than you can imagine or imploding toward a point. The crucial thing is its direction. If things come apart enough, they will have started to come together.

0001. Members of the class: feral children, hermits, street people, gamblers, prisoners, missing persons, forest fire wardens, freaks, permanent invalids, recluses, autistics, road tramps, the sensory deprived. (See also astronauts.)

We borrowed an ordinary precinct car and went looking for one. Contact on Fourteenth Street and Avenue A, time of contact ten thirteen P.M. Subject going east on southside Fourteenth Street. White, female indeterminate age. Wearing WW II issue khaki greatcoat over several dresses, gray fedora over blue watch cap, several shawls, some kind of furred shoes overlaid with galoshes. Stockings rolled to ankles over stockings. Pushing two-wheeled grocery cart stuffed with bags, sacks, rags, soft goods, broken umbrellas. Purposeful movements. Subject went directly from public trash receptacles to private trash deposits in doorways, seemed interested in anything made of cloth. Subject sat down to rest back to fence East Fifteenth Street. This is the site of Consolidated Edison generating plant. Subject slept several hours on sidewalk in twenty-degree weather. At four A.M. awakened by white male derelict urinating on her.

Bancroft suggests as an organizing principle we make the distinction between simple and profound dereliction. Ignore bums in the pokey and the poor slobs who shoot up. Always the snob, Bancroft. He wants only middle-class and above material? Still there's something to be said: If the brain is overrun where is the act of separation? If nothing is excluded the significance is lost. Interesting he designates as profound that which is incomplete.

·

In the city of New Rochelle, N.Y., a man was apprehended as a peeping tom. He'd been found in the landscaping behind the residence of Mr. and Mrs. Morris Wakefield, 19 Croft Terrace. He had the aspect of a wild man, bearded, unkempt, ragged. Reported to have been glimpsed several times over a period of months in back yards of the better neighborhoods of the city. No identification.

Slater sat up and took notice. The incident had so shocked Mrs. Morris Wakefield that she had been placed under sedation. Poor woman was in no shape. Already under severe stress as a result of the disappearance of her husband, Morris Wakefield a partner in a bridge construction firm, an engineer of considerable reputation in his field, no known enemies. Exemplary life. Gone. The couple was childless. They had been married twelve years. We went up there. Alone and grieving in her home, Mrs. Wakefield had prepared for bed and came downstairs in her negligee for a glass of warm milk. Two eerie eyes rolled along the rim of the windowsill. She screamed and ran upstairs and locked herself in her bedroom where she phoned the police. I find, not infrequently, quote New Rochelle Police detective Leo Kreisler, trouble breaks out in a rash, we have people in our community we have no dealings with for twenty years, and suddenly everything goes at once, someone is robbed, then hurt in a car a week later, or someone is beat up and a relative steals money, and just like that one family is in multiple crisis in the space of a few days. We asked to see him. Sure why not, quote Detective Kreisler. Who knows maybe he'll like you. He doesn't talk, he doesn't eat, he looks at you like he's thinking of something else.

The prisoner wore floppy chino slacks torn down one leg and belted with a piece of clothesline, dirty white Stan Smith tennis sneakers, no socks, a stained and greasy work shirt. He was not a trim person, but a person who looked formerly fat. Pants and shirt hung on him. Badly needed a haircut and in the fluorescent light of the slammer blinked with the weak eyes and pale doughy undereyes of a person who wears glasses without his glasses. His beard white although his matted hair reddish. He sat crosslegged on the vinyl floor. He sat with the fingers of his hands intertwined stiffly. Slater contemplated him. He was all connected, his legs crossed, his fingers laced. Under observation he raised his knees still crossed and roped his wrists around them his fingers still locked.

Slater: Are you in fact the owner of the property on which you were apprehended, the bridge engineer Morris Wakefield, the missing husband?

The peeper nodded yes.

An item from the files of the security department of National Dry Foods Corporation: One of their young marketing executives had been relocated from Short Hills, New Jersey, to Flint, Michigan. It was discovered sometime thereafter that in Flint he was living in domicile with a woman not his wife and two children not his children, although he represented them as such. Six months it took them to find his legal wife and two children still in place in their Short Hills, New Jersey, home, but living in domicile with an executive of the company who had been relocated from Flint. The two executives had been fraternity brothers at Duke University.

Slater, do you fuck around?

A long time before answering. No.

So do I. Let me tell you about the lunch I had yesterday. A very beautiful lady whom I've had my eye on for years. She and my wife are pals, they go to the galleries together. Well we were all at this party and I make a joke, a signal joke, clearly funny if she doesn't pick up on it but a signal in case she wants to. Is that how you do it?

No, I usually come right out with it.

Well I'm older than you are. I'm a different generation. Wit counts for me, the double entendre. So we had lunch. I could hardly hold her down. She was ready to avenge fifteen years of faithful marriage. Not only that her husband cheated on her but that he was nasty at home. Not only that he was nasty and mean, but that he had no respect for what she did and made fun of the causes she supported. Not only that he lacked respect but that he was infantile and went all to pieces when he cut himself shaving. And not only that, but that he spent no time with the children and complained when he had to shell out money for their school.

Slater smiled.

Oh god, it was uncanny. Like she had held a mirror up. I found myself getting defensive, wanting to argue. It finally comes down to a smile, a small kindness, a bit of good cheer she said. Those are the important things. Your husband is a cheerful man, I said, and by this time in the conversation I didn't want to have anything more to do with her. An amiable charming man I said with a good sense of humor. Oh yes, she said, so was Dr. Jekyll.

What is the essential act of the Leather Man? He makes the world foreign. He distances it. He is estranged. Our perceptions are sharpest when we're estranged. We can see the shape of things. Do you accept this as a principle? All right then, consider something as common as philandering. I'm an old-fashioned fellow and I use old-fashioned words. After a while your marriage becomes your cover. Don't laugh. I'm quite serious. Your feelings are broken down by plurality, you don't stop, you keep moving, it becomes your true life to keep moving, to emotionally keep moving, you find finally the emotion in the movement. You are the Leather Man, totally estranged from your society, the prettiest women are rocks in the stream, flowers along the road, you have subverted your own life and live alone in the wild, your only companion your thoughts.

I think what I'm proposing is a structure, not a theory of a subversive class, but an infrastructure of layered subversion, perhaps not conspiracy at all. That something has happened like a rearrangement of molecules, and that since we are political persons here we are sensitive to the crude politics of it, we think of it as some sort of ground for antisocial action when it might not be that at all. So I'm saying the way to understand it for our particular purposes might be not the usual thing of getting inside, penetration, but distance, putting it away from us, getting as far from it as possible to see what it really is. Because if it has gotten outside us, and we're inside and we can't see the shape of it, it comes to us as reality and it has no meaning at all.

We've got this astronaut who went bad, James C. Montgomery who took a hero's welcome in 1966 and since then has been picked up for stock fraud, embezzlement, forgery, drunken driving, you name it he's done it, stealing cars, assault, assault with a deadly weapon. This sometimes happens to individuals in whom history intensifies like electroshock, leaves them all scattered afterwards. We've got him quiet now but his wife keeps talking to reporters down in Florida and threatens suit.

I'll read you part of the interrogation by one of the staff psychiatrists:

Were you ever frightened? Did anything happen on the mission you didn't report?

No sir.

Did anything unexpected happen?

No sir.

Did the idea of space hold any terror for you? Being out there so far from home?

Question repeated.

No, well, you do your job, you're busy as hell, there's no time to think. And you're always in touch, almost always in touch, control voice in empyrean void. No. I would say not. (Pause.) You just keep your nose to the panel. Make community with the switches, little lights. Everything around you is man-made, you have that assurance. (Pause.) American made.

But then you did the landing, right?

Yes sir.

You walked.

Yes sir.

You got out of the machine and walked around.

Yes sir. Oh — for a while there I was alone and miserable inside my space suit. Is that what you mean?

I have the feeling you're trying to tell me what you think I want to hear.

Well shit. (Pause.) Look, the truth is I don't remember. I mean I remember that I walked on the moon but now I can see it on television and I don't feel it, you know what I mean? I can't believe it happened. I see myself, that I did it, but I don't remember how it felt, I don't remember the experience of it.

Can I just try a quick simple experiment here? Five minutes of your time? Silence. Slater looked around the table. Someone lit a pipe. The grudging tribal assent. I'm going to give you a list

of simple nouns and ask you to respond — just fill me in on
what's happening. All right?

Night. Ladder. Window. Scream. Penis.

Have you been talking to my wife, someone said. Everyone
laughed.

Patrol. Mud. Flare. Mortar.

All right, someone said.

President. Crowd. Bullet. Slater said, We've got thousands of
people in this country whose vocation it is to let us know what
our experience is. Are you telling me this is not a resource?

Slate, we're going to have a fight on our hands if you want to
admit that kind of material. You don't know the minds you're
dealing with. They're not going to understand, they're going to
read it as source. Then you know how messy it'll get? You're
going to have to interrogate these resources, the most articulate
people in the land, the ones who already have their hackles up
and you're going to ask them where they got their information?

No, you're not hearing me, Slater said. We'll know where they
got their information. We gave it to them.

MARGARET EDWARDS

Roses

(FROM THE VIRGINIA QUARTERLY REVIEW)

THE WOMAN, who likes to be called Susan, not Sue, looks down at her hands in her lap; and when she looks up, still listening, the man once again catches her eye. He has dark, curly hair and a mustache. His look is steady, absorbed, savoring, unabashedly sexual. She has no idea how long he has been staring.

The audience for the lecture is arranged in a horseshoe around the lectern, which places Susan and the man, though 20 feet apart, virtually face to face. If she looks straight ahead, she cannot avoid him.

At first, she looks away. She turns her head to the windows which open greenly onto the perfect lawns of a Southern campus. Stuck into the grass at intervals are various impromptu signs, hand-lettered and lashed to pointed sticks, which serve to guide the members of the conference from one building to the next. She has never been to Mississippi before. She has been flown here this morning as an invited guest and speaker. It is May, and roses are blooming in carefully groomed plots. She is still experiencing the wonderment of disorientation. Her mind is putting down rudimentary paths in what is otherwise a blank acreage of the unfamiliar. Directly in her line of sight sits a handsome man.

The speaker continues to drone facts, to make points, to pose rhetorical questions. When the demonstration begins, with charts and graphs, Susan must crane her neck to see them. The man with the mustache is not bothering to lean forward. He is still observing her. He tilts his head backward, very slightly. This movement lowers his lids so that his gaze changes from a commanding regard to one more relaxed, more wistful and amused. In such a manner he acknowledges her having seen him.

"Do you enjoy that sort of stuff?" he asks later. He has ambled up to her immediately after the stiff applause and the shuffling departures. People are drifting to the next forum and Susan intends to follow them.

" 'That sort of stuff' is my field. I'm in business. And you?" She is brisk and direct.

He isn't wearing one of the plastic-coated greeting tags that would announce his name and company. Hers is pinned inefficiently to her blouse. It sags on the silk. He is quite young and carries no jacket, wears no tie. "No, I'm not in business," he says. They laugh as if this were funny.

"Susan," he says, touching her tag very lightly with his fingertip. "Susan Vaughan."

"Not Sue," she says.

"I like it." He shakes her hand with a gruff formality. He is called Edwin, and he doesn't volunteer a surname.

"Not Ed?" she says, and they laugh again.

They walk together out of the hall. Susan holds her program in front of her and takes her direction from a mineographed map. "Straight along here," she says.

"No. We turn."

"That's an exit."

"Right." He gives her a quick cut of his eyes, conspiratorial.

"No, I'm sorry," she says. She won't leave.

Somewhat to her surprise, he follows her down the corridor and through heavy metal doors which lead them into a huge, acoustically perfect auditorium in which she fancies she hears paper tearing. Someone is merely arranging notes on the lectern. A booming thump is a pitcher of water being set by an empty glass. They sit down. As they wait, she learns he is twenty-four, originally from Virginia, now living in Atlanta. He has been hired to take pictures for a slide presentation called "Art and the Business Environment." He will man the projector while the lecturer explains what is being shown.

"Tomorrow," he says.

"I'm just the brawn of the operation," he adds.

She can tell he wants to be reassured. "I would have said you were the artist. You look like one."

An hour of packaging and profit margins makes him restless. When Susan turns her head to him and gestures slightly toward the door, meaning that he can leave if he wishes, he at once stops slouching and stretching and, like a reprimanded child, sits stock still, rigid with effort. He's too young, she thinks.

"You bore that very well," she says, "for someone whose field is photography." They are finding their way to the cafeteria. He has been issued a conference member's pass. His card is blue. Hers is yellow, the special ticket.

"I'll enjoy lunch," he says. "I eat anything. If I'm hungry."

"I see. And you're hungry?"

"Always. But mostly when I see something good." He keeps smiling at her, giving his words double meaning. His drawl is exceptionally mild, softening all that he says though not blurring it, as a mist softens but doesn't blur a landscape.

Susan feels she is blushing. "Already a glutton? Discipline yourself now so that later you won't get fat."

"Oh, beer will get me in the end. Like it does all us Dixie boys."

In the cafeteria they must separate. Blue cards eat in the main dining area. Yellow cards go to the reserved section, to the tables behind a velvet cordon, where the utensils are wrapped in cloth napkins and there are vases of flowers. Susan sits by two people who are experts in her field. The conversation is lively. She forgets all about the young man named Edwin until she sees him walking on a gravel path outside in the sunshine.

They confront each other beside one of the large plantings of roses. The earth has been thoroughly turned till it is brown and weedless, and the clipped bushes emerge individually from the soil, sending out buds and blooms in corollas of color. She points to one particularly lovely blossom which is apricot-shaded, tipped with pink. "Imagine naming it Mudge," she says, for its tag reads Mudge's Twentieth Anniversary.

"What does that mean?" he asks, baffled.

"That's the name of the rose. Each variety has a name."

He falls into stride beside her when he learns she is heading for her room. She is staying in a motel adjacent to the campus.

"They've put you up in style, haven't they?" he says. "I'm supposed to be sleeping in one of the dorms."

Now Susan remembers having seen him in the airport this morning. He must have arrived on another flight, but had been waiting for his luggage when she had been. His large blue canvas backpack had contained something that had broken.

"A bottle of Jack Daniel's," he says in reply to her question. "Black label too."

"I saw you picking the pieces of glass out of a towel."

"Yeah. And my underwear stinks of it. I'll be smelling like I'm drinking on the job." He shakes his head. "I would have been doing just that if I hadn't had such bum luck."

"Too bad."

The conversation falls. They walk in silence. Susan stares straight ahead, aware that his next words will be personal, and they are.

"You're married, aren't you?"

"No."

"I would have thought you were. Divorced?"

"No."

"Living with a guy?"

"No."

He is silent. She says, "Give up?"

He looks to make sure she is smiling. Finding that she is, he takes the joke. "So what are you, a nun?"

"I've separated from the man I used to live with and I'm about to get married. To someone else."

"Complicated."

"Aren't we all?"

She is not more than moderately beautiful, with regular features, acceptable slimness, a clear complexion, large eyes. She has a vibrancy which some men find disagreeable, and in close conversation she seems sometimes not to listen, then turns with a disconcerting flash of attention and proves by her response that she has heard every word. She is attractive to men who fear being needed. Her level gaze, her matter-of-factness, and her quiet alarm at being physically approached reassure them she will back away, keep her own counsel, not grieve if they change their minds. She would seem cold, except that she moves with the ease of contentment, and the veiled stroke of her eyes across a male body is quick for the crucial details and appreciative.

"I live with my girlfriend," he says. "We've been together four years." He tells her name, describes how she sews patchwork pillows and stuffs toy dragons for a crafts store by day, then goes to school at night. She is studying for a real-estate license. She wants to buy a house.

Susan notices how sad he looks. "Do you have a job?" she says. "I mean, besides your photography."

"Yeah. I work for my uncle on and off. Mostly off."

They have arrived at the motel. Susan takes the key out of her purse to read its number, then walks down the row of doors until she stands before 22.

"You're twenty-two?" he says, right beside her as she unfastens the lock.

"No, thirty-three, Edwin. And just for now, good-bye. I want to bathe and take a nap." She has slid through without him and she shuts the door.

The afternoon's hot sun is gone. The room is dark. She doesn't open the blinds. After her bath, she lies on the bedspread nude in the cool, humming gloom. The air conditioner is on. Whoever cleaned the room must have turned it on, routinely, for Susan hasn't touched it. The breeze from its vents stirs the long panel of beige curtains.

There are beige walls, beige spreads, and even the plaid of the armchair upholstery has beige stripes. She thinks of the Someone Somewhere whose job it was to choose the wall color and the fabrics, who sat and thumbed through many samples and considered what went with what, holding swatches together. Perhaps to reconstruct such a scene in her mind will make this dull cubicle become more personal and real. But beige is a coward's color, she concludes. She closes her eyes.

She imagines making love to him, this Edwin. Under him at first, with his arms encircling. Then looking down on him, his mustache like a winged moth. Being kissed, his dark mustache tickling. With eerie exactitude, she can imagine her hands gripped on his back and his muscles working. She opens her eyes. The gentle purr of artificial wind makes the curtains' hems ripple. Even the ceiling is beige here. The speech she must deliver crosses her mind. She doesn't like the second paragraph, and she now knows how she can change it to make it better. She is suddenly very happy, with the guilty happiness of the traveler who never really wants to go home.

Whenever she leaves where she belongs, she becomes immediately detached and misses nothing and no one she has left behind. It is something she never confesses about herself. She keeps a list of names and addresses of the people she will write to. As if she were missing them. This exercise with postcards and stamps seems necessary for sanity, for otherwise she feels cut adrift. She likes the thought that she can step out of her regular life, then step back in it again. Being in a completely different place, with no ties to her friends or past, excites her. The sensation reminds her of acting, of her days in college theater, when she would dress and paint herself into a stranger, then walk from the wings into the fierce brilliance of the stage, a place where silence was a vast, rustling attentiveness in the greenish black cavern beyond the footlights. Such moments of speaking her lines were her most intense experiences of privacy. Now travel takes her there, into deep solitude.

He finds her later as she climbs a flight of stairs heading for a seminar. Is she planning to waste more time listening to "pontificators"? He wants to know. She smiles, because it's so evident he has thought carefully to come up with a word like "pontificators" to impress her.

"I know it all seems a waste to you," she says.

He nods.

"But these are my subjects. I'm working my way up the corporate ladder, you see. I've got to pay attention to the rungs."

He wants her to come for a walk. While she was napping, he discovered a park. "It isn't far. You'll like it."

"I'm sure I would." She shakes her head.

"No. really."

Then she notices that the seminar room is small, unventilated, and drab. Two men, already seated, are smoking cigars. Does she need to know more about profit sharing? Will the speaker even know that much more than she? Thus far the conference hasn't impressed her.

"I'm with you," she says, turning suddenly, and he flushes

with surprise, beaming, set aglow. She is reminded how uniquely attractive young men can be, men who are still novices at disguising their feelings, whose dissimulations fail. Perhaps this is because their circulatory systems are excellent. Their colors change. They redden with delight and pale with dismay. They are prone to unanticipated erections. "Edwin," she says, "you're delightful."

He pretends he hasn't heard.

As they walk along the shaded boulevards (to his directions, no longer to hers) he is talking. She listens. He knows only that she lives and works in Philadelphia, that her parents are alive, that she doesn't smoke. This is enough for him. He isn't curious. Instead, he is rapturously enthusiastic on the subject of his own life. He has built a cabin in a plot of woods his father owns. It's hardly a cabin, just a three-walled shelter with a concrete floor and screens, a place to set up the folding cots and aluminum chairs, a roof to shade the beer cooler. He and his friends go there to drink and to swim in the lake. He's building a platform cantilevered over the water. "You'll be able to run out and dive off the end," he says, as if Susan might actually come there and see it.

"Is the water deep enough?" she answers.

"Always deep enough. And there are snakes in there swimming around." He makes a zigzag in the air with one finger, looking at her to see how she will react.

She smiles.

"But harmless snakes," he says. "They crook up their heads and look at you. Don't bite or do much of anything. The mosquitoes are the ones that bite." His girl friend hates going to the lake because of the mosquitoes.

The park is typical of any small-town Southern park. It is part zoo, part garden, part war memorial. Two dogs chase each other. There are swings whose metal seats and chains have been heated in the strong sun to such a degree that a small boy in shorts, lifted up to take a seat, shrieks and cries. The azaleas are past their prime. Clusters of their last flowers, limp pink handkerchiefs, still cling to the branches.

"Disappointed?" he says. "It looked better earlier when it was cooler and I was here alone."

"No, I like being here. It's just that it's hot."

They walk under the shade of magnolias. When they reach the other end of the park, he shows her a deep concrete basin painted mint green, filled with a dozen alligators, none of which is over five feet long. All of them float motionless in the mud-colored water.

Susan has braced her arms on the basin's rim as she looks down. "They look comfortable, don't they?" she says.

"Or dead."

"But they have their eyes open."

"Dead people's eyes are often open." He says this wisely, as if this were something he has known for a long while. "You can't keep them shut too easily. They tend to come open again." He explains that the uncle for whom he works owns a mortuary. "I'm an assistant, and it's good money."

Again, as when he described the snakes, he is looking at her, measuring her reaction.

Susan nods gravely, wondering why men feel the urge to shock the very women whom they wish to please. Men are always doing this, she thinks. They tell her horrid stories, use coarse words, confess crimes, hoping for what? Her disgust? Her approbation? She has never figured this out, but she accepts it as a part of the seduction ritual.

She says, "I've never seen a body. I mean, a dead human being's body."

"It can make you sad. If they're young."

"Not if they're old?"

"Then you feel sad they got old. Not so much that they died."

As they begin to walk back to the park gates, he says, "I took my gear over to the dorm, and I met a girl there."

"Oh?"

"Yeah. She's a nice one."

Susan smiles and arches her brows. "Lucky you." She does not slow her pace. She lifts her hair off the back of her neck, to cool herself.

He is waiting for her to say more. Forcefully, he pulls a switch off a tree, strips it of leaves, then flicks it over and over. It makes a dull, savage hiss through the air.

She is silent.

He says, "So maybe I won't sleep alone tonight."

"Not if your luck holds."

She avoids his eyes, which are on her. She doubts he has met another woman, for if he has, why isn't he there, not here? Or is he flattering her that he prefers her? Or challenging her that she must take him or another will? Whatever his aim, his effect has been to make the Mississippi humidity more oppressive. The small of her back and her underarms are damp.

They pass the swing set again. No children swing there. The two dogs that have been chasing each other now move in a tight circle, nose to tail. The bigger, fluffy dog, the male, is licking the ass of the short-hair. This gives a new meaning, thinks Susan, to the expression "Dog eat dog."

"You want a drink?" he says, pointing to a water fountain under the last tree in the line of magnolias. The cement-cradled public drinking font has smooth pebbles crusting its pedestal's surface and a burnished brass button. As he presses the button, the water spurts in a high arc, lifting over the chrome rim and falling to the ground. Susan notices how the grass grows much greener in that very spot.

"I'm not thirsty," she says.

He sticks his face into the water, squirting his squinting eyes, opening his mouth fishlike, spluttering. Then he jumps backward, releasing the button and shouting, "Wooo——eee!"

The arc of water dies.

He does the same thing twice more, then shakes his wet, curly hair. "Feels good," he says. "And the water's cold."

On the campus, she leaves him at the bed of roses and continues on to her room. His last words were, "See you at dinner," but she has decided to go late to avoid him. She will sit with her peers. She will recoup her professionalism. She will settle to the task of making contacts, gleaning news, trading facts. She will take some time to look over her speech. She will linger at the interminable cocktail party. She will get a night's sleep.

The next morning, she sees him across the empty tables, eating his breakfast alone. He is a late riser just as she is. She joins him with her tray.

"Good morning, Edwin."

"Hi." He glowers. He won't smile at her.

She sits across from him. He is drinking black coffee and eating toast spread thickly with jam. His plate has already been cleaned. He had drunk two glasses of juice.

He tells her that breakfast is always the best meal in any cafeteria. "It's harder to louse up, I guess. The cook has two ingredients — bread and eggs, eggs and bread. Gets lots of practice." Still he won't smile.

"You look tired," she says.

"No sleep."

"She kept you up then?"

When he raises his eyes, perplexed, Susan knows he has forgotten his line of the day before. "What about the girl back at the dorm?" she prompts him. "Weren't you lucky?"

"No."

He tells her his hard-luck story. Not only would the girl not have him, but his room was taken by someone else. He returned very late from drinking at a bar only to find that there was no place for him to sleep. His belongings had been placed out in the hall. "There was nothing for me to do but unroll my sleeping bag and sack out right there."

"On the floor?"

He nods.

Susan feels he should complain to the conference managers. "They shouldn't have flown you here, then not provided you with a place to stay. Have you told someone?"

"Not yet."

He hasn't been able to take a shower either, he says. Something is wrong with the plumbing in the wing where he slept. There has been no running water. In the other wing, there was such a long line of students waiting turns that he gave up.

"Well, that's outrageous," she says. "Here. Take my key. I won't be using my room at all this morning. You can take your shower there."

He smiles and refuses. Has she forgotten that he's going to show his slides? "I thought you'd come see the work of the artist." He pronounces "artist," with irony, deprecating himself. She can tell he is eager for her to agree to be there.

Instead of concentrating, as she should, on advances in marketing techniques, Susan sits through the lecture that is illustrated with Edwin's slides. Most art, she concludes, makes big buildings more depressing, not less so. There seems to be a dead eye in the business world, which fills recessed-lit foyers, corridors, and offices with paintings that look programmed, flat, and cost-efficient. Even more dismal are the chunky welded-steel sculptures that dwarf any courtyard's spindly potted trees.

"What did you think?" Edwin asks her afterward.

She is evasive, of course. "It was nice."

"You didn't like it. I can tell."

"You take good photographs. I merely wish your subjects had been more worthy."

This pleases him. "You mean they *were* good, my photographs?"

"Of course they were. They were clear. They seem well-composed. You'll have to forgive me for not knowing more about it."

Mollified, he says, "I complained about what happened last night. I've been promised another room. But so far nothing's happened."

They are walking on the now familiar path. The roses send up a heavenly smell. Blooms that were full and perfect just the day before are now showering petals, and buds that were tightly bound are loosening. There is a rose named Bliss.

She says, "What is your last name? I've been meaning to ask you."

"Hunter."

It seems too apropos, and she laughs. Hunter, stalker, trapper. Seeker of quarry.

"See?" he says, and he has flipped open his wallet to show his driver's license. She realizes this is what he still has to do occasionally when he buys a drink.

Then he says abruptly, in a burst, "I like being with you. It's easy to be with you." This tiny affirmation appears to have cost him a great effort, for he has struggled to get it out, and now, with its weight gone, he walks as if he just set down a burden. He bounces on his toes. He flexes his shoulders.

Amused, she touches his forearm, a signal for him to halt, and she lets her hand rest on him even when he stops. "See that?" she says, nodding her head.

"See what?"

"That. The bush with those three different types of roses on it. They do that by grafting. Aren't they clever?"

He holds her touch by remaining breathlessly still. Then he moves slightly closer, leaning with such imperceptible insistence forward that her hand resting lightly becomes a soft pressure on his muscle. She can scent what he would smell like if she were to turn into his shoulder and rest her face on him, as she could very easily do. He parts his lips and lowers his head, for kissing.

She chooses to pull back but squeezes his arm as she releases him. He knows enough about women to take her lead, withdrawing himself, to mask any resentment, and to resume walking beside her, measuring his steps to hers. In complete silence they walk the full length of the long rose bed until they have reached the point where they usually part.

"Well, Mr. Hunter," she says quietly, "I have a bed that's big enough for two and a shower that works. Would you like to spend the night with me?"

"Yes, I would." His voice is tremulous, a little high, and more tender than a whisper.

She doesn't have to look to confirm that his face is suffused with color and gently tilted, like the blooms she stands beside. She says, "Will you come after dinner, after it gets dark?"

"I will."

As quickly as that, it has happened. He turns stiffly and begins to walk away until the walk is too much for him and he must break irrepressibly into a run. She watches. Moments before making him her offer, Susan Vaughan, with her pinned name tag and her conference notes, wouldn't have predicted she would make such a departure from the official schedule. What am I doing, she wonders. And why?

Because, she thinks, while washing herself carefully in the spotless tiled bathroom, he gave no wrong answers. Because he said, simply, forthrightly, "I like being with you. It's easy to be with you." Because he knew how to lean forward very slowly and responsively, and equally he had understood he should pull away. Because his arm was lean and lithe, and he smelt of the ocean.

The Mississippi twilight, when it finally begins, is prolonged. At least it seems so to Susan. The sun has set for hours before the streetlights blink on and some of the cars take the signal to use their headlights. Still it is far from dark. The heat haze becomes a vast purple mist. She sits on the bed, fully dressed again, and tries to read.

She anticipates suggesting that they go out together to a bar, for she is having her usual second thoughts. All men are risks. And *why* sleep with them, she asks herself, anxious now. Her hands sweat, and her stomach is tight. Men are either wonderfully sweet, physically magical, in which case their power to compel is great and relinquishing them is hard. Or else they are disappointing, petty, arrogant, ridiculous, demanding, and one would so much rather be alone. She rises and begins to pace the floor.

She wishes she had said nothing to Edwin Hunter. Taking him on is unnecessary, promiscuous, perhaps even dangerous. Instantly she represses the fear that he might abuse her or harm her. This sort of bad experience has never happened to her. (*Yet*, she concedes. The worst has never happened to me *yet*.) Like a sportsman, though, who weighs the chances, she prides herself on her luck, her deft choices, her shrewd timing. She has known which men to trust. She has never guessed wrongly. Her loving father gave her a sixth sense in sex.

I will enjoy him, she tells herself. She goes to the mirror and looks. There she is, her remembered self and all her changes, her own composite, which no new friend, certainly no stranger, can ever see. She feels inviolate. She feels wreathed in a luxurious peace and desired, for a moment. Then, very suddenly, she's lonely in a silence murmuring with traffic. What if he doesn't come? But he will, of course, because she remembers the inadvertent jolt he gave at the moment she propositioned him. She smiles at the recollection. It was as if she had delivered him a physical blow violent enough to have made him stagger. He's an experienced but not a jaded twenty-four.

And he has no place to stay the night, she thinks, imagining him stretching out in a bedroll on a linoleum floor. Being glad to offer creaturely comforts to win his gratitude, she gives up for good her thought of writing a note, sticking it to the door, turning off the lights, and hiding. She sits at what serves as a dressing table and opens her mouth to examine her teeth. His teeth still have their little scalloped flutings, the mark of youth. Hers are worn. Two lines in the skin of her neck won't vanish, no matter which way she holds her head. These lines are new? No, she has had them always, but they used to disappear when she lifted her chin. Like this.

She is exposing her pale neck to the strong light when she hears a soft tap-tap-tap. She rises at once and opens the door to find him standing there. His head is bowed, and slowly he lifts it. He is nervous and unsmiling. His pack looks heavy on his shoulders. At first she thinks he has come with terrible news, for his face looks stricken. Wild-eyed, startled. His eyelids are open preternaturally. He reminds her of a panicked horse.

"You're here," she says. "I'm glad you're early."

"Yeah."

"You'll have plenty of time for your shower."

He is looking around the room as he enters it.

"Is anything wrong?"

"No." He shrugs off the straps and eases the pack to the floor.

"Why not put it there?" She points to a corner near her suitcase.

He swings the pack into the corner, then stands looking at it. When he turns to her, he folds his arms. He is still unsmiling and pale. He looks so terrified that she is afraid she will laugh. She realizes he had hoped to find her undressed.

"Would you like a drink?" she says.

"No, don't bother."

"It's no bother. The ice machine is just down the way."

"No, no. I'm fine. I don't need it."

"I've been working on my speech," she says, nodding at the papers spread out on the bureau. He walks over to them and examines her briefcase, slim, expensive, of black leather with brass fastenings. He opens it, then shuts it. Hearing the click of its locks seems to intrigue him.

In the lamplight, his skin is very smooth, and standing there as he does, slender and slouching, he makes her feel what she rarely feels for men — protective.

"Your shower, Mr. Hunter? Here's a bit of soap, especially

for you." She hands him a sample-size soap cake still in its wrapper. "That's the bathroom." She points to the door. "And extra towels are folded on the back of the toilet. You'll see them."

Obediently, fully clothed, he goes into the bathroom, closing the door.

She takes off her clothes. When she hears the shower running, she goes in. He is momentarily invisible, standing just beyond her on the other side of the frosted glass. Under the rush of water, his body is a tanned rippling and his head a dark rose.

She pulls open the panel and steps into water and into his arms.

"You're like a regular girl," he says, looking at her, laughing with pleasure. "Like the others."

"You expected something else?" She's amused. He has obviously taken the age difference too seriously. Now he is confident again, stroking and teasing her body with his hands.

As she lathers him with soap, he suddenly says, "Hey, please, let's stop this. I've had two showers already. I don't want to wait any longer. Can't we just go to bed?"

It will be later, after they have spent their first energies and lie curled together, that she confronts him with "You slipped up, didn't you?" She is smiling. "What was this about your having had *two* showers before showing up here? You said so."

He is silent.

"Come, come. I'm not angry. I just want to know the truth."

He grins with satisfaction, rubbing her hip gently with his palm. His hands by being calloused from his carpentry create new sensations on her skin.

"Now, own up," she says. "Tell me. You've been fibbing to me, haven't you?" (Another part of the ritual: men tend to lie.)

"Me?"

"Admit it. You had access to a bathroom of your own, didn't you?"

In the half-dark, he chuckles.

"Not that I mind." She squeezes his arm. "I like being wanted for something more than my plumbing."

"Okay, I confess to a bathroom."

"One that worked?"

"Yep, that worked."

"Furthermore, you were using a room all to yourself, now weren't you? A firm mattress, a bureau, etcetera."

"Yes."

"Ah, I should've known it. You *didn't* sleep on that hallway floor."

"No." He raises himself on his elbow so as to look down on her. His erection under her hand is pink as a rose, petal soft.

"And all my sympathy's been wasted!" She laughs. "Why, you rogue, you naughty cheat, there was *nothing* wrong with your room!"

"Oh, but there was," he says.

"What?"

"Sugar," he leans to tell her in his lowest, loveliest voice, "they forgot to put a woman in my bed."

This next time, with ebullience, with style, he moves into her as one who knows his way. He is looking directly into her face as he takes her. His tentative movements and questioning probes give way to the full stroke of pleasure-giving that makes her cry out. At another point, when he lifts her shoulders to shift her, repositioning her, she is aware how he moves a body's weight often in his work. Practiced. And that revelation — of his laying out the dead — chills her momentarily; then, with mysterious force, stimulates her to reoffer herself even more passionately.

Later, in the complete dark, Susan says, "Edwin?" Lights from the street cannot penetrate the curtains and he is invisible, yet she knows by his breath's new rhythm and how his head lolls too carefully on her breast that he is awake.

"Yeah."

"How deep is your lake?"

He moves even closer. "Twenty feet after a solid rain."

"I'm sorry I'll never see it."

"Well, it's not so pretty really. And the mosquitoes are bad."

The next morning she walks back and forth from closet to suitcase, packing, clenched against feeling depressed. She is scheduled to deliver her paper, then answer questions, then be driven to the airport. The man named Edwin Hunter is still there. Under the drawn sheet, his long body is stretched out as immobile as an alligator's. His eyes are open. He watches. The morning light turns the bedroom's beige a rose's pink.

Methodical action soothes her. She clips the typed pages together and arranges them in her briefcase. She puts stamps on her postcards. From the bathroom, she gathers a Givenchy soap in a plastic case, a zippered make-up bag, a bottle of *L'air du Temps*, a toothbrush made for travel that retracts into a silver cylinder, and deposits these in the suitcase. She slips over her head a long chain with carnelian pendant, then loops up her hair and fastens it, holding the pins in her teeth.

"When do you give your speech?" he says, sitting up.

She reads her wristwatch. "An hour and a half."

"Come here."

As he lifts her skirt and begins to strip her of her pants, she takes hold of his wrists. She kisses his coarse, curly hair.

"Wicked," she says.

"Who's the man you're supposed to marry?"

Because the question is surly and rhetorical, she doesn't answer.

They make love again. When they have finished and she has dressed once more and he has pulled on a pair of bourbon-scented jeans and a shirt, he takes from his pack a dog-eared spiral-bound notebook. He borrows her pencil. "I want to give you my address," he says, tearing an edge from a page.

She shakes her head.

"What? Why not?" He gives her a rueful look.

"Thanks, but I can't write you."

"Okay."

He wads the paper and with a quick grace tosses it. She watches its slow, perfect arc. It vanishes into the wastepaper basket. "But I'll think of you," he says. "May I do that?"

"And I of you." She means it.

He leaves first. In the full light, he makes his way across the parking lot. She watches him from behind folds of the beige curtain. This moment is utterly real to her. Without detachment. From the way he holds his head and saunters, tapping lightly with one hand the hoods of the cars he passes, she guesses he is whistling.

STARKEY FLYTHE

Walking, Walking

(FROM NORTHWEST REVIEW)

"SLEEP," ROSA SAID. "If I don't get sleep."

Not sleeping, her son David had told her when he worked at the hospital, would make you go crazier than anything, and the competition, he said, was pretty stiff.

He had been dead these two years and she saw him now, walking, walking.

"He can't sleep," she said, explaining to herself there was no such thing as ghosts, "I can't sleep."

She saw him perilously close to some edge. The world? Or their flat neighborhood spread like a poor supper on a table above the town. Then saw him veering away from the edge, stiffly sober as he never had been in life, canny when once he had been foolish and vulnerable. He was tired, and she had tried to transfer some of his tiredness to herself by worrying, a burden added to the overwhelming fatigue she already felt from not sleeping. But tired as he must've been, he kept on walking, and she felt she had to keep up her vigil with him.

Rosa's head, wrapped in a napkin, was ball-like so that coming at her from the side it seemed you might be seeing her from the front. The head looked something like a frog's, the eyes large, the mouth rounding inward. But not a real frog, rather an obsidian or carnelian frog, or some rare hard stone.

She had seen Little David laid out in the tuxedo they had told her the burial insurance didn't cover and she had had to pay extra for. She had paid that $2.98 a week virtually forever, since she was eighteen, fifty some-odd years ago. For herself. How could she have known she'd outlive him? The insurance people had argued the policy wasn't transferable, but it was, finally, if she made up the difference of the better box and went on paying the $2.98, now upped to $4.98, and she had wished more — David's death, his little body — could've been transferable too so that she would've been lying there surrounded by the cool peach of pink gladiolus and he would've been in her place, puzzled, sleepless, alone, but alive. Alive, anything might happen: dead, nothing would. Except for this which she couldn't figure out, her seeing him, his seeming to want to explain something.

She had walked by the casket a thousand times. She had thought of his saying one day about a friend of hers who had died and worse than died, been pursued, by pain, by people who wanted her to pay money she didn't have, that the friend had gone "where nobody could touch her."

"And where's that?" Rosa had said.

He had seemed embarrassed. Then he'd said, turning around, "Religion's ignorant. You learn that in nursing school. What makes people sick or well isn't faith, hope or charity!"

What was odd about what he had said was that the same things that made you well made you sick. After a lifetime she wasn't sure about religion, only that she took any help she could get, and that religion went beyond her idea of peace as lying in a satin-lined box surrounded by heavy-smelling flowers. It was useful, she thought, like the friend she had invented to keep from going crazy.

"I see him!" she exclaimed to the woman, her creation, a reasonable, straight-haired creature who spoke about "her people" and was in politics, as invisible as Little David though Rosa saw her, light-skinned, smooth-faced, as falsely soothing as cornbread with sugar in it.

"Where?" the woman demanded by Rosa's changing her voice. "Not in your dreams if you ain't sleeping. Not around here because everything you see in this house I see! His room, your room, this room!"

This room was the main room, kitchen, living room, dressing room, because of the stove. Rosa was proud of the house, its working, the pump in the sink that froze up and only she could get going, the stove she got red hot even with wet wood, the unwired, unplumbed house behind the 7-Eleven that was such a surviving oddity the historical society had asked to come in, once, to see it and make a tape-recording of "what she remembered." Rosa wouldn't talk, said she couldn't remember.

"I was forty-two when I got him." Rosa said to the imaginary companion, a woman she deemed childless in her imagination, and for whom she remembered everything. "I remember the night — clean — as if it was tonight! He in me a year, no nine months." The woman nodded agreeably as if such biological inaccuracies were part of the suffering of their race.

"A year! They say, 'Rosa, you stick out any more they can't get to you to deliver that baby!' You ever notice how mens know everything about having babies?" The smooth-faced woman chuckled softly. "Experience don't count for nothing in this place. And he won't come and he won't come. They say he dead in me. You know what that is? They have to deliver it the same way they deliver a live baby. You sitting there waiting a year and they got to reach way up inside you and haul out a itty bitty corpse."

The woman made a sour face and said, as if the potential horrors of childbirth were well dispelled by the fact, "But David's alive!"

"They turn over and over in you," Rosa said. "He's turning over in me now." She looked up at the door to indicate Little David was walking across the porch.

"Watch out!" she yelled. "If you fall into them rotten boards I can't get you!"

"You'd get him no matter where he fell," the woman said sympathetically.

And Rosa had, when he'd fallen into easy ways, drinking the health of tomorrow before the evil of today was taken care of, being led by loose ends, friends who could not pick up the string, she had sworn she'd go with him to the end, bitter only because she could see it was an end and she couldn't stop its being one. They could still have been going on, mother and son, worrying about such minor difficulties as whether she was making a mama's boy of him at thirty. She asked herself if she had let him fall then, into a shallow hole, she might've saved him from the worse he was walking around in now.

A raspy-tongued cat, she had scrubbed him from a child, going over his groin, pushing the washcloth hard as steelwool against a pot, seeing his growing up, the moment of becoming a man, bending him over the hide-bottomed ladderback chair in front of the stove. Fourteen, he had said: "No, I'm too big." Rosa thought now, wrong not to let him go; she had confused his small size with his maturity, but she should've looked inside his head: he was independent there. He died the same small size. She had picked up the iron she pressed shirts with and heated on the stove when he said no more scrubbing, had come across his face, missing, she told herself years since on purpose, hitting his shoulder with the glancing blow that caused him to lean to the left the rest of his life, a glancing blow because the iron was so heavy she could not manage it once it had left the power of her hand, the power that made his shirts dazzling.

David had got his job at the hospital, Rosa knew, on the strength of the dazzling shirts she had ironed for him and for his willingness to wash and change incontinent patients. She had beamed when the head nurse told her, "We got plenty nuclear medical specialists and space doctors out here and *one* common laborer: *Him.* I trade you five nuclear medical specialists for one *him!*"

Rosa could've blamed everything on Little David's father but she didn't know him past being glad he had gone. He had loved her for periods of quarter hours. He had had no thought for time beyond those periods and she had had thoughts for nothing else. Little David had been half him. But he hadn't stopped at half a bottle. The other half must've been her. There was some desire she had passed on to him that kept him thirsty then, walking now.

The trouble with Little David was he couldn't amuse himself. He had had the good job driving Dr. Murphy. Dr. Murphy delivered every baby in town though he only had one leg. His name was legion, almost as legion as Washington. And while Dr. Murphy was delivering, Little David was nipping.

When the county replaced Dr. Murphy and his midwives with its own hospital (and baby deaths shot up, the old doctor said) he had his bird collections to occupy him. David, at twenty-one, was too shaky to climb trees and bring down eggs from the nests. "I'd go myself but for the leg," Dr. Murphy said, and hired a younger, soberer, agile boy. He got David into practical nursing classes. He was quick, he understood the courses. But between classes. In the bathroom? Standing outside the hospital in the alley on fine days? Rosa couldn't teach him to amuse himself because she couldn't understand what spare time was herself.

Rosa lay down, closed her eyes and was wide awake. The others — how was it a person could be completely alone, lose her husband, her son, parents, all sisters, one brother and still have relatives? — came and went, saying she was crazy, or asking to see him, agreeing, sharing the vision. "Yes! I see him! There!" "In a white robe? The peace on his face? Yes!"

The relatives explained it was all perfectly normal, or had they said perfectly natural? They said it was God's footprint on her brain, that it — did they mean him? — would go away. With time. Time! There was no such thing. You had only to be in a hurry to learn that.

Rosa thought and thought, it was not normal. Or natural either. Something was causing Little David to pad about. Wearing the tuxedo.

That meant he had come straight on from the funeral instead of going anywhere else first, home or purgatory, and the tuxedo itself was unnatural, a flimsy sort of facade like a building in a ghost town or the starched bibs that Chaplin used to wear in movies. What a church that Chaplin must've run, she thought. In heaven since it seemed unlikely she would ever get to California, she would like to visit that man's church, hear him preach, see the bib pop off from the trouser button they didn't even put on new pants now and slap him in the face. Little David's tuxedo was like that. Only it had no pants, just sort of a black apron that went to his knees. No back. For what they charged her, she thought, it should have had a train. Angels to hold it up. His poor little legs! The walking, walking, pushing against the sleazy black apron. The little clip-on bow tie. He needed a real one, a satin butterfly she would tie as lightly as the ribbon around his baby neck she had bowed the day of his baptism.

Her age, she was afraid, was closing in on her. She had to get him to bed or to sleep before she went. Or, dead too, there would be two of them. Moving around an inch or two above the ground, like a hydrofoil she'd seen, floating on air above the water unable to get themselves down without going under.

The letter that came was almost a note from him. He leaned towards her across the distance, motioning her to read it as she saw on the envelope titles and styles ("Mrs.," her husband's names) she had not worn for so long she wondered who they were talking to. "Madame." Dear Madame: They were going to dig up his grave. With her permission. They were going to dig up the whole cemetery. It was harder, they hinted, to get permission from the dead than the living and so would appreciate cooperation. "They bought a stamp to tell you that?" the woman said, reading over her shoulder.

"Eminent domain," the letter stated, "To connect a vital access to another." " 'They' would dig to China if you let them," the woman murmured. "Wake my people up from their only rest!" Rosa thought she was going to sing.

The highway was coming. They would pay for the exhumation. They had the permission of the state. The county coroner. The coroner's physician would be in attendance. There was a hearing scheduled. She could attend with her lawyer or other "representative." Rosa did not understand how that could be as the letter was *from* a representative.

She held the letter up to the light. It seemed almost to take on the shape of David's face, losing its square edges, the paper matching, equaling the face, his face paler and paler next to it in the distance, his body thinner and thinner like winter sun through the clouds. He seemed to grow towards her, flatter and flatter, to fix her with his stare.

The second letter — Little David had come very close this time — so close she thought she could grab him and "put him down" — she used to say that for putting him to bed when he was a baby — but when she reached, her hands went through air. She had not chosen to attend the hearing, it said, or even to send her "representative"; they understood this as consent. The exhumation would take place "on or about" December 21st at an hour she couldn't somehow remember.

It was the shortest day of the year. Rosa was grateful for that.

David, half naked, the cold cracking his poor skin, the very light skin that anything, even a mosquito bite, scarred, his tiny butt that never quite filled out his underwear pants, exposed to the gaping people digging up his grave, would have less time in the merciless winter light that never warmed.

She dressed carefully. Out the front door the intense winter sun blinding her, she realized she was wearing the black dress she had worn to his funeral. The light-skinned woman smiled: her perfect teeth, Rosa saw in the dazzling light, were not her own. The minted scent of properly soaked dentures wafted past her nose. She saw David's nostrils flare. He was leading them.

At the street he pointed to her shoe that was untied. She bent over to tie it and just as she tightened the knot, lost her balance, the wind spanking her, and she sat down hard on the cold pavement. She had not put on underwear believing somehow he might try to get back inside her. That the year he had spent there had not been enough and she must present no hindrance to his journey back. Or forward. He threw up his arms in front of her, closer to her than he had ever been, even in life. The weariness in his face gave way to glee. He mouthed the words, "You see?" She nodded to him, as unable to understand his meanness as his wanting to be separate from her in life, her dreams for him. Maybe, she thought hoping, he had learned to amuse himself. In life he had been sweet, he had been obedient, but he didn't want to be part. He had had the extra job when he was able, to try to earn money for the refrigerator they told him couldn't be plugged into the house. He had tried to help, but he didn't want to be with her or anybody else. He liked the company of drinking, *doing* it as much as the taste of wine itself. When he had become visible after death, she knew there would be plenty of company for him out there, people who couldn't rest, things like drinking and girling that liked to get the best of you, forces, powers that made you drop things and gave the falling things the anger they would have had had they been thrown! A biscuit dropped from the table could break your foot if it wanted to, it gained such momentum from somewhere. Things could hurt you hard as people; stub your toe, cut you, worry you crazy.

Rosa thought the woman with her should've offered her comfort, her arm or some short cut to the cemetery. The sidewalk was overgrown. Everyone who passed this way had cars now. Children went to school on the bus.

Rosa was not used to walking long stretches anymore. She felt dizzy. The sun burned her eyes. She wished she'd worn a broad brim hat. She even wished for a moment he would go away, leave her to ordinary grief. She'd go back to her cold bed and lie down; now, she felt she could sleep. Maybe she could pity him better when she woke up. But the woman took on a superior look that said, We must go on. Rosa could hear some spiritual proclaiming strength in suffering.

At the cemetery, Rosa's presence had not been needed to begin. The backhoe had already dug up graves, the truck was loaded with muddy caskets. Over Little David's grave — she knew it by the cedar tree, almost red now from the winter cold — the arm of a derrick raised like the hand of a blessing, held a dangling empty concrete rectangle, coffinless, Little Davidless. There was no bottom, no top to the vault which the funeral home man had said was permanent. She approached the grave. A man in waders, startlingly close, peered up at her from the mud in the hole. For a moment she thought the man was trying to take David's place. The mud seemed like quicksand, and the man shifted his weight, left foot, right foot. He must've been cold too, in the grave with mud and ice water around his feet.

Two men came towards her. It was her grave, her son's. No, she saw nothing in it, either. It had been, she told them, *solid bronze*. It would last, the funeral home had said, forever. She had the written guarantee. Not a handle, the men told her, a hinge, or a screw had been found. There'd be something, they said. It might be rusty, but there'd be something. Wasn't it just two years? Two years wouldn't destroy everything. "She could argue that," her friend, stepping around the excavations, said. Across what was now a field, the cedars and yews having been largely bulldozed, she saw David, his teeth exposed, Rosa couldn't tell, in a grimace or a smile.

They drove her, which was a relief, warm, in their car, to an office in the court house and explained and asked questions about who buried David and whether she had put any gold or silver in the box, things like jewelry or a watch, or "money," they said winking at each other, "for the trip." Then they drove her

to the medical school where a young woman who seemed
frightened of Rosa and wouldn't look her straight in the eye
told them *their* bodies came from the state asylum or she (it was
part of her job) asked for the bodies from the relatives of indi-
gents who wanted to avoid the final payment of a funeral. They
would never buy a body from "a questionable source." She had
her records, they could look at them. They turned then to Rosa.
Had she? What did they take her for? They hadn't meant that,
they said. Had only turned to ask her if she had an idea. What
did they do with the cadavers, they asked the young woman,
when the medical students were finished? The young woman
had an answer though Rosa's friend who had squeezed into the
car with them looked skeptical, as if her people were being
exploited. The sanitation department came, the girl said she
alerted them, they came especially, nothing else in the truck, no
garbage, she put it, and they carried the remains off to the city
incinerator. The pathology lab got bits and pieces.

The path, Rosa thought, then led to the funeral home. The
owner stood on the porch defending himself, the high columns
that had been sewer pipes and had no relation to the rest of the
house except for being painted white rising behind him.

He listened to the woman, the men. Representatives from the
district attorney's office he had dealt with before, even contrib-
uted to. But this woman's eyes didn't blink.

"You said it was solid bronze," she said, fairly quietly.

"Solidbronz!" he told her, "a registered trademark! Nothing
lasts forever." With his luck today, the same box was sitting in
the salesroom waiting like some girl at a dance, to be chosen,
and this woman — and he knew her — was the sort to have
scratched her initials in the side when she knelt, wailing by the
bier of her son, two years ago, the sort to run her hands under
the box and feel the little trap door that allowed the frail body
to exit the strong box. It was foolish, wasn't it, he thought,
almost asking her, she seemed so reasonable, to waste a three
thousand dollar box. When it was as good as new? So foolish to
give in to wet ground when wet eyes had to dry and go home.
Unchristian! Where your treasure lies so also lies your heart!
Leave it in the ground?

One of the men, he thought, to frighten him, recited another case, said something about greed: "They resold the shrouds twice! Thirty cents each. Piece of sheet!" The man from the D.A.'s office looked at him as though he were recounting a parable from the Bible, its weight past the necessity of explanation. There was a reason the man had mentioned money. He was running for office on this visit. The funeral home man grasped the equation. He turned to Rosa. She was so reasonable, what people used to call "wise," when you could afford to be poor, before water bills and light bills could change your life.

She understood people making money. But this was supposed to be a place of necessary grief. You came here in your last hour, not to God. Nothing was free; everybody knew that, but even God listened a moment for the money you paid. The undertaker and the D.A. man seemed to be splitting apart here, the D.A. more sympathetic. David, pale as the false columns outside that held up the roof, stood square behind the undertaker. Odd, Rosa thought, he would've sided with the man who'd cheated her. Paying the money, she thought, for the coffin, was like saying a prayer, a necessary ritual; results anybody's guess; like guarantee, a word that no longer obtained. The man's gypping her had turned back on him. David wasn't in the box. David had got out. David had broken his bonds. David was loose. He could improve now. The figure, walking alone that had worried her, now pleased her, slowly, like the heat in the car which after the long walk in the cold, had seeped sweetly, complete, around her swollen knees and thighs, soothed them and made the motion and comfort of the body possible and infinite. Jesus had let that woman wash his feet with her hair and oil him up good. Little David was moving, lifting. She had seen his pitiful little backside and shivered for him. He had washed the backsides of the sick and dying when nobody else would and carried out the buckets. Not everybody saw that side in people, she thought, some just saw the tuxedo side. Those people would do the same thing to live people this funeral home man had done to the dead, dress them up, box them. She knew David now couldn't blame her for anything. He'd have been better off if he'd let her follow him the way she scrubbed him.

Suddenly, she turned, asked the man if he saw David. The quick consummation in the undertaker's eyes, his thinking this craziness would go against her, that they would excuse him because of her, thrilled her with its connivance. Like her relatives, the man caught the tone.

"Yes!" he fairly shouted. "I see him! Crowned!" and his eyes, yellowish and bulging, rolled back in his head so the people from the D.A.'s office could see. They were smart enough to give no sign; Rosa knew they were thinking about elections: she was only one vote; the undertaker was a precinct power.

Still the men paused, staring at her, her strangeness, her virtue in letting go. They saw that the knowledge the man had cheated her seemed to please her as much as any damages might.

"David's in the sky," she said, quietly satisfied.

"Escaped," the undertaker whispered under his breath.

The men might smile at each other later, over a drink, though now they were unable to, staring at this minor revelation that was somehow disturbing. They kept looking at Rosa, looking for a way to understand her without giving her any credit, to find themselves back on the concrete of their own beliefs and certainties. She returned the stares, blinkless, forcing upon them the enigma of differences. There was no noise in the room. Rosa's steady eyes grew, never leaving the men. They looked uneasily at the ring of caskets around the room, the choices, the dull tones of silver, bronze, gold, the thin metal — no more than foil — covering the wood (or plastic?) boxes. It was as though they could hear something through the silence: Rosa's anguish. Flesh whining. Damned of earth, damned of air. But staring at Rosa they knew they could hear nothing.

Home, Rosa felt she could sleep. She took off her dress slowly, squinted hard at the image of David, his feet thick and crusty from years of going barefoot, the tuxedo front no more than a black veil covering his nakedness now. The edges of his hands and feet, like a leper's, began to blanch and fade.

The light-skinned friend glanced at her with pity and contempt — a woman whose grasp had exceeded her reach — and moved into the light surrounding the softening form of David. Rosa made one more desperate lunge for him. Her hands came back wet. Everything she could remember was wet: the man standing in the grave with his feet in water. The little drops that would find the leaks in the roof above her and trickle in, travelling halfway across the house along a beam to find an opening, water always seeking the lowest level. It was raining outside, bright slashes that would turn to ice before dark.

Rosa smoothed the clean, cold sheets. The force of her weariness pressed down on her. She tried to find the mind that had found David, known he was not where she had buried him, but there was only a feeling of loss, like static from the radio during a storm. The people today had not been able to count the dead much less the living. She thought of souls, numberless souls, still wandering around in the void. She wished she could follow each of them the way she had David. Through her flickering eyelids she saw less and less of him until there were only bright bits fighting against the rain. Even as he dissolved the lilt of his body where she had struck him stayed and she felt the iron in her hand, lighter than her sleep.

H. E. FRANCIS

The Sudden Trees

(FROM PRAIRIE SCHOONER)

BY SPRING SHE WAS uncannily thin and stumbling frequently. And though her classmates, with a naturalness as uncanny, leaped to her and caught and straightened and supported her, even making comedy of it, his principal and fellow teachers and some parents insisted she be taken out of classes: She should be kept in the Home, first thing you knew she'd be breaking bones, there would be outrage and shock and trauma, and the children would never forget.

"But what of her future?" he said.

Breath sliced air. Faces froze.

"Her what?"

"Future."

Future.

There was a future — until there was nothing. Unless nothing.

"She'll spend it alone — in a bed. The State will send her to the hospital — to lie and do nothing but vanish — when she's unmanageable."

"She's almost that now."

"But *not* that," he said. "You see how the children help her — and there's only until June to go until the end of classes. She'd want to finish them."

But they were a wall of faces too wordless and still, eyes deliberately elsewhere. Oh, he knew they understood. How *could* they defend themselves but through staunch silence? They were parents, they paid taxes, they went faithfully to PTA. And wasn't it their town, their children's future?

But he could do nothing. Their unity was stone.

"If you could let it be natural," he said.

In two days, when she fell and tried to get up but could not, he asked Alice Dempsey to monitor his class and carried Rhoda out to his car and drove her to the Home.

The next morning he did not want to think her face, but in class the empty place — third row, third seat — gaped. The box on his seating chart was a grave. Absence cried out her presence.

When the children went yelling and shouting home and he said, "See you tomorrow, Alice," and waved down the corridor to Bill Brown, he went outside — and his breath caught: at the suddenness of trees, veils of instant spring gold glowing in the sun, the yellow burn of forsythia, and a warm weight of air that pressed at his mouth, nostrils. Off the road the bay moved with a glitter and heave that threatened to spill over the edge and carry him. This. And he went past his turn and took the old dirt road up slope and came abruptly onto a high flat rise overlooking the Sound, where the wind grew and the Home loomed barren. Its walls and uncurtained windows and long porch futile to sea wind, the great house looked hollow. From the playground below came shrieks and yells.

Inside, he did not look far. In the enormous hall beyond the desk where Ella Trask usually sat, Rhoda was standing. How tiny she was! A wind might whisk her off.

"I knew your car." She did not move.

He laughed. "You were right then. Well, you can't do without a history lesson, can you? Suppose —" He took her hand. "Suppose we do it in the little room. It's quiet and there are always gulls out the windows.

"I'll carry you."

"I don't hurt." Her voice, which in the chorus of class borrowed strength from the others, was as wobbly as her legs.

From the corridor Ella Trask called, "She said you'd come, Mr. Trueblood. Have a good lesson, Rhoda."

"Today Four B got to the hardest part, fractions, in math, and to India in geography, and a big battle in Africa in history. First for math. You ready? If I bought a quarter of a pound of butter — write it this way — and bread weighed —"

"I love fractions!"

Precocious, she had skipped third and usually left 4B behind too; and despite distracting cries from the playground and a tumble of children in other rooms, she did now. Her fingers moving the pencil caught the problems almost before his words fell — she was that adept. Her brown eyes rolled in quick thought, and the long brown hair rode over the table, flicked and lashed as she bent close.

Repeating names carefully, she followed through India. But in history, in the midst of Carthage, her hands had to hold her head in place.

"Well, that was a long long siege Hannibal went through and *he* didn't do it in one afternoon. Why should we?" he said.

"Because Four B did, you said." Not to accuse. Fact was fact.

"That's because so many heads were working together. Sometimes that's fast."

"But it's easiest alone with you 'cause your head is much bigger and full of things." Though she laughed, her face stayed pale.

"Now we've got time for a go around the building and then your suppertime. On my back?"

All the next week was the interlude after school. She was confined to sitting, but when *he* (there was only one *he*, she let them know) came, by special permission it was her hour on the grass. Though they watched earthworms' probing mouths and pushing corrugations and girdles, she wouldn't let him ease up on her lessons. She would follow Hannibal. "I hate the Romans and love Hannibal and Hamilcar Barca! Ugh. Someday I'll climb the Alps, I'll plant a dandelion for Hannibal, it will bloom in the snow. You just wait." He let her crawl. Together they gathered a bouquet of dandelions to put in a glass on her windowsill, a yellow splash in the sun.

On Monday the bouquet was gone.

And Rhoda was not waiting.

"They've taken her to the hospital up-island," Ella Trask said. "But they'll take good care of her. We had to think of the children. They couldn't really bear it."

Bear it?

You did not know what children could bear. And forever.

At school Laura or Anne or Millie shifted roles, so losing Rhoda did not cripple their games, but after their cries and shrieks and laughter at recess, when they came in and took their seats around that dark center, the class asked, "How's Rhoda?" "When's Rhoda coming back?" And Anne, out of the blue, said, "We all want to *see* her."

So, with permission from parents, a station wagon full, they made the long ride with gifts and his promise of a homeward-bound stop at McDonald's for hamburgers and fries.

You could see Rhoda's eyes could not contain — they darted from face to face as all spurted at once: "Listen you know Mrs. Berg hates games and scolded Timmy and Mill shoved Mary's head down the toilet she screamed and —" All the while her hands clutched the compass and hair ribbons and sketchbook they'd brought. Her own voice made a quiver softer than a veil over them, she listened so hard her eyes never blinked, even *they* listened: "Mr. Berry is sick and Mama gave me a birthday party and we went to the beach but the water's too cold to swim yet and Mary hid Mr. Trueblood's box of chalk and we all stayed in for recess and then Dennis squealed on Mary and —"

But how quickly they were bored. Their attention wandered to a nest outside the window, to the children in the other beds. Corridors — down, up — called. They pursued wagons and trays, tracked nurses. He was all voice and hands to tame them. But she — how in her stillness she blotted them up!

When he called time to go, everybody scrambled, leaped with laughter, sending volleys of "Bye, Rhoda," "So long," "Bye, bye, bye," making children in the beds turn heads, wave. Despite his voice and hand, his "I'll see you soon," her gaze turned stone.

Looking back, he saw she had not moved.

By the time they saw the big M blazing yellow arches over the trees, they were all screaming. Rhoda was virtually forgotten. The outing was over.

But Rhoda did not forget. Her presence startled: In his box in the teachers' lounge lay the letter with the jolt of her hand-writing. She wrote in awkward clumps.

Dear Mr. Trueblood:
    Tell the class thanks.   I have all the gifts on the bed.   It is cold at night but their gifts keep me warm.   Sometimes it's

dark.   But there are lots of faces here.   Mr. Trueblood we
didn't finish Hannibal.   Is anyone sitting at my desk?   Tell
hello to Miss Samples and Anne and Terry and . . .

He saw each face take its desk. The room filled. She had not
left one name out.

After the last hour he read the letter to the class. They listened as if words stood Rhoda before them. Lines said special
things to some — they emitted laughs, sighs, murmurs, but once
he began reading their names, the tense expectation made them
say "Shhhhh, *lis*ten —" till he dismissed them.

But the letter did not dismiss him. At home he saw it when he
lowered his books in halts and stares at the sea. Words stood in
the waves: It is cold at night. Sometimes it's dark. There are lots
of faces here. Blocks of words stood harder than glaciated stone.
If his hand reached, it would touch words. Marie. He could not
turn to her now. There was silence and the sea he had been
maddened and consoled by when she left. He swore, I won't
live with anyone else, I won't ever live with anyone else. She had
turned life quicksand — not only by going, but despite all warn-
ings, suddenly. Her going had told him that to her what was
love was sex; what was companionship, time filled; what was
hope, desperation; what was a dream of a long life together, a
lie. She said, I can't live small town and be confined to salt water
and your papers and books and sometimes a niggardly night's
reprieve — to what? the same faces, same streets. I'm hemmed
in — and Jesus, how can you stand it? I'm breaking, Darren.
But, Marie, he said, this is my life.

Gone. Day after day, weeks, all he heard, relentless, in the
beat of the waves was Marie, Marie, Marie.

He dropped the book and went out onto the deck. The sea
was a great heaving. Waves beat, beat. He stared — all he saw
was that face, stone, Rhoda sitting there stone — stared until he
was sitting there, he was Rhoda sitting there, beating day after
day — "No," he said, so loud it halted wind and sea in him for
an interval. No. *Not* day after day after day — or what did it all
mean?

He called Esther.

"Darren!"

"Esther, listen — I've decided to do something, and I may need your help, but first, don't think I'm crazy. You know me best, you'll understand, though I'm not even sure *I* do."

"Your voice is vibrating like wire."

"You know Rhoda Marsh?"

"The child you've just visited?"

"Im going to try to get her."

"Get her?"

"Bring her here."

"To town? I don't understand."

"To my house. Keep her here."

"But, Darren — Do you know what you're asking for?"

"Yes. But no."

"You know she hasn't long. She may die there."

"Yes."

"But you're willing?"

"Yes."

"Do you know — oh, it's not your prime consideration right now — but do you know what it will do to us — I mean, to your friends, relationships . . . ?"

"I've all summer free. I can."

"But — may I ask it? — *why*, Darren?"

"I don't know."

"You don't know why?"

"I told you — I don't know. But I must. Perhaps I'll find out why. Esther, *will* you, if I need it, help me, stand by my character, whatever this requires? I'll talk to Arnold Bingham — he's a fine lawyer — if there are complications. But why should there be? The doctors know her condition, she has no parents, to be practical the State will be glad of one expense less, they need hospital beds, so except for legalities you name the objections. Will you? You trust me, don't you?"

"Who more? But do you realize what it will do?"

"To all of us? But for a summer, one summer in our — her — life!"

"Well, I do have objections, but you know I'll help. You come first."

"Rhoda does."

"Well, Rhoda does."

"You're a prize!"

And despite his urgency, which Bingham echoed, he had not considered Rhoda's choice, he had assumed she would come. But Farnley, head of the hospital, had to protect. "You know rights these days, free will is public will or no will, and I, if I were Rhoda, would want to be asked. You agree, Mr. Bingham? Shall we all go see her together?"

In the corridor Bingham said, "You know what you're doing to yourself, Darren?"

"No." But his hand assured Bingham.

The presence of three official visitors alerted all the children, brought silence, all attention on Rhoda.

"You're blushing," he said.

"I knew you'd come, Mr. Trueblood." She was trembling.

"Mr. Trueblood wants to take you home to spend the summer vacation with him, Rhoda," Farnley said.

She did not once turn her eyes to Farnley.

"Yes."

"Well!" Eased, Farnley was smiling. "No doubt about that decision."

"Now?" Rhoda said.

"That's up to Mr. Trueblood."

Darren laughed. "Now."

"The nurses will dress Rhoda. Barbara, she's going home."

"Home?" the nurse said. "Oh. Of course."

When she was ready, he would have scooped her into his arms but for Farnley's warning glance: He was responsible for her now. He raised her gently. When word of her leaving passed down the beds, all sorts of nervous laughs and cries came from the others, and clapping. "Home!" "Come see us, Rhoda." "Have a swim for me." A few forlorn faces gazed, too still. Rhoda waved and for the first time a laugh, loud, broke from her throat. He felt it reverberate in her chest.

How she came to life! She slept in his brother's old bed in the room next to his, the door between open unless she wanted it shut — that way he could hear her any minute. But mostly he kept her at his side. She loved the spread of the Sound, especially when, roused, it thrashed at the shore below and swirled about rocks half the size of the house; and when it threatened to mount the cliff to the deck, she screamed with the thrill of it.

"Can I go down the steps?" Long wooden stairs went down the slope to pure white stones and then sand and water. He put on his bathing trunks.

"On my back?" But her clutch failed so he carried her. "Now, we'll take off your clothes and go in —"

"I don't have a suit!"

"Tomorrow I'll buy you one. Right now — don't tell a soul! — you'll wear pants in, okay?"

She buried her head in his neck, a huddle in his arms, and he walked deep into the water, and they bobbed awhile.

"I can swim. Let me."

He held her while she feebly flapped and kicked till, fearing her fragility, he gathered her up like a delicate web.

She helped him cook. "Hand me the package? That's a spatula. In that drawer's an apron —" In her attempts to move about, she would forget and when she toppled, vigilant as he was, he swept her up. "Must be grease on the floor . . . That chair . . . Something wrong with your sole? . . . Let me see . . ." until she said, "It's all right. I fall. I'm weak. You have to get used to that."

At such moments he wanted to stand in her place, in her thin body, behind those eyes — and see this house, sea, him. You made some adjustment. The body told you. You did what it told you. Did you know what the body was doing? He wanted to see from Rhoda, be Rhoda.

"And don't you worry," she said. "I'll tell you."

"Tell me what?"

"When I can't do something."

Some afternoons they would ride till she waned. "How 'bout an ice cream?" She would glow. But in her cup, hardly touched, it would melt.

Was she doing it for him?

When he had to stop by Dr. Spurling's, the M.D. shingle nearly stopped breath.

"Don't run off now. I need a word with the doctor."

"You sick?"

"Nope. Just need advice."

"You can go then." She made a deep laugh.

And Spurling confirmed: Of course she would dwindle, bones could easily break, coordination go, speech go muddy, lumps and swellings appear, pain . . .

But could a hospital save? prolong? do more?

"You check with me for anything you're not sure about handling, the least thing, and at any time."

At home she said, "Hannibal! We didn't cross the Alps yet. We're stranded." She struck the table. Pain cracked her porcelain face. She gripped into laughter, bit, but he felt her pain dart up his own arm.

"Okay. Hannibal. But only for thirty minutes. Starting today we're having a schedule for what you missed, if you like, but only weekdays because . . . Guess what's coming to the playgrounds this Saturday?"

Her eyes grew awesome. "Not — !"

"Yes."

She screamed, "The circus!"

Instantly he regretted saying it, then as instantly ashamed at his regret because she clapped and her eyes glowed so, she vibrated with excitement; but something in him did not want her to go. Why? He was perplexed by his own probing, his own perplexity.

Half the nights she was awake — at intervals he heard her — until Saturday.

"It's today, and it didn't rain!"

By one she was nearly breathless with anxiety. She had gone over her four dresses — for him, happy because the blue was his blue. "Wonderful!" he cried.

"I'm ready." She yelped, pure joy, crawling about slowly on all fours.

"Stalking like that, you'll be joining the tigers."

"It's elephants I want to see."

"There'll be plenty of those."

All down the road she talked a blue streak, not one minute taking her eyes off things to look at him. Was she hoarding? "Down that dirt road're the best blackberry bushes! — you get quarts at a time, last summer Terry and me and Tina Lewis went, then we'd hunt things in the dump before they burned them all up, that's old Hinkelman's house, we steal green apples and he chases us and he swears to make you stop up your ears —"

In her excitement she was grinding and slurring words. Did she know?

"And did you stop up your ears?"

"No." She giggled. "*We* know all the words. Ohhhhh!" The woods fell away, sky fanned out, the big top loomed, colored flags galore raged in the wind, and the lot glittered with cars. "The whole town's here. Listen!" The band, tinny in the blow off the sea, came in spotty bursts.

Light in his arms, she was twisting, turning, waving. "Amy! Terry!" She called name after name.

"It's Mr. Trueblood and Rhoda!"

A crowd gathered around them at the entrance: Dr. Walker and Jenny, the Wardwells, and Charlotte Fay, half her classmates . . .

Nervous somewhat annoyed, if smiling, he said, "We'd better find a seat," for it was bleachers catch-as-you-can; and they sat, but a wound opened in him when they said, "What, Rhoda?" "What'd you say?" "It must be the wind, but I can't hear —"

"Here come the clowns!" Red-white yellow-white motley atumble and berserk, leaps beatings falls screams whistles laughter. Confetti sprayed rainbows over the audience, in Rhoda's hair, everywhere. A joyful heat filled the tent.

She was not even blinking: Trapezes swung in her eyes, bangles glittered, cycles flipped, lions leaped to a whip — with each act the wider her gaze. She reveled in it, sometimes in a frozen stillness of ecstasy. When she pressed close, he felt her heart quick quick quick against him; but when at last through the great flaps *they* appeared — "Elephants!" — she screamed. "Look! Gold and silver! Wow!" And the trainers glittered silver blue yellow red glitter, with batons — one touch and the elephants moved, surged, raised gigantic feet, knelt on front on rear legs; and when one woman lay under an elephant's foot, Rhoda's nails dug deep into his arm and she shrilled as the woman rose "Safe!" But when the trainers stopped the elephants and a man announced a ride on the back of each elephant for the lucky person whom a trunk pointed straight toward, alone she rose, she stood, her arms reached out — At once, as if the elephant spotted her, its trunk rose and pointed. "Yes!" she cried, but it came taut as a whisper. And the crowd around her shrieked as all the elephants pointed at their lucky chosen.

Down he carried her. Down slowly sank the elephant. He set her in the howdah. Slowly the elephant rose. Around the arena she rode, smiling, her hair asway as she sat, stunned with joy, as the tent filled with applause and cheering. Before the descent she threw him a kiss, and when she slipped down he could feel the hot palpitation and the thud in her chest. She could not speak, but she gripped louder than words.

Then the band struck up and clowns reeled into the arena, and amid final catcalls and shouting, it was over.

Not till they were in the car did she burst: "Did you see me? Did you? Did you?"

By morning she was in a fever, talking elephants and Alps and Hannibal. Hot and so dry, yet she pushed water and juice back, murmuring, "Nnnnnnn," and on into the second night, "Nnnnnnnn."

She saw something. Something would not leave her eyes. ". . . nnnns. ark."

"What is it, Rhoda?"

He looked where she looked. He lay beside her, stared at walls, objects, following her hand and eyes, tried to think what she saw, how. The metal light disc made a dark shadow against the ceiling. If you watched long, it came down at you, it grew. ". . . nnnns . . . dar . . ." The sun's dark? He removed the disc and brought in a table lamp. She stopped staring at the ceiling, but kept up her mumbles Elephant Hannibal Terry Lee Anne till he knew he had to ease her, had to. It was the first time he must give her anything. The needle did ease. She slept. And when she finally closed her eyes, he felt a sudden hard choke that caught him so unaware it blinded him an instant.

But it frightened: She slept almost steadily for two days.

At night, straining, he could hardly hear her breath. By the night light he watched the sheets for the vaguest rise and fall of her chest — and stood long, looking, till reassured. Often she lay so motionless he had to sit on the edge of the bed or lie beside her to catch a sound or even the slight warmth of her breath.

Now he was learning her: the shape of bone, the thin skin, where it lay taut to ribs, taut over belly, vague blue veins, her dry forehead turning a pale translucence with the finest lines and lines down her cheeks, through her dry lips. Despite her small body, in the face so serious in repose, the expression of long experience, a woman was emerging. He pressed back the hair, surprised at how cool it was over the hot flesh. Her breath had a rancid odor, she expelled puffs of burnt chestnut, yellow smears he quickly washed. He came to know when each motion would come, could say It is time, and rise and go to her, as if she'd called. Awake or in half sleep she too responded to his motions, knew when to cling, roll, ease down with his hands.

Occasionally she would open her eyes, wide, still, unrecognizing. Was she confused? lost? disoriented? She would sigh back into that other world or let her head slump against him. Nights he lay with her, vigilant, fearful he might roll over, break bones. Her quiet throb slowed his own till her breath was his, her heat came from his body, the odor of her mouth from his.

When at last she woke fully, she smiled.

"You," she said. "You're back."

His throat filled with a rush.

He was cramped, but he picked her up and carried her onto the deck. "What a glorious morning!" The water burned, enough heaving gold to blind you.

That very afternoon Esther drove up.

"I've come to invade the recluse. Do you mind? I've something for Rhoda. A surprise. Do you like surprises, Rhoda?"

"Everybody likes surprises!"

"What? *Oh!*" She set the box down.

Rhoda's fingers gripped so hard they turned white.

The top shot off. "A kitty!" Fur leaped and veered, climbed, ran circles till their laughter exhausted Rhoda and the little ball found its way into the crook of her neck and finally fell asleep with her.

"You've been so cooped up, you must need an escape. Could I relieve you?"

"Relieve?"

"Well, it must be wearing."

Wearing.

"No." He realized how strange his view (Was it a view?) must seem to her. She was, if nonchalantly, observing — in her own way, probing.

"We miss you, though we're aware you can't have anyone in. But don't cut yourself off too completely — you'll have to come back to us, you know. That — dreadful as it sounds! — is inevitable." She tried to laugh, but it was measured, testing.

"And she's holding the line?"

"We are, yes."

Esther's glance encompassed the house, conditions, arrangements.

When she was leaving, she drew his head down and kissed him full. She said, "I believe you've forgotten that too," smiling but considerate, letting her hand linger on his cheek, and then "Goodbye."

He shut the door, leaned. Why was breath so restricted all the while she was there? He was glad he had not moved the daybed into Rhoda's room until now. He set it against the wall so he could be sure to hear the least movement.

But that night all he heard was the kitten, its meow and purr, and actual bleat at times, overriding her sounds. And when he checked, the kitten was so close to her he feared it would block her nose or mouth, steal her breath, drain her warmth. And it was so playful and lashing, he feared for her eyes. You fool, you! Yet he resented it to jealousy; and with the kitten he felt Esther intruding, reminding that she was out there. So they made three here. She had set flesh between him and Rhoda.

One afternoon Rhoda cried out.

No, *not* —

But it was the kitten. It had drawn a long fiber of blood. Her arm was so thin the blood going out of her appalled him. He must stop it. He sucked at it, held his tongue there till it stopped, then washed and bandaged it.

She was petting the frightened kitten and murmuring to assure it, but when he said, "The little devil's got sharp claws," she set it aside and sank back on her pillow.

Waking in dark, she said, "I don't think I want the kitten."

He felt a leap of joy and, as quickly, shame.

"Can you give it away?"

"Yes."

"All right."

"Rhoda?"

He heard her turn over.

Afternoons she went back to modeling the clay he had bought. Because she could not walk now, he had set the armchair before the picture window so she could watch the people along the beach and the ships on the Sound. He carried her down to the sand to watch gulls and hunted shells for her collection, took her into the water and laid her on a blanket to sun until she slept, then carried her back up and into the shower with him or, if she was too sleepy, sponged her down.

An afternoon came when she said, "Can we read?" and he knew she could not go down. For the first time he knew walls, how quickly walls surrounded, how quickly flesh enclosed you, how you could move no farther than bones. And he felt frenzy at the thought: Whatever you were, it was contained in those walls. All of it? He felt it, a mysterious prisoner, moving inside the flesh, trying every moment to break free. The kitten had scratched her and given it a fine split to escape through. He clutched Rhoda — too hard: Her eyes widened, her breath rasped, though she did not cry out.

Angles hurt her now. She was comfortable only when she sat in his lap, slumped against him so long she was no longer a separate thing. She said, "I can hear your heart." Her fingers touched the throbbing in his neck; her own lay tilted, and he watched the barely visible pulsing in her throat. And after he lay her in bed, almost flat now, with a very thin pillow because bulges hurt her neck, he moved about the house, bereft, incomplete.

Soon she could not leave the bed and he feared lifting her too frequently.

"Read me more of your book. I like Rebecca."

She was too much bone, her head seemed larger, her neck too thin and long to support it. As flesh dwindled, her eyes grew and her hair seemed to thicken and spread. Long he would read *Ivanhoe*. After, he passed a damp wash cloth over her, with his fingertips teasing the hollows and sinks he knew so well until she laughed.

She wanted sea.

"*I've* got an idea. Let's make the living room our bedroom."

"You mean it?" She wanted to help. She tried to rise but no bone moved.

He dismantled the beds and set them up so she would wake on sea, fall asleep to waves, though it was as much, yes, for himself. He would not stand the separation from her at night by walls.

Below, time mocked. It stood visible in the monolithic boulders. He could touch time. Yet with Rhoda there was no time, they lived a perpetual now.

But Esther brought time. Though she had been incredibly discreet in staying away, she phoned regularly. And she did help — by keeping everyone else away. "They understand." Her voice reminded: September was approaching, school threatened the world of the house.

"Don't you need anything?"

"I think not." His only venture out now was for food.

"I'd like to see you . . ."

"Right now, I can't see anyone."

"Darren, you'll be back?"

"Back?"

"To school. When the time comes. You wouldn't risk that?"

Risk?

"Of course. To school. But, Esther, it would be better — she's particularly sensitive to sounds — if you didn't call. Let *me*. Do you mind?"

"Well, if you *will* . . . ?"

How she put up with him was a remarkable tribute to her goodness, for he felt cold, distant, not really grateful for the protection.

"Rhoda?"

She wanted sun.

"Promise you won't move," he said, "and I'll be back in a jiffy."

In an hour he returned with a rollaway and moved her onto it. Now he could push her out onto the deck and she could lie in the sun a while. She opened her mouth to catch wind, her hands reached to feel the flow.

And she began to tell him stories:

"There was a crab crying because she was lost in a field, and a hungry cat found it. The cat would have swatted her with his paw and eaten her, but he felt sorry for her and said, 'Why are you crying, crab?' and the crab answered, 'I'm lost. I can't find the ocean.' 'Well,' said the cat, 'I'm hungry and if you wait I'll show you my house and feed you, and then show you the way to the ocean if you'll show me your house and feed me!' 'Oh, yes, I will,' said the crab. So they went to the cat's house and they ate and then the cat led the crab to the ocean. The crab was very happy to see water again and the cat was surprised to see the crab lived in such a big house. He did not want the crab to see he was afraid of water so he followed her in, and the cat loved the crab's house so much he married the crab and stayed forever. And that's why we have fish with cat's whiskers!"

He wiped her forehead for the effort forced a fever and damp in her hair, which he would kiss, his lips wet with her. But she would talk now, talk tale after tale, a fever of invention — Where did it come from? — poured out of her, a slurred cascade of words. Though her body hardly moved, her eyes were wonderful — large, shining: She saw stories, she was in them — somewhere beyond sea, beyond cloud and sky; and her sound, after, even when she slept, went on in him, a higher pitch, refined to thinness now.

Suddenly the stories ceased.

She sat silent.

In stillness her eyes, brown seas filled with worlds, would gaze long. They grew glazed. When he spoke, she did not respond. Where was she? And if he touched her, the longest interval passed before her eyes turned and actually encompassed him. Then she smiled, so serene, with a calm look so comforting and assuring — she made him feel such a boy — and weakly her hands cupped his face. Her face was a woman's now, the wear of a lifetime, bones stark, stale skin, so little flesh, finely wrinkled. Surrendering to her smile, he would bow his head, and she would caress his hair. The breath, soap, dank acrid expulsion came into him. Since she ate almost nothing, "More?" he kept encouraging, "More?" for the yellow stains testified to how little came through her. Where did it go? She seemed to hold nothing, nothing stayed. What fed breath and bone? the voice that remained? heat? the motion of her eyes? What lived?

Inexplicably she wanted him, she sank against him; he held her until she eased into sleep, reluctant to let her go. He felt whole. What was he holding? He wanted what it was. He wanted to hold back what it was.

"Cold," she murmured. He set the thermostat up, for now was dog-days August. In the fields all the white potato flowers had long since vanished, the green life been drawn down into potatoes. Tractors sounded over the fields along the cliffs. Their sounds pained over her flesh. He quivered with her. The last summer heat lay a turgid body over the land and crystal shimmering over the sea. Inside, the least effort made him sweat.

And she sweat. He could not find the exact temperature for her comfort; she veered hot, cold, restless with starts and whimpers, for swellings multiplied, and lumps. When she reached for him, he raised her — so light, yet heavy with bone. Carefully he set her head — she could scarcely hold it up — against his cheek, and walked, sat, rocked, listening to her mumbles. She would of a sudden blurt, blurred, "Italy is a peninsula, it is in the Mediterranean Sea, it is shaped like a boot, the Mediterranean is a basin," a whole lesson verbatim; but it was her sound he listened to — it filled her hollow and vibrated in him; and her eyes he watched, expecting something, but he found she was searching his — and she smiled a smile filled with such pity. Did she know something she could not say? Rhoda! He saw an abyss in her, an endless fall — he wanted to sink down, know bottom. He was sure she did, sure she was going there, leaving bit by bit, sure she could in fact leave and return. She must carry him to somewhere in himself he could know — which in her stillness *she* knew — but not yet. Rhoda, have pity! But he was instantly ashamed, for didn't she have?

And he feared now — in darkness especially the fear besieged — that she might not take him there but go, not leave a trace. The thought roused a frenzy in him, but *she* startled: for her hand groped, her fingers touched his chin. "What?" she said uncannily, smiling up at him. And it calmed him.

Sometimes now it cost her to breathe. He must lie beside her. He must not leave her bed at night. The least break in her rhythm and his eyes flicked open. He whispered, "Rhoda?" A stir would answer. By aura of sky, light of moon, he watched

the ridges of the sheet, straining to see the rise and fall. Like
her, he was near collapse. He could not bear that she lie in the
silence without him. He must touch her to feel her motion in
his hands.

He fed her bit by bit. She would ask for nothing.

"The TV hurts." She bit her lips. He turned it off.

She griped. "I feel things." Spurling had warned him he
would have to be patient. There would be the unexpected.
Should he call? But he did not *want* Spurling. He had even
unplugged the phone. Feel things? If she could tell! She was
listening to what she saw. Moments, she stared so hard, not
blinking, he was sure she was watching something out there. He
was afraid of her staring. Yet he was afraid to call her back. And
when her eyes finally flagged and she returned to him, she said,
"Where were you?"

Where was he?

"I was right behind you. I was with you all the time," he
hazarded.

Now even her bones seemed to sleep against him, sink deeper
into his flesh. And he wanted to enclose her. He would like to
stand, walk, run *her*, be certain he held that motion, as long as
he kept it it was his. If he wandered while she slept, her sudden
whispers brought him back:

"Ssss . . . chool?"

"Yes, soon."

"Cat 'n 'y bed?"

She was wandering. He fibbed: "She's outside, doing her
duty."

Despite the agony of her flesh, skin, swellings, he was almost
afraid to take his hands off her now, fearful of *bereft*; and she
depended on the strength in him. She was all eyes and hair. He
combed it gently, not to pull at her scalp, let it hang soft, sank
his face into it, drawing in the heavy oil. She lay docile.

"I'm cold."

But he had days since cut off all air conditioning because the
sound needled her flesh so.

He lay close to her. "That's warm." Her head lay against his
chest. "I hear you."

And he thought: I have never been so happy, not with Marie

or at home or as a child, never. He could feel happiness running warm through him from her. He wanted to say it, if he dared say it, if she could know the meaning: You could touch happiness, you could hear happiness. And how could that stop? It would go on, it had to go on, he knew it would —

While she slept, he lay listening to the waves hush-hushing. He saw his classroom, all the children's faces, and Esther in her doorway across the corridor. The bell rang and the children dashed for recess, but they stopped — Rhoda had struck the desk and gone headlong. He bolted —

His eyes opened. He was sitting straight up in bed.

He heard the silence. His heart seemed to stop to listen. Then everything rushed.

"Rhoda?"

He touched her. Nothing passed into his hands.

"Rhoda?"

He stared into her open eyes. He could not believe the distance her eyes touched.

Rhoda.

For an instant he was seeing her from a great height: She was so small. There was almost nothing. Nothing.

And quickly she was close, she filled him, he could not contain her. The wrenching at his heart made him alive with pain.

Rhoda!

He wanted to tell her the pain she had left him.

And he felt an agony for what he had never said.

Had she known?

He bent over her.

"You're me," he said to her.

At last — after what hiatus? — he plugged the phone in and called Spurling.

"You'd better come. Rhoda's dead. And have them come take her. I won't be here."

He went out to walk the beach. Wind and sky moved, waves beat Rhoda, Rhoda,. Rhoda. Water rushed over his feet, filled the sand, sank deep. It came with the rush of love that filled and sank far down in you, deeper than knowing — and unceasing.

He went through the days of the death, through stillness and

ceremony and grave and nights of waves relentless against the
shore, and Hannibal and the kitten, at last returning to his
books to read those voices which would never die and to September and town, Esther and the other teachers warm with
welcome, back to texts and chalk and the blackboard, the classroom empty but ready.

And to his place.

He went to the first window. He raised the shades. The room
filled with the fire of morning. Green spilled, and trees, houses.
The bay rose far off, shimmering.

He went back to his desk.

The bell rang and the children rushed, mumbling and shouting, to their seats.

He almost dared not raise his eyes to the class.

But he raised them.

For the briefest interval they were all skulls.

Then Jimmie Riley said, "Good morning, Mr. Trueblood."

And the air broke, the class chorused, thirty good mornings
pealed.

When he sought at last the other place, the seat was taken:
Her hair gleamed gold and blue eyes glittered, and she had her
hand up.

"I'm Ella Claire."

He mouthed it: Ella Claire.

He lined the other name through on his seating chart and
wrote hers in its place.

"Ella Claire." He smiled at her.

"Now," he said. And surveying the class, he began.

BEV JAFEK

You've Come a Long Way, Mickey Mouse

(FROM COLUMBIA)

THE NAME'S John Q. Slade. I'm a talk show host. Been at it for fifteen years and damned clever at it. It's hard work, and it takes plenty of energy, creativity, and plotting, believe me. It's not the only way for a talkative guy like me to move up, but it's a damned good one. Anyway, Mickey was on last night, third time for him, and the hell if I know whether I ever want to see him again. He takes these liberties. Pompous as hell, that's Mick. But I wish I could do the non-verbal thing like he can.

The non-verbal thing! Is he *cool!* He started out a great show, believe me. I had a feeling it would be memorable, one of those things that stew in the old brain box awhile. He looked great, that was part of it. He's tall now, about six feet four, slender, kind of twiny. And that fur! He's got it real plush — shiny, soft, almost downy. You see it and you want to pet the guy. And of course they've done a lot with his teeth. He really had a bite once but now they've whittled them down and whited them over. A beautiful, dazzling smile with the teeth just a little apart. One of those sensual, half-grimacing smiles that black talk show hosts have. And then that suit — sharpest cut you ever saw and like it's made of his own fur.

And I almost forgot the *ears!* Out of this world! So *soft!* These little tiny pink veins all over in and out, so *tiny.* And then the fur, so *fine!* The ears are all to the side and resting, just resting like a little baby, and so round and soft. It either just plain hypnotizes you or you put your damned hand up there and it goes straight through. We all know he's an image, so it's kind of embarrassing.

I mean, here's this great-looking guy — tall and all velvety everywhere, his eyes shining like wet coal and wet diamonds, dressed fit to kill, and every bit of fur combed and glowing, that dazzling smile that says, "It's O.K., do what you damned well please," slinking in and sitting down on my show. Jeez, I think I clapped as loud as the little old ladies in the audience.

We knew they'd done a good job on him. After all, he came in long after the screen stars were processed. They were a kick for a while — real moving, talking people, but then again not; images programmed for personality and volition. I even heard one of them say she didn't know where the black box was anymore. But Mickey! Nothing like him. He was a superb processed image, plus the fact that there once was a real Mickey Mouse. I'm not kidding, once in the twentieth century. Lots of people know about it; one of the first cartoons.

So he sits down with that smile and arranges his legs with that twiny, sinuous movement. The non-verbal thing, across the board, the non-verbal thing. The guy's a prince! Now the image-processed people, they were nowhere near as slick. They were kind of bumpy when they moved — like people. Too real. But Mickey — he's anyone's dream, maybe even his own.

Even his own. That's what bugs me! So anyway, first we gave them a little hype of intellectual b.s. You know, carbon versus silicon evolution and stuff like that. Mickey's good for that, he knows the stuff people like in little bits. He draws his long black fingers together in a thoughtful, prayer-like thing. And the dramatic dark eyebrows. All like the urbane young guy *thinking* and *thinking* and telling you like it is. That's what he did, you see? He spiced it up with these little witticisms. Just what everyone wanted, the non-verbal thing. Their mouths all hung open at once — it was like we were in an aquarium.

"Silicon evolution," he was saying, "produces a more serene life-form, it is true," and a little smile, highlighting the soft, grey-black complexion. "You're really a funny lot," and the smile just picking up that velvety moustache below the nose, oh he can do it! "Perhaps you need someone like me to really

appreciate you," and a wide gesture to the right taking it all in,
you know, the world. "I sometimes wonder when you think
you're really comfortable. Eh, Jack?"

I didn't say anything, just watched him for the next move. So
he said, "When the fond old flesh just lies in a heap, eh?" And
the smile. And then real lights in those coal-black eyes. *Style.*

"A nice warm bath?" he said. "Just letting your mind wan-
der?" And here he lost the smile, and his delicate little paw
wandered distractedly over his pocket as though he were
dreaming on a hot day, all the time in the world, baby . . .
Really, he's better if you don't listen to him.

"You couldn't stand it for long." Then he looked real serious,
no smile, just looking straight at me. "You're so ill-adapted to
simple living that you set up stimulants continually." And here
he even moves forward. "I sometimes think your greatest pleasure is blanking out in a warm tub, and your greatest fear remaining there just a moment too long."

You see how it was? That's when I really started wondering
about him. Had he tapped into another information source? I
had to think fast or it was going to get sticky. It's a hell of a day's
work getting things simple again. I tried a little question of my
own. "Well, Mick, where's the old black box these days?"

Now, that got to him. He shot right back in his chair with
nothing but venom in those black eyes and even a little mad
working with the teeth. Mussed his moustache real good. That's
when I noticed how really well-trimmed his snout whiskers
were. It was a low blow but after all, why should the guy be so
damned critical when he's an image generated by an image-
processor, right? Just remind him of the black box from whence
he came, and we're back on the right track.

Then slowly the guy starts to relax while that little smile comes
across his face. And he reaches behind him and pulls out — can
you believe it? — his own tail. And that tail was *something!* Long,
covered with the softest gray fur ever imagined, kind of plump,
round, glowing a bit. God, you wanted to pull or caress the
damned thing. And he pulls it right out for anyone to see while
twining his lovely black fingers all around it. And then that
smile. Something about it just said: *obscenity, obscenity.* Like a
whore doing a dance naked or something.

You have to watch for these things on TV. You can't just let somebody get obscene. That's why Mick and the non-verbal thing were so great. He could be obscene, alright, and it wasn't down there in incriminating words. Something about the way he just twined those fingers around the tail said: This body is *obscene, lovely, potent.*

The audience went nuts. They called, cried, hooted as much as they wanted to. Mick, he's like a happening. He invites you to just *do* something. Then a big whopper of a smile and those eyes. As the sound came down, he just said, "Well, did I press a button on the little black box?"

We didn't say a thing. Why should we? The guy's a showman.

It's a little wild with an image on the air, but dull moments there are none. So I said to him, "Let's show the folks the historical Mick. Remember that one?" Well, for sure he remembered because images don't decay. And no sooner has the guy taken everyone's breath away than he disappears. Or rather, he vaporizes foot by foot. They're programmed to alter their own shapes, you know. Some do it on request, compulsive types. Mick's really special — he only does it on a whim. So then, who wobbles out from behind the curtain but the old Mickey; this cartoon with big, heavy lines all around the edges and a round little body only three feet tall. And the way it moves! Real rough, back and forth, the little round head bobbing up and down along with it. Wearing that baggy suit of — I don't know what — railroad driver's pants? And the eyes with never a spark, teeny little frightened buttons if you ask me. And on top of it all, he doesn't want to come out, just holds on to the curtain! That was one of the folks' biggest belly laughs of the year. He had them jumping like popcorn. Looks like a poor little animal that burrows all day, sleeps all night. And that's a fact. The life back then was brutal, absolutely brutal.

Then blam! It's gone in a puff. And nothing comes out. I keep waiting for good old Mick to show, but he doesn't. Then just plain the weirdest thing. It was, it was — like a little cool flow all over you, say, like being touched but then, all over like no touch. First it's cool, then prickly, then numb. And no Mick. So I think, what's all this? I looked at the folks and I knew the same thing was happening to them. Nobody knows the exact substance of an image. We know how to make them and use them, but what it is is something else. As soon as they could change their own forms, they started bringing in a little surprise or two that we didn't put there. Like suddenly from behind my back this, well, this *thing* starts rising up. First it's just a bunch of squares, cubes, triangles, arcs, we don't know what. Then it kind of soars in place, lots and lots of stretching and bagging around and more stretching and a real big lump here, then there, and we don't know what kind of shape it's going to have. Sometime I ought to have an image describe these things. Well, then we kind of begin to make out what it is. It's Mick, or what's left of him. You could just make out the shape, so I said, "Hey, fella — still with us?"

And of course he came out with a decent sort of "yes," so we knew he was O.K. Then we got a real big smile — all jiggling rectangles, but it was his for sure. I confess I was getting a little bit nervous, because I really didn't know what the guy was going to turn into next, and I do like to have a little control over my own show. That, coupled with the fact that we're all supposed to be sitting around chewing the fat, not turning ourselves into piles of cubes and triangles. So I said, "Want to come back, Mick?" and the guy doesn't answer for a while. But then there's a pop, like a magician would make when he pops something, and there he is sitting right in front of us, velvety and cool like before. The great old Mick — didn't even muss his fur. So I said, "That was the twentieth century Mick, right?" and he just beamed yes while the audience was clapping. So I said, "That last one, did we put that into you?"

"Tossed it together myself, Jack," he said. The audience was still clapping, and he held two fingers up in a little black V to them. I always like to see that kind of thing on a talk show. I really do. Makes everyone feel at home, like they've got alot in common.

So I decided, what the hell, I'll just drive the whole cart down lovers' lane. "What's Minnie doing these days?" I asked him. Well, the smile washes off his face like soap, and he caves in the middle and stares straight at the folks with eyes like fried eggs.

"I haven't seen the woman in years." His face was the ashen tone of a really expensive wool suit. Sometimes you have to watch alot of daytime TV to really know human emotions, but I'd say we're in for a long story full of the painful truth. And I say a talk show's no good without one. "At first, she was just a lovely girl, perhaps a little different from any other. At times, when I saw her, it was in a perfect, static pose. You know it: against the background of bright sunlight or pure dark, the very rich tones and colors of hair and skin, the intensity of the eyes. And then this pose, this image, becomes the thing you love. And when you are loving, even surface to surface, the image is there in your thoughts, your private obsession.

"You have no idea what your poetry is to an image experiencing love for the first time — what an incredible catalogue of mannerisms and obsessions: the line of the cheek, depth of the eyes, the long, slender hands, the quiet, gracious hands, the gestures — excitable, elegant, feverish. As she distilled further into this pose, my desire was continually rekindled. It had the most marvellous, violent way of expanding. I could not even conceive of it as sane or insane, emotional or mental. I was chasing an atom into the sky.

"And then I understood the enormity I had become: I was like you. My life was lived on a line parallel to yours, but my capacity to reflect my own essence was so horribly perfect. I had discovered, as only an image can, that all your ability to think and feel is based upon truncated images. What an uncomfortable creature you are — how prone to obsession, myopia, how divided from all you survey, what a watcher, defender, conqueror. And so it is with love — the more distant I was from her, the more incited I became.

"Then I truly saw the world you had created. For you are the species who creates a world to invite images. I found that vehicles, parks, whole streets, even cities had been created to incite images. It was astounding — I now understood what your kind had been feeling, what so much of your world was intended for. I became fascinated with the dialectics of people alone — driving in cars, hidden away with their books, sitting in their homes, drinking in whatever corner the world allowed. For I now knew a human secret: When alone, people have a truly horrifying hunger for another person, a hunger beyond satisfaction, a life of images held like a hand of cards against fate."

Well, the audience hung on all of that like a cliff, then dropped away limp. Jeez, it was like he broke an egg on a skillet.

"I began to have a riotous inner life based upon my discovery. As I walked on the street, I saw myself simultaneously as a huge, open pore gushing fluid and as a hollow within a solid that never knows its shape; in rain as rain itself."

The guy was excitable. And his face, I swear, looked like a bottle of ketchup thrown into a wind of coal dust. Everything said, and all the time he said it, had the shock of intense, of really wild and crazy feeling. "Well whoa boy," I thought, "time to bust up." So on came the commercial, and we all had a breather. Mick's a funny guy, as the folks could plainly hear; but fact is, things don't quite happen to them like they do to Mick and frankly, it was breathtaking. They love the guy. He puts the spark back in the old spark.

So when we get back, we find out that's only half the story. A new mood comes over him — I can only call it a stillness, maybe even a stillness before rain. He's stock-still in the midst of a crushing, a lollapalooza, emotion. "Well, we've got the time and the audience, so let her rip," I thought.

"Eventually," Mick said, "we did what all people do: we attempted to merge our images. What we longed for most was satiety and boredom; relief rather than possession. I suddenly began to notice several of her rather eccentric mannerisms — a peculiar shining black on her inner knees and elbows, a strange tendency to hiccough upon rising, her rather poor and inefficient sinuses and — this she could have spared me — her love of sleeping with a sheet wound up over her head. So I lay beside, I was forced to think, a rather erratically blackened, hiccoughing, senseless mummy. She could become ridiculous, revolting, even horrifying, but she could not bore me. Boredom generates so few images. Eventually our union, our colocation of images was something impossible for us to take seriously. If I may attempt a vulgar generalization: Images are not made to be joined but to stand in static poses. They are the essence of what you think of as abstract thought, even of your world's dynamic laws, yet all the while they completely subvert them.

"I tried not to despair. The image of despair is so horrifying that I could not tolerate it for a moment. I kept her at a distance, both physical and psychological, such that she neither attained nor lost focus for me. In our home, I took the top floor and she the bottom. And then, wonderfully enough it occurred to us both that we might set up an interim fantasy room between us, and so reapproach one another. We gave it all the surfaces of fantasy — dark walnut, wind instruments, candlelight, chimes. For you, conscious fantasy is enthralling. For images, on the other hand, it is the blackest despair. All the acts we might have carried out we knew in advance to be artifice. So we sat in that quiet, horrible room, unable to speak or raise our heads or even cry.

"One day I saw her standing before me, nearly coming into focus. Then I knew how utterly miserable she was. I stood up, intending to embrace her. She came toward me in such a wavering, hesitant way, as though she both loved and hated what she did. Then she gently took my face in her hands and bit my cheek and throat until I could feel the warmth and moisture of blood. I knew a pure metaphysical horror: She had actually altered my image. In our passion, we had become fully imaginable to one another and therefore vulnerable. At that moment, she disappeared to me and I to her. That was the end."

You can imagine what a tussle it was getting the show back on its feet after that one. That's the kind of thing you want to sit still awhile after. Or go to sleep. Or just plain blow your nose. And that's why old John Q.'s worth every penny they pay me.

"Buck up, man," I said to him. "You'll ride it out. I mean, how long are you going to remember it, anyway? Like a dream, probably."

"That's kind of you, Jack," he said, still real deflated.

So I went on, "And what's more, that old love muckety-muck is pretty much the human condition." He didn't say anything and didn't look like he was going to. The folks looked great, though — mellowed out and comfy as hell. Mick can do that. He can scare the pants off them, take their breath away, then bow out. The best talk show material, without a doubt.

"We all got to get close to one another, and sometimes we get bit for it, sure enough," I said. "Intimacy, communication, that's what makes life tick."

"Not quite, Jack," he said in that cool, remote voice, and here he crosses his twiny legs again and smiles. I was glad to see something sparkling in his eyes, but just the same, it always scares me.

"What you love is the image of intimacy. You have no idea what it is. Images and abstractions are the most graceful assailants; who can stop the warring of dancers?"

Now that wasn't so bad as it sounds. The folks like a little obscurity now and again. They all rested a little more deeply into their chairs and a few lit cigarettes, thoughtful like. "Well," I said, "talk shows seem to be as eternal as what beats in the human breast." Afterall, a little promo for yourself now and again never hurts.

"The image of communication. You're in love with your images, even the most insipid ones. Alone, in your homes, you're far too self-conscious to talk to yourselves. It would reveal your truth to you. It would terrify you."

"Well, I guess we're the restless, curious species, Mick. We just go off and explore one thing, found another, learn to control this and that. The up side of carbon. Our heads really light up, it's true. It may seem a little bright for someone out of silicon, but these things are just the biological truth of life. Your kind has the efficiency, we've got the nerve."

"I wonder, Jack . . ." he said. He's been getting deeper and deeper into the chair, and I confess, I thought either something scary or another bunch of rectangles and cubes was going to come flying out. "I think of you as rather blank, as perhaps having few attributes outside of your images. But you and the folks are plenty dazzling with them. You're restless and curious for them, for little else, perhaps least of all for one another."

You see what a tough guy he is to have around! He's velvet, he's funny, he vaporizes, and then he just throws some more dust in your eyes. It was getting late and, frankly, I thought it might be a better thing for the folks to hear a bunch of decent, honest commercials than listen to Mick anymore. So I said, "Hey, you're one of our images, too, old fella." Close it on a little bonhomie. The strangest light came on in his eyes — bright, angry, violent, even brilliant. It's like I popped him on the snout. "Mick, get it together," I whispered. And aloud I said, "You've come a long way, Mick." And still he didn't say a thing, just lounged back in the chair like something that wants to coil up in a cave. God, what a strange, powerful guy to have on my show! I suppose you know I admire the hell out of him, but he's scary as they come.

Then he smiled that bright old Mick smile and said, "So have you, Jack, so have you," but I really wonder what he was thinking before he said that. A fascinating guy — you want to know what's in the gaps and peeps and silences. Then good old Mick! He made his eyes sort of wan and milky and held up his fingers in those Vs again. The folks roared. I mean, what a perfor-mance!

Still, I never want to see the guy again. On the other hand, it'll be damned exciting.

JOHN L'HEUREUX

Clothing

(FROM TENDRIL)

CONOR HAD BEEN a Jesuit for sixteen years now, and an ordained priest for three of those years. He was a member of the long black line; he had faded into the woodwork; he was a minor cog in a vast machine. This is how he thought of himself, in images not his own but drawn from the rules of the Society of Jesus, from conversations in the rec room, from admonitions of Superiors. Life was bland, uneventful, with few successes and no dangers to speak of. The habit does finally make the man, he told himself.

There were sources of anxiety, to be sure, but not really dangers, not terrible temptations. A drink too many, perhaps, or imprudence in speech (telling sophomores in a high school English class that "Cardinal Spellman, quite simply, is a fascist"), or undue intimacy with the mother of one of his students (Mrs. Butler and that funny business at the pool). But nothing serious, nothing to worry about. Still, habit or no habit, there was something very wrong. Something — he searched for the word — hopeless.

And then, in the spring of his fourth year as a priest, he was officially transferred from the prep school where he taught in Connecticut to the retreat house in downtown Boston, the transfer to be effective in summer. Suddenly it all seemed impossible to him: the vow of obedience, the awful loneliness, the waste of his talent as a poet. He had published two books, and they had been well received by reviewers, but what was he doing — as a priest — writing poems at all? And why? He went into a prolonged depression. He prayed. He drank too much. He flirted, deep in his subconscious, with the idea of suicide. Finally, while there was still a week to go before his transfer to Boston, it came to him that he did not have to die to get out, he just had to get out.

Conor went to his major superior, the Provincial, and said he wanted some time to consider his vocation, he had come to a point where he had to do this one thing, for himself. It was the 1960s and in the aftermath of Vatican II half his priest friends had already left, but Conor did not want to just leave. He wanted to make a decision at least as rational and prayerful as the decision he had made sixteen years earlier when he entered. Conor paused in his declamation and appraised the Provincial, who looked bored, and so he took a deep breath and said that while he was thinking through this problem, he did not want to work in, did not even want to live in, the retreat house.

"I see," the Provincial said. "How's your drinking?"

Conor thought about that for a while, rejected the idea of a smart aleck response, and said, "Well, the drinking will always be a problem . . . for any of us, I suppose, but I think I've got it under control. What I'm talking about, Father, isn't a crisis of booze, or even a crisis of faith. It's a crisis of hope. I don't hope anymore."

"Hope, schmope," the Provincial said. "Look. You're just one of over a thousand men we have to deal with, Conor. Things are changing. In the old days I'd have simply told you to go to the retreat house or get the hell out, but we can't do that anymore. Superiors have to *confer* with a subject now, we have to consult his *needs*, we have to *adapt*. So look, I'm short on time; I've conferred and I've consulted and I've adapted. What do you want?"

"Well, I thought . . ."

"Where are you going to live, first of all?"

"Well, I thought I'd stay right where I am."

"And do what?"

"Well, I thought I'd continue to write my poetry, and reviews. And give readings. I thought I'd . . . pray."

"And who's supporting you, please, while you're writing this poetry?"

"Well, I thought, the Jesuits. I've given sixteen years of my life, after all, and . . . well, I thought . . ."

"Well, you thought. Well, you thought. Think again, my friend, and when you do, be very clear on one thing." He leaned across the desk to make his point. "The Society of Jesus owes you . . . *nothing*. Got it? Nothing."

Conor felt hot, and dizzy. The Provincial seemed to come in very close to him, their faces almost touching, and then he pulled away, and his desk with him. Conor was isolated suddenly, lost, a small ridiculous figure in a world that in seconds had become distant from him. He saw himself as he was: self-absorbed, pretentious, absurd. As if, in this huge organization of brilliant and holy men, he could possibly matter: ridiculous. He had deceived himself with this self-important talk about hope. The room tipped away from him and he wanted to hide.

Then all at once, something inside him said no, and at that instant the room righted itself. Words came to him and Conor leaned forward to say, But I want my life. I have a right to my life. It's my only hope.

But instead, he heard himself saying in a strange voice, almost a child's voice, "Of course you're right, Father. I'll go to the retreat house. I'll try harder."

And in the long silence that followed, he said, "Hope isn't that important anyway."

A year later — after seventeen weekend retreats to laymen and laywomen, after thirty talks to high school students on sex and marriage, after five Cana conferences and many baptisms and innumerable confessions, after a brief love affair with a divorcée (Mrs. Butler, who left her husband and family and came to Boston to find herself; she found herself, eventually, in AA) and a long love affair with a former nun (Alix, whom he intended to marry as soon as he got his walking papers from the Jesuits) — a year later, Conor made formal application to leave the Jesuits and to be reduced to the lay state. He was assigned an interrogator, Fr. Casey, a man in his seventies with a perpetual cough and a bad cigarette habit.

"*Interrogator?*" Conor asked. "*Reduced* to the lay state?"

"Just technical terms, boy," Fr. Casey said. "Don't get jumpy now; they told me you're the jumpy type. Poetry."

Conor said nothing. He was doing this not for himself but for Alix, who had her own code of morality. She would have sex with him, she would even live with him, but she would not marry him except in the Catholic Church. Love is fine, she said, and so is sex, so long as there is love, but marriage outside the Church was unthinkable; it did violence to her integrity. And so he was doing this for her, submitting himself to a final humiliation so that they could be married as Catholics.

For over an hour Conor sat with his right hand on the little blue book that enshrined the Rules of the Society of Jesus, the blue book itself resting on a Douay version of the Holy Bible, while he answered questions about whether his parents had married from love or obligation, whether he was a wanted or an unwanted baby, whether they had proposed the priesthood to him or he had come upon the idea himself. Conor answered and contradicted himself and then answered again. Fr. Casey dutifully wrote down everything he said.

Telling himself he had only to hang on and eventually this nightmare would be over, Conor concentrated on the priest's handwriting: perfect little letters of the same height and slant, perfectly controlled, perfectly legible. Perfection in the smallest of things. Would this never end? Finally Conor's patience gave out.

"Why are you writing down every word I say? This is going to take forever!"

Fr. Casey looked up, amused. He had all eternity ahead of him. "I have to," he said. "This is a legal document. It will be sent to Rome. You've been in the Jesuits for seventeen years; it doesn't seem to me very unreasonable to ask you to spend a few hours getting out."

"But who could answer these questions?" Conor said, exasperated. "This whole process is designed to prove that I never really had a vocation, that somehow I was forced into this. But you're not going to make me say that. I was *not* forced into the priesthood. I did *not* enter the Jesuits under any misconceptions. I *did* understand fully what I was doing."

There was a long silence in the room. Conor was about to apologize, but said instead: "I entered the priesthood of my own free will, and now it's because of my own free will that I want out. I want to be my own man. I want to make my own mistakes. I want to be free."

"Free," Fr. Casey said, the word loaded with meaning.

"To make my own mistakes," Conor said.

Another long silence. "We'll try again." Fr. Casey lit a new cigarette and said, "This is going to take hours, son, so I'd suggest you cool down. Now, as to the question of your vocation: to what do you attribute it; to what exact person or event or moment? It's very important, so I want you to think. Are you thinking?"

Conor thought, and said nothing. It was as if the priest had not heard a word he'd said.

An hour later Fr. Casey had moved on to other topics. How often did Conor masturbate? Never. Very good, but when did you stop? I never began. Never? Never at all? No, never. Why? What was the matter? A long pause, and then another cigarette, and more irritation on Conor's part, but no explosion this time.

"And has there been any sexual congress with *others* during the past years?"

"Yes," Conor said; a non-equivocal answer.

"Frequently?"

"Sometimes."

"Women? More than one?"

"Two."

"Men?"

"No men."

"Ah." Fr. Casey took out his handkerchief and mopped his brow. Conor laughed, thinking the priest meant to be funny.

"Yes?" Fr. Casey was puzzled.

"No. I mean, we're nervous. Or at least I am."

"Now, about these women." He paused, significantly.

"The first was an affair. It was just sex. I broke it off after two weeks. Confessed it, of course. The other is love; a love affair, if you want; but it's permanent. We're going to marry as soon as my papers come through."

"*If* they come through."

"*When* they come through."

"Be careful." Fr. Casey held his pen suspended for a moment in air.

"Father, I've been careful and I'm all done. I've given sixteen years of honest service to God, and one year of very muddled service that was meant to be for God but that ended up being for me, I guess, because it's getting me out. Out. And I don't particularly care what *you* think of me or what *Rome* thinks of me, because it's myself I've got to live with. And all I want from you is *out*. I'm done. Like it or not, I'm free."

"You go too far." Fr. Casey's voice was suddenly the voice of God. "You go too far."

I'll do it for Alix, Conor told himself, and bowed his head as if he were sorry for his outburst.

"You are dealing with Mother Church, and she is a very indulgent Mother indeed. But even mothers can be pushed too far. Do you understand me?"

Later, hours later, when Conor was leaving Fr. Casey's room, he turned and said with a kind of innocent surprise: "I suddenly remembered. Your question about my vocation, about when exactly I knew I had one? It's just come back to me: I was a child, about five or six, and I had a terrible quarrel with my mother about something or other. It was shortly after that quarrel that I began thinking I'd be a priest; not because I wanted to, but because it just seemed inevitable."

"It doesn't matter now," Fr. Casey said. "I've finished taking notes."

Months went by and Conor moved from the retreat house into a studio apartment. At last a letter arrived asking that he come to the Provincial's office to sign and receive his decree of laicization. He signed and, with that signature, he was reduced to the lay state.

But when he moved from his studio into Alix's apartment just before the wedding, Conor discovered that — for some reason he could not explain — he still had in his possession his Jesuit habit: the cassock, the cincture, the roman collar.

What was he to do with them? Obviously he couldn't keep them. Nor could he just throw them out.

The awful session with Fr. Casey came back to him, and then the scene in the Provincial's office where he had signed away his Jesuit allegiance, surrendered the practice of his priesthood. No, he did not want to see those men again. Anger, resentment, shame; none of these described what he felt, but he knew he could not face them again for a long long time.

"Betrayal," he said aloud, and though there was no connection in his mind between the word he said and the idea that came to him, he realized at once what he would do.

He folded the habit carefully and lay it on the bed. He folded the cincture in halves, and then in halves again, and then once more. He lay the white plastic collar on top of the habit and cincture.

He stared at the clothes for a moment and then, with purpose, he picked them up and draped them over his left arm.

He walked the five blocks to the retreat house and went in the door to the public chapel. Though it was early afternoon, the chapel was very dark, and it was a moment or two before Conor was certain that no one was there.

He knelt and said an Act of Contrition. Then he stood and placed the cassock carefully in the pew in front of him. He lay the cincture on the cassock, crossways, with the white plastic collar on top.

He turned to go, hesitated, and then quite deliberately turned back. He picked up the collar and, with no thought that it was sentimental or melodramatic to do so, he lifted it to his lips for the ritual kiss that custom and devotion had required of him for so many years.

He genuflected and walked out of the chapel, hopeful, free.

II

Conor sat in the rocking chair reading *Swiss Family Robinson* while his mother peeled carrots for the stew. They often spent Saturday mornings like this, Conor reading in the big rocker while his mother watered her plants or prepared meals or did the baking.

Conor was eight years old and there was nobody his age in this new neighborhood; his mother, trapped here by marriage and the Depression, missed her old chums in Springfield; and so they were friends, really; more like companions than mother and son.

But she was cross this morning, Conor could see, and she was not going to keep her promise.

"You should be outside, playing," she said.

"But what about the shoes?" Conor said, not looking up from his book. "We've got to go buy the shoes."

"I'm busy," she said, and tossed the last of the carrots into the pot.

Conor had been invited to Marianne Clair's birthday party that afternoon, and he had a present for her (one of his Thornton Burgess books; you couldn't tell it wasn't new), and so he was all set to go. Except for one thing. He had to have a new pair of shoes. He had only a single pair that he wore for school and for best, and somehow he must have scuffed the top of the toe on his right shoe because the leather had worn away and when he stood in front of the class to read, everybody could see his sock showing through.

Conor had not been able to tell his mother this, or tell her what happened yesterday in school when Miss Moriarty made him stop reading and insisted that Marianne share with the whole class whatever it was that she found so funny. He could never tell her this; he could never tell anyone. But last night he had prayed over and over that he would get the new shoes soon.

Two weeks ago his mother had said that maybe next Saturday they would take a bus downtown and buy him a new pair of shoes. A week later she had said the same thing again. But this morning she had already mentioned several times how busy she was, how many things she had to do. It would be only a while longer — he could tell — before she said he would just have to wait another week for the shoes.

She finished preparing the stew and in no time spread the kitchen table with newspaper, got out her bag of soil and her pots, and was busy transferring the first of the window plants from a small pot to a larger one.

Conor looked over at her without raising his head; this way he could watch without her knowing it. She rapped the plant out of its pot and held it upside down in her left hand while she scooped soil into the new pot with her right. Conor liked to watch her do this; she was quick and certain, juggling the plant and the pot, pressing down the new soil with her knuckles, making it all come out right. Everything she touched grew.

She looked up at him suddenly. "You should be outside, in the nice sun," she said. "It's too nice a day not to be outside."

"But when are we going to buy the shoes?" he asked, even though he had begun to suspect it was hopeless.

She said nothing.

"Mother? What about the shoes?"

"They'll have to wait," she said, her hands busier than ever with her potting.

"But you promised. You said."

She started on another plant, ignoring him.

"You promised. You never keep your promises."

"That's enough. Now stop, or you won't go to the party at all."

"What a cheater you are!"

"Conor!" she said, the last warning.

"You lied to me. You never intended to buy the shoes."

"That's it. That does it," she said. "You're spoiled and you're fresh and you're selfish, and you are not going to that party. Period."

"You just don't want to take me, that's all. You just don't want to buy me shoes."

"Go to your room! Now!"

"I hate you," Conor said, and headed — fast — for the door. "Besides, you're as homely as Mrs. Dressel."

It had popped into his head from nowhere. He had heard Mrs. Waters from next door say she thought Emily Dressel was the homeliest woman in town, and he had heard his mother repeat the comment to his father. He had heard them laugh and agree that it was probably true. His mother had said, "That poor woman; if I looked like that, I'd wear a hat with a veil."

So now he sat in his bedroom wondering why his mother had said nothing back to him. He had wanted to make her angry, to hurt her, badly, because she had ruined everything. Even if he said he was sorry and they were friends again, it wouldn't be the same. Even if she took him to get the shoes now, it wouldn't be the same. It was too late.

He would ignore her. He would be nice to her from now on, but never again the way he used to be. Well, that was what she deserved. She had earned her punishment.

He tried to go back to *Swiss Family Robinson* which, despite the speed of his escape from the kitchen, he had had the sense to take with him, but he couldn't concentrate on the words.

He wondered if she knew. Did she know that he was punishing her? And did she suspect that, in a way, he was relieved not to have to go to the party with all new kids?

She probably did. She probably knew, as he himself knew, that in a day or so, after he'd been punished for being fresh and after they'd gone without talking for a while, it would all be the same, and that next Saturday he would read some new book and she would bake cookies and all of this counted for nothing. He wanted to hurt her back, for good.

Instantly he realized how to do it.

He marched firmly out to the kitchen and stood beside her at the kitchen sink. She was holding one of the repotted plants near the faucet, getting it wet, but not too wet. She said nothing and so he waited. He would give her one more chance. But when she still remained silent, he said, "Do you want to know something? You really *are* as homely as Mrs. Dressel. And tomorrow or the next day when we're not mad at each other anymore, I'll tell you I didn't really mean it. I'll tell you I just said it to pay you back. But I do mean it, and — you know what — I'll mean it *then*, too, even when I say I don't. Because it's the truth."

His mother said nothing, but her face got hard-looking, and she shook. Suddenly the plant fell from her hands. The fresh soil spilled into the sink and the water from the faucet drilled hard on the plant until even the old soil fell away and the roots were exposed, but still she did nothing to save it. She only stared straight ahead.

Conor turned smartly and walked down the hall to his room. He shut the door behind him.

His face was hot and he felt dizzy, but not sick-dizzy. He was dizzy with a kind of power, a strange sense of who he was and what he could do. He looked around the room and everything seemed different. His bed was so small, and the chair too, and his bureau. Not exactly small, but distant; as if he had moved away from them, as if he had nothing to do with them anymore. Even his books looked different; they looked old, ancient; he knew everything that was in them. With one finger, with a single word from his mouth, he could dismiss them from existence. He was capable of anything now.

And at once he knew he must hide. But where? He went to

his closet and climbed in among the slippers and boots and old toys, but that was not enough.

He took his bathrobe down from its hook and put it over his head. No. He was still not hidden.

He pulled down his shirts from the shelves, his pajamas, his underwear; in a frenzy he tore everything from the hangers, heaped the clothes in a mound on the closet floor. Still it was not enough.

He stripped himself then, adding his shirt and trousers to the pile on the floor, and, pulling the door tight behind him, crawled beneath the heavy pile of clothing and lay, for a time, hidden.

Hours later his mother found him there, still shaking with power and terror.

III

Alix was dying of metastatic liver cancer.

Hers was the typical case. While shaving beneath her arms one evening, she had noticed an odd little lump near the nipple of her left breast. The next morning she phoned her gynecologist, and almost before she had time to realize what was happening, she was recuperating from a radical mastectomy. At her third month checkup she seemed fine, but three months later a tumor appeared in her right breast and she had to undergo another mastectomy.

Two years passed, filled for Alix and Conor with a kind of desperate hope, and then the hoping was over. Alix developed a nagging cough, she began to lose weight, her fine white skin began to turn sallow. Even before the doctor examined her, he pronounced it cancer of the liver — final and fatal. Alix had been in the hospital for over a month now, with the promise of days to live, or hours. And still she had not complained.

Whenever he had a cold, Conor always said — by way of apology to her and acknowledgment to himself — that on his tombstone he wanted carved this simple inscription:

He Suffered No Pain Without Complaint.

What he could never understand, therefore, was how Alix could suffer so much and complain so little. Or rather, not at all.

He had sat by her bed each day, telling her about his classes (he taught English at Sacred Heart College), about her friends from school who had phoned to inquire how she was doing (she taught English at Sacred Heart Prep), about their German shepherd, Heidi. She had smiled, her hand resting lightly on his, and in her new voice — husky, strained, exhausted — she had done her best to cheer him up.

But now she slept all the time, or perhaps she was unconscious. Conor sat beside her bed, forcing himself to look at her emaciated hand or at the small mound her feet made beneath the covers, or at the reproduction of the Madonna della Strada on the wall opposite. Anywhere, but at her face.

Because the last time he had looked at her sleeping face, he had thought, Go. Please Go. I have never known you anyway. And he could not bear to think that again.

Conor had known her since that last terrible year in the priesthood, when he had prayed and drunk and made love to her and then gone to confession, promising he would end this affair, and he meant it, and then he would start all over again. How had she endured it? Endured him?

He shot a quick glance at her face. Her skin was smooth, taut to her skull, and with the advance of the disease the color had darkened from its natural white to a pale yellow and then to a deep tan; now it was a reddish brown, thin and hard to the touch. Her face was a deathmask made of copper.

This was not Alix.

He tried to summon some image of her, some proof that he had known her after all. He saw them walking on the beach with the dog; he saw them fighting, spitting out the angry words they would take back later; he saw them making love. But that was not it; that was not what he was looking for. He thought of her as she had been for the past two years, broken with cancer, and he remembered kissing the pink flesh where her breast used to be and looking up to see the single tear on her cheek. He thought of her in bed with him, her head twisting on the pillow, the sounds of her pleasure in his ear. But that was not the right image either. It was hopeless.

Then, just when he had given up, it came to him: the photo of Alix on the swing. She was five years old and she was wearing a birthday dress. She sat on the swing with both feet planted on the ground; her hands gripped the ropes solidly, easily; she looked straight into the camera. There was a smile on her face, a look of confidence, a sureness about everything in her world. Her eyes saw, and liked what they saw, and she was perfectly content. Hope was not even a question.

Conor fixed the picture firmly in his mind, smiled at the freshness, the inviolability of that child, and then he turned to look at Alix.

"The relentless compassion of God," he said aloud, and as if she had been waiting for him to say that, Alix opened her eyes and looked at him.

"Never," she said, and then something else which Conor could not make out.

He leaned over her to catch the words, and at once her eyes tipped upward in her head and she began to push away the sheets. "Help me," she said. "Oh help me with these." She sat up somehow and managed to kick the sheets free of her body. She clawed at the johnny tied loosely at her back; the string broke and she flung the thing to the floor. She was sitting up in the bed now, naked, staring, her eyes empty in her copper face. "Help me," she said once more. "I never loved."

"No," Conor said, taking her by the shoulders, turning her to look into his face. "No, that's not true," he said again, desperate this time. "You loved me. You always loved me."

She focused on Conor then and something came into her empty eyes, a kind of promise.

"And I loved you," he said, but already her eyes had begun to close. He lay her back on the bed, slowly, gently, and she seemed finally to be without life altogether. "No," Conor sobbed. "Oh, God, no. No." And then he thought he heard her echo him, "No. No."

He did not cover her dead body, but left it as it was, naked, decent. He stood by her bed and prayed, hoping against hope.

PETER MEINKE

The Piano Tuner

(FROM THE ATLANTIC MONTHLY)

THE PIANO TUNER was a huge man, crowding the doorway. I hadn't known he was coming, but I got up from my desk to let him in; my wife was still out shopping. His head was small for his body, and his belt was almost hidden by the belly folding over it. I suppose I came up to about his shoulders, and the reek of his sweat was stunning. His stained T-shirt announced THE PIANO EXCHANGE.

"Where's the piano?" he said.

"In there." I pointed toward the music room. "But there's nothing much wrong with it."

"Yeah, we'll see." His voice resonated like the bass in a barbershop quartet.

I led him through the living room to the small music room. In one corner, the mahogany of my wife's Russian-made harp glowed in the late-afternoon sunlight. By the casement windows on the right stood my old piano, painted black.

"It's an 1899 Kimball," I told him. I was proud of this handsome antique, with its scrolled legs and matching bench.

"No, it's not that old," the piano tuner said sourly, "but it looks like a Kimball, all right."

"It *says* Kimball." I pointed to the gold lettering.

He bent over the keys, shaking his little head. "That means zilch. This'll take some time; I'll go get my tools." He straightened up with a sudden intake of breath, as if someone had kicked him in a kidney. "Jesus," he said.

I wanted to go back to my desk to continue my work. Fredericks would be furious if my review was late again, but this one was proving particularly troublesome. The problem was, I knew all the authors; there was no one I could attack with relative impunity. Van Buren was clearly the weakest, but he had said such good things about *my* last book, I had to reciprocate somewhat. Prokol was a friend of Fredericks's. I had just about decided to stick it to Foreman, who was pretty good but without influence, when the piano tuner had rung.

I wished my wife wouldn't make these appointments without telling me. Besides, it was my piano, and it sounded all right to me. I had been practicing Durand's *Valse,* a not-too-difficult but flashy piece, with lots of runs on the right hand and oompah on the left, and I hadn't noticed anything. Maybe the B-flat stuck a little now and then. I practiced hard when my wife was out, though I pretended never to practice at all. She was a pretty good harpist, but had to work hard at it.

I wouldn't feel right going back to my study with this massive lout of a piano tuner lumbering through the house. Who was he to say my piano was not that old? We had a lot of expensive — irreplaceable, really — souvenirs scattered around; he might just slip our Wedgewood ashtray into his pocket, or a wooden plate from Poland into the khakis bunched below his gargantuan stomach. Where was he, anyway? I looked out the front door.

He was standing in our driveway, next to a dilapidated VW van, talking to a thin black man about half his size. The van's windows were painted crudely, in childlike strokes, with a continuous forest scene; on the back were what appeared to be the turrets of a castle. Whenever a car wandered down our narrow, curving street, the black man would lean back and deliver a sharp karate-style kick toward the car, which would swerve to the other side and then move on. The piano tuner paid no attention to this but kept talking intently, crouched over, fingers jabbing the air. When he saw me watching, he called out, "Help me with these will you?" I noticed two large metal toolboxes at his feet.

The thought occurred to me that there were just two boxes and he had two hands, but his tone was so peremptory that I walked down the driveway to comply. Up close, the black man was startling to look at: the skin on his face, arms, and hands had large, irregular patches of pink. I was consciously not staring at him, but he said, "What you lookin' at, man?" Of course, I didn't reply, and turned to the piano tuner instead.

"If I was a little more diseased," the black man said, stepping between us, "I be white like you." He leaned away, aiming his foot at me, but as I jumped backward he reversed and bent steeply toward me, snapping his foot behind him into the side of the van, leaving a good-sized dent.

The piano tuner had already started toward the house, carrying one of the toolboxes as lightly as if it were empty, and he didn't turn around. I hefted the other one and lurched after him. "Watch out for the flowers!" I shouted, not knowing whether to look in front or in back of me. His great square-toed boot had just crushed one of our azalea cuttings alongside the driveway. I had told my wife it was asking for trouble, planting them so close to where people walk, but she was an incurable optimist, believing somehow that everyone would be careful and sensible, would keep within the proper boundaries. Twice a year she pruned our azaleas, potting the cuttings for two months in just the proper mixture of vermiculite and peat moss before transferring them to various parts of our property in her ongoing beautification program. She was the neighborhood's answer to Lady Bird Johnson.

The piano tuner paused on the doorstep, waiting for me to open the door for him. "My wife loves azaleas," I said, "so please be careful of them."

"I don't like flowers, myself," he said. "They bother my asthma." I had already noticed his heavy breathing. With a sinking heart, I opened the door and led him in, trying to get him to follow my example of not stepping on our delicate Persian rugs, mementos of our year in Iran. But he blindly and heavily — greasily, muddily — tramped straight across them into the music room.

With remarkable dexterity and speed for such a heavy man, he had the top and front panels of the piano off in a minute. The exposed keys huddled together like ranks of suddenly naked soldiers. He set up the tuning hammer and began hitting single notes over and over.

"I think it's all right," I said.

"It's flat," he replied, without looking at me. "I'll have to bring it up almost a whole tone. That'll cost you fifty dollars."

"Sometimes the B-flat sticks," I said, trying to show some knowledgeability about the subject. I could read music, but I was tone-deaf; his jarring notes meant nothing to me.

"Yeah, you need some new hammers. Some turkey tried to fix them with Scotch tape. That'll cost extra." I could see the dried-out tape peeling off the pegs like old gauze bandages. The piano tuner did not sit down but stood humped over the keyboard, left hand prodding the notes, right hand working the tuning hammer. His fingers were so large it was hard to believe he could press down a single key at a time.

I went back to my study but was unable to work in that comfortable, windowless room; the repetitive striking of notes was too irritating. At the same time, I felt I needed the door open so I could keep an eye on the piano tuner, whom I instinctively mistrusted. After sitting immobile at my desk for what seemed hours, I got up and made myself a drink. What was keeping my wife? Evening was coming on. Looking out the living-room window, I saw the black man still in the driveway. Now he had headphones on, and an expensive-looking portable stereo sat against the pole supporting the basketball backboard our son had loved so much before he ran away. The man was dancing to the silent music, making Eastern motions with his chin, neck, and hands, not unlike his earlier karate movements.

I walked over to the music room. "That man is still out there," I announced somewhat superfluously, since he could be clearly seen through the casement windows.

"It's a free country," said the piano tuner, looking up. Rivulets of sweat ran down his face, and his thin hair gleamed on the bullet-shaped head. Dark wet spots patched his T-shirt, and his chin was going black with stubble, rougher and thicker than when he arrived. He was staring at my drink.

"Do you want a glass of water, or a beer?" I asked.

"No," he said, "maybe a little whiskey. Beer hurts my stomach. You got some Jim Beam or something?"

"I've got a little bourbon, I forget what it is."

"Sure, a little bourbon, it's good for the digestion. My digestion is terrible."

"Have you eaten?" I said. My conversation seemed to pop out of me against my will.

He pulled on the tuner with a grunt. "No, when could I eat? I'll eat later, I'm used to it. I meant to say, if a string breaks, you got to pay for that, too."

When I brought him his drink, he sat down with a sigh, hiking his pants up tight around his crotch. I asked him how long the tuning would take; if it was going to take too long, maybe he should come back another day.

"No," he said, "you got to work nights, overtime, if you're a piano tuner. And even then, you can't afford to buy a woman." He banged the piano so hard that some whiskey splashed out of his glass.

I spoke smiling into the silence, trying to be man to man. "I didn't know people still had to buy women nowadays."

He looked at me as if I had thrown up on his boots. "Are you kiddin'? Do you live under a rock, or what? Y'ever been downtown, see those babes on the street corners? What d'you think they are, goddamn city engineers?" He finished his bourbon in a gulp. "These felts are all eaten by roaches," he continued, peering into the piano. "That's going to cost ya."

I looked over his shoulder; the felt pads were indeed ragged and in places completely gone.

"And if you don't buy a woman," he went on, "you get in terrible trouble. I had a best friend once, and I was getting it on with his old lady; they had four kids. When he found out about it he just up and left, after twenty years! Took the car, too. God knows where he went." The piano tuner's sweat was splashing on the keys as he tightened the strings; his lower lip stuck out as though he might burst into tears, or perhaps he was just pouting at the world's injustices, or straining with the effort of his work.

"Look," I said, "don't feel bad. If you could ruin a marriage like that, it probably wasn't worth saving anyway. It would've collapsed sooner or later. Don't blame yourself."

"Yeah," he said. "We're all going to die sooner or later, so I might as well strangle you now."

There was another silence while he stared at me. I was trying to smile.

"Am I right?" he said.

I couldn't believe my wife wasn't home yet. It was past supper time. This had happened before, but she had always left something in the oven for me. It wasn't like her to be so careless. I kept looking around, half expecting her to materialize through the walls.

The piano tuner sat down again and groped a cigarette out of a wrinkled pack. I dashed out to the kitchen for one of our old glass ashtrays and brought it to him.

"My wife and I are trying to give up smoking," I explained.

"People who smoke have more lead in their pencil," he said with conviction. "What do you think of just four smokes a day?"

"I heard you could smoke up to six a day without bad effects, but I could never hold myself down to that few." The smoke from his cigarette was making me dizzy; some of his ashes fell on the keys.

"I have four a day," he said. "I can't afford to get sick, but you got to have something to enjoy."

"Yes, everyone does."

"The rich don't get sick. They get all the women they want, and good food, too. The poor get exercise and diet."

"It's a tough life," I said, trying to back out.

"Could be worse." He hit a few chords on the piano. "I pass blood every day but they won't give me one of those scans; I don't know why. I did five push-ups three days in a row and I haven't recovered. I told the doc I'm a right-handed piano tuner, I can't afford to get arthritis in my right hand."

"How's the piano sounding?" I asked, trying to switch the conversation to more professional ground.

He ran a series of scales, starting from the bass and winding up high in the treble. "Some uprights are lemons, but this old Kimball is worth keeping up. I know a guy that refinished one and sold it for twenty-nine hundred dollars. The dampers are stuck, though," he said, working the pedals. "That has to be extra too."

By now it was dark out. I brought him another bourbon. "How long is this going to take?"

"A long time," he wheezed, pulling on the tuner. "This is really flat. I have to bring it up a long way. It could take all night, but after nine o'clock I get double time." This was a depressing prospect in several ways, so I said, "I don't know if I can afford it."

"Listen, it's worth it. This is a good instrument here. Almost as good as that harp." The harp looked outrageously expensive in the soft light.

"Well, we got that in Russia," I said. "It wasn't too expensive over there."

"Over here it's plenty expensive; this is real money," he said, waving his hand vaguely around. "You know, that harp's got over two thousand moving parts?" He peered backward toward the harp. "And that's gut string, the real thing. A lot of dead animals in this room, I'll tell you. Look" — he lifted his sloping shoulders with a groan — "I could use another bourbon." He had swallowed it like water, but I was ready for another one myself, so I went obediently to the kitchen.

After I got him the drink — a small one this time; I didn't want a drunken piano tuner on my hands — I went back to my study and sat down. I was worried about my wife. She really was very dependable. I had been taking her too much for granted, getting irritated by her high nasal voice, which, after all, was hardly her fault. She was still very attractive. When she came home, I would tell her that. She had probably gone to a matinee with Iris and they had stayed to discuss the movie over a bite to eat. I hated talking about movies. I never knew what to say. But why hadn't she called me?

On impulse I got up and went to the phone. I had avoided it before because the phone was on the wall near the music room, and it was somehow embarrassing to be looking for my wife in front of the piano tuner. He was working on the higher register now. Iris's line was busy. He hadn't paused while I was dialing, but when I hung up he stopped, and the quiet was a great relief from the insanely repetitious notes.

"I've got a Reserve meeting tomorrow," I told him. "I have to find out what time I should leave." This was true enough, though my reluctance to speak about my wife in front of him puzzled me.

"You in the Army?" he asked.

"Yes," I said, "I'm a captain in the Reserve. It brings in some nice extra income." At once, I regretted saying that; he seemed to make me babble like an idiot.

"Were you in the war?" he asked — ambiguously, considering recent history.

"Yes, but I was stationed in Washington, reading documents."

"I was in the Navy in the sixties, during Vietnam." The piano tuner sighed. "Didn't do much, but you know what I liked?" His square-tipped left fingers kept striking notes while his right hand pulled the tuning key to tighten the strings. His little head bent close to the keys. "I liked laying in bed listening to the engine and feeling it shake the bunk, like a big cat purring or something. Sometimes I'd wake up and there'd be this bird outside my porthole movin' right along with the ship without waving its wings or anything, just like it was painted there, its little black feet tucked under its belly like miniature bombs. That was a helluva way to sleep." He stood up, gasping, suddenly towering over me. "Now I got me a bad back and nobody gives a shit. Look, you got a vacuum? I need to clean the inside of this thing."

"Sure, in the bedroom upstairs. I'll get it for you."

"No need." With the swiftness that kept catching me off-guard, he stepped by me onto the stair landing. "I got to stretch these legs." As soon as he disappeared, I called Iris again; this time it rang, but there was no answer.

It was totally dark by now. I peered out the window. His van squatted like an armored car in the driveway, the streetlamp throwing the trees' shadows across it like camouflage; no one was near it. The piano tuner was using the bathroom upstairs, so I made myself a stiff drink and sat down in my study to wait him out. If only my wife were here! It came to me that she was the one who threw people out of the house — that was *her* job. She slammed the door in salesmen's faces, hung up on telephone solicitors. While I had a reputation as a stinging, even withering, critic, I was not programmed for face-to-face confrontations. I had even been known to lie on the kitchen floor while the Seventh Day Adventists prowled our neighborhood with their books, leaflets, and sermons; the alternative, for me, was suffering through a dreary, hour-long lecture-debate. My wife, on the other hand, would just give them the raspberry and send them on their way.

Now the vacuum cleaner was going, and I breathed a relieved sigh. It must be almost over. A man's home *is* his castle, after all. I settled down at my typewriter and tried to concentrate on the review. After a while, I was aware that the piano tuner was padding to the kitchen and back again, but I was determined to ignore him. Time passed, though I got little done. I found myself thinking about when I first met my wife. She stood at the top of a staircase in a summer dress, her eyes bright with energy and good will, her long legs tan and slim. No one expected more from the world than she, and right then and there I resolved that I would get it for her. Now, looking around, I realized I didn't even have a picture of her on my desk, just one of our son shooting baskets in the driveway. I remembered how the endless bouncing of that ball had driven me crazy.

Suddenly the piano burst into song: the piano tuner was playing, of all things, "The Battle Hymn of the Republic." "Mine eyes have seen the glory of the coming of the Lord"; his low voice accompanied the piano. I stuck my checkbook into my back pocket and walked to the music room. The piano was still apart and the bottle of bourbon sat beside the vacuum cleaner; the tools were spread across the floor — I couldn't believe the mess.

"I thought you were finished!" I shouted. I almost felt like crying.

"God, I love this song," he said, his deep voice slurred. He was playing it slowly, ponderously. "Listen, what do you think of it?"

"It's all right," I said, dragged in again, trying to control myself, thinking of the best way to get rid of him. "I've always liked the sound of the words, like *vintage* . . ."

"No! No! I mean it makes me feel like flying the flag, you know what I mean? Gettin' out there, marching down the streets." He struck the chords again.

"Well," I tried to smile, humoring him. "I've never been what you call patriotic, 'My country right or wrong' . . ."

The piano tuner swiveled his bloated body toward me and glared.

"Look," I said, "you're through. You must be tired. I know I am. Let me pay you and you can go home."

"I haven't done the felts yet; that's a big job. That'll cost quite a bit. I just vacuumed the old felts out of here."

"Look," I repeated, "that's enough. You've been here long enough today. Call us tomorrow and we'll make an appointment for you to finish."

He picked up the bottle and sloshed some whiskey into his glass. He took a large sip and began to cough. His face turned purplish red. "Don't bother me," he said between coughs. "I'll just put the felts in. We got a contract."

"What contract? There isn't any contract, for God's sake!" I put my hand on his shoulder, where his crumpled cigarettes were rolled up in his T-shirt sleeve, the way tough high school kids had carried them in the fifties.

He sprang up and staggered through the debris on the floor, miraculously missing the bourbon bottle. He held me two inches above the elbow. "You just work at your desk till I finish," he said, propelling me across the living room. The only way for me to resist would have been to twist around and hit him or to sag to the floor. Naturally, I did neither.

"You'll get in trouble, you know," I said, feeling cowardly and humiliated. But he was a hundred pounds heavier than I was; what was I supposed to do? He gave me one last shove, a flick of his thick and hairy wrist, and I stumbled into my office. The door banged shut behind me and the key, always in the keyhole, turned in the lock.

He had locked me in my own office! For the first time in several hours I was no longer nervous or afraid — just furious. I banged on the door, I shook it, I kicked it. Suddenly, it swung open. The thought occurred to me that he was joking — this was the idiot's sense of humor; but I was not amused.

He was standing right there, of course, and I said, *"Get out of my house,"* with all the force I could muster. Like a frog snatching a fluttering moth, his right hand shot out and caught my left. He bent my little finger in on itself and the joints popped as I sank down on my knees. I felt a searing pain in my neck and dug my fingers under the piano wire he had looped over my head. He jerked me to my feet, four of my fingers still under the wire.

"Listen, the next time you bother me I'll pop your eyes out," he whispered. He shoved me back into the study and locked the door.

I lay on the floor a long time. For a while, the piano tuner played as if bashing the piano with his fists. Keys were breaking, wood splintering, in some sort of devil's symphony. Radio music, turned up, competed with the piano. Absurdly I thought, What will the neighbors think? Where are my neighbors? And I remembered that I didn't even know their names. After some time, I became aware of my own sobbing, and something else, frail and familiar. I rolled over and put my ear to the door. Under the din I could hear my wife's voice. "Oh," she was saying. When had she come in? "Oh, my God," she cried. "Oh! Oh!"

WRIGHT MORRIS

Fellow-Creatures

(FROM THE NEW YORKER)

NOTHING SPECIAL, just a leghorn pullet, the pet of children who lived in a nearby trailer, its feathers soiled by too much handling, the little bird had escaped from its pen and found shelter in the garage of Colonel Huggins, U.S. Army, retired. The malfunctioning garage door stood half open, offering a dark and convenient sanctuary that had attracted the pullet at an early hour of the morning. Huggins had been awakened by the mournful clucking. When it persisted, he investigated. In the dawning light, the little bird looked ghostly, but cast a huge shadow in the beam of the flashlight. Her jewelled eye seemed to flash; the clucking became shrill and agitated. Huggins crouched, extending one hand, and the bird, with some reluctance, took a few steps toward him. When Huggins clucked encouragement, the pullet responded. Huggins had grown up in a farmyard cackling with chickens without remarking that they were so expressive. He was amazed to note the range of emotion in the cluck of a chicken. Fear and anxiety soon gave way to a soft, throaty warbling for reassurance. Huggins responded. Soon the little bird pecked at the button on his shirt cuff; then, with a minimum of flutter, she allowed him to slip a hand beneath her breastbone, cradle her on his arm. She liked that, being accustomed to it.

As Huggins left the garage and entered the house, the pullet's cackle was troubled and anxious. Huggins stroked her throat feathers to calm her. The bird was quiet while he dialled the neighbors' number and heard the excitement of the children, their cries of relief. The pullet's name proved to be Lucy.

In a moment, three of the children came scrambling through the brush on the slope, trampling whatever it was Huggins' wife had planted. Had he fed her, they cried. She was probably starving! The youngest of the three hugged the little pullet like a package, and off they all raced, hooting. High on the slope Huggins heard the shrill voice of their mother, a liberated young woman who had set up her trailer in her parents' back yard; she was urging them to thank the nice man.

Was Huggins a nice man? For three years, he had endured the cackling of chickens (originally a flock), the honking of geese (now down to two), the bleating of a goat, and the bloodcurdling cry of a peacock kept in a cage too small to strut in or display his plumage. All of this illegal in an exclusively residential area. Even the trailer the young woman and her brood lived in (the tires now flat) required a special permit she had not been granted. Huggins, that nice man, had said nothing. Over the years, he *had* written several letters, all unmailed, to her father, Albrecht, a prominent figure in the foreign-car business. Huggins wondered how he himself would have handled a grown daughter (a squatter on his property) who had brought a court suit against her own father for polluting the air with his diesel-engine Mercedes. Huggins had never met her. She called her cats, her chickens, her geese, and her children by clapping her hands — a racket he found distracting. The pullet had left bits of dirt and feathers on his sleeve. How light she had been! Like a feather duster. He stood as if waiting for something to happen, plucking at his sleeve.

Huggins' daily morning walk was altered to bring him past the pen where the little pullet did her scratching. With a little coaxing, Huggins persuaded her to take birdseed from his palm. Imported Irish oatmeal also caught her fancy. He inquired in the local pet shop what was recommended to brighten up a young bird's feathers. He added the vitamin mixture to her water. He was caught red-handed by Mrs. Albrecht, the young woman's mother, who appeared with vegetable hulls and cuttings. She, too, had a weakness for chickens! Just in passing, she let it drop that this little pullet was the last of the fryers but hadn't fleshed out like the others — had he noticed? There was nothing to her. For which the bird could be thankful. Mrs. Albrecht (she drove a non-diesel Mercedes) could hardly wait to tell the children that their neighbor, Colonel Huggins, had taken on the chore of feeding their chicken — that's how starved it looked!

Huggins would surely have explained what led him to feed his neighbors' chicken, but the word "fryer" had so unsettled him that he was speechless. Was it new to him that young chickens were *fryers*? Hardly. He had once even barbecued fryers in batches — a *spécialité de la maison*, as he had put it.

A few days later, Mr. Albrecht, a jovial type with a strong, booming voice, called across from his deck to say that Huggins was welcome to the whole damn zoo if he would like it, so long as he took the peacock, too. How did Huggins stand it? Albrecht thought it sounded like some female screaming "Help!"

During the war in Europe, Colonel Huggins had enjoyed the hospitality of a French family proud of their cuisine. He had been instrumental in providing them with hard-to-find gourmet necessities. At war's end, they cooked him a five-star dinner, featuring steak. Huggins had admitted to being a connoisseur of steak.

"So," the host asked him, "how you like?"

His mouth full of the steak, Huggins smiled and nodded.

"A *spécialité, mon vieux — filet de cheval Américain!*"

Huggins was calm enough to swallow what he had already chewed. Moments later, however, he was obliged to excuse himself, leaving most of the *filet de cheval* on his plate. He perspired a good deal. A damp towel was applied to his face.

"You Americans!" his host exclaimed. "You like it fine till you know what it is. What you eat is not on your plate, it is in your mind!"

Then there was the time Huggins' wife cried out from the kitchen, "Oh my God!" Fearing the worst, he went to her rescue. But at the door to the kitchen he saw nothing unusual. His wife had prepared a plump bird for roasting with a coat of olive oil that made it glisten.

"Yes?" he said.

She took a moment to slip off the bib of her apron. Then she said, almost flatly, "It looks just like a newborn baby!" and left Huggins alone with it.

•

A cow, somewhat on the small side — not so large that Huggins found her intimidating — was tethered to pasture in a field that Huggins passed on his long daily walk. He was in the habit, when the spirit moved him, of pulling up the grass that grew along the bank where the cow was unable to reach it. When she raised her head to crop the sweet, fragrant offering from his hand, the breath she exhaled smelled of clover. On the instant, Huggins experienced a time displacement, familiar to poets. A boy, he stood in the shadow of a freight car down the tracks from the town, peering into a great vat of sorghum as sweet and thick as Karo syrup. Bees droned in a cloud above it. A thick green scum spotted its surface. He almost swooned at the thought that he might topple into it. So rich and fragrant had been its smell that he felt no need to taste it. The whole great vat of it, swarming with bees, the scum on the top softly undulating, had put him in mind of the old movie serials where if the hero toppled into one of the pits of terror he would be preserved like a bee in a jar of honey.

On occasion, the cow shared the pasture with a swaybacked horse. In the rainy season Huggins might pull up a tuft of the new grass, earth still clinging to the roots, and toss it to where the horse could munch it. The animal showed no interest whatever. The horse's owner occasionally forked hay from the back of a pickup, but he never checked to see what the horse thought about it. He drove in, made his drop, and drove off. Some days Huggins would stand on the bridge over the creek, where he and the animals had a good view of each other; the bare spots on the horse, worn by the harness, were the shiny black of old oilcloth. In bad weather, the beast took shelter in a shed, where Huggins, attentive as he passed, might hear a snort and the stomp of a hoof. Somehow it troubled him that it was a mare. On cold mornings he saw her breath smoke. He thought it especially disturbing that she was both so big and so useless. He had read about pet food, but he tried to put it out of his mind.

Occasionally, this pasture also nourished several black-faced sheep, adored by children. Seen close up, their faces were like felt masks, the heads like carnival toggery on a stick. At no time did Huggins entertain any notion that he and the sheep shared a common doom or aspiration. He did feel the creatures' ill-starred need to be led somewhere, anywhere — even to slaughter. Nevertheless, for no particular reason, Colonel Huggins — a lover of roast spring lamb — passed up the seasonal special called to his attention by Angelo, the butcher, well known for his own hopeless love for steak tartare with three raw eggs.

"So what is new?" queried Angelo, sensing a change.

"Less fat," replied Huggins, patting his midriff. It was old advice he was now moved to take. What did that leave him? Perhaps a mozzarella pizza from the freezer. One day — not today — he would ask Angelo how horses did so well on just hay and cereal.

Escaped or missing pets — now that Huggins had been alerted — were having one of their high seasons. Urgent requests for their return were posted on abandoned cars, telephone poles, and supermarket bulletin boards, citing rewards along with descriptions of their character, identifying marks, the names to which they sometimes responded, or — in the case of parrots — what they would say if questioned. What parrots might say often shocked Huggins; he had always teased them to speak with a mere "Polly want a cracker?" but lately one had told him to buzz off.

One day, a big cottontail rabbit, with feet like snowshoes, hopped from behind a shrub to startle Huggins. The sight of Huggins did not give the rabbit cause for alarm; it hopped so close that Huggins might have seized it if he had not been so unnerved. When he mentioned this incident to his cousin, Liz Harcourt — a woman who had hatched several batches of quail eggs in her kitchen and raised the broods to eat from her plate and nest in her apron pockets — she said, "You should have grabbed him. I love chicken-fried rabbit!"

Some years back, during a rainy season with bad mud slides and considerable flooding, a herd of Holstein cows pastured somewhere behind the ridge had made their way, pursued by a pack of baying dogs, through groves of oak and laurel, through a dense tangle of brush that streaked their hides with red as if raked with barbed wire, to where they exited, mooing distractedly, at the foot of the driveway Huggins shared with the Albrechts. He saw them from his deck, where he was barbecuing spareribs. As they made their mooing way up the driveway, he worried that they would trample his azaleas. Single file, following the leader, they continued up the slope to the Albrecht house (at that time the trailer was not there) and followed the walk around the house onto the deck at the rear. The rail fence around the deck confined them; there they formed an assembly, casually informal, like guests at a cocktail party. Peering down at Huggins, one or two mooed plaintively. He could see the red streaks on their flanks and udders. The bizarre spectacle brought to Huggins' mind a fantastic, fanciful painting. Fear that the deck might collapse — his neighbors were out that afternoon — aroused him to call the fire department for some quick action. The man who owned the cows, a shaggy, bearded fellow who did not trouble to greet Huggins, finally appeared to herd them peaceably back down to the street.

At the time, the incident seemed merely bizarre. But that night, as Huggins put his mind to it, his eyes on the play of shadows on the bedroom ceiling, it came to him that the face of a cow, a craggy primitive mask, was like a piece of the landscape seen in closeup. That congress of cows assembled on a house deck, their gaze centered in judgment on Huggins, had led him to forgo the ribs smoking on his barbecue.

Another day — it had been overcast, with a bit of drizzle, obliging him to plod along with his head down — Huggins heard a raucous clamor above and behind him. A flock of grackles, their wet feathers gleaming, sat along one of the telephone wires. On an impulse, he threw up his arms and hooted hoarsely. The birds rose about him like a leaf storm, scattered for a moment, then gathered on a wire on the street below. Did Huggins detect, as he passed by, a change in the tone of their discussion? Several flew ahead to strut about on a plot of grass. As he approached them they took off, flying in crisp military formation. He wheeled to watch them, blinking his eyes at the pelting stream of their forms. After several orderly strategic flights, they congregated in a tree along the curb walk. The tree itself was not much — a dark clump of leaves without visible branches. It was Huggins' impression, however, as he walked toward it, that the gabble of the birds caused the leaves to tremble, as if stirred by a breeze. He sensed their hovering, inscrutable presence. From beneath the tree, he peered upward just as the flock noisily departed, like bees from a hive. Bits of leaves and feathers rained on him. The agitation Huggins had observed in the leaves he now felt within himself — a tingling, pleasurable excitement. Squinting skyward, he could see strips of sky as if through cracks in leaky shingles. High at the top, perched at an angle, was a single black bird. Either that bird or another just like it — among birds it seemed unimportant — fluttered along with Huggins, its hatpin eyes checking on his interests and curious habits, all the way back to the foot of his drive, where he heard, high on the slope above him, the expectant clucking of the little pullet, and he responded in kind.

BHARATI MUKHERJEE

Angela

(FROM MOTHER JONES)

ORRIN AND I ARE in Delia's hospital room. There's no place to sit because we've thrown our parkas, caps, and scarves on the only chair. The sides of Delia's bed have metal railings so we can't sit on her bed as we did on Edith's when Edith was here to have her baby last November. The baby, if a girl, was supposed to be named Darlene, after Mother, but Edith changed her mind at the last minute. She changed her mind while she was being shaved by the nurse. She picked "Desirée" out of a novel.

My sisters are hopeless romantics.

Orrin loves Delia and brings her little gifts. Yesterday he brought her potted red flowers from Hy-Vee and jangly Mexican earrings I can't quite see Delia wearing; the day before he tied a pair of big, puffy dice to the bedrails. Today he's carrying *One Hundred Years of Solitude*. Delia can't read. She's in a coma, but any day she might come out of it.

He's so innocent! I want to hold his head in my hands, I want to stop up his ears with my fingers so he can't hear Dr. Menezies speak. The doctor is a heavy, gloomy man from Goa, India. Hard work got him where he is. He dismisses Orrin's optimism as frivolous and childish.

"We could read twenty or thirty pages a day to her." Orrin pokes me through my sweater. "You want to start reading?" It's a family joke that I hate to read — my English isn't good enough yet — and Orrin's almost family. "It's like *Dynasty*, only more weird."

"You read. I'll get us some coffee."

"A Diet Coke for me."

Dr. Vinny Menezies lies in wait for me by the vending machines. "Hullo, hullo." He jerks his body into bows as I get myself coffee. "You brighten my day." He's an old-fashioned suitor, an unmarried immigrant nearing forty. He has put himself through medical school in Bombay and Edinburgh, and now he's ready to take a wife, preferably a younger woman who is both affectionate and needy. We come from the same subcontinent of hunger and misery: that's a bonus, he told me.

I feel in the pockets of my blue jeans for quarters, and the coffee slops out of the paper cup.

"I'm making you nervous, Angie?" Dr. Menezies extracts a large, crisp handkerchief from his doctor's white jacket, and blots my burning finger tips. "You're so shy, so sensitive."

He pronounces the *s* in *sensitive* as a *z*.

"Do you have a nickel for five pennies? I need to get a Coke for poor Orrin."

"Of course." He holds a shiny nickel out to me. He strokes my palm as I count out the pennies. "That boyfriend of Delia's, he's quite mental with grief, no?"

"He loves her," I mumble.

"And I you."

But Dr. Menezies lightens the gravity of his confession by choosing that moment to kick the stuck candy machine.

A week before the accident, Orrin asked Delia to marry him. Delia told me this. I've been her sister for less than two years, but we tell each other things. Bad and good. I told her about the cook at the orphanage, how he'd chop wings off crows with his cleaver so I could sew myself a sturdy pair of angel wings. He said I was as good as an angel and the wings would be my guarantee. He'd sit me on the kitchen floor and feed me curried mutton and rich, creamy custards meant for the Bishop Pymm. Delia told me about her black moods. Nobody knows about the black moods; they don't show, she's always so sweet-tempered. She's afraid she's going crazy. Most of the time she loves Orrin, but she doesn't want him to marry a nut.

Orrin calls me by name, his special name for me. "Angel," he says. "Tell me, was she going to say yes?"

I pull open the flip-top of his Diet Coke. He needs looking after, especially now.

"You've come to know her better than any of us." He sits on the windowsill, his feet on the chair. His shoes squash our winter things. "Please, I can handle the truth."

"Of course she loves you, Orrin." In the dry heat of Delia's hospital room, even my smile is charged with static.

Delia's eyes are open. We can't tell what she sees or hears. It would have been easier on us if she'd looked as though she were sleeping. Orrin chats to her and holds her hand. He makes plans. He'll quit his job with the United Way. He'll move back from Des Moines. When Delia gets out, they'll fly to Nicaragua and work on a farm side by side with Sandinistas. Orrin's an idealist.

I believe in miracles, not chivalry.

Grace makes my life spin. How else does a girl left for dead in Dacca get to the Brandons' farmhouse in Van Buren County?

When I was six, soldiers with bayonets cut off my nipples. "They left you poor babies for dead," Sister Stella at the orphanage would tell me, the way I might tell Desirée bedtime stories. "They left you for dead, but the Lord saved you. Now it's your turn to do Him credit."

We are girls with special missions. Some day soon, the mysteries will be revealed. When Sister Stella was my age, she was a Muslim, the daughter of a man who owned jute mills. Then she fell in love with a tourist from Marseilles, and when he went home she saw him for what he was: the Lord's instrument for calling her to Christianity. Reading portents requires a special kind of literacy.

Mrs. Grimlund, the nurse, steals into the room with her laced, rubber-soled shoes. Dr. Menezies is with her. "Hullo, again." At the end of a long afternoon, his white doctor's jacket looks limp, but his voice is eager. "Don't look so glum. Delia isn't dying." He doesn't actually ignore Orrin, but it's me he wants to talk to.

Orrin backs off to the window. "We aren't looking glum," he mutters.

Dr. Menezies fusses with Delia's chart. "We're giving her our best. Not to worry, please."

Mrs. Grimlund, deferential, helps out Dr. Menezies. "My, my," she says in a loud, throaty voice, "we're looking a lot livelier today, aren't we?" She turns her blue watchful eyes on Orrin. As a nurse and a good Christian she wants to irradiate the room with positive thinking. She marches to the window and straightens a bent shutter. Then she eases the empty Coke can out of Orrin's hand and drops it into the wastebasket. She can always find things that need doing. When I first got to Iowa, she taught me to skate on the frozen lake behind our church.

Dr. Menezies plucks Delia's left hand out from under the blanket and times her pulse. His watch is flat, a gold wafer on a thick, hairy wrist. It looks expensive. His silk tie, the band of shirt that shows between the lapels of his jacket, even the fountain pen with gold clip look very expensive. He's a spender. Last Christmas he gave me a choker of freshwater pearls he'd sent for from a Macy's catalog.

"Splendid," he agrees. But it's me he's looking at. "Very satisfactory indeed." In spite of my bony, scarred body and plain face.

Sometimes I visualize grace as a black, tropical bat, cutting through dusk on blunt, ugly wings.

"You wonder why a thing like this happens," Mrs. Grimlund whispers. She lacks only imagination. She tucks Delia's hand back under the blanket, and tidies up Orrin's gifts on the night table. I brought a bag of apples. For Orrin, not Delia. Someone has to make him keep up his energies. "She's such a sweet, loving Christian person."

Orrin turns on her. "Don't look for the hand of Providence in this! It was an accident. Delia hit an icy patch and lost control of the wheel." He twists and twists the shutter control.

"Let me get you another Coke," I beg.

"Stop mothering me!"

Orrin needs to move around. He walks from the window to the bed, where Dr. Menezies is holding his flashlight like a lorgnette, then back to the window. He sits on the chair, on top of our parkas. I hate to see him this lost.

"Delia always carries her witness," Mrs. Grimlund goes on. "I never once saw her upset or angry." She's known Delia all of Delia's life. She told me that it was Delia who asked specifically for a sister from Bangladesh. She was dropping me off after choir practice last week and she said, "Delia said, 'I have everything, so I want a sister who has nothing. I want a sister I can really share my things with.'"

I never once saw her angry, either. I did see her upset. The moods came on her very suddenly. She'd read the papers, a story about bad stuff in a day-care center maybe, about little kids being fondled and photographed, then she'd begin to cry. The world's sins weighed on her.

Orrin can't seem to stay in the chair. He stumbles toward the door. He isn't trying to leave Delia's room, he's just trying to get hold of himself.

Once Orrin goes out of the room, Mrs. Grimlund lets go a little of her professional cheeriness. "It just pulls the rug from under you, doesn't it? You wonder why."

I was in the back seat, that's how I got off with a stiff neck. I have been blessed. The Lord keeps saving me.

Delia was driving and little Kim was in the bucket seat, telling a funny story about Miss Wendt, his homeroom teacher. Mother says that when Kim first got here, he didn't speak a word of anything, not even Korean. He was four. She had to teach him to eat lunch slowly. Kim was afraid the kids at school might snatch it if he didn't eat real fast.

He braced himself when we went into that spin. He broke his wrist and sprained his ankle, and the attendant said probably nothing would have happened if he'd just relaxed and sort of collapsed when he saw it coming.

"There's no telling, is there?" The world's mysteries have ravaged Mrs. Grimlund. Her cap has slipped slightly off-center. "Who'll be taken and who'll be saved, I mean."

Dr. Menezies gives her a long, stern look. "Our job is not to wonder, but to help." He reaches across Delia to touch my arm.

Mrs. Grimlund reddens. What was meant as rebuke comes off as a brisk, passionate outburst. The dingy thicknesses of coat and shirt envelop a wild, raw heart. In the hospital he seems a man of circumspect feelings, but on Sunday afternoons when we drive around and around in his Scirocco, his manner changes. He seems raw, aimless, lost.

"I didn't mean anything wicked," Mrs. Grimlund whispers. "I wasn't questioning the Lord's ways."

I calm her with my smile. My winning smile, that's what the Brandons call it. "Of course you didn't." I am Angela the Angel. Angela was Sister Stella's name for me. The name I was born with is lost to me, the past is lost to me. I must have seen a lot of wickedness when I was six, but I can't remember any of it. The rapes, the dogs chewing on dead bodies, the soldiers. Nothing.

Orrin rushes us from the hall. Dr. Menezies, his passion ebbed, guides Orrin to the chair and I grab the parkas so Orrin will have more room to sit. He needs looking after. I imagine him among Sandinista farmers. He tells slight, swarthy men carrying machetes about rootworms and cutworms. His eyes develop a savior's glittery stare.

"We shouldn't be just standing around and chattering," he shouts. "We're chattering in front of her as though she's dead."

He's all wired up with grief. He was up most of last night, but he doesn't look tired. He looks angry, crazy, stunned, but not tired. He can be with Delia two more days, then he has to go back to Des Moines.

"Take him home." Dr. Menezies is at his best now. He takes charge. He helps Orrin into his jacket and hands him his scarf, cap, mittens. "He isn't doing Delia any good in this state. We have our hands full as it is."

Mrs. Grimlund watches me pull a glove on with my teeth. "I didn't mean it should have been you, Angie." Her lower lip's chewed so deep that there's blood.

Then Dr. Menezies' heavy arm rests on my shoulder. If his watch were any closer to my ear, I'd hear it hum. "Give my regards to your dear parents," he says. He makes a courtly, comical bow. "I shall be seeing you on Sunday? Yes, please?"

On Sunday, after church, we sit down to a huge pork roast — pigs aren't filthy creatures here as they are back home — and applesauce, mashed potatoes and gravy, candied carrots, hot rolls. My older sister Edith and Mary Wellman, the widow from two farms over, have brought dessert: two fruit pies, a chocolate cake, and a small jar of macaroons. My brother Bill's wife, Judy, is studying for her master's in library science, so she usually brings something simple, like tossed salad.

I love these Sunday dinners. Company isn't formal and wearying as it was in the orphanage. The days that the trustees in their silk saris and high heels sat at our tables were headachy and endless. The Brandons talk about everything: what the Reverend Gertz said about the Salvadoran refugees, the blizzard we've just gone through, the tardy bank officers who still haven't authorized the loan for this season's plantings. Dad's afraid that if the money doesn't come through by the end of March, he and a whole lot of farmers in the county will be in trouble.

"It'll come through." Mother's the Rock of Gibraltar in our house. She forks carrot slivers delicately and leans her head a wee bit toward Judy, who is telling us about her first husband. "I wouldn't let him near the children, I don't care what the judge says." Bill just melts away from conversations about Judy's first husband. Mother wanted to be a schoolteacher, Delia told me. She wanted to help kids with learning difficulties. Delia wants to be a physical therapist.

"I shouldn't be so sanguine," Ron says. Ron is Edith's husband. He worked for John Deere until the big layoff, but he's not waiting for recall. He's training himself for computers at the community college, and during the day he sits in a cubicle in a hall full of cubicles and makes phone calls for a mail-order firm. The firm sells diet pills and offers promotional gifts. Ron thinks the whole thing's a scam to misuse credit cards.

"Oh, you always look on the negative side," Edith scolds. She eats at the small table — to the left of the dining table — with Kim and Fred. Fred is Judy's six-year-old. She's expecting a baby with Bill in the spring. Desirée is propped up and strapped into her white plastic feeding seat. Edith lifts teaspoonfuls of mashed potatoes to Desirée's full, baby lips. "She really goes for your gravy, Mom. Don't you, darling?"

Ron reaches into the basket of rolls. "Well, life hasn't been too upscale lately for any of us!"

Dr. Menezies bobs and weaves in his chair, passing the plate of butter curls and the gravy boat. He's clearly the most educated, the most traveled man at the table but he talks the least.

He is polite, too polite, passing platters and tureens, anticipating and satisfying. This Sunday his hair springs in two big, glossy waves from a thin parting, and his mustache has a neat droop. He tries to catch my eye as he passes the butter.

"I don't know what we'd have done without you, Vinny," Dad says. Dad looks away at the yard, and beyond it at the fields that may not get planted this season.

We have deep feelings, but we aren't a demonstrative family. Fellowship is what we aim for. A parent's grieving would be a spectacle in Bangladesh.

Dr. Menezies tugs at his mustache. It could be a pompous gesture, but somehow he manages to make it seem gracious. "It was my duty only, sir."

I can tell he is thrilled with Dad's praise.

Around 3:30, after Edith and her family and Bill and his family have driven away, and Mary Wellman, Mother, and I have washed and dried the dishes, I play Mozart on the piano for Dr. Menezies. He likes to watch me play, he says. He's tone-deaf, but he says he likes the way the nuns taught me to sit, straight and elegant, on the piano bench. A little civility is how he thinks of this Sunday afternoon ritual. It's one more civility that makes the immense, snowy Midwest less alarming, less ambiguous.

I throw myself into the Fantasy in C Minor. The music, gliding on scarred fingers, transports me to the assembly hall of the orphanage. The bishop sits in the front row, flanked by the trustees in their flowered saris, and a row or two behind, blissful Sister Stella, my teacher. The air in the hall is sweet and lustrous. Together, pianist and audience, we have triumphed over sin, rapacity, war, all that's shameful in human nature.

"Bravo!" the doctor shouts, forgetting himself, forgetting we're in a farmhouse parlor in the middle of America, only Mary Wellman, my parents, and himself to listen. He claps his soft hands, and his gold watch reflects, a pure white flame, on a window pane. "Bravo, bravo!"

When I've lowered the lid, Mary Wellman gathers up her coat and cake pan. I've wrapped what was left of the chocolate cake in tin foil and she carries the small, shiny package breast-high as if it is a treasure. Then Mother excuses herself and goes up to her room to crochet an afghan for Christmas. She doesn't know whom she's making it for, yet. She knits, she crochets. On Sundays, she doesn't read, not even the Des Moines *Register*.

Dad joins Kim in the basement for basketball. Dr. Menezies doesn't care for basketball. Or football or baseball. He came to America as a professional, too old to pick up on some things. The trivia and the madness elude him. He approaches the New World with his stethoscope drawn; he listens to its scary gurgles. He leaves the frolicking to natives. Kim and I are forced to assimilate. A girl with braids who used to race through wet, leechy paddy fields now skates on frozen water: that surely is a marvel. And the marvels replicate. The coach has put me on the varsity cheerleading squad. To make me feel wanted. I'm grateful. I am wanted. Love is waving big, fluffy pompoms with the school colors; it's wearing new Nikes and leaping into the air. I'd never owned shoes in Bangladesh. All last spring, when Delia played — they said, she was tough on the boards, she was intimidating, awesome, second team all-state, from a school of only 200 — I shook my pompoms fiercely from the court's edge, I screamed my sisterly love. Delia sent for me from Dacca. She knew what her special mission was when she was just in tenth grade. I could die not knowing, not being able even to guess.

"We're alone. At last."

Dr. Menezies floats toward me in squeaky new leather shoes. He's the acquisitor. His voice is hoarse, but his face is radiant. He should not alarm me now. After 3:30 on Sunday afternoons, the Brandons leave the front room to us, and nothing untoward ever happens.

I retreat to the upright piano. Shockingly, my body trembles. "Where did everyone go? We seem to be the only idle ones around here."

The doctor laughs. "Idleness is the devil's workshop, no?"

I suggest a walk. But my suitor does not want to walk or go for a drive. He wants to sit beside me on the piano bench and whimper from the fullness of love.

I hold my shoulders pressed back, my spine taut and straight, so straight, the way Sister Stella taught me. Civilities to see us through minor crises.

"You must be worrying all the time about your future, no?" He strokes my hair, my neck. His inflection is ardent. "Your school will be over in May."

"In June."

"May, June, OK. But then what?" He rubs the lump scars between my shoulder blades.

There's a new embarrassing twitchiness to my body. My thighs squeezed tight, begin to hurt.

"In America, grown-up children are expected to fly the coop," my suitor explains. "You will have to fly, Angie. Make your own life. No shilly-shally, no depending on other people here."

"I thought I'd go to Iowa City. Study physical therapy, like Delia."

"Delia will never study physical therapy, Angie." His voice is deep, but quiet, though we are alone. "You are the strong one. I can tell you."

Mrs. Grimlund dances a sad, savage dance on weightless feet. There's no telling who'll be taken and who'll be saved. I wait for some sign. I've been saved for a purpose.

"Anyway, you're going to make the Brandons shell out three or four thousand? I don't think you're so selfish." He gives a shy giggle, but his face is intense. "I think when school is over, you'll be wanting to find a full-time job. Yes. You'll want to find a job. Or a husband. If it is the latter, I'm a candidate putting in an early word."

He slips a trembling arm around my waist and pulls me close. A wet, shy kiss falls like a blow on the side of my head.

Tomorrow when I visit Delia, I'll stop by the personnel department. They know me, my family. I'll work well with handicapped children. With burn-center children. I'll not waste my life.

But that night, in the room with two beds, Dr. Menezies lies on Delia's pink chenille bedspread. His dark, ghostly face rests on pillow shams trimmed with pink lace. He offers me intimacy, fellowship. He tempts with domesticity. Phantom duplexes, babies tucked tight into cribs, dogs running playfully off with the barbequed steaks.

What am I to do?

Only a doctor could love this body.

Then it is the lavender dusk of tropics. Delinquents and des-
titutes rush me. Legless kids try to squirm out of ditches. Packs
of pariah dogs who have learned to gorge on dying infant flesh,
soldiers with silvery bayonets, they keep coming at me, plunging
their knives through my arms and shoulders. I dig my face into
the muddy walls of a trough too steep to climb. Leeches, I can
feel leeches gorging on the blood of my breasts.

BETH NUGENT

City of Boys

(FROM THE NORTH AMERICAN REVIEW)

MY LITTLE SWEETHEART, she says, bringing her face close enough for me to see the fine net of lines that carves her skin into a weathered stone. You love me, don't you, little sweetheart, little lamb?

Whether or not she listens anymore, I am not sure, but I always answer yes, yes I always say, yes, I love you.

She is my mother, my father, my sister, brother, cousin, lover; she is everything I ever thought any one person needed in the world. She is everything but a boy.

— Boys, she tells me. Boys will only break you.

I know this. I watch them on the street corners, huddled under their puddles of blue smoke. They are as nervous as insects, always some part of their bodies in useless agitated motion, a foot tapping, a jaw clenching, a finger drawing circles against a thigh, eyes in restless, programmed movement, from breasts to face to legs to breasts. They are never still, and they twitch and jump when I walk by, but still I want them. I want them in the back seats of their cars, I want them under the bridge where the river meets the rocks in a slick slide of stone, I want them in the back rows of theaters and under the bushes and benches in the park.

— Boys, she says, don't think about boys. Boys would only make you do things you don't know how to do and things you'd never want to do if you knew what they were. I know, she says, I know plenty about boys.

•

She is everything to me. She is not my mother, although I have allowed myself the luxury of sometimes believing myself her child. My mother is in Fairborn, Ohio, where she waits with my father for me to come home and marry a boy and become the woman into whom she still believes it is not too late for me to grow. Fairborn is a city full of boys and parking meters and the Air Force, but most of all it is a city full of my mother and in my mind she looms over it like a cloud of radioactive dust. If I return it will be to her. She is not why I left, she is not why I am here; she is just one thing I left, like all the things that trail behind us when we go from place to place, from birth to birth and from becoming to becoming. She is just another bread-crumb, just another mother in the long series of mothers that let you go to become the women you have to become. But you are always coming back to them.

Where I live now is also a city full of boys, and coming here I passed through hundreds of cities and they were all full of boys.

— Boys, she tells me, are uninteresting, and when they grow up, they become men and become even more uninteresting.

I know this too. I see how boys spend their days, either standing around or playing basketball or engaged in irritating persistent harangue, and I can draw my own conclusions as to what they talk about and as to the heights of which they are capable and I see what they do all day, but still I want them.

The one time I pretended she was a boy, she knew it because I closed my eyes and I never close my eyes, and I imagined it was a boy there doing that, soft tongue between my thighs, and when I came she slapped me hard.

— I'm not a boy, she said, just you remember that. You know who I am and just remember that I love you and no boy could ever love you like I do.

Probably she is right. What boy could love with her slipping concentration; probably no boy could ever achieve what she lets go with every day that comes between us, what she has lost in her long history of love.

What I do sometimes is slip out under her absent gaze. — Where are you going, what are you going to do, she says, and wallowing in the luxury of thinking myself a child, I answer

Nowhere, nothing. In their pure undirected intoxicating mean-inglessness, our conversations carry more significance than either of us is strong enough to bear, together or alone, and I drag it out into the streets today, a long weight trailing behind me, as I look for boys.

Today, I tell myself, is a perfect day for losing things, love and innocence, illusions and expectations; it is a day through which I will walk and walk until I find the perfect boy.

Where we live, on the upper west side, the streets are full of Puerto Rican men watching women. Carefully they examine each woman that walks by, carefully they hold her with their eyes, as if they are somehow responsible for her continued existence on the street. Not a woman goes by untouched by the long leash of their looks.

Oh, they say, Mira Mira sssssssssssss. In their eyes are all the women they have watched walk by and cook and comb their black hair; all the women they have touched with their hands, and all the women they have known live in their eyes and gleam out from within the dark. Their eyes are made only to see women on the streets.

Where we live, on West 83rd and Amsterdam, there are roaches and rats, but nothing matters as long as we're together, we say valiantly, longingly. Nothing matters, I say, stomping a roach and nothing matters, she agrees, her eyes on a low-slung rat sidling by in the long hallway toward the little garbage room across from the door to our apartment. I told the super once that if he kept the garbage out on the street, perhaps the building would be less a home for vermin. — What's vermin, he wanted to know. — Vermin, I told him, is rats and roaches and huge black beetles scrabbling at the base of the toilet when you turn on the light at night. Vermin is all the noises at night, all the clicking and scratching and scurrying through the darkness. — No rats, he said, maybe a mouse or two, and maybe every now and then you'll see your roach eggs, but I keep this place clean. Together we watched as a big brown-shelled roach tried to creep past us on the wall. Neither of us moved to kill it, but when it stopped and waved its antennae, he brought his big fist down in a hard slam against the wall. He didn't look at the dead roach, but I could hardly take my eyes off it, perfectly flattened as though it had been steamrolled against the side of his palm. — Maybe a roach here and there, he said, flicking the roach onto the floor without looking at it, but I keep this place clean. Maybe if you had a man around the house, he said, trying to look past me into the apartment, you wouldn't have so much trouble with vermins.

I pretended not to understand what he meant and backed into the room. Rent control is not going to last forever in New York, and when it goes and all the Puerto Ricans have had to move to the Bronx, we will have to find jobs or hit the streets, but as long as we're together, as long as we have each other. — We'll always have each other, won't we, she says, lighting a cigarette and checking to see how many are left in her pack.

— Yes, I always say, wondering if she's listening or just lost in a cigarette count. You'll always have me, I say. Unless, I think, unless you leave me, or unless I grow up to become the woman my mother still thinks is possible.

Today is a day full of boys. They are everywhere, and I watch each of them, boys on motorcycles, in cars, on bicycles, leaning against walls, walking, to see which of them in this city of boys is mine.

I am not so young and she is not so old, but rent control is not going to last forever, and someday I will be a woman. She wants, I tell myself, nothing more than me. Sometimes I think she must have been my mother, the way she loves me, but when I asked her if she was ever my mother, she touched my narrow breasts and said Would your mother do that, and ran her tongue over my nipple and said Or that. Would your mother know what you want, Sweetheart? I'm not your mother, she said, I stole you from a mattress downtown, just around the corner where all the winos lie around in piss and wine and call for help and nobody listens. I saved you from that, she says, but I remember too clearly the trip out here, in the middle of a car full of people full of drugs, most of them, and I remember how she found me standing just outside the porn theater on 98th and Broadway and she slipped me right from under the gaze of about four hundred curious Puerto Ricans. — Does your mother know where you are? she said. I laughed and said, My mother knows all she needs to know, and she said, Come home with me, I have somebody I want you to meet. When she brought me home, she said to a big man who lay on the couch watching television, Tito, this is Princess Grace, and Tito raised his heavy head from the end of the couch and said, She don't look like no princess to me.

I never thought much of Tito, and she never let him touch me, even though our apartment is only one room, and he was sick with wanting it from me. At night after they'd done it just about as many times as anyone could, she crept over to me on little cat feet and whispered into my ear, Sweetheart you are my only one. As Tito slugged and snored his way through the nights, we'd do it at least one more time than they had, and she would sigh and say, Little sweetheart, you're the one I wanted all the time, even through all those boys and girls that loved me it was always you that I was looking for, you that I always wanted.

This is the kind of talk that kills me, this is the kind of talk that won me, in addition to the fact that she took me in from the hard streets full of boys and taxicabs and cops and everywhere I looked the hard eyes of innocence turned.

What it felt like with her that first time was my mother come back and curled up inside me, giving birth, so that I came out of her at the exact same second that I moved closest into her center.

The long car pulls up to the sidewalk and I bend to see if it has boys in it. It is full of them, so I say,
     — Hey, can I have a ride.
     — Hey, they say, Hey, the lady wants a ride. Where to, they ask.
     — Oh, I say, wherever.
     I look to see where they are heading; — Uptown, I say and the door swings open and I slide in. The oldest boy is probably sixteen and just got his driver's license and is driving his mother's car, a big Buick, or Chevrolet, or Monte Carlo, a mother's car. Each of the boys is different, but they are all exactly alike

in the way that boys are, and right away I find the one I want.
He's the one who does not look at me, and he's the oldest, only
a couple of years younger than me, and it is his mother's car we
are in.

— How about a party, they say, we know a good party uptown.

— Let's just see, I say, let's just ride uptown and see.

Sometimes I wake up to see her leaning on her thin knees
against the wall that is stripped down to expose the rough brick
beneath the plaster. I dream that she prays to keep me, but I
am afraid that she prays for something else, a beginning or an
end, or something I don't know about. She came to bed once
and laid her face against my breast and I felt the imprint of the
brick on the tender skin of her forehead.

She herself is not particularly religious, although the apartment is littered with the scraps of saints — holy relics of one sort
or another; a strand of hair from the Christ child, a bit of
fingernail from Paul, a shred of the virgin's robe. They are left
over from Tito, who collected holy relics the way some people
collect lucky pennies or matchbooks, as some kind of hedge
against some inarticulated sense of disaster. They are just clutter here, though, in this small apartment where we live and I
suggested to her once that we throw them out. She picked up a
piece of dried weed from Gethsemane and said, I don't think
they're ours to throw out. Tito found them and if we got rid of
them, who knows what might happen to Tito. Maybe they work
is what I mean, she said; I don't think it's spiritually economic
to be a skeptic about absolutely everything.

When Tito left, his relics abandoned for some new hope, she
was depressed for a day or two, but said that it was really the
best for everybody, especially for the two of us, the single reality
to which our lives have been refined. Tito said he was getting
sick of watching two dykes moon over each other all the time,
though I think he was just angry because she wouldn't let him
touch me. I was all for it, I wanted him to touch me. That's what
I came to this city for, to have someone like Tito touch me,
someone to whom touching is all the reality of being, someone
who doesn't do it in basements and think he has to marry you,

someone who does it and doesn't think about the glory of love. But she wouldn't have it, she said if he ever touched me, she would send me back to the 98th Street porn theater and let the Puerto Ricans make refried beans out of me, and as for Tito, he could go back to Rosa, his wife in Queens, and go back to work lugging papers for the *Daily News* and ride the subway every day and go home and listen to Rosa talk on the telephone all night, instead of hanging out on street corners and playing cards with the men outside the schoolyard. Because, she said, because she was paying the rent, and as long as rent control lasted in New York she would continue to pay the rent and she could live quite happily and satisfactorily by herself until she found the right sort of roommate; one, she said, fingering the shiny satin of Tito's shirt, who paid the rent.

So Tito kept his distance and kept us both sick with his desire and when she finally stopped sleeping with him on the bed and joined me on the mattress on the floor, even Tito could see that it wasn't going to be long before he would have to shift himself to the floor. To save himself from that he said one day that he guessed he was something of a fifth wheel around the joint, huh, and he'd found a nice Puerto Rican family that needed a man around the house and he guessed he'd move in with them. I think he was just covering for himself, though, because one day when she was out buying cigarettes, he roused himself from the couch and away from the television and said to me, You know, she was married before, you know.

— I know that, I said, I know all about that. How she pays the rent is with alimony money that still comes in from her marriage, and I know all about that and Tito wasn't telling me anything that I didn't know, so I looked back at the magazine I was reading and waited for him to go back to the television.

He kept looking at me, so I got up to look out the window to see if I could see her coming back and if she had anything for me.

— What I'm trying to say, he said, What I'm trying to tell you, is that you're not the only one, not you. I was the only one once too, the one she wanted all those years; I was the one before you and you're just the one before someone else.

I could see her rounding the corner from 83rd and Broadway and could see that she had something in a bag, doughnuts or something, for me. I said nothing but looked out the window and counted her steps toward our building. She was reeling slightly, and leaning toward the wall, so I guessed that she must have had a few drinks in the bar where she always buys her cigarettes. When I could hear her key turning in the lock to the street door, I went to open our door for her and Tito grabbed me by the arm and said, Listen, you just listen. Nobody is ever the only one for nobody, don't kid yourself.

I pulled away and opened the door for her and she came in, cold skin and wet, and I put my face in her hair and breathed in the smell of gin and cigarettes and all the meaning of my life.

The next day Tito left, but he didn't go far, because I still see him hanging out on street corners. Now all the women he has known are in his eyes, but mostly there is her, and when he looks at me, I cannot bear to see her, lost in the dark there. Whenever I pass him, I always say

— Hey, Tiiiiiiiito, Mira Mira, huh? and all his friends laugh, while Tito tries to look as though this is something he's planned himself, as though he has somehow elicited this remark from me.

One day I suppose Tito will use the key he forgot to leave behind to sneak in and cover me with his flagging desire, his fading regrets, and his disappointments, and she will move on, away from me; but rent control will not last forever in New York, and I cannot think ahead to the beginnings and the ends for which she prays.

The boys in the car lean against one another and leer and twitch like tortured insects and exchange glances that they think are far too subtle for me to understand, but I've come too far looking for too much to miss any of it. We drive too fast up Riverside, so that it's no time before the nice neighborhoods become slums full of women in windows and bright clothing slung over fire escapes, and salsa music laid over the thick city air like a layer of air all itself. Like the sound of crickets threading through the Ohio summer nights, it sets the terms for everything.

— So, one of them says to me, so where are you going, anyways.

— Well, I say, Well. I was thinking about going to the Bronx Botanical Gardens. The Bronx Botanical Gardens is no place

I'd ever really want to go, but I feel that it's important to maintain, at least in their eyes, some illusion of destination. If I were a bit more sure of myself, I'd suggest that we take the ferry over to Staten Island and do it in the park there. Then I could think of her. When we went to Staten Island, it was cold and gray and windy; we got there and realized that there was nothing we wanted to see, that being in Staten Island was really not all that different from being in New York. — Or anywhere, she said, looking down a street into a corridor of rundown clothing stores and insurance offices. It was Sunday, so everything was closed up tight and no one was on the streets. Finally we found a coffee shop near the station, where we drank Cokes and coffee and she smoked cigarettes while we waited for the boat to come in.

Lezzes, the counter man said to another man sitting at the counter eating a doughnut. What do you want to bet they're lezzes?

The man eating the doughnut turned and looked us over and said

— They're not so hot anyways, no big waste.

She smiled and held her hand to my face for a second; the smoke from the cigarette she held drifted past my eyes into my hair.

— What a moment, she said, to remember.

On the way back I watched the wind whip her face all out of any shape I knew, and when I caught the eyes of some boys on the ferry, she said, not looking at me, not taking her eyes off the concrete ripples of the robe at the feet of the Statue of Liberty just on our left, What you do is your own business, but don't expect me to love you forever if you do things like this. I'm not, she said, turning to look me full in the face, your mother, you know. All I am is your lover and nothing lasts forever.

When we got off the ferry, I said, I don't expect you to love me forever, and she said I was being promiscuous and quarrelsome, and she lit a cigarette as she walked down into the subway station. I watched her as she walked and it seemed to me to be the first time I had ever seen her back walking away from me, trailing a long blue string of smoke.

•

Something is going on with the boys, something has changed in the set of their faces, the way they hold their cigarettes, the way they nudge each other. Something changes when the light begins to fade and one of them says to me

— We have a clubhouse uptown, want to come there with us?

— What kind of club, I ask, what do you do there?

— We drink whisky, they say, and take drugs and watch television.

My boy, the one I have picked out of this whole city of boys stares out the window, chewing at a toothpick he's got wedged somewhere in the depths of his jaw, and runs his finger over the slick plastic of the steering wheel. I can tell by his refusal to ask that he wants me to come.

This, I suppose, is how to get to the center of boys, to go to their club. Boys are like pack creatures, and they always form clubs; it's as though they cannot help themselves. It's the single law of human nature that I have observed, in my limited exposure to the world, that plays and plays and replays itself out with simple mindless consistency: where there are boys there are clubs, and anywhere there is a club it is bound to be full of boys, looking for the good times to be had just by being boys.

— Can I join? I ask. This is what I can take back to her, cigarettes and a boys' club; this will keep her for me forever, that I have gone to the center of boys and have come back a woman and I have come back to her.

— Well, they say and smirk and grin and itch at themselves, Well, there's an initiation.

The oldest of the boys is younger than me, and yet like boys everywhere, they think that I don't know nearly so much as they do, as if being a woman somehow short-circuits my capacity for input. They think they have a language that only boys can understand, but understanding their language is the key to my success, so I say, I will not fuck you all, separately or together.

My boy looks over at me and permits himself a cool half smile and I am irritated that he now holds me in higher regard because I can speak a language that any idiot could learn.

Between us there are no small moments; we do not speak at all or we speak everything. Heat bills and toothpaste and dinner and all the dailiness of living are given no language in our time together.

I realize that this kind of intensity cannot be sustained over a long period of time and that every small absence in our days signals an end between us. She tells me that I must never leave her, but what I know is that someday she will leave me with a fistful of marriage money to pay the rent as long as rent control lasts in New York, and I will see her wandering down the streets, see her in the arms of another, and I say to her sometimes late at night when she blows smoke rings at my breasts, Don't leave me, don't ever ever ever leave me.

— Life, she always says to me, is one long leavetaking. Don't kid yourself, she says, Kid, and laughs. — Anyways, you are my little sweetheart, and how could I ever leave you and how could I leave this — soft touch on my skin — and this, and this.

She knows this kills me every time.

Their clubhouse is dirty and disorganized and everywhere there are mattresses and empty bottles and bags from McDonald's, and skittering through this mess are more roaches than I thought could exist in a single place, more roaches than there are boys in this city, more roaches than there are moments of love in this world.

The boys walk importantly in: This is their club, they are New York city boys and they take drugs and they have a club and I watch as they scatter around and sit in chairs and on mattresses and flip on the television. I hang back in the doorway and reach out to snag the corner of the jacket my boy is wearing. He turns and I say

— How about some air.

— Let me just get high first, he says, and he walks over to a chair and sits down and pulls out his works and cooks up his dope and ties up his arm and spends a good two minutes searching for a vein to pop.

All over his hands and arms and probably his legs and feet and stomach are signs of collapse and ruin, as if his body has been created for a single purpose and he has spent a busy and productive life systematically mining it for good places to fix.

I watch him do this while the other boys do their dope or roll their joints or pop their pills and he offers me some; I say no, I'd rather keep a clear head and how about some air.

I don't want him to hit a nod before any of it's even happened, but this is my experience with junkies, that they exit right out of every situation before it's even become a situation.

— Let's take the car, he says.

You are my sweetheart, she says, and if you leave me, you will spend all your life coming back to me. With her tongue and her words and the quiet movement of her hand over my skin, she has drawn for me all the limits of my life and of my love. It is the one love that has created me and will contain me and if I left her I'd be lonely, and I'd rather sleep in the streets with her hand between my legs forever than be lonely.

In the car, the boy slides his hand between my legs and then puts it on the steering wheel. A chill in the air, empty streets, and it's late. Every second takes me further into the night away from her; every second brings me home. We drive to Inwood Park and climb the fence, so that we are only a few feet away from the Hudson.

— This is nothing like Ohio, I say to him, and he lights a cigarette and says

— Where's Ohio.

— Don't you go to school? I ask him; Don't you have to take geography?

— I know what I need to know, he says, and reaches over to unbutton my blouse. The thing about junkies is that they know they don't have much time, and the thing about boys is that they know how not to waste it.

— This is very romantic, I say, as his fingers hit my nipples like a piece of ice; Do you come here often?

What I like about this boy is that he just puts it right in. He just puts it in as though he does this all the time, as though he doesn't usually have to slide it through his fingers or in between his friends' rough lips; he just puts it in and comes like wet soap shooting out of a fist and this is what I wanted. This is what I wanted and I look at the Hudson rolling by over his shoulder;

this is what I wanted but all I think about is the way it is with us; this is what I wanted but all I see is her face floating down the river, her eyes like pieces of moonlight caught in the water.

What I think is true doesn't matter anymore; what I think is false doesn't matter anymore. What I think at all doesn't matter anymore because there is only her; like an image laid over my mind, she is superimposed on every thought I have. She sits by the window and looks out onto West 83rd Street as if she is waiting for something, waiting for rent control to end, or waiting for something else to begin. She sits by the window waiting for something and pulls a long string through her fingers. In the light from the window, I can see each of the bones in her hand; white and exposed, they make a delicate pattern that fades into the flesh and bone of her wrist.

— Don't ever change, I say to her, Don't ever ever change.
She smiles and lets the thin string dangle from her hand.
— Nothing ever stays the same, she says. You're old enough to know that, aren't you, little sweetheart? Permanence, she says, is nothing more than a desire for things to stay the same.
I know this.

— Life is hard for me, the boy says. What am I going to do with my life? I just hang around all day or drive my mother's car. Life is so hard. Everything will always be the same for me here in this city; it's going to eat me up and spit me out and I might as well have never been. He looks poetically out over the river.
— I wanted a boy, I say, not a poet.
— I'm not a poet, he says. I'm just a junkie, and you're nothing but a slut. You can get yourself home tonight.
I say nothing and watch the Hudson roll by.
— I'm sorry, he says. So what. So I'm a junkie and you're a slut, so what. Nothing ever changes. Besides, he says, my teacher wants me to be a track star because I can run faster than anyone else in gym class. That's what he says.
— Well, that sounds like a promising career, I say, although I can imagine the gym teacher's cock pressing against his baggy sweats as he stares at my boy and suggests after-school workouts. Why don't you do that?
— I'd have to give up smoking, he says, and dope.

Together we watch the Hudson roll by and finally he says
— Well, it's about time I was getting my mother's car home.
— This is it? I ask him.
— What were you expecting? he says. I'm only a junkie. In two years I probably won't even be able to get it up anymore.

— Look, I say, coming in and walking over to where she sits by the window. Look, I am a marked woman. There is blood between my legs and it isn't yours.

She looks at me, then looks back at what she was doing before I came in, blowing smoke rings that flatten against the dirty window.

— Did you bring me some cigarettes, she says, putting hers out in the ashtray that rests on the windowsill.

— A marked woman, I say. Can't you see the blood?

— I can't see anything, she says, and I won't look until I have a cigarette. I give her the cigarettes I bought earlier. Even in the midst of becoming a woman, I have remembered the small things that please her. She lights one and inhales the smoke, then lets it slowly out through her nose and her mouth at the same time. She knows this kills me.

— Don't you see it? I ask.

— I don't see anything, she says, I don't see why you had to do this.

She gets up and says, I'm going to bed now. I've been up all day and all night and I'm tired and I want to go to sleep before the sun comes up.

— I am a marked woman, I say, lying beside her, Don't you feel it?

— I don't feel anything, she says, but she holds me, and together we wait patiently for the light. She is everything to me. In the stiff morning before the full gloom of city light falls on us, I turn to her face full of shadows.

— I am a marked woman, I say, I am.

— Quiet, she says, and puts her dark hand gently over my mouth then moves it over my throat onto the rise of my chest. Across town, no one notices this, nothing is changed anywhere when she does this.

— Quiet, she says. She presses her hand against my heart

and touches her face to mine and takes me with her into the motherless turning night. All moments stop here, this is the first and the last, and the only flesh is hers, the only touch her hand. Nothing else is, and together we turn under the stroke of the moon and the hiss of the stars and she is everything I will become and together we become every memory that has ever been known.

JOYCE CAROL OATES

Raven's Wing

(FROM ESQUIRE)

BILLY WAS AT the Meadowlands track one Saturday when the accident happened to Raven's Wing — a three-year-old silky black colt who was the favorite in the first race, and one of the crowd favorites generally this season. Billy hadn't placed his bet on Raven's Wing. Betting on the 4:5 favorite held no excitement, and in any case, things were going too well for Raven's Wing, Billy felt, and his owner's luck would be running out soon. But telling his wife about the accident the next morning Billy was surprised at how important it came to seem, how intense his voice sounded, as if he was high, or on edge, which he was not, it was just the *telling* that worked him up, and the way Linda looked at him.

"— So there he was in the backstretch, looping around one, two, three, four horses to take the lead — he's a hard driver, Raven's Wing, doesn't let himself off easy — a little skittish at the starting gate, but then he got serious — in fact he was maybe running a little faster than he needed to run, once he got out front — then something happened, it looked like he stumbled, his hindquarters went down just a little — but he was going so fast, maybe forty miles an hour, the momentum kept him going — Jesus, it must have been three hundred feet! — the poor bastard, on three legs. Then the jockey jumped off, the other horses ran by, Raven's Wing was just sort of standing there by the rail, his head bobbing up and down. What had happened was he'd broken his left rear leg — came down too hard on it, maybe, or the hoof sunk in the dirt wrong. Just like that," Billy said. He snapped his fingers. "One minute we're looking at a million-dollar colt, the next minute — nothing."

"Wait. What do you mean, nothing?" Linda said.

"They put them down if they aren't going to race anymore."

" 'Put them down' — you mean they kill them?"

"Sure. Most of the time."

"How do they kill them? Do they shoot them?"

"I doubt it, probably some kind of needle, you know, injection, poison in their bloodstream."

Linda was leaning toward him, her forehead creased. "Okay, then what happened?" she said.

"Well — an ambulance came out to the track and picked him up, there was an announcement about him breaking his leg, everybody in the stands was real quiet when they heard. Not because there was a lot of money on him either but because, you know, here's this first-class colt, a real beauty, a million-dollar horse, maybe two million, finished. Just like that."

Linda's eyelids were twitching, her mouth, she might have been going to cry, or maybe, suddenly, laugh, you couldn't predict these days. Near as Billy figured she hadn't washed her hair in more than a week and it looked like hell, she hadn't washed herself in all that time either, wore the same plaid shirt and jeans day after day, not that he'd lower himself to bring the subject up. She was staring at him, squinting. Finally she said, "How much did you lose? — you can tell me," in a breathy little voice.

"How much did *I* lose?" Billy asked. He was surprised as hell. They'd covered all this ground, hadn't they, there were certain private matters in his life, things that were none of her business, he'd explained it — her brother had explained it too — things she didn't need to know. And good reasons for her not to know. "How much did *I* lose — ?"

He pushed her aside, lightly, just with the tips of his fingers, and went to the refrigerator to get a beer. It was only ten in the morning but he was thirsty and his head and back teeth ached. "Who says I lost? We were out there for five races. In fact I did pretty well, we all did, what the hell do you know about it," Billy said. He opened the beer, took his time drinking. He knew that the longer he took, the calmer he'd get and it was one of those

mornings — Sunday, bells ringing, everybody's schedule off —
when he didn't want to get angry. But his hand was trembling
when he drew a wad of bills out of his inside coat pocket and let
it fall onto the kitchen counter. "Three hundred dollars, go
ahead and count it, sweetheart," he said, "you think you're so
smart."

Linda stood with her knees slightly apart, her big belly straining at the flannel shirt she wore, her mouth still twitching. Even
with her skin grainy and sallow, and pimples across her forehead, she looked good, she was a good-looking girl, hell,
thought Billy, it was a shame, a bad deal. She said, so soft he
almost couldn't hear her, "I don't think I'm so smart."

"Yeah? What?"

"I don't think I'm anything."

She was looking at the money but for some reason, maybe she
was afraid, she didn't touch it. Actually Billy had won almost a
thousand dollars but that was his business.

Linda was eight years younger than Billy, just twenty-four
though she looked younger, blond, high-strung, skinny except
for her belly (she was five, six months pregnant, Billy couldn't
remember), with hollowed-out eyes, that sullen mouth. They
had been married almost a year and Billy thought privately it
was probably a mistake though in fact he loved her, he *liked* her,
if only she didn't do so many things to spite him. If she wasn't
letting herself go, letting herself get sick, strung-out, weird, just
to spite him.

He'd met her through her older brother, a friend of Billy's,
more or less, from high school, a guy he'd done business with
and could trust. But they had had a misunderstanding the year
before and no longer worked together.

Once, in bed, Linda said, "— If the man had to have it, boy,
then things would be different. Things would be a lot different."

"What? A baby? How do you mean?" Billy asked. He'd been
halfway asleep, he wanted to humor her, he didn't want a fight
at two in the morning. "Are we talking about a baby?"

"They *wouldn't* have it, that's all."

"What?"

"The baby. Any baby."

"Jesus — that's crazy."

"Yeah? Who? Would you?" Linda said angrily. "What about your own?"

Billy had two children, both boys, from his first marriage, but as things worked out he never saw them and rarely thought about them — his wife had remarried, moved to Tampa. At one time Billy used to say that he and his ex-wife got along all right, they weren't out to slit each other's throat like some people he knew, but in fact when Billy's salary at GM Radiator had been garnisheed a few years ago he wasn't very happy; he'd gone through a bad time. So he'd quit the job, a good-paying job too, and later, when he tried to get hired back, they were already laying off men, it was rotten luck, his luck had run against him for a long time. One of the things that had driven him wild was the fact that his wife, that is his ex-wife, was said to be pregnant again, and he'd maybe be helping to support another man's kid, when he thought of it he wanted to kill somebody, anybody, but then she got married after all and it worked out and now he didn't have to see her or even think of her very much: that was the advantage of distance. But now he said, "Sure," trying to keep it all light. "What the hell, sure, it beats the Army."

"*You'd* have a baby?" Linda said. Now she was sitting up, leaning over him, her hair in her face, her eyes showing a rim of white above the iris. "Oh don't hand me that. Oh please."

"Sure. If you wanted me to."

"I'm asking about *you* — would *you* want to?"

They had been out drinking much of the evening and Linda was groggy but skittish, on edge, her face very pale and giving off a queer damp heat. The way she was grinning, Billy didn't want to pursue the subject.

"How about *you*, I said," she said, jabbing him with her elbow, "— I'm talking about *you*."

"I don't know what the hell we are talking about."

"You do know."

"What — I don't."

"You do. You do. Don't hand me such crap."

When he and Linda first started going together they'd made love all the time, like crazy, it was such a relief (so Billy told himself) to be out from under that other bitch, but now, married only a year, with Linda dragging around the apartment sick and angry and sometimes talking to herself, pretending she didn't know Billy could hear, now everything had changed, he couldn't predict whether she'd be up or down, high or low, very low, hitting bottom, scaring him with her talk about killing herself (her crazy mother had tried *that* a few times, it probably ran in the family) or getting an abortion (but wasn't it too late, her stomach that size, for an abortion), he never knew when he opened the door what he'd be walking into. She didn't change her clothes, including her underwear, for a week at a time, she didn't wash her hair, she'd had a tight permanent that sprang out around her head but turned flat, matted, blowsy if it wasn't shampooed, he knew she was ruining her looks to spite him but she claimed (shouting, crying, punching her own thighs with her fists) that she just *forgot* about things like that, she had more important things to think about.

One day, a few months before, Billy had caught sight of this great-looking girl out on the street, coat with a fox-fur collar like the one he'd bought for Linda, high-heeled boots like Linda's, blond hair, wild springy curls like a model, frizzed, airy, her head high and her walk fast, almost like strutting — she knew she was being watched, and not just by Billy — and then she turned and it *was* Linda, his own wife, she'd washed her hair and fixed herself up, red lipstick, even eye makeup — he'd just stood there staring, it took him by such surprise. But then the next week she was back to lying around the apartment feeling sorry for herself, sullen and heavy-hearted, sick to her stomach even if she hadn't eaten anything.

The worst of the deal was, he and her brother had had their misunderstanding and didn't do business any longer. When Billy got drunk he had the vague idea that he was getting stuck again with another guy's baby.

The racing news was, Raven's Wing hadn't been killed after all.

It *was* news, people were talking about it, Billy even read about it in the newspaper, an operation on the colt's leg estimated to cost in the six-figure range, a famous veterinary surgeon the owner was flying in from Dallas, and there was a photograph (it somehow frightened Billy, that photograph) of Raven's Wing lying on his side, anesthetized, strapped down, being operated on like a human being. The *size* of a horse — that always impressed Billy.

Other owners had their opinions, was it worth it or not, other trainers, veterinarians, but Raven's Wing's owner wanted to save his life, the colt wasn't just any horse (the owner said) he was the most beautiful horse they'd ever reared on their farm. He was insured for $600,000 and the insurance company had granted permission for the horse to be destroyed but still the owner wanted to save his life. "They wouldn't do that for a human being," Linda said when Billy told her.

"Well," Billy said, irritated at her response, "— this isn't a human being, it's a first-class horse."

"Jesus, a *horse* operated on," Linda said, laughing, "and he isn't even going to run again, you said? How much is all this going to cost?"

"People like that, they don't care about money. They have it, they spend it on what matters," Billy said. "It's a frame of reference you don't know shit about."

"Then what?"

"What?"

"After the operation?"

"After the operation, if it works, then he's turned out to stud," Billy said. "You know what that is, huh?" he said, poking her in the breast.

"Just a minute. The horse is worth that much?"

"A first-class horse is worth a million dollars, I told you, maybe more. Two million. These people take things *seriously*."

"Two million dollars for an animal — ?" Linda said slowly. She sounded dazed, disoriented, as if the fact was only now sinking in, but what *was* the fact, what did it mean? "Hey I think that's *sick*."

"I told you, Linda, it's a frame of reference you don't know shit about."

"That's right. I don't."

She was making such a childish ugly face at him, drawing her lips back from her teeth, Billy lost control and shoved her against the edge of the kitchen table, and she slapped him hard, on the side of the nose, and it was all Billy could do to stop right there, just *stop*, not give it back to the bitch like she deserved. He knew, once he got started with this one, it might be the end. She might not be able to pick herself up from the floor when he was done.

Billy asked around, and there was this contact of his named Kellerman, and Kellerman was an old friend of Raven's Wing's trainer, and he fixed it up so that he and Billy could drive out to the owner's farm in Pennsylvania, so that Billy could see the horse, Billy just wanted to *see* the horse, it was always at the back of his mind these days.

The weather was cold, the sky a hard icy blue, the kind of day that made Billy feel shaky, things were so bright, so vivid, you could see something weird and beautiful anywhere you looked. His head ached, he was so edgy, his damn back teeth, he chewed on Bufferin, he and Kellerman drank beer out of cans, tossed the cans away on the road. Kellerman said horse people like these were the real thing, look at this layout, and not even counting Raven's Wing they had a stable worth millions, a Preakness winner, a second-place Kentucky Derby finisher, but was the money even in horses? — hell no it was in some investments or something. That was how rich people worked.

In the stable, at Raven's Wing's stall, Billy hung over the partition and looked at him for a long time, just looked. Kellerman and the trainer were talking but Billy just looked.

The size of the horse, that was one of the things, and the head, the big rounded eyes, ears pricked forward, tail switching, here was Raven's Wing looking at last at him, did he maybe recognize Billy, did he maybe sense who Billy was? Billy extended a hand to him, whispering his name. Hey Raven's Wing. Hey.

The size, and the silky sheen of the coat, the jet-black coat, that skittish air, head bobbing, teeth bared, Billy could feel his warm breath, Billy sucked in the strong *smell* — horse manure, horse piss, sweat, hay, mash, and what was he drinking? — apple juice, the trainer said. *Apple juice*, Christ! Gallons and gallons of it. Did he have his appetite back, Billy asked, but it was obvious the colt did, he was eating steadily, chomping hay,

eyeing Billy as if Billy was — was what? — just the man he
wanted to see. The man who'd driven a hundred miles to see
him.

Both his rear legs were in casts, the veterinarian had taken a
bone graft from the good leg, and his weight was down — 1,130
pounds to 880 — his ribs showing through the silky coat but
Jesus did he look good, Jesus this was the real thing wasn't it?
— Billy's heart beat fast as if he'd been popping pills, he wished
to hell Linda was here, yeah the bitch should see *this*, it'd shut
her up for a while.

Raven's Wing was getting his temper back, the trainer said,
which was a good thing, it showed he was mending, but he still
wasn't 99 percent in the clear, maybe they didn't know how easy
it was for horses to get sick — colic, pneumonia, all kinds of
viruses, infections. Even the good leg had gone bad for a while,
paralyzed, and they'd had to have two operations, a six-hour
and a four-hour, the owner had to sign a release, they'd put
him down right on the operating table if things looked too bad.
But he pulled through, his muscle tone was improving every
day, there he was, fiery little bastard, watch out or he'll nip you
— a steel plate, steel wire, a dozen screws in his leg, and him not
knowing a thing. The way the bone was broken it wasn't *broken*,
the trainer told them, it was smashed, like somebody had gone
after it with a sledgehammer.

"So he's going to make it," Billy said, not quite listening. "Hey
yeah. *You*. You're going to make it, huh."

He and Kellerman were at the stall maybe forty-five minutes
and the place was busy, busier than Billy would have thought, it
rubbed him the wrong way that so many people were around
when he'd had the idea he and Kellerman would be the only
ones. But it turned out that Raven's Wing always had visitors.
He even got mail. (This Billy snorted to hear — a horse gets
mail?) People took away souvenirs if they could, good-luck
things, hairs from his mane, his tail, that sort of thing, or else
they wanted to feed him by hand: there was a lot of that, they
had to be watched.

Before they left Billy leaned over as far as he could, just
wanting to stroke Raven's Wing's side, and two things happened
fast: the horse snorted, stamped, lunged at his hand; and the
trainer pulled Billy back.

"Hey I told you," he said. "This is a dangerous animal."

"He likes me," Billy said. "He wasn't going to bite hard."

"Yeah? — sometimes he does. They can bite damn hard."

"He wasn't going to bite actually *hard*," Billy said.

Three dozen blue snakeskin wallets (Venezuelan), almost two dozen up-scale watches (Swiss, German) — chronographs, water-resistant, self-winding, calendar, ultrathin, quartz, and gold tone — and a pair of pierced earrings, gold and pearl, delicate, Billy thought, as a snowflake. He gave the earrings to Linda to surprise her and watched her put them in, it amazed him how quickly she could take out earrings and slip in new ones, position the tiny wires exactly in place, he knew it was a trick he could never do if he was a woman. It made him shiver, it excited him, just to watch.

Linda never said, "Hey where'd you get *these*," the way his first wife used to, giving him that slow wide wet smile she thought turned him on. (Actually it had turned him on, for a while. Two, three years.)

Linda never said much of anything except thank you in her little-girl breathy voice, if she happened to be in the mood for thanking.

One morning a few weeks later Linda, in her bathrobe, came slowly out of the bedroom into the kitchen, squinting at something she held in the air, at eye level. "This looks like somebody's hair, what is it, Indian hair? — it's all black and stiff," she said. Billy was on the telephone so he had an excuse not to give her his fullest attention at the moment. He might be getting ready to be angry, he might be embarrassed, his nerves were always bad this time of day. Linda leaned up against him, swaying a little in her preoccupation, exuding heat, her bare feet planted apart on the linoleum floor. She liked to poke at him with her belly, she had a new habit of standing close.

Billy kept on with his conversation, it was in fact an important conversation, and Linda wound the several black hairs around her forearm, making a little bracelet, so tight the flesh started to turn white, didn't it hurt? — her forehead creased in concentration, her breath warm and damp against his neck.

NORMAN RUSH

Instruments of Seduction

(FROM THE PARIS REVIEW)

THE NAME SHE was unable to remember was torturing her. She kept coming up with Bechamel, which was ridiculously wrong yet somehow close. It was important to her that she remember. A thing in a book by this man lay at the heart of her secret career as a seducer of men — three hundred and twelve of them. She was a seducer, not a seductress. The male form of the term was active. A seductress was merely someone who was seductive and who might or might not be awarded a victory. But a seducer was a professional, a worker, and somehow a record of success was embedded in the term. "Seducer" sounded like a credential. Game was afoot tonight. Remembering the name was part of preparation. She had always prepared before tests.

Male or female, you couldn't be considered a seducer if you were below a certain age, had great natural beauty, or if you lacked a theory of what you were doing. Her body of theory began with a scene in the book she was feeling the impulse to reread. The book's title was lost in the mists of time. As she remembered the scene, a doctor and perhaps the woman of the house are involved together in some emergency lifesaving operation. The woman has to assist. The setting is an apartment in Europe, in a city. The woman is not attractive. The doctor is. There has been shelling or an accident. The characters are disparate in every way and would never normally be appropriate for one another. The operation is described in upsetting detail. It's touch and go. When it's over, the doctor and the woman fall into one another's arms — to their own surprise. Some fierce tropism compels them. Afterward they part, never to follow up. The book was from the French. She removed the Atmos clock from the living room mantel and took it to the pantry to get it out of sight.

The scene had been like a flashbulb going off. She had realized that, in all her seductions up to that point, she had been crudely and intuitively using the principle that the scene made explicit. Putting it bluntly, a certain atmosphere of allusion to death, death fear, death threats, mystery pointing to death, was, in the right hands, erotic, and could lead to a bingo. Of course, that was hardly all there was to it. The subject of what conditions conduce — that was her word for it — to achieving a bingo, was immense. One thing, it was never safe to roll your *r*'s. She thought, Everything counts: chiaroscuro, no giant clocks in evidence and no wristwatches either, music or its absence, what they can assume about privacy and *le futur*. That was critical. You had to help them intuit you were acting from appetite, like a man, and that when it was over you would be yourself and not transformed before their eyes into a love-leech, a limbless tube of longing. You had to convince them that what was to come was, no question about it, a transgression, but that for you it was about at the level of eating between meals.

She was almost fifty. For a woman, she was old to be a seducer. The truth was that she had been on the verge of closing up shop. The corner of Bergen County they lived in was scorched earth, pretty much. Then Frank had been offered a contract to advise African governments on dental care systems. They had come to Africa for two years.

In Botswana, where they were based, everything was unbelievably conducive. Frank was off in the bush or advising as far away as Lusaka or Gwelo for days and sometimes weeks at a time. So there was space. She could select. Gaborone was comfortable enough. And it was full of transient men: consultants, contractors, travelers of all kinds, seekers. Embassy men were assigned for two-year tours and knew they were going to be rotated away from the scene of the crime sooner rather than later. Wives were often absent. Either they were slow to arrive or they were incessantly away on rest and recreation in the United States or the Republic of South Africa. For expatriate men, the local women were a question mark. Venereal disease was pandemic and local attitudes toward birth control came close to being surreal. She had abstained from Batswana men. She knew why. The very attractive ones seemed hard to get at. There was a feeling of danger in the proposition, probably irrational. The surplus of more familiar white types was a simple fact. In any case, there was still time. This place had been designed with her in mind. The furniture the government provided even looked like it came from a bordello. And Botswana was unnerving in some overall way there was only one word for: conducive. The country depended on copper and diamonds. Copper prices were sinking. There were too many diamonds of the wrong kind. Development projects were going badly and making people look bad, which made them nervous and susceptible. What was there to do at night? There was only one movie house in town. The movies came via South Africa and were censored to a fare-thee-well — no nudity, no blue language. She suspected that for American men the kind of heavyhanded dummkopf censorship they sat through at the Capitol Cinema was in fact stimulating. Frank was getting United States Government money, which made them semi-official. She had to admit there was fun in foiling the eyes and ears of the embassy network. She would hate to leave.

Only one thing was sad. There was no one she could tell about her life. She had managed to have a remarkable life. She was ethical. She never brought Frank up or implied that Frank was the cause in any way of what she chose to do. Nor would she ever seduce a man who could conceivably be a recurrent part of Frank's life or sphere. She assumed feminists would hate her life if they knew. She would like to talk to feminists about vocation, about goal-setting, about using one's mind, about nerve and strength. Frank's ignorance was one of her feats. How many women could do what she had done? She was modestly endowed and now she was even old. She was selective. Sometimes she felt she would like to tell Frank, when it was really over, and see what he said. She would sometimes let herself think he would be proud, in a way, or that he could be convinced he should be. There was no one she could tell. Their daughter was a cow and a Lutheran. Her gentleman was late. She went into the pantry to check the time.

For this evening's adventure she was perhaps a little too high-priestess, but the man she was expecting was not a subtle person. She was wearing a narrowly-cut white silk caftan, a seed-pod necklace, and sandals. The symbolism was a little crude: silk, the ultra-civilized material, over the primitive straight-off-the-bush necklace. Men liked to feel things through silk. But she wore silk as much for herself as for the gentlemen. Silk energized her. She loved the feeling of silk being slid up the backs of her legs. Her nape hairs rose a little as she thought about it. She had her hair up, in a loose, flat bun. She was ringless. She had put on and then taken off her scarab ring. Tonight she wanted the feeling that bare hands and bare feet would give. She would ease off her sandals at the right moment. She knew she was giving up a proven piece of business — idly taking off her ring when the occasion reached a certain centigrade. Men saw it subliminally as taking off a wedding ring and as the first act of undressing. She had worked hard on her feet. She had lined her armpits with tissue which would stay just until the doorbell rang. With medical gentlemen, hygiene was a fetish. She was expecting a doctor. Her breath was immaculate. She was proud of her teeth, but then she was married to a dentist. She thought about the Danish surgeon who brought his own boiled-water ice cubes to cocktail parties. She had some bottled water in the refrigerator, just in case it was indicated.

Her gentleman was due and overdue. Everything was optimal. There was a firm crossbreeze. The sightlines were nice. From where they would be sitting they would look out at a little pad of healthy lawn, the blank wall of the inner court, and the foliage of the tree whose blooms still looked to her like scrambled eggs. It would be self-evident that they would be private here. The blinds were drawn. Everything was secure and cool. Off the hall leading to the bathroom, the door to the bedroom stood open. The bedroom was clearly a working bedroom, not taboo, with a night light on and an oscillating fan performing on low. He would sit on leather; she would sit half-facing, where she could reach the bar trolley, on sheepskin, her feet on a jennet-skin karosse. He should sit in the leather chair because it was regal but uncomfortable. You would want to lie down. She would be in a slightly more reclining mode. Sunset was on. Where was her gentleman? The light was past its peak.

The doorbell rang. Be superb, she thought.

The doctor looked exhausted. He was greyfaced. Also, he was older than the image of him she had been entertaining. But he was all right. He had nice hair. He was fit. He might be part Indian, with those cheekbones and being from Vancouver. Flats were never a mistake. He was not tall. He was slim.

She led him in. He was wearing one of the cheaper safari suits, with the S-for-something embroidery on the left breast pocket. He had come straight from work, which was in her favor.

When she had him seated, she said, "Two slight catastrophes to report, doctor. One is that you're going to have to eat appetizers from my own hand. As the British say, my help are gone. My cook and my maid are sisters. Their aunt died. For the second time, actually. Tebogo is forgetful. In any case, they're in Mochudi for a few days and I'm alone. Frank won't be home until Sunday. *And,* the Webers are off for tonight. They can't come. We're on our own. I hope we can cope."

He smiled weakly. The man was exhausted.

She said, "But a cool drink, quick, wouldn't you say? What would you like? I have everything."

He said it should be anything nonalcoholic, any kind of juice would be good. She could see work coming. He went to wash up.

He took his time in the bathroom, which was normally a good sign. He looked almost crisp when he came back, but something was the matter. She would have to extract it.

He accepted iced rooibos tea. She poured Bombay gin over crushed ice for herself. Men noticed what you drank. This man was not strong. She was going to have to underplay.

She presented the appetizers, which were genius. You could get through a week on her collations if you needed to, or you could have a few select tastes and go on to gorge elsewhere with no one the wiser. But you would remember every bite. She said "You might like these. These chunks are bream fillet, poached, from Lake Ngami. No bones. Vinaigrette. They had just started getting these down here on a regular basis on ice about a year ago. AID had a lot of money in the Lake Ngami fishery project. Then the drought struck, and Lake Ngami, poof, it's a damp spot in the desert. This is real Parma ham. I nearly had to kill someone to get it. The cashews are a little on the tangy side. That's the way they like them in Mozambique, apparently. They're good."

He ate a little, sticking to mainstream items like the gouda cheese cubes, she was sorry to see. Then he brought up the climate, which made her writhe. It was something to be curtailed. It led the mind homeward. It was one of the three deadly W's: weather, wife, and where to eat — in this country, where not to eat. She feigned sympathy. He was saying he was from British Columbia so it was to be expected that it would take some doing for him to adjust to the dry heat and the dust. He said he had to remind himself that he'd only been here four months and that ultimately his mucous membrane system was supposed to adapt. But he said he was finding it wearing. Lately he was dreaming about rain. A lot, he said.

Good! she thought. "Would you like to see my tokoloshi?" she asked, crossing her legs.

He stopped chewing. She warned herself not to be reckless.

"Dream animals!" she said. "Little effigies. I collect them. The Bushmen carve them out of softwood. They use them as symbols of evil in some ceremony they do. They're turning up along with all the other Bushman artifacts, the puberty aprons and so on, in the craft shops. Let me show you."

She got two tokoloshi from a cabinet.

"They call these the evil creatures who come to you at night in dreams. What you see when you look casually is this manlike figure with what looks like the head of a fox or rabbit or zebra, at first glance. But look at the clothing. Doesn't this look like a clerical jacket? The collar shape? They're all like that. And look closely at the animal. It's actually a spotted jackal, the most despised animal there is because of its taste for carrion. Now look in front at this funny little tablet that looks like a huge belt buckle with these x-shapes burned into it. My theory is that it's a Bushman version of the Union Jack. If you notice on this one, the being is wearing a funny belt. It looks like a cartridge belt to me. Some of the tokoloshi are smoking these removable pipes. White tourists buy these things and think they're cute. I think each one is a carved insult to the West. And we buy loads of

them. I do. The black areas like the jacket are done by charring
the wood with hot nails and things."

He handled the carvings dutifully and then gave them back
to her. He murmured that they were interesting.

He took more tea. She stood the tokoloshi on an end table
halfway across the room, facing them. He began contemplating
them, sipping his tea minutely. Time was passing. She had various mottoes she used on herself. One was: Inside every suit and
tie is a naked man trying to get out. She knew they were stupid,
but they helped. He was still in the grip of whatever was bothering him.

"I have something that might interest you," she said. She went
to the cabinet again and returned with a jackal-fur wallet, which
she set down on the coffee table in front of him. "This is a
fortune-telling kit the witch doctors use. It has odd things inside
it." He merely looked at it.

"Look inside it," she said.

He picked it up reluctantly and held it in his hand, making a
face. He was thinking it was unsanitary. She was in danger of
becoming impatient. The wallet actually was slightly fetid, but
so what? It was an organic thing. It was old.

She reached over and guided him to open and empty the
wallet, touching his hands. He studied the array of bones and
pebbles on the tabletop. Some of the pebbles were painted or
stained. The bones were knucklebones, probably opossum, she
told him, after he showed no interest in trying to guess what
they were. She had made it her business to learn a fair amount
about Tswana divination practices, but he wasn't asking. He
moved the objects around listlessly.

She lit a candle, though she felt it was technically premature.
It would give him something else to stare at if he wanted to and
at least he would be staring in her direction, more or less.

The next segment was going to be taxing. The pace needed
to be meditative. She was fighting impatience.

She said, "Africa is so strange. You haven't been here long,
but you'll see. We come here as . . . bearers of science, the scientific attitude. Even the dependents do, always telling the help
about nutrition and weaning and that kind of thing.

"Science so much defines us. One wants to be scientific, or at least not *un*scientific. Science is our religion, in a way. Or at least you begin to feel it is. I've been here nineteen months . . ."

He said something. Was she losing her hearing or was the man just unable to project? He had said something about noticing that the tokoloshi weren't carrying hypodermic needles. He was making the point, she guessed, that the Batswana didn't reject Western medicine. He said something further about their attachment to injections, how they felt you weren't actually treating them unless they could have an injection, how they seemed to love injections. She would have to adapt to a certain lag in this man's responses. I am tiring, she thought.

She tried again, edging her chair closer to his. "Of course, your world is different. You're more insulated, at the Ministry, where everyone is a scientist of sorts. You're immersed in science. That world is . . . safer. Are you following me?"

He said he wasn't sure that he was.

"What I guess I mean is that one gets to want to really *uphold* science. Because the culture here is so much the opposite. So relentlessly so. You resist. But then the first thing you know, very peculiar things start happening to you. Or you talk to some of the old settler types, whites, educated people from the protectorate days who decided to stay on as citizens, before the government made that such an obstacle course. The white settlers are worse than your everyday Batswana. They accept everything supernatural, almost. At first you dismiss it as a pose."

She knew it was strictly pro forma, but she offered him cigarettes from the caddy. He declined. There was no way she could smoke, then. Nothing tonight was going to be easy. Bechamel was right next door to the name she was trying to remember: why couldn't she get it?

"But it isn't a pose," she said. "Their experiences have changed them utterly. There is so much witchcraft. It's called *muti*. It's so routine. It wasn't so long ago that if you were going to open a business you'd go to the witch doctor for good luck rites with human body parts as ingredients. A little something to tuck under the cornerstone of your bottle store. People are still being killed for their parts. It might be a windpipe or whatever. It's still going on. Sometimes they dump the body onto the

railroad tracks after they've taken what they need, for the train
to grind up and disguise. Recently they caught somebody that
way. The killers threw this body on the track but the train was
late. They try to keep it out of the paper, I know that for a fact.
But it's still happening. An undertow."

She worked her feet out of her sandals. Normally she would
do one and let an intriguing gap fall before doing the other.
She scratched an instep on an ankle.

She said, "I know a girl who's teaching in the government
secondary in Bobonong who tells me what a hard time the ma-
tron is having getting the girls to sleep with their heads out of
the covers. It seems they're afraid of *bad women* who roam
around at night, who'll scratch their faces. These are women
called *baloi* who go around naked, wearing only a little belt made
out of human neckbones. Naturally, anyone would say what a
fantasy this is. Childish.

"But I really did once see a naked woman dodging around
near some rondavels late one night, out near Mosimane. It was
only a glimpse. No doubt it was innocent. But she did have
something white and shimmering around her waist. We were
driving past. You begin to wonder."

She waited. He was silent.

"Something's bothering you," she said.

He denied it.

She said, "At any rate, don't you think it's interesting that
there are no women members of the so-called traditional doctors' association? I know a member, what an oaf! I think it's a
smoke screen association. They want you to think they're just a
benign bunch of herbalists trying out one thing or another a lot
of which ought to be in the regular pharmacopeia if only white
medical people weren't so narrow-minded. They come to semi-
nars all jolly and humble. But if you talk to the Batswana, you
know that it's the women, the witches, who are the really potent
ones."

Still he was silent.

"Something's happened, hasn't it? To upset you. If it's anything I've said, please tell me." A maternal tone could be death.
She was flirting with failure.

He denied that she was responsible in any way. It seemed
sincere. He was going inward again, right before her eyes. She

had a code name for failures. She called them case studies. Her attitude was that every failure could be made to yield something of value for the future. And it was true. Some of her best material, anecdotes, references to things, aphrodisiana of all kinds, had come from case studies. The cave paintings at Gargas, in Spain, of mutilated hands . . . handprints, not paintings . . . stencils of hundreds of hands with joints and fingers missing. Archaeologists were totally at odds as to what all that meant. One case study had yielded the story of fat women in Durban buying tainted meat from butchers so as to contract tapeworms for weight loss purposes. As a case study, if it came to that, tonight looked unpromising. But you could never tell. She had an image for case studies: a grave robber, weary, exhausted, reaching down into some charnel mass and pulling up some lovely ancient sword somehow miraculously still keen that had been overlooked. She could name case studies that were more precious to her than bingoes she could describe.

She had one quiver left. She meant arrow. She hated using it.

She could oppose her silence to his until he broke. It was difficult to get right. It ran counter to being a host, being a woman, and to her own nature. The silence had to be special, not wounded, receptive, with a spine to it, maternal, in fact.

She declared silence. Slow moments passed.

He stirred. His lips stirred. He got up and began pacing.

He said, "You're right." Then for a long time he said nothing, still pacing.

"You read my mind!" he said. "Last night I had an experience . . . I still . . . it's still upsetting. I shouldn't have come, I guess."

She felt sorry for him. He had just the slightest speech defect, which showed up in noticeable hesitations. This was sad.

"Please tell me about it," she said perfectly.

He paced more, then halted near the candle and stared at it.

"I hardly drink," he said. "Last night was an exception. Phoning home to Vancouver started it, domestic nonsense. I won't go into that. They don't understand. No point in going into it. I went out. I went drinking. One of the hotel bars, where Africans go. I began drinking. I was drinking and buying drinks for some of the locals. I drank quite a bit.

"All right. These fellows are clever. Bit by bit I am being taken

over by one, this one fellow, George. I can't explain it. I didn't
like him. He took me over. That is, I notice I'm paying for
drinks but this fellow's passing them on to whomever he
chooses, his friends. But I'm buying. But I have no say.

"We're in a corner booth. It's dark and loud, as usual. This
fellow, his head was shaved, he was strong-looking. He spoke
good English, though. Originally, I'd liked talking to him, I
think. They flatter you. He was a combination of rough and
smooth. Now he was working me. He was a refugee from South
Africa, that always starts up your sympathy. Terrible breath,
though. I was getting a feeling of something being off about the
ratio between the number of drinks and what I was laying out.
I think he was taking something in transit.

"I wanted to do the buying. I took exception. All right. Remember that they have me wedged in. That was stupid, but I
was, I allowed it. Then I said I was going to stop buying. George
didn't like it. This man had a following. I realized they were
forming a cordon, blocking us in. Gradually it got nasty. Why
wouldn't I keep buying drinks, didn't I have money, what was
my job, didn't the Ministry pay expatriates enough to buy a few
drinks? So on ad nauseam."

His color was coming back. He picked up a cocktail napkin
and touched at his forehead.

He was looking straight at her now. He said, "You don't know
what the African bars are like. Pandemonium. I was sealed off.
As I say, his friends were all around.

"Then it was all about apartheid. I said I was Canadian. Then
it was about Canada the lackey of America the supporter of
apartheid. I'm not political. I was scared. All right. When I tell
him I'm really through buying drinks he asks me how much
money have I got left, exactly. I tell him again that I'm through
buying drinks. He says not to worry, he'll sell me something
instead. All right. I knew I was down to about ten pula. And I
had dug in on buying drinks, the way you will when you've had
a few too many. No more buying drinks, that was decided. But
he was determined to get my money, I could damned well see
that.

"He said he would sell me something I'd be very glad to know.
Information. All right. So then comes a long runaround on

what kind of information. Remember that he's pretty well three sheets to the wind himself. It was information I would be glad to have as a doctor, he said.

"Well, the upshot here was that this is what I proposed, so as not to seem totally stupid and taken. I would put all my money down on the table in front of me. I took out my wallet and made sure he could see that what I put down was all of it, about ten pula, change and everything. All right. And I would keep the money under the palm of my hand. And he would whisper the information to me and if I thought it was a fair trade I would just lift my hand. Of course, this was all just facesaving on my part so as not to just hand over my money to a thug. And don't think I wasn't well aware it might be a good idea at this stage of things to be seen getting rid of any cash I had, just to avoid being knocked down on the way to my car."

"This is a wonderful story," she said spontaneously, immediately regretting it.

"It isn't a story," he said.

"You know what I mean," she said. "I mean, since I see you standing here safe and sound I can assume the ending isn't a tragedy. But please continue. Really."

"In any event. There we are. There was more back and forth over what kind of information this was. Finally he says it's not only something a doctor would be glad of. He is going to tell me the secret of how they are going to make the revolution in South Africa, a secret plan. An actual plan.

"God knows I have no brief for white South Africans. I know a few professionally, doctors. Medicine down there is basically about up to nineteen fifty, by our standards, despite all this veneer of the heart transplants. But the doctors I know seem to be decent. Some of them hate the system and will say so.

"I go along. Empty my wallet, cover the money with my hand.

"Here's what he says. They had a sure way to drive out the whites. It was a new plan and was sure to succeed. It would succeed because they, meaning the blacks, could bring it about with only a handful of men. He said that the Boers had won for all time if the revolution meant waiting for small groups to grow into bands and then into units, batallions and so on, into armies that would fight the Boers. The Boers were too intelligent and had too much power. They had corrupted too many of the blacks. The blacks were divided. There were too many spies for the Boers among them. The plan he would tell me would take less than a hundred men.

"Then he asked me, if he could tell me such a plan would it be worth the ten pula. Would I agree that it would? I said yes."

"This is extraordinary!" she said. *Duhamel!* she thought, triumphant. The name had come back to her: *Georges Duhamel.* She could almost see the print. She was so grateful.

"Exciting!" she said, gratitude in her voice.

He was sweating. "Well, this is what he says. He leans over, whispers. The plan is simple. The plan is to assemble a shock force, he called it. Black people who are willing to give their lives. And this is all they do: *they kill doctors.* That's it! They start off with a large first wave, before the government can do anything to protect doctors. They simply kill doctors, as many as they can. They kill them at home, in their offices, in hospitals, in the street. You can get the name of every doctor in South Africa through the phone book. Whites need doctors, without doctors they think they are already dying, he says. Blacks in South Africa have no doctors to speak of anyway, especially in the homelands where they are all being herded to die in droves. Blacks are dying of the system every day regardless, he says. But whites would scream. They would rush like cattle to the airports, screaming. They would stream out of the country. The planes from Smuts would be jammed full. After the first strike, you would continue, taking them by ones and twos. The doctors would leave, the ones who were there and still alive. No new ones would come, not even Indians. He said it was like taking away water from people in a desert. The government would capitulate. That was the plan.

"I lifted my hand and let him take the money. He said I was paying the soldiery and he thanked me in the name of the revolution. Then I was free to go."

He looked around dazedly for something, she wasn't clear what. Her glass was still one-third full. Remarkably, he picked it up and drained it, eating the remnants of ice.

She stood up. She was content. The story was a brilliant thing, a gem.

He was moving about. It was hard to say, but possibly he was leaving. He could go or stay.

They stood together in the living room archway. Without prelude, he reached for her, awkwardly pulled her side against his chest, kissed her absurdly on the eye, and with his free hand began squeezing her breasts.

DEBORAH SEABROOKE

Secrets

(FROM THE VIRGINIA QUARTERLY REVIEW)

OH HOW I LOVED HER! my father said on the plane back to the States. But he said it was over now, his affair with the girl at the Institute, Clara Springel. How she had wept at my grandmother's book party in London, what a scene she had made.

The boy I was with wanted to know who the redhead was. That's Clara Springel, my father's lover, I said.

My mother wrote to say she had big welcome home plans, had arranged for another doctor to be on call so she could pick us up at Kennedy and we could all go out to eat. My father handed the letter to me. Now isn't that nice of her? he said. She doesn't have to do that. I was planning. . . . I had hoped you and I could just take a quiet ride home in a taxi.

My mother was a pediatrician in New York. She kept toy whistles in her pocket and passed out sugarless gum at the desk.

In the crowd at the buffet table, I stuffed myself with something fried in tempura and watched my grandmother, whose nose was as red as her garden gnome's, hug an older man in the book business around his neck. Impossible to imagine, I actually had to see my English grandmother having a good time. My mother's mother, an Italian Mama from Far Rockaway, never stopped laughing, her fat neck and great bosom, everything jiggling at once. My mother was beginning to take after her, her bosom already hung low, and she wore polyester pants with elasticized waists and flowered tunic tops. The boy I was with, something my English grandma had arranged, loved to hear me talk Long Islandese. He really wanted to get to the States someday, he said. He held a copy of my grandmother's new gardening book, *From Aubergine to Zucchini with Mrs. Slipper,* waiting for her to sign it for his mother as a birthday present. "I say," he said, "I wish I'd met you earlier, Liz. And what a lovely party. That girl's your father's lover? She looks rather unhappy. My father doesn't have a lover."

Yes, Clara Springel. The one hanging on to the arm of the man with the big head of steely curls, my father, whose shoulder looks good to lean on. That's her, turning her face into his shoulder when someone comes up and wants to talk to them. Because he can't introduce her as his wife, he calls her his "friend," and she says the word frightens her, but she understands. "Oh why do you have to be married? It must be something to have two women love you at the same time," she says. My father scoops up a glob of chick-pea pâté on a piece of toast and guides her to a tattered pink love seat. The boy I'm with, named Jasper, suggests a look at the Parliament building by night and leads me away from the food to the balcony of the hotel. He puts the book down. I let him kiss me, and then see my father looking for me inside at the party. It's time to take Clara back to her hotel, crying in the taxi.

My father, a geneticist, is somewhat of a celebrity in scientific circles. My grandmother is proud of him, but she still said sternly to me, "There is nothing wrong with being ordinary, Elizabeth."

Clara would say the same thing when I told her I was not cut out for science and doubted I would write books like my grandmother. "I like you just the way you are," she said. We stood in the park at the edge of the duck pond, in the town of Bath, on her break from the Institute, where she sat at a Bunsen burner all day. I'd met her before my father did, feeding the big, sloppy ducks pellets from a paper cone. We met in the George Lillo Park. It was named for a minor eighteenth-century English playwright in my literature book, with its muddy duck bank and groups of boys who liked to call to Clara and me over the water and push each other into trash cans. Clara's red hair always attracted attention.

Then when I told her whose daughter I was, she was flustered. Her hand flew up to her identification badge on her breast. "Dr. Slipper's a great man. How lucky you are." I was amused, but then everyone here thought he was wonderful. Clara asked me his first name.

"George," she murmured. "Such a refined name. Does it fit him?"

"Except when he's playing the saxophone," I said.

Every Wednesday morning, my father and I would leave Oxford on the six A.M. bus for his lecture in Bath at the Institute. Out of the dusty, rattling windows at the back of the bus I'd watch dawn break over Oxford's spires. Below us, students huffed up the streets on their bicycles, oblivious to the roar and soot from our tailpipe. My grandmother said the air in Oxford was unbreathable with its exhaust and factory smoke. I thought worse of the damp chill that the ancient stone gave off.

I was always glad for our weekly excursion to Bath, though it meant an encounter with my grandmother in her garden. Since 1954, her eggplants had won first prize at the Bath Fair, and last year the London *Times* had sent a photographer to immortalize her spading around the foxgloves. The first day we met, in late August, she gave me a present of gardening gloves, and together we ripped out the dying annuals. She had the hands of an Irish potato farmer, and for a writer she didn't talk much. I did all the talking and told her about home, our unmown yard, and the wild woods so different from all this English order. At home, we swam in a private cove in Cold Spring Harbor. I did my homework upstairs at my window overlooking squirrels' nests and my dilapidated treehouse. When my father wasn't working in his lab down in the woods, he blew his cheeks out on his saxophone in the basement. "Road Runner" was his showpiece, but I liked better the bluesy improvisations that sounded like a big fish undulating in the current. The Cold Spring Harbor Fish Hatchery was only a mile away from our house. We would leave a block of my mother's frozen spaghetti sauce out to thaw for dinner and walk down to see the bass in their concrete houses. We fed them Purina Fish Chow you could get out of a gumball machine for a dime and watched them flip and dive for the pellets.

My English grandma didn't understand how my mother could live in the city during the week and only come home on weekends. My mother was now five years into building her pediatrics practice. "But she should be home with her family," Grandma said to me in an anger so strong that she tore a five-foot rope of mint out of the ground and went tumbling backwards.

She knew the Springels of Bath. Clara's father was a butcher. They were a little too High Church for my grandmother's blood but still very nice. Clara was their only child, born the year my father left for his freshman year at Oxford. If my grandmother could have predicted that there he would meet Anna Maria Multari from Far Rockaway and run off to America with her, she would have done anything to stop him. She would have welcomed the saxophone in a Blackpool jazz band over the microscope and months of silence from overseas. When he did write, she said, they were the letters of a lonely man, swamped in the chores of maintaining a household while his wife went off to medical school. "Baby doctor!" she said. "Why didn't your mother want to stay home and tend to her own baby?

". . . but your father was marvelous. He didn't complain. He kept your boopy clean and your fingernails cut and in the meantime made a name for himself. A great man, he is. The great minds of England appreciate him."

Clara Springel wasn't everything she could have hoped for for his mate either, but at least she knew Clara's parents, and Clara was an English girl. Clara wasn't brought up having her diaper rash rubbed with olive oil. And Clara's mother, the butcher's wife, could vouch that she was ambitious, yes, but basically a good, ordinary girl who mainly wanted a family of her own.

The fact that my father still had a wife in the States while carrying on an affair with Clara didn't embarrass my grandmother. Her best friend, Mrs. Feeney, had a nephew who was a convicted bigamist. And my grandmother's deep kinship with the natural world also enhanced such freethinking. She had the butcher's wife agreeing with her that the artificial bonds of matrimony would not make the crows or foxes lead more happy lives.

Clara, the butcher's daughter, my father's lover, threw a handful of pellets to the ducks and leaned back next to me on the bench. "My mother ought to stick with slicing sausage," she said to me. "And my father, he'll like it when your Dr. Slipper leaves for the States again and I marry a nice local boy."

Their lovemaking took place in Oxford, most of it clandestinely in the house we rented on Beaumont Street, after I had gone to bed. But some of it in a punt on the river in broad daylight in the pious presence of the swans. Clara left her flat in Bath to move in with us, but the commute every day to the Institute was too exhausting, and she and my father quarreled. Clara would accuse him of having an easier life than hers because all he had to do was teach one Monday afternoon tutorial at Oxford and present a Wednesday lecture at the Institute. Seeing the newspaper in the bathroom would send her into a rage because he'd had the luxury of sitting there reading. He, in turn, roared about her wet stockings hanging in the shower. He insulted her television shows. When my mother telephoned, Clara was difficult to talk to for days afterward. Although my friendship with her began before she became his lover, I found myself barely able to tolerate her moods. My attitude — I could not seem to help it — was that if she were going to make my father unfaithful, she had better make him happy. I didn't think she had any right to demand that same happiness herself.

After a long winter of rain and quarreling, she moved out. Spring came, and sunlight broke across the pocked stone and shot through stained glass windows. My father's students brought him daffodils. Clara sometimes telephoned before breakfast with a breezy "Good morning" and then an intense interest in what my father had prepared himself to eat and what we had done the evening before. I finally realized who she was, a girl only seven years older than I, hopelessly locked in a situation sordid even in the eyes of my father. By spring, he still would not consider divorcing my mother for her. I certainly did not want that either, and Clara, wisely, never asked my help in the matter.

In the spring, we resumed meeting at the George Lillo Park on Wednesdays during her break from the Institute. When my

father couldn't get away to join us, we had a better time because
Clara would let herself relax. She never acted silly when he was
around, but if it were only me, she would bend over the fence
at the ducks and insult them, calling them cows, sluts, ignora-
muses. Still, they waddled up to her and let her stroke their
sleek heads. When she was sad, she called them her beauties. I
told her she'd love the fish hatchery at home. There was nothing
more beautiful than a school of big brown bass swimming in
perfect synchronization along the slippery walls of their tanks.

In some ways, it would have been fun to have Clara come
home with us. She thought my father's saxophone improvisations exquisite and encouraged him to practice on the roof. She
would love the cove and the woods. I could show her around
New York. When June came, my father's tutorials at Oxford
would end, and we would be going home. Thinking there might
be something more she could have done, Clara permed her hair
and bought a tailored suit to make herself look older. She took
French cooking lessons and wore the opal ring my father gave
her on her left hand. He still introduced her to his acquain-
tances as his friend. Or worse, his "daughter's friend," which
would make her inconsolable.

London. The dim corridor of her hotel which stood across
the Thames from ours. We had moved into London for a week
before our plane left for New York. My grandmother's book
party. My stomachache from the rancid mayonnaise in the sea-
food dip. That boy Jasper trailing me on and off buses and
leaving messages at the desk. Clara refused to board at our
hotel, let alone sleep with my father. It was part of breaking
away, she said. I shouldn't have even followed him to London.
In the excitement of seeing London for the first time, I dreaded
Clara's brave, buttoned-up face every morning when we met for
breakfast, either at her hotel or ours. She put up a fuss if my
father offered to take her out somewhere alone. In the booth,
she insisted on sitting across from us. If my father ordered
coffee, she would order tea.

Our last day, we stood at Piccadilly Circus. My father told me
as I fed the pigeons some popcorn that if you stood here long
enough you always saw someone you knew. Not five minutes
later, I saw my third grade teacher from home. And not ten

minutes after that, I saw Clara edging her way off a bus with a crisp paper shopping bag. Two teenage boys barged past her, and she lost her balance at the curb. A little crowd milled around her, and someone helped her up. Then I caught sight of her again, bag torn, glumly looking at a menu in a cafe window. If she turned her head but a few degrees, she would see us. My father yanked me up by the arm and pulled me down the steps, through the traffic circle, away. He explained later, as I examined my arm in the taxi, that no matter how pathetic Clara looked, he must now try to think only of my mother. Because he would be going home to love her just the same as before he left.

Our first Saturday back home, the three of us went for a sail at my mother's instigation in my little boat. While we'd been gone in England, she'd sent it to the marina for new tackle and bottom paint so that I might get interested in sailing again. "Take advantage of your last free summer," she said. Once I entered college, I was to get a summer job to help pay. I'd value my studies more that way. She hung her beeper in a plastic bag from the mast, we stowed away a motor in case she should get called, and off we set. She opened a Thermos of tomato soup and passed around mugs. She was very pleased at having us home.

Then the wind picked up as we left the lee of the land, and we flew in sleek elegance toward a public beach across the harbor. Elegant until I forgot to head the boat into the wind as we approached, and scraped us along the rocks. She said nothing about the bottom paint, but rolled her pants as I held the boat steady, and slowly lowered herself over the other side. We fastened a line, and my father took the anchor to dig into the sand up the beach. I helped her over the shells and slippery rocks. Summers ago, my mother had worn a bathing suit with a little pleated skirt that my father used to flick up in back to annoy her. Now he seemed to prefer to be alone, thinking no doubt of how Clara would look in a bikini.

Clara sunned herself in my grandmother's eggplant patch that summer and wrote him letters, parts of which he read aloud to me when I walked down to the lab for a visit. As I looked at the pages in his hand, I saw not one crossed-out word. Obviously, she had toiled over her letter on scratch paper and copied the whole thing over to please him with her neatness. I learned she had joined a badminton team and had to have a tooth filled. She wrote like a child and not a very clever one. Her letters came in scented pink envelopes to the post-office box he used in town for his scientific correspondence.

Barnacles attacked the underside of my boat where the paint had been scraped. One hot August morning, I dragged it up onto our beach and cracked at them with a kitchen spatula. Chips of calcium flew, but after an hour I'd made no significant progress, so I heaved her back over and pushed her into the water on her tether. My mother would have stayed at it until the job was finished.

That same August, one of her patients got leukemia, a five-year-old boy named Daniel who was now being kept alive with transfusions. My mother was sleeping at the hospital, most weekends included, so determined she was to be with him when he died. Talking to me one night on the phone, she said she'd never had a patient die before. It was terrible but a great relief in a way. She'd known that eventually she would have to face it with one of them, but which one would it be? When it didn't happen and didn't happen, she began to dwell on any idiosyncrasy and wrote pages of notes after each child she examined. Daniel had been with her since she'd opened her practice, a 9½-pound healthy newborn. She'd given him his first examination in the delivery room and swore now that she remembered his trembling tongue inside that screaming blue mouth, and how her gloves felt on his slippery skin, and that the mother had said to her from the table, "I don't know what I'm going to do with another boy. Please doctor, tell this one he has to be good."

My lack of interest in the boat aggravated her. Here was a five-year-old fighting for his life, who tried to slap a hockey puck down the hospital corridor from his wheelchair. Daniel had become her child for the summer.

On a Sunday when my father and I had risen late and were having newspaper and coffee at the bottom of the stairs, the phone rang. My father grumbled and rose to get it, the sash of his bathrobe trailing into the kitchen.

"Oh hello, Baby," he said. It was my mother. There was a

long stretch of silence after which I heard him hang up, but he didn't come back. "What did she want?" I called. I walked into the kitchen and saw him looking into the refrigerator.

"Do we have any eggs?" And then, bump, he shut the door and leaned back against it. "Oh dear. Oh what have I done?" he said.

And then my heart took a leap. She had found out about Clara at last.

My mother had called to say that she had had lunch yesterday with an old friend of *hers* from Oxford, Lavinia Stewart. "She's a widow now, your mother told me. Poor, dear, prying Lavinia."

Lavinia was in Oxford last April for a reunion of her class and stayed over to browse in the bookstores. "And crossing Magdalen Bridge in her widow's weeds, whom do you think she saw in a punt? And whom else do you think she saw in that punt? And what do you think these two people were doing?" my father asked.

But an hour later, a towel around his waist, he was laughing at himself in the mirror. He had called me in to powder his back before he dressed. "Your mother's going to make me sweat it out, but I'll win her over, don't you worry." As my fingers slipped over the moles and gray hairs that grew out of them, I wondered how Clara had overcome such a sight during their lovemaking. He was going into the city to deliver a confession and apology to my mother over lunch. He asked me if I thought he ought to wear some aftershave.

"She can't be won over that easily," I said.

"You make me sound like a buffoon." He ordered me downstairs to the kitchen junk drawer to find a Long Island Railroad schedule. I opened my mouth to say, do it yourself, but I wanted him to go through with this. He needed to give Clara up before things could go back to normal. One evening recently, I had brought his supper to the lab and saw him hastily shove a pink letter under some magazines. He was supposed to be injecting duck eggs with mutant cells. But ducks reminded him of Clara. I told him I was sick of his absurd passion for an assistant lab technician. I didn't care if he now hated the cancers he'd manufactured and loved the duck eggs. The great minds of England who so appreciated him were waiting for the genius to do something.

So now I ran upstairs with a train schedule, with all my will trying to muffle my excitement, when I heard him call, "Elizabeth!" He lay on the bed clawing at his tie. I loosened the knot and tore it off. "I can't breathe!" he said. He grabbed his chest, his nostrils snorting for air. I called an ambulance and then my mother's office. But it was Sunday. I only reached her answering service. She was on her rounds at the hospital. What was the nature of the call? In an emergency, here was a number I could call. I beat his jacket pocket for a pencil. I looked in the nightstand. "I don't have a pencil!" I shouted at the woman. "Look, just tell her to call home right away."

"Am I going to die?" my father asked.

"No. Just keep calm. Try to breathe normally."

"It's beating again."

"Good."

"I'm frightened."

"Don't talk."

"I was thinking of Clara when it happened. Did she ever say anything bad about me? Anything to make you think, even for a moment, that I was disgusting?"

"No. Will you shut up and save your breath?"

"I wouldn't blame her if she had. It was wrong. It was wrong."

The ambulance arrived before my mother called back. We shot to the local hospital, siren and all. Sitting next to his stretcher, I watched the road rip away through the back window. Cars pulled off at odd angles. People coming out of a church heard us and were riveted there on the marble steps. The pristine steeple reminded me of Oxford's sooty spires and gargoyles. I heard Clara's midnight giggling. My father's eyes held on to me. His cheeks felt like stone.

His heart attack turned out to be nothing more than palpitations, something everyone under stress feels now and then. But it took all morning to convince him of that. He ran a treadmill test to prove there was something wrong, as if he thought my mother would go easy on him if she saw him in a hospital bed. But his heart pumped beautifully. The doctor said he had the heart of a twenty-year-old man.

"Get me out of here," my father said, and I rushed off to call a taxi while the doctor removed the wires from his chest.

While we waited outside the hospital, my father paced the walk from the flagpole to the brick wall where I sat. "When we were in the ambulance, I knew you were worried. What were you thinking?" he asked.

"I was in a trance. You know the way you feel in an emergency. I wasn't thinking much about anything other than that I didn't want you to die."

"Were you thinking that I deserved to die, maybe just a little, for my behavior with Clara?" He looked hard at me.

"No," I said. Yes, the old bitterness had flickered in me for a moment in the siren's screaming.

A breeze came up, sending a paper cup clattering across the hospital drive. It blew my hair in front of my eyes and obscured his image. And I pretended for a moment, the way I sometimes did when I watched them together in Oxford, that I wasn't connected to him, not connected and therefore not responsible for an opinion.

Sometimes when I would first look into a tank at the hatchery, the brown fish blended so well with the water, I couldn't discern that anything was down there at all. I saw mostly my reflection and the sky behind me. The fish saw me, of course, and were waiting for their food. And I used to wonder what I looked like to them. Did they think I swam in the light on the other side of the water? If I waited long enough, one of the fish would try to dive at me, and the surface would break into a thousand ripples; and in between the shattered pieces of light I would see them all swaying in harmony down below. I would have to throw them their food then, because they had revealed themselves.

I heard a motor. "Taxi's coming."

Inside the car, in the stuffy air which open windows didn't seem to help, I told him for the first time how I had hated him for his unfaithfulness. Sometimes I had hated him so much I *had* wished him dead and that was what I was remembering in the ambulance. But I hadn't been glad when it looked like it was truly happening. Then Clara seemed insignificant in the scope of his whole life. I remembered the crowd of doctors at the Institute nattering him with questions. I saw him once again locked in awesome concentration over his microscope. The way it had been before Clara.

The taxi passed along the same route the ambulance had taken. My father leaned forward and spoke through the dingy partition at the driver's ear to give directions to our house. Soon the taxi turned into our dirt road. Sunlight flashed through the trees; the jouncing car sent up graceful plumes of dust in its wake. As we climbed the hill, my father said that in the ambulance a picture had come to his mind of a crab apple tree in his mother's garden that blew over one spring. It had never bloomed more profusely; its brilliance took your breath away, and it seemed that that day the color was at its peak. "It was windy," he said, "and my mother and I were eating a lunch of buttered potatoes in the kitchen. We saw it topple. She stood up and screamed, 'It can't be!' She had shown far less emotion when my father died.

"So I was glad to see your worried face in the ambulance, Elizabeth." The taxi stopped with a jolt. He paid the driver, and we walked across the tall grass toward the front door. A rabbit skittered for the woods.

The air always smelled good here in summer, with the sun on the dry grass and a salty breeze blowing up from the water. Why hadn't we ever spread out our lunch here? Or my father practiced his saxophone and sent the rabbits running? Maybe it would have made things too heavenly, to tap the beauty here, and we would have fallen like the crab apple from the weight of too many blooms.

"I'm going to go upstairs to change," he said, "then try to pull the day together at the lab." Pull the day together. That was what you did. When the water's surface broke and gave you glimpses of the harmony below, of how we could all have gently swum together like a school of fish, it only made you realize such beauty wasn't in you. It might have been beautiful if I had run up the stairs after him, butted my head under his chin, and we had held each other close. The inspiration did set my foot on the stair, forgiveness was in my heart, and if he had turned around to look at me, some speck of loveliness inside would have set me free. But I stopped on the second step. Sometime later. Let me pull my day together first. At some other time I'll tell him I love him.

So I got a spatula and rubber gloves and walked to the cove.

All afternoon until high tide, I chipped and scraped at the barnacles on the bottom of my boat. The ambulance and my father's stone-cold cheeks on the stretcher all seemed to have happened years ago. My jeans were slick and green with algae. Flies crawled among the ruined barnacles all afternoon. When my gloves became cut in too many places and began to tear, I left the boat beached and walked up to the lab.

Through the window I saw my father injecting eggs. It sounded like Bartók on the radio, but I could hear it only faintly. Leaf shadows played over the film of dirt on the window and made it hard to distinguish much else besides his silhouette as he held each egg up to the Tensor lamp like a jeweler looking for flaws.

Judging from the row of eggs in front of him, he still had a lot of work to do, so I left and walked to the house for a shower.

Out front in a lawn chair, in the din of the crickets, I picked at a cold breast of chicken. The sky was wild and red, but it was one of those summer nights that portended autumn in the chill as soon as the sun went down. I set my iced tea in the grass and warmed my fingers inside my shirt. And then tires rumbled as a car entered our driveway. I saw headlights clear the hill and bounce as the car strained to keep up its speed over the ruts. Her left parking light was out. She drove halfway up the lawn when the drive ended, got out and stood against the car. I put my plate in the grass and stood, too, looking away where the drive became a scrappy path to his lab, where I could just make out a light in his window, as if my father could know she were here and come help me explain.

"Dad's all right. I guess you know by now," I said trying to sound breezy. "I guess we forgot to call you back."

"I checked with my answering service when he didn't show up for lunch," my mother said. "They told me you sounded upset, but no word about ambulances. No explanation. If I'd been given a hint, I could have called Dad's doctor and found out what happened."

For the first time I noticed she wasn't wearing polyester pants, but a skirt and blouse, a bit tight across the bosom, but a pretty blue silk with a bow at the neck. When she was piqued, her chin and cheeks burned. It looked better than makeup. "It turned out to be only palpitations. They did some tests. He was fine," I said.

"Oh I know . . . now. His doctor kindly phoned me this afternoon. I'd been trying to reach you for hours."

"I'm sorry. I just wasn't thinking. I got really involved scraping the boat."

She didn't seem to hear me. She bent at her reflection in the car window and retied her bow. "The Expressway was hell tonight. I *did* look a little crisper at lunchtime."

I tried to smile, but inside I was bucking against being blamed. It wasn't all my fault. He was her husband, and he could have remembered to phone.

Then she looked over the roof of her car at his light in the woods. "Maybe I'll just walk down and surprise him," she said. Fireflies flickered in her wake as she plowed through the grass toward his path.

MARJORIE SANDOR

The Gittel

(FROM THE GEORGIA REVIEW)

THERE IS A TRADITION in our family that once in a while a dreamer is born: an innocent whose confused imagination cannot keep up with the civilized world. This person walks around in a haze of dreams, walking eventually right into the arms of the current executioner, blind as Isaac going up the mountain with his father. Nobody knows who started this story — my mother used to say it was a second-rate scholar out to impress the neighbors — but apparently there are characteristics, traits peculiar to this person, and two hundred years ago people knew a catastrophe was on the way if such a person came into their midst. Once, when I was a little girl, I asked Papa to name the traits. He said he couldn't; they'd been lost. All he knew was that this dreamer, before vanishing, always left behind a dreaming child, and that sometimes he thought he was such a child.

My father was a modest man; he came to Ellis Island with his eyebrows up, and they never came down. Furthermore he was the kind of storyteller who rarely got past the scenic details, since every time he let his imagination go his children had nightmares for a week. I remember: I was eight years old, sitting with him on the kitchen stairs, my bedtime cup of milk between us. My mother was scrubbing a pot with steel wool, making that sound that hurts the smallest bones in the body, and in the parlor the alabaster lamp had been lit for my grandmother Gittel's yahrzeit.

The lamp looked different than it does now. We hadn't converted it yet to electric, and it glowed pale orange behind the alabaster. As a child I could look at it for hours, imagining miniature cities on fire, or ladies in a golden room. It didn't have the long crack you see running down the left side. My daughter Rachel did that when she was ten years old, running like a maniac through the room and tripping over the cord. She won't go near it now; at nineteen she thinks it's her destiny to break it. She's a little careless, it's true, but nothing some responsibility wouldn't cure. I'm waiting for her now — she said she was taking the 4:30 bus from the city. I've been thinking about things, and tonight, after we eat, I'm going to tell her she can have the lamp when she and Daniel move into the new apartment.

So, where was I? With Papa? Yes, he was looking away from me, at the lamp in the parlor.

"We don't really know when she died," he said. "Not the exact date. But sometimes I wonder — what if these dreamers are common, nothing extraordinary, people you have to fight to recognize as a sacrifice, a warning. . . ." He bent lower, opening his mouth to speak again. Something rough and wet scratched my wrist; it was the steel wool, all soapy, in my mother's hand.

"Don't romanticize, Bernard," she said. "It's common knowledge that Gittel was a selfish woman who should have had the good sense to stay single. Sacrifice, my foot."

Sometimes I wish I were more like her and less like my father. No matter how many questions a daughter had, she knew when to talk and when to keep quiet. Before my wedding, young as I was, she didn't tell me anything. "Why frighten a person unnecessarily?" she said later. Papa was different. He couldn't hide anything from me. It's from him we get the insomnia and the bad dreams — he always left his children to finish his stories in their sleep.

"The Gittel," he used to say, as if she were a natural phenomenon. A little beauty at sixteen, she had red-gold hair to her waist, fine features, and tiny feet. Thank God, Rachel inherited her feet and not mine. Lucky girl. Tiny feet, this Gittel, and a good dancer and musician. The red in her hair and the musical sense came from the Hungarian; the rest was German going all the way back to the seventeenth century, when the Shapiros settled illegally in Berlin. By 1920 the family was in a good position: respected by the new Berlin intellectuals. Of course it wasn't really the brains, but the red-gold hair and the fine noses that made them comfortable. You can bet if they'd looked more Semitic they'd have caught on sooner to the general news.

She was eighteen then. Her father, along with a handful of other Jewish scholars, had been granted a professorship in the University of Berlin, and the family was able to establish itself in a brick house on Grunewaldstrasse, with real lace curtains and a baby grand. Being her father's pet, Gittel took whatever she liked from his library shelves, and sometimes sat with him when a colleague came to visit. Soon after her eighteenth birthday, she came into his study to borrow a book — without knocking, just like my Rachel. She had just mastered the art of the entrance, and paused where the light from the alabaster lamp would shine best on her hair.

"Papa," she announced. "Where is the Hoffmann?"

Shapiro was deep in conversation with a slender, bearded visitor whose trousers, according to Gittel's standards, were a little short. "Read something else," said her father. "The Romantics are anti-Semitic."

"Not Hoffmann," cried Gittel.

The visitor turned. He cursed himself for having put on his reading glasses, since at that distance he could not see her face or her eyes. He saw hair lit to the color of his own carefully raised flame roses and a brown merino skirt, very trim at the waist. "You enjoy Hoffmann as well?" he asked, squinting.

His name was Yaakov Horwicz: thirty-five years old and a scholar from Riga, Latvia. Like Shapiro he was enjoying the new generosity of his government. For the first time in his professional life he had had enough money to take the train to Berlin for a lecture series: Shapiro's on Western Religions. After the lecture and a three-hour discussion in the Romanische Café, he had received an invitation to coffee in the professor's home.

He was delirious, first to stand in Shapiro's study, then to make the acquaintance of his household. And still wearing those ridiculous spectacles, the cheap frames warped from the weight of the lenses. He took off his glasses for the formal introduction. His eyes, which had seemed to Gittel to be unnaturally large behind the lenses, now had a fine, granular brilliance, like her mother's antique blue glass vase. It was his eyes that kept her standing there, and his eyes that made Shapiro think to himself: he can't help but be honorable. It's not in his veins as a possibility, unfaithfulness. She's young, but better to send her with a scholar than watch her run off at twenty with a young gentile going through his mystical phase.

Professor Shapiro is not to be blamed. I can imagine his concern, for Gittel was famous for her lively behavior with students. A young man would come to the house on Grunewaldstrasse, stand in the front hall, and within minutes a figure in petticoats would appear running down the curved staircase, shouting "Mama, Mama, I can't get the buttons in back!" Mrs. Shapiro was no help either, in the long run. She wore her hair in a neat coil, fastened her own innumerable buttons without assistance, and on top of that made bread from scratch. Just like my mother, she wouldn't let her daughter into the kitchen until dinner was safe in the oven. "You're a little girl yet," she'd say. "There's plenty of time to learn." I vowed I'd be different with mine. She would make her bed the minute she started to talk back, and help me in the kitchen whenever it was convenient. I wasn't going to make the same mistake.

Mrs. Shapiro got the message from her husband and invited Horwicz to stay to supper that evening. That meal nearly cost them a suitor, for despite the intensity of his vision and the shortness of his trousers, Horwicz had a fondness for table manners, and Gittel's were wretched. She tapped her fingers on the white linen, rearranged her cutlery, and sometimes hummed a phrase of music, as if she were alone in her room. He blushed, torn between embarrassment and desire. She, on her side, glanced at him only long enough to compare his eyes to those of Anselmus, the student-hero of a Hoffmann tale, noting that each time she looked at him, a feverish color stained his cheeks. I know this kind of girl: not happy unless she's in the midst of charming someone into his downfall. Gittel hummed and smiled and asked Horwicz if, after supper, he would turn the piano music for her.

Horwicz raised his napkin awkwardly to his lips.

"Go ahead," said Shapiro. "We'll finish our discussion later."

Horwicz had never before turned pages of music for a lady,

young or otherwise, and here Gittel sealed her fate. *Turn*, she said, trying out a low, husky cabaret voice. *Turn*. It was easy to obey such a voice. Horwicz imagined going on and on, watching her narrow, lightly freckled hands touch the keys and lift under the lamplight. Her fingers trembled a little; his heart swelled under his ribs, wanting to protect. . . . When at last she released him into her father's study, he had forgotten Western Religions and inquired after Gittel's status. Shapiro was standing by his desk, a book in his hand.

"Tell me about Latvia," he said. "Things don't flare up there the way they do here, isn't that so?"

"That's true," said Horwicz. "The nationals have been very liberal."

Shapiro smiled a small, lopsided smile. "She will be a lovely wife, a delight," he said. "And Latvia is good."

Picture the night Gittel was told of her destiny. They stand in the front parlor, and she turns pale yellow, like a late leaf, and begins looking through her music for something she says she's been missing for a long time. Finally she stops looking and says to Horwicz: "We will live here, in town?" He takes her hands, surprised at the firmness of the thin fingers, the tautness of the palm. The hands don't tremble now.

"I have a house of my own, and a garden," he says. "In a suburb of Riga."

"Mother," cries Gittel. *"Riga?"*

Mrs. Shapiro ushers her daughter from the parlor. Imagine the sounds of their two skirts rustling, and how Horwicz felt watching them leave the room — the upright mother and the daughter, long fingers gripping her skirt. The two men wait in the parlor like displaced ghosts; Professor Shapiro trying over and over to light his pipe; Horwicz holding himself perfectly still, blinking and pale as if he'd just stepped out of his study into broad daylight.

When Gittel appeared in the doorway again her back was needle-straight. She stepped up to Horwicz and held out her hand. "Let me play you something," she said.

"Chopin," muttered her father. "Another anti-Semite."

Horwicz escorted her to the piano, where she played for him the Sixth Prelude, her favorite. It's a strange piece: half delight, half dirge. They say he wrote it during a night of terrible rains.

A messenger came to his door: George Sand and her three children had been killed in a carriage accident. He kept composing, unable to leave the piano bench. He wrote the last notes in the morning, just as there was another knock on the door, and her voice . . .

Mrs. Shapiro did not come back into the parlor until Horwicz was ready to leave. She was as gracious as ever, a remarkable woman; I know how she felt. I can see her face, almost as fragile as her daughter's, the eyelids only a little pink, only a little. I admire that woman.

The wedding picture is right there — on the mantel. When my Rachel was small, she used to take it down and touch her tongue to the dusty glass.

"Don't do that," I'd say.

She'd look at me, already the archaeologist, and say, "I'm cleaning it off for you."

Somewhere in her teens she lost interest; she could walk by that picture without even a glance. I can't do that. I walk past and there's Gittel in the dress her mother made for her by hand: a creamy, flounced thing. Her waist is unbelievable. She's tiny, but then the bridegroom is no giant himself. Great mustaches hide his lips, and he's not wearing his glasses. Without them his eyes appear pale and wide awake, as if when the shutter came down he saw something astonishing. I don't know anything about his childhood or bachelor circumstances; why he should have such eyes on his wedding day I can only attribute to foresight. He was like Shapiro that way. So much foresight he couldn't enjoy the wedding cake.

Beside him the Gittel is serious too; only on her, seriousness doesn't look so sweet. Her lips are set tight together, and her pupils are so dilated that her green eyes look black as caves. Rachel used to look at those eyes.

"I don't like her," she'd say. Somehow even a child knows it's not the usual bridal worry that's in Gittel's eyes. Ten years old, holding that picture in her hand. "Mom," she says to me. "Do I have to leave home like her if I'm bad?"

She gave me a nice shock. When had I ever spoken of Gittel leaving home at eighteen? I played innocent. "Who told you that, Rachel?" I asked.

"You talk in your sleep," she said.

She made me nervous then, she makes me nervous now. At the time, I thought: what good will it do to tell a ten-year-old that when the time comes, she'll be good and ready to leave home?

"You're not a Gittel," I said. "Nobody is going to make you leave home. We just want you to be happy."

She bit her lower lip and big terrible tears dropped on her T-shirt.

"Rachel, you're breaking my heart," I said. "What's the matter?"

"It's okay," she said. "I'll go and pack."

Thank God that phase is over — although with Rachel it's hard to tell. Last month when we looked at that picture together she laughed.

"I used to have nightmares about her," she said.

I acted nonchalant. "Like what?"

"I don't remember. Big melodramas, everybody in the world disappearing —"

"Go on," I said.

Then she gave me such a look. "Mom," she said. "All kids have dreams like that."

"About the end of the world?" I asked.

"Yes."

Sometimes she hurts me with her quick answers. Every family has its stories, why should she deny hers? Besides, she traps me. She was all eagerness: "Mother, what finally happened to Gittel?"

What am I supposed to do? If I start to tell it, and she's in a modern mood, she cuts me off. If she's not, she gets all dreamy on me. Naturally I start thinking about her and Daniel and their archaeology studies, and so I say to her, "Rache, tell me honestly what you plan on doing with those old pots? Read the newspapers, look around you!" I raised her to read the newspapers so nothing should take her by surprise, and she winds up in the ancient ruins. Last week on the phone she said to me: "Mother, I read the newspapers and so does Daniel," and I knew she was biting her lip. It's a bad habit. "I'm coming this weekend," she said, "so you and I can have a talk." I made up my mind right then and there that I wouldn't mention Gittel unless she promises not to interrupt . . .

Gittel bore her husband seven sons in ten years. Papa was number four, Gittel's favorite because he had his father's eyes and could listen to her at the piano without speaking or tugging on her skirt every three minutes. Sometimes she would stop playing and say to him: "Shut your eyes, Bernard, and imagine that this is a baby grand instead of an upright, and that across from us is a maroon divan, where grandpapa sits reading, his glasses slipping down his nose." Other times she took him into the courtyard and lifted her fine nose into the air. "Smell," she said. "Today it smells exactly like April at home." He listened to her describe where the alabaster lamp had stood in the other house (she had it next to the piano in Riga) and how her mother had given it to her, along with the brass candlesticks, the five handmade lace doilies, and her own key ring to wear at her waist. "A good housekeeper is never without her keys," her mother had said, knowing everything in advance.

Once a week a letter arrived from Grunewaldstrasse, and the family gathered in the parlor to hear Gittel read it. Papa remembered later how his father leaned against the mantel listening carefully to letters that seemed to be about nothing but the weather and fifteenth-century religion. His mother's hands trembled as she read — her voice, too — and sometimes afterward he heard them talking in their bedroom, their voices soft to begin with, then rising, rising.

Gittel captured the little suburb. For months after her departure people talked of how the young mother would be stirring soup in the kitchen and suddenly remember a dream she'd had the night before. Off she'd run to the neighbor's house, bursting in: "Marta, I forgot to tell you what I dreamed about your boy!" Her friends seemed to love this, especially the burning of the soup that went hand in hand with the piece of news, the almost forgotten dream, the stories about Grunewaldstrasse. It was rare in that time and place to find a woman for whom dreams and stories came before soup, and a miracle that, given her dizzy mind and her husband's library heart, any of the seven boys grew up. "Luck," Papa would say to me if Mother was in the room. "Destiny," he'd say if she wasn't.

He was five years old when his father died. Diabetes: that's where Papa got it, and now I have to be careful too. Gittel was twenty-eight, and after the seven boys she still had her figure and her lovely hair. Papa's memory of her is of a woman in a new black silk dress and fine shoes, hushing a baby. It was at his father's funeral that he began to be afraid of her.

The service was held on a little rise in the Jewish cemetery outside Riga. It was a fine March day, the kind of day when the tips of the grass look caught on fire, and gulls go slanting across the sky as if they can't get their balance. The kind of day where you want to run in one direction and then turn and see the figures of people you've left behind, tiny and unreal as paper dolls. Papa wanted to break out of the circle of mourners and run across the knolls and valleys of the cemetery, all the way down to the shore, where the Gulf of Riga stretched endlessly away.

"Come here, Bernard," said Gittel. "Stand in front of me."

She placed one hand lightly on his shoulder, but every time he shifted his weight, her fingers tightened. His brothers stood all around him: Johan, the eldest, almost ten and already a tall boy; Aaron and Yaakov beside him. Pressed tight to their mother's skirt were the two young ones, whose names Papa later forgot, and on her hip, the baby. She stood absolutely still, while around her Horwicz' friends and relatives rocked back and forth. Papa turned once and looked up at her face. Her narrow jaw was marble white, and her eyes, clear and unreddened, were trained on a tuft of grass blowing beside the open pit. People whispered: "Poor thing, she's in shock. He was everything to her." Only Papa, watching the dark pupils, knew that she was not thinking about her husband. When the rabbi closed his book, Gittel sighed and bent down to Bernard.

"Very soon," she said, "we can go back."

"Back to the house?" said Bernard.

"No," she replied. "Grunewaldstrasse."

For five years no one but Papa knew Gittel's mind. They thought she would pull herself together and become a good manager with all the help she was offered by her women friends. Everybody should be so fortunate; Horwicz' cousins in the city came by often to take the boys out for a drive, and ladies were always bringing hot dishes by. "With seven boys she must be desperate," they said. The neighbors began to wonder, though, how with seven wild boys they would be hearing Cho-

pin and Mozart four hours together in the morning. Certain
shopkeepers began to talk. The dishes stopped coming, and the
cousins, after a lecture or two, stopped coming to get the boys.
"Let her suffer like other human beings," they said. "A lesson is
what she needs."

Maybe by that time it was too late for lessons. I suppose she
tried. She worked in her husband's garden, coming up with
small, deformed carrots and the smallest heads of cabbage imaginable. She sent the three eldest boys to serve one-year appren-
ticeships in town, and when they came home for the Sabbath
they brought her things from the city, and part of their wages.
Bernard she sent to school: Bernard, who wanted nothing more
than to be a carpenter like his big brother Johan, whom he
worshiped for his muscles and his talk of America. Every day
after school Bernard went to the carpenter's house to drink tea
with Johan, and every day Johan showed him the tin with the
money in it. "They say you can't keep kosher there," he'd say.
"But otherwise it's paradise."

Home in the evenings, Bernard let his mother caress his face.
"You have the eyes of your father, and the brains of mine,"
she'd say. "He is a great teacher in Berlin, and so will you be,
when we go home."

"We are home," he'd say, looking at his feet.

"No," she said. "You wait and see."

Gittel's looks were beginning to go. Her hair was no longer
that burnished gold color, although the ladies told her she could
fix it easily with a little lemon juice and a walk in the sunlight.
But Gittel wasn't listening. She played loud, crashing pieces by
Chopin and Liszt, and sent Bernard to do all her errands in
town so she wouldn't have to face the helpful remarks of the
shopkeepers. When he left for school she sent him with letters
to mail to Grunewaldstrasse, which came back marked *wrong
address.*

One day a letter came from the Shapiros — with another address, in a district of Berlin Bernard had never heard his
mother mention. In the morning, he waited beside her writing
table while she finished a letter. Over her shoulder he read: *I
don't care if it's smaller, we're coming. People stare at me in the street.*

"I'll be back in a minute, Mama," he said. Upstairs in his room he packed a school satchel and hid it in his closet. He would know when she began to pack up her lamp and her candlesticks.

That night Gittel went to the carpenter's house and wept at his table. "We're running out of money," she said. "Can you keep Johan for another year?" The carpenter was surprised; he knew Gittel's people in Germany were well off, that she could get money any time she wanted. He told people later that his first reaction was to refuse: "Lie in your own bed," he wanted to say, but she looked almost ill. Her lovely skin seemed blue, as if she were turning to ice inside. "All right," he said.

Two days later the shoemaker received a visit, and under the pressure of her tears, offered to keep Aaron for a second year. "He works like the devil," he said later, "better than my own sons, and doesn't waste his money." But telling the story, he shook his head: "It's a terrible thing to see a woman trying to give away her children."

The third boy, Jacob, was finally taken by the Horwicz cousins, though not until they had given Gittel a piece of their minds. Now that Horwicz had passed on, they revered him like a saint. "If our Yaakov were alive, what would he say to all this?" "If your Yaakov were alive," she answered, "would any of this be happening?" She was gaunt and smoky-eyed as a gypsy, and sometimes, in the two weeks that followed, she looked at Bernard with such passion that he ran out of the house and took a streetcar to Johan's, where he stayed till suppertime. Late one night, as he was working in his copybook for school, she knelt beside him.

"Bernard," she said. "Are you still having your special dreams?"

He hadn't been able to remember his dreams for weeks. Instead he heard voices all talking at once: the voices his father had called "demons" because they distorted every word that came into the mind. "No," he said.

"I have," she said, touching his arm. "You are now my eldest son, and we are taking our family home."

"We are home," he said.

"Home," she repeated. "My mother's —"

Something was kicking inside his ribs. Where his heart should be was a small, clawed animal coming loose. He scrambled up onto his chair and stood towering over his mother. "You can't make me," he shouted. "Because I am going to America with Johan and Yaakov and Aaron."

She stayed on her knees a moment, then tried to get up — too suddenly — and swayed forward as she did. Bernard flushed with shame; she looked like a drunk girl clutching the table edge.

"You are my son, and you will do as I say," she said.

The pressure in his chest built higher. He looked at the woman before him, and for an instant, the curve of her nose, the tiny velvet mole beside her mouth, were as alien to him as the landscapes of Asia in his schoolbook. "I don't know you," he cried, closing his eyes against the sight of her hand rushing toward his face.

"Go to bed," said Gittel. "In the morning we will talk."

At dawn Bernard crept out with his satchel and took the first streetcar to the carpenter's house. Every day he waited for the knock on the door, for the sight of his mother and the three children standing on the step, a cart piled high with belongings. The world seemed to him to have closed its mouth; the gulls, the bright grass, the wide and silent gulf — all seemed to have grown bolder in their colors to judge him. A week passed.

One evening Johan came home from work and took his hand. "Come," he said. "I want to show you something." They took a streetcar out of the city and walked down the street to their own house. It was unlocked. Inside the furniture gleamed, the rug lay bright and soft on the floor, and the pots and pans — always before in the sink — hung clean and polished on the kitchen wall. Under the alabaster lamp was a sheet of paper. *To my beloved Bernard I leave my mother's alabaster lamp, her brass Shabbas candlesticks, and the key ring, so that in America he will remember his mother.* The rest of the letter divided up the household items among the other boys. In an envelope they found the deed to the house.

It was the station porter who had told Johan; he was the last person in the suburb to see Gittel and the three children. He said her fingers quivered when she tried to hand him the four tickets to Berlin. He had never seen her up close before, and told people later that she was a little girl. "Magnificent hands, though," he said. "Like a slender man's, strong and nicely shaped. The kind of hands you don't expect to tremble, and she didn't expect them to either. I could see she was embarrassed, so I said, 'Going for long?' ' Oh no,' she said. 'Just to visit my parents and take the children to a magic show.' She put her hands in her coat pockets. 'I'm terrible about traveling,' she said, smiling."

The silence of the world then was different; it wasn't the silence of waiting, but the kind that comes after a mistake, with disbelief caught in it like a maimed bird. The three oldest brothers swore never to allow their mother's name to cross their lips as long as they lived — not even if she wrote and begged their forgiveness, or became ill. They worked hard, and Johan spoke continually of passage costs and departure dates. And Bernard began to dream. He dreamed he was sitting beside his mother on the piano bench, both of them dressed for his father's funeral service. Suddenly she rose from the bench and gripped his arm. "Come with me," she cried, "into the piano where it's safe." Bernard looked out the window. At the door and all the windows of the house stood a hundred men in fine suits, knocking politely. He bit his mother's hand, but she kept her grip, drawing him to her and into the open piano. The lid came down, suffocating . . .

After school Bernard sometimes went to the station to listen to the porter, who was still elaborating on Gittel's departure: how she looked, how the three little boys clung about her asking, "Will there be an acrobat there? Will there be a fat lady and a thin man? Will they cut somebody in half and make him come out whole?" Every day the story got longer. The porter got better tips, and his tongue lightened as if it were a balance scale tipping in one direction. "Terrible circles under her eyes," he said. "And the children: I swear the youngest knew it was for more than three days —"

Such stories the Gittel could tell you — about strangers in town, or what happened to the neighbors yesterday, or a terrifying dream that would haunt you for weeks, as if you yourself had dreamed it. But when it came to newspapers, she was a fool. Thank God that's not the case with Rachel, although from the look on her face sometimes, and the news of the world, I think:

"What's the difference?" She will argue with me about Gittel, too, but newspapers or not, Gittel wasn't thinking about current events. She was sleepwalking, imagining the lovely carpets, the curved staircase, her mother coming down the hall to greet her, her father sitting down to chat with a student.

I should stop the story here. For one thing, Rachel's bus gets in any minute, and the way she walks, she'll be here before I can clear the table of these papers. . . . But I remember how it used to drive me crazy when Papa began to describe the tiniest details of Gittel's traveling dress and people and things he had never seen. He could never get to the end of the story. *Next time,* he'd say, and next time he'd start all over at the beginning, lingering until Mother called us in to supper. Some habits are hard to break, he used to say.

On the train Gittel took her children into an empty compartment, but you know how it is; someone always comes to interrupt your dreams. This time it is an elderly gentleman, the first German she's seen since she got on in Riga. During the first hour of the ride nobody speaks. The children keep their heads lowered, once in a while glancing up at the stranger, who is smart and alternates his gaze between the countryside and his own shoes. You know how the eye roams when you're traveling. Maybe at this moment my own daughter is sitting in the window seat of a bus, a stranger beside her. Any minute he could turn and look at her face and say, "Going home?" The stranger in Gittel's compartment is polite, and Gittel is busy telling her children about magic shows and lace curtains and hot potato kugel. "Grandpa and Grandma have moved," she says, "but I'll take you to look at the old house. She'll have a lunch for us, too. A hot lunch."

She has a nice voice, thinks the stranger. He lets his eye rest on a piece of hand luggage at her feet, and suddenly, coming awake, he sees the name *Shapiro.* He turns pale and leans forward.

"Frau Shapiro?"

She looks at him, startled, and the children hide their faces in her coat.

So much goes through the stranger's mind when he sees the face of the Gittel: a face that cannot shed its innocence, even

when the eyes in it look out the compartment window at the
new red and black flags in the station windows — seen quickly,
because the train goes so fast. The stranger holds out his hand.

"I knew a Shapiro at university," he says. "I am proud to say.
I am proud."

He holds her hand too long; he won't let it go even when the
conductor comes into the compartment and says: "Passports,
please." Her eyes grow dark with surprise.

"Excuse me, please," she says, pulling her hand away, reaching into her bag for her passport.

"Wait," he says.

But Gittel, with a nervous laugh, has handed hers over. She
doesn't change expression when the conductor takes a long look
at it and says: "You will report to the Bureau of Immigration as
soon as you arrive. Your passport needs changes."

The conductor is gone. The stranger wants to tell her something, but her face speaks to him like marble, like a desert statue
that knows either everything or nothing.

What can he do but ask her where she is going, keep her in
conversation until the train comes into the station? So he asks,
and she begins a story. A story about a lovely house, a mahogany
mantel, a fireplace, a smoking chimney, a girl who is coming at
this moment through the front door, having for once remembered her key; a girl capable, after all, of surprising her mother.

JANE SMILEY

Lily

(FROM THE ATLANTIC MONTHLY)

CAREERING TOWARD Lily Stith in a green Ford Torino were Kevin and Nancy Humboldt. Once more they gave up trying to talk reasonably; once more they sighed simultaneous but unsympathetic sighs; once more each resolved to stare only at the unrolling highway.

At the same moment, Lily was squeezing her mop into her bucket. Then she straightened up and looked out the window, eager for their arrival. She hadn't seen them in two years, not since having won a prestigious prize for her poems.

She was remarkably well made, with golden skin, lit by the late-afternoon sun, delicately defined muscles swelling over slender bones, a cloud of dark hair, a hollow at the base of her neck for some jewel. She was so beautiful that you could not help attributing to her all of your favorite virtues. To Lily her beauty seemed a senseless thing, since it gained her nothing in the way of passion, release, kinship, or intimacy. Now she was looking forward, with resolve, to making the Humboldts confess really and truly what was wrong with her — why, in fact, no one was in love with her.

A few minutes later they pulled up to the curb. Nancy climbed the apartment steps bearing presents — a jar of dill pickles she had made herself, pictures of common friends, a cap knitted of rainbow colors for the winter. Lily put it on in spite of the heat. The rich colors Nancy had chosen lit up Lily's tanned face and flashing teeth. Almost involuntarily Nancy exclaimed, "You look better than ever!" Lily laughed and said, "But look at you! Your

hair is below your hips now!" Nancy pirouetted and went inside
before Kevin came up. He, too, looked remarkable, Lily
thought, with his forty-eight-inch chest on his five-foot-nine-
inch frame. Because of Nancy's hair and Kevin's chest, Lily
always treasured the Humboldts more than she did her current
friends. Kevin kissed her cheek, but he was trying to imagine
where Nancy had gone; his eyes slid instantly past Lily. He
patted her twice on the shoulder. She cried, "I've been looking
for you since noon!" He said, "I always forget how far it is across
Ohio," and stepped into the house.

That it had been two years — two years! — grew to fill the
room like a thousand balloons, pinning them in the first seats
they chose and forbidding conversation. Lily offered some food,
some drink. They groaned, thinking of all they had eaten on
the road (not convivially but bitterly, snatching, biting, swallow-
ing too soon). Lily, assuming they knew what they wanted, did
not ask again. Immediately Kevin's hands began to fidget for a
glass to jiggle and balance and peer into, to turn slowly on his
knee. Two years! Two days! Had they really agreed to a two-
day visit?

Although the apartment was neat and airy, the carpet vacuumed and the furniture polished, Lily apologized for a bowl
and a plate unwashed beside the sink. Actually, she often wondered whether cleanliness drove love away. Like many fastidi-
ous people, she suspected that life itself was to be found in dirt
and disorder, in unknown dark substances that she was hesitant
to touch. Lily overestimated her neatness in this case. The win-
dowsills, for example, had not been vacuumed, and the leaves
of the plants were covered with dust. She began to apologize for
the lack of air-conditioning, the noise of cars and trucks through
the open windows, the weather, the lack of air-conditioning
again; then she breathed a profound sigh and let her hands
drop limply between her knees.

Nancy Humboldt was moved by this gesture to remember
how Lily always had a touch of the tragic about her. It was
unrelated to anything that had ever happened, but it was dis-
tinct, always present. Nancy sat forward and smiled affection-
ately at her friend. Conversation began to pick up.

After a while they ate. Lily noticed that when Kevin carried his chest toward Nancy, Nancy made herself concave as she sidestepped him. Perhaps he did not exactly try to touch her; the kitchenette was very small. Jokes were much in demand, greeted with pouncing hilarity; a certain warmth, reminiscent of their early friendship, flickered and established itself. Conversation ranged over a number of topics. Nancy kept using the phrase "swept away." "That movie just swept me away!" "I live to be swept away!" "I used to be much more cautious than I am now; now I just want to be swept away!" Kevin as often used the word "careful." "I think you have to be really careful about your decisions." "I'm much more careful now." "I think I made mistakes because I wasn't careful." Lily listened most of the time. When the discussion became awkwardly heated, they leaped as one flesh on Lily and demanded to know about her prizewinning volume, her success, her work. Nancy wanted to hear some new pieces.

Lily was used to reading. Finishing the fourth poem, she wondered, as she often did, why men did not come up to her after readings and offer love, or at least ask her out. She had won a famous prize. With the intimacy of art she phrased things that she would not ordinarily admit to, discussed her soul, which seemed a perfectly natural and even attractive soul. People liked her work: they had bought more copies of her prizewinning volume than of any other in the thirteen-year series. But no one, in a fan letter, sent a picture or a telephone number. Didn't art or accomplishment make a difference? Was it all invisible? Lily said, "I think Kevin was bored."

"Not at all, really,"

"I wasn't in the slightest," Nancy said. "They're very good. They don't have any leaves on them." Nancy grinned. She rather liked the occasional image herself.

Now was the time to broach her subject, thought Lily. The Humboldts had known her since college. Perhaps they had seen some little thing, spoken of it between themselves, predicted spinsterhood. Lily straightened the yellow pages and set them on the side table. "You know," she said with a laugh and a cough, "I haven't gone out in a month and a half. I mean, I realize it's summer and all, but anyway. And the last guy was just a friend, really, I —" She looked up and went on. "All those years with Ken, nobody even made a pass at me in a bus station. I didn't think it was important then, but now I've gotten rather anxious."

Kevin Humboldt looked straight at her, speculating. Yes, it must be the eyes. They were huge, hugely lashed, set into huge sockets. They were far more expressive and defenseless than anything else about her. The contrast was disconcerting. And the lids came down over them so opaquely, even when she blinked but especially when she lowered her gaze, that you were frightened into changing any movement toward her into some idle this or that. Guys he'd known in college had admired her from a distance and then dated plainer women with more predictable surfaces.

"Do you ever hear from Ken?" Nancy asked.

"I changed my number and didn't give him the new one. I think he got the message."

"I'll never understand why you spent —"

"Nine years involved with a married man, blah blah blah. I know."

"Among other things."

"When we were breaking up, I made up a lot of reasons, but now I remember what it was like before we met. It was just like it is now." Kevin thought of interrupting with his observation. He didn't.

"Everyone has dateless spells, honey," said Nancy, who'd had her first dateless spell after her marriage to Kevin. She had always attributed to Lily virginal devotion to her work. Nancy thought a famous prize certainly equaled a husband and three children. Love was like any activity, you had to put in the hours, but as usual Kevin was right there, so she didn't say this and shifted with annoyance in her chair. "Really," she snapped, "don't worry about it."

Kevin's jaws widened in an enormous yawn. Lily jumped up to find clean towels, saying "Does it seem odd to you?" Kevin went into the bathroom and Nancy went into the bedroom with her suitcase. Lily followed her. "I have no way of knowing," she went on, but then she stopped. Nancy wasn't really listening.

In the morning Nancy braided and wound up her hair while Lily made breakfast. Kevin was still asleep. Nancy had always had long, lovely hair, but Lily couldn't remember her taking such pride in it as she was now, twisting and arranging it with broad, almost conceited motions. She fondled it, put it here and there, spoke about things she liked to do with it from time to time. She obviously cherished it. "You've kept it in wonderful shape," Lily said.

"My hair is my glory," Nancy replied, and sat down to her eggs. She was not kidding.

When Kevin staggered from bedroom to bathroom an hour later, Nancy had gone out to survey the local shops. Kevin looked for her in every room of the apartment and then said, "Nancy's not here?"

"She thought she'd have a look around."

Kevin dropped into his seat at the table and put his head in his arms. A second later he exclaimed, "Oh, God!" Lily liked Kevin better this visit than she had before. His chest, which had always dragged him aggressively into situations, seemed to have lost some of its influence. He was not as loud or blindingly self-confident as he had been playing football, sitting in the first row in class, barreling through business school, swimming two miles every day. Thus it was with sympathy rather than astonishment that Lily realized he was weeping. He wiped his eyes on his T-shirt. "She's going to leave me! When we get back to Vancouver, she's going to leave me for another guy!"

"Is that what she said?"

"I know."

"Did she say so?"

"I know."

"Look, sit up a second and have this piece of toast."

"He's just a dumb cowboy. I know she's sleeping with him."

She put food in front of him and he began to eat it. After a few bites, though, he pushed it away and put his head down. He moaned into the cave of his arms. Lily said,

"What?"

"She won't sleep with me. She hasn't since Thanksgiving. She never says where she's going or when she'll be back. She can't stand me checking up on her."

"Do you check up on her?"

"I call her at work sometimes. I just want to talk to her. She never wants to talk to me. I miss her!"

"What do Roger and Fred say?" Roger and Fred were friends
from college who also lived in Vancouver.

"They don't understand."

Lily nodded. Unlike Lily, Roger and Fred had wavered
in their fondness for Nancy. Many times she had been selfish about certain things, which were perhaps purely femi-
nine things. She thought people should come to the table
when dinner was hot in spite of just-opened beers and half-
smoked cigarettes or repair projects in the driveway. She
had screamed, really screamed, about booted feet on her
polished table. Roger and Fred especially found her too punc-
tilious about manners, found her slightly shrill, and did not
appreciate her sly wit or her generosity with food and lodg-
ing and presents (this liberality they attributed to Kevin,
who was, simultaneously, a known tightwad). And they overlooked her capacity for work — willing, organized, unsnob-
bish bringing home of the bacon while all the men were
looking for careers and worrying about compromising themselves. Lily and Kevin at least agreed that Nancy was a valuable
article.

"Okay," Lily said, "who's just a dumb cowboy?"

"His name is Hobbs Nolan. She met him at a cross-country ski
clinic last year. But he's not really outdoorsy or athletic; he just
wears these pointy-toed cowboy boots and flannel cowboy shirts.
Out there guys like him are a dime a dozen. . . ."

"You know him?"

"I've seen him. He knows people we know. They think he's a
real jerk."

"You blame him for all of this, then?"

Kevin glanced at her and said, "No." After a moment he
exclaimed "Oh, God!" again, and dropped his head on his arms.
His hair grazed the butter dish, and Lily was suddenly repelled
by these confidences. She turned and looked out the window,
but Nancy was nowhere in sight. The freshness of the morning
was gone, and the early blue sky had whitened. She looked at
her watch. It was about ten-thirty. Any other morning she
would already have sat down to her work with an apple and a
cup of tea, or she would be strolling into town with her list of
errands. She glanced toward the bedroom. The blanket was half

off the bed and a corner of the contour sheet had popped off the mattress. Nancy's and Kevin's clothes were piled on the floor. They had left other items in the living room or the kitchen: Nancy's brush, a scarf, Kevin's running shoes and socks, two or three pieces of paper from Nancy's purse, the map on which they had traced their route. But hadn't she expected and desired such intimacy? He sat up. She smiled and said, "You know, you're the first people to spend the night here in ages. I'd forgotten —"

"I don't think you should worry about that. Like Nancy said, we all go through dry spells. Look at me, my —"

"Oh, that! I wasn't referring to that."

"My whole life was a dry spell before Nancy came along."

Lily sat back and looked at Kevin. He was sighing. "Hey," she said, "you're going to have a lot better luck if you lighten up a little."

"I know that, but I can't." He sounded petulant.

Lily said, "Well —"

"Well, now I'd better go running before it gets too hot." Kevin reached for his shoes and socks. But Nancy walked in and he sat up without putting them on. Nancy displayed her packages. "There was a great sale on halter tops, and look at this darling T-shirt!" She pulled out an example of the T-shirt Lily had seen on everyone all summer. It said, "If you live a good life, go to church, and say your prayers, when you die you will go to OHIO." Lily smiled. Nancy tossed the T-shirt over to Kevin, saying, "Extra extra large. I'm sure it will fit."

He held it up and looked at it and then said, glumly, "Thanks."

"Are you going for your run now?"

"Yeah."

But he didn't make a move. Everyone sat very still for a long time, maybe five minutes, and then Lily began clearing plates off the table and Nancy began to take down her hair and put it back up again. Kevin seemed to root himself in the chair. His face was impassive. Nancy glared at him, but finally sighed and said, "I got a long letter from Betty Stern not so long ago. She stopped working on her Chinese dissertation and went to business school last year."

"I heard that Harry got a job, but that it was in Newfoundland or someplace like that," Lily said.

"Who'd you hear that from?" Refusing even to look in Kevin's direction, Nancy combed her hair.

"Remember Meredith Lawlor? Did you know she was here? She's teaching in the pharmacy school here in Columbus. She raises all these poisonous tropical plants in a big greenhouse she and her husband built out in the country."

"Who's her husband?"

"She met him in graduate school, I think. He's from Arizona."

"I'd like to raise plants for a living. I don't know necessarily about poisonous ones." Nancy glanced at Kevin. Lily noticed that she had simply dropped her packages by her chair, that tissue paper and sales slips and the halter tops themselves were in danger of being stepped on. In college they had teased Nancy relentlessly about her disorderly ways, but Lily hadn't found them especially annoying then. Kevin said, "Why don't you pick that stuff up before you step on it?"

"I'm not going to step on it!"

"Well, pick it up anyway. I doubt that Lily wants your mess all over her place."

"Who are you to speak for Lily?"

"I'm speaking for society in general, in this case."

"Why don't you go running, for God's sake?"

"I'd rather not have a heart attack in the heat, thank you."

"Well, it's not actually that hot. It's not as hot as it was yesterday, and you ran seven miles."

"It's hot in here."

"Well, there's a nice breeze outside, and this town is very shady. When you get back we can have lunch after your shower. We can have that smoked turkey we got at the store last night. I still have some of the bread I made the day we left."

Kevin looked at her suspiciously, but all he said finally was, "Well, pick up that stuff, okay?"

Nancy smiled. "Okay."

Still Kevin was reluctant to go, tying his shoes with painful slowness, drinking a glass of water after letting the tap run and run, retying one of his shoes, tucking and untucking his shirt. He closed the door laboriously behind him, and Nancy watched out the window for him to appear on the street. When he did, she inhaled with sharp, exasperated relief. "Christ!" she exclaimed.

"He doesn't seem very happy."

"But you know he's always been into that self-dramatization. I'm not impressed. I used to be, but I'm not anymore."

Lily wondered how she was going to make it to lunch, and then through the afternoon to dinner and bedtime. Nancy turned toward her. "I shouldn't have let all these men talk to you before I did."

"What men?"

"Kevin, Roger, Fred."

"I haven't talked to Roger or Fred since late last winter, at least."

"They think I ought to be shot. But they really infuriate me. Do you know what sharing a house with Roger was like? He has the most rigid routine I have ever seen, and he drives everywhere, even to the quick shop at the end of the block. I mean, he would get in his car and drive out the driveway and then four houses down to pick up the morning paper. And every time he did the dishes, he broke something we got from our wedding, and then he would refuse to pay for it because we had gotten it for free anyway."

"Fred always said that being friends with Roger showed you could be friends with anyone."

"Fred and I get along, but in a way I think he's more disapproving than Roger is. Sometimes he acts as if I've shocked him so much that he can't bear to look at me."

"So how have you shocked him?"

"Didn't Kevin tell you about Hobbs Nolan?"

"He mentioned him."

"But Hobbs isn't the real issue, as far as I'm concerned. Men always think that other men are the real issue. You know, Roger actually sat me down one night and started to tell me off?"

"What's the real issue?"

"Well, one thing I can't bear is having to always report in whenever I go somewhere. I mean, I get in the car to go for groceries, and if I decide while I'm out to go to the mall, he expects me to call and tell him. Or if I have to work even a half hour late, or if the girl I work with and I decide to go out for a beer after work. I hate it. I hate picking up the goddamned telephone and dialing all the numbers. I hate listening to it ring, and most of all I hate that automatic self-justification you just slide into. I mean, I don't even know how to sound honest anymore, even when I'm being honest."

"Are you —"

"No, most of all I hate the image I have of Kevin the whole time I'm talking to him, sitting home all weekend with nothing to do, whining into the phone."

"I think Kevin is mostly upset because you don't sleep with him."

"Well —"

"I really don't see how you can cut him off like that."

"Neither does he."

"Why do you?"

"Don't you think he's strange-looking? And everything he does in bed simply repels me. It didn't used to but now it does. I can't help it. He doesn't know how big or strong he is and he's always hurting me. When I see him move toward me, I wince. I know he's going to step on me or poke me or bump into me."

"Well, you could go to a therapist. You ought to at least reassure Kevin that you're not sleeping with this other guy."

"We did go to a therapist, and he got so nervous he was even more clumsy, and I am sleeping with Hobbs."

"Nancy!"

"Why are you surprised? How can this be a reason for surprise? I'm a sexual person. Kevin always said that he thought I was promiscuous until I started with him, and then he just thought that I was healthy and instinctive."

"Well, Nancy —"

"I have a feeling you aren't very approving either."

"I don't know, I —"

"But that's all I want. I realized on the way here that all the time I've known you I've wanted you to approve of me. Not just to like me, or even respect me, but to approve of me. I still like being married to Kevin, but all of us should know by now that the best person for being married to isn't always the best person for sleeping with, and there's no reason why he should be." She glanced out the window. "Anyway, here he comes." A moment later the door slammed open. Lily thought Kevin was angry, until she realized that he had simply misjudged the weight of the door. Sweat was pouring off him, actually dripping on the carpet. Nancy said, "Jesus! Go take a shower." Lily wanted to tell him not to drip over the coffee table, with its bowl of fruit, but said nothing. He looked at them with studied ingenuousness and said, "Four miles in twenty-five minutes. Not bad, huh? And it's ninety-three. I just ran past the bank clock."

"Great." Nancy turned back to Lily and said, "Maybe I should try to call Meredith Lawlor while I'm here. We were pretty good friends junior year. I've often thought about her, actually." Kevin tromped into the bathroom.

Washing lettuce for the sandwiches, Lily watched Nancy slice the turkey. It was remarkable, after all, how the other woman's most trivial mannerisms continued to be perfectly familiar to her after two years, after not thinking about Nancy or their times together for days and even weeks at a stretch. It was as if the repeated movement of an arm through the air or the repeated cocking of a head could engrave itself willy-nilly on her brain, and her brain, recognizing what was already contained in it, would always respond with warmth. In fact, although she did feel this burr of disapproval toward Nancy, and sympathy for Kevin, Kevin's presence was oppressive and Nancy's congenial. Nancy got out the bread she had made, a heavy, crumbly, whole-grain production, and they stacked vegetables and meat on the slices and slathered them with mustard and catsup. The shower in the bathroom went off and Nancy sighed. Lily wondered if she heard herself.

Lily remembered that the kitchen workers in the college cafeteria had always teased Kevin about his appetite. Certainly he still ate with noise and single-minded gusto. His lettuce crunched, his bread fell apart, pieces of tomato dropped on his plate and he wiped them up with more bread. He drank milk. Lily tried to imagine him at work. Fifteen months before, he had graduated from business school near the top of his class and had taken a risky job with a small company. The owner was impressed with his confidence and imagination. In a year he'd

gotten four raises, all of them substantial. Lily imagined him in
a group of men, serious, athletic, well-dressed, subtly dominat-
ing. Was it merely Nancy's conversation about him that made
him seem to eat so foolishly, so dependently, with such naked
anxiety? To *be* so foolish, so dependent? When he was finished,
Nancy asked him whether he was still hungry and said to Lily,
"Isn't this good bread? I made up the recipe myself."

"It's delicious."

"I think so. I've thought of baking bread for the healthfood
store near us. In fact, they asked me to, but I'm not sure it would
be very profitable."

"It's nice that they asked you."

"A couple of guys there really like it."

Kevin scowled. Lily wondered if one of these guys was Hobbs
Nolan. Nancy went on, "I make another kind, too, an herb
bread with dill and chives and tarragon."

"That sounds good."

"It is."

Lily was rather taken aback at Nancy's immodesty. This exchange, more than previous ones, seemed to draw her into the
Humboldts' marriage and to implicate her in its fate. She felt a
brief sharp relief that they would be gone soon. She finished
her sandwich and stood up to get an apple. It was before one
o'clock. More stuff — the towel Kevin had used on his hair,
Nancy's sandals, Nancy's other hairbrush — was distributed
around the living room. Lily had spent an especially solitary
summer, with no summer school to teach and many of her
friends away, particularly since the first of August. Some days
the only people she spoke to were checkers at the grocery store
or librarians. Her fixation on the Humboldts' possessions was a
symptom that her solitary life certainly was unhealthy, that she
was, after all, turning back into a virgin, as she feared. It was
true that her apartment never looked "lived in" and that she
preferred it that way. Suddenly she was envious of them; in
spite of their suspicions and resentments their life together had
a kind of chaotic richness. Their minds were full of each other.
Just then Kevin said, with annoyance, "Damn!" and Nancy
shrugged, perfectly taking his meaning.

"There's a great swimming pool here," Lily said. "I've spent

practically the whole summer there. You must have brought
your suits?"

Kevin had been diving off the high board steadily for at least
forty-five minutes. At first, when Nancy and Lily had been talking about Kenneth Diamond and Lily's efforts to end that long
relationship, Nancy had only glanced at Kevin from time to
time. Lily remarked that she had slept with Ken fewer than
twenty times in nine years. Nancy stared at her — not in disbelief but as if seeking to know the unfathomable. Then, for four
dives, Nancy did not take her eyes off Kevin. He did a backwards double somersault, tucked; a forward one-and-a-half layout; a forward one-and-a-half in pike position; and a double
somersault with a half-gainer, which was astonishingly graceful.
"I knew he dove in high school," she said, "but I've never seen
this." A plump adolescent girl did a swan dive and Kevin
stepped onto the board again. Other people looked up, including two of the lifeguards. Perhaps he was unaware that people
were looking at him. At any rate, he was straightforward and
undramatic about stepping into his dive. The board seemed to
bend in two under his muscular weight and then to fling him
toward the blue sky. He attempted a forward two-and-a-half,
tuck position, but failed to untuck completely before entering
the water. In a moment he was hoisting himself out and heading
for the board to try again. Nancy said, "It's amazing how sexy
he looks from a distance. All the pieces seem to fit together
better. And he really is a good diver. I can't believe he hasn't
practiced in all these years."

"Maybe he has."

"Maybe. I mean he looks perfect, and no older than twenty-
one. That's how old he was when we first met — twenty-one.
I was dating Sandy Ritter. And you were dating Murray
Freed."

"I could have done worse than stick with Murray Freed. But
he was so evasive that when Ken approached me in a grown-up,
forthright way, I just gave up on Murray. He's got a little graph-
ics company in Santa Barbara, and I hear he spends two or three
months of the year living on the beach in Big Sur."

"Well, don't worry about it. I've always thought leisure and beauty were rather overrated, myself." She grinned. "But look at him! He did it! That one was nearly perfect, toes pointed and everything."

"I guess I'm sort of surprised that you think he's funny-look-ing. Everybody always thought he was good-looking in college."

"Did they? It's hard to remember what he looks like, even when I'm looking at him. I mean, I know what he looks like, but I don't know what I think about it. This diving sort of turns me on, if you can believe that."

"Really?" But Lily realized that she was vulnerable, too, and when Kevin came over, dripping and fit, toweling his hair and shoulders with Lily's own lavender towel, his smile seemed very white, his skin very rosy, and his presence rather welcome.

Actually, it was apparent that they all felt better. Lily had swum nearly half a mile, and Nancy had cooled off without getting her hair wet. Kevin was pleased with the dives he had accomplished and with Nancy's obvious admiration. All three of them had an appetite, and it was just the right time to begin planning a meal. "This is a nice park," Kevin said. "The trees are huge."

"We should get steak," Nancy said.

In the bedroom, putting on her clothes, Lily smiled to hear Nancy's laugh followed by a laugh from Kevin. Really, he was a good-humored sort of person, who laughed frequently. Al-though she could not have said how the visit had failed that morning, or why it was succeeding right then, she did sense their time filling up with possibilities of things they could do together. She heard Nancy say, "I think the coals must be ready by now," and the slam of the door. She pulled a cotton sweater over her head and went into the kitchen thinking fondly of the Humboldts' driving away the next morning with smiles on their faces and reconciliation in their hearts. She hadn't done any-thing, really, but something had done the trick. Kevin was sit-ting at the table wrapping onions and potatoes in foil. Lily opened the refrigerator and took out a large stalk of broccoli, which she began to slice for steaming. Kevin had put on a light-blue tailored shirt and creased corduroy slacks. His wet hair was combed back and he had shaved. He said, "Why did you stick with Diamond all those years? I mean" — he looked at her cautiously — "wasn't it obvious that you weren't going to get anything out of it?"

"I got a lot out of it. Ken's problem is that nobody thinks he's anything special but me. I do think he's quite special, though, and I think I got a good education, lots of attention, lots of affection, and lots of time to work. It wasn't what I expected but it wasn't so bad, though I wish there had been some way to practice having another type of relationship, or even just having dates."

"What did he think about your winning the prize?"

"I don't know. I broke up with him right after I applied for it, and I didn't read the letter he sent after I got it."

"Last night, when you were talking —" But the door opened and Nancy swept in. "The coals are perfect! Are these the steaks in here? I'm famished! Guess what? I got three big ears of corn from your neighbor, who was out in his garden. He's cute and about our age. What's his name? He was funny, and awfully nice to me."

"I've never even spoken to the guy," Lily said.

"What do you do? Cross the street when you see an attractive man?" Nancy teased.

"It's not that. It's that some curse renders me invisible. But Kevin was about to say something."

He shrugged.

"Put on you by Professor Kenneth Diamond, no doubt," Nancy said. She handed a potato back to Kevin. "Do that one better. The skin shows. Seriously, Lily" — Kevin took the potato back with a careful, restrained gesture — "you can't keep this up. It's impossible. You're the most beautiful woman anyone we know knows. You have to at least act like you're interested. I'm sure you act like you wouldn't go on a date for a million dollars. You don't prostitute yourself simply by being friendly." Kevin rewrapped the potato and handed it back to Nancy. Then he smiled at Lily and she had a brief feeling that something dramatic and terrible had been averted, although she couldn't say what it was. Nancy ripped the paper off the rib eyes and dropped it on the table.

•

The wine was nearly finished. Kevin had chosen it, a California red that he'd tried in Vancouver. He kept saying, "I was lucky to find this so far east. That isn't a bad liquor store, really." Lily hadn't especially liked it at first because of its harsh flavor and thick consistency, but after three glasses she was sorry to see the second bottle close to empty. She set it carefully upright in the grass. There was a mystery to its flavor that made her keep wanting to try it again. Nancy was talking about the play she had been in, as the second lead, with a small theater group in Vancouver. She had loved everything about it, she said. "The applause most of all," Kevin said, smiling. "She got a lot of it, too. The third night, she got more than anyone in the cast. She was pretty funny."

"I was very funny."

"Yes, you were very funny."

Nancy lay back on the chaise longue. "The director said that he thought I should take acting classes at the university. They have a very good program. I had never acted before, and they gave me the second lead. You know, there are tons of professional actors in Vancouver."

"It wasn't exactly a professional show. Only the two leads were getting paid, and the guy wasn't even an Equity actor," Kevin said.

"I know that."

Lily took a deep breath. Neither Kevin nor Nancy had changed position in the past five minutes. Both were still leaning back, gazing into the tops of the tress or at the stars, but their voices were beginning to rise. She said, "It must be lovely to live in Vancouver." She thought of it vividly, as if for the first time: thick vegetation, brilliant flowers, dazzling peaks, lots to eat and do, the kind of paradise teaching would probably never take her to.

"It's expensive," Nancy said. "And I've found the people very self-satisfied."

"I don't think that's true," Kevin said.

"I know you don't. Kevin likes it there just fine. But the university is good, and they send acting students off to places like Yale and England and New York City all the time."

"By the time you could get into acting school, you would be

thirty-one at the very least." Kevin had sat up now, but casually. He poured the last of the mysterious-tasting wine into his glass.

"How do you figure that?"

"Well, frankly, I don't see how you can quit working for another two years, until I get established." He looked at the wine in the glass and gulped it down. "And maybe thirty-one is a little old to start training for a profession where people begin looking for work before they're out of their teens. And what about having kids? You can't very well have any kids while you're going to school full time. That play had you going eighteen hours a day some days. Which is not to say that it wasn't worth it, but I don't know that you would even want to do it six or eight times a year."

Nancy was breathing hard. Lily leaned forward, alarmed that she hadn't averted this argument, and put her hand on Nancy's arm. Nancy shook it off. "Kids! Who's talking about kids? I'm talking about taking some courses in what I like to do and what some people think I'm good at doing. The whole time I was in that play you just acted like it was a game that I was playing. I have news for you —"

"It was a community-theater production! You weren't putting on Shakespeare or Chekhov, either. And it's not as if Bill Henry has directed in Toronto, much less in New York."

"He's done lights in New York! He did lights on *The Fantasticks!* And on *A Chorus Line!*"

"Big deal."

Nancy leaped to her feet. "I'll tell you something, mister. You owe it to me to put me through whatever school I want to go to, no matter what happens to our relationship or our marriage. I slaved in the purchasing department of that university for three years so that you could go to business school full time. I lived with those crummy friends of yours for four years so we could save on mortgage —"

Lily said, "Nancy —"

Kevin said, "What do you mean, 'no matter what happens to our relationship'? What do you mean by that?"

"You know perfectly well what I mean! Lily knows what I mean, too!"

Lily pressed herself deep into her chair, hoping that neither of them would address her, but Kevin turned to face her. In the darkness his deep-set eyes were nearly invisible, so that when he said, "What did she tell you?" Lily could not decide what would be the best reply to make. He stepped between her and Nancy and demanded, "What did she say?"

"I think you should ask her that."

"She won't tell me anything. You tell me." He took a step toward her. "You tell me whether she still loves me. I want to know that. That's all I want to know." The tone of his voice in the dark was earnest and nearly calm.

"That's between you and Nancy. Ask her. It's not my business."

"But you know. And I've asked her. She's said yes so many times to that question that it doesn't mean anything anymore. You tell me. Does she still love me?"

Lily tried to look around him at Nancy, but seeing the movement of her head, he shifted to block any communication between them. "Does she?"

"She hasn't told me anything."

"But you have your own opinion, don't you?"

"I can't see that that's significant in any way."

"Tell me what it is. Does she still love me?"

He seemed, with his chest, to be bearing down on her as she sat. She had lost all sense of where Nancy was, even whether she was still outside. Wherever she was, she was not coming to Lily's aid. Perhaps she too was waiting for Lily's opinion. Lily said, "No."

"No, what? Is that your opinion?"

Surely Nancy would have stepped in by now. "No, it doesn't seem to me that she loves you anymore." Lily broke into a sweat the moment she stopped speaking, a sweat of instant regret. Kevin stepped back and Lily saw that Nancy was behind him, still and silent on the chaise longue. "Oh, Lord," said Lily, standing up and taking her glass into the house.

The Humboldts stayed outside for a long time. Lily washed the dishes and got ready for bed; she was sitting on the cot in the guest room winding her clock when Nancy knocked on the door and came in. "We had a long talk," she said, "and things are all right."

"Did you —"

"I don't want to talk about it anymore. This may be the best thing. At least I feel that I've gotten some things off my chest. And I think we're going to leave very early in the morning, so I wish you wouldn't get up."

"But I —" Lily looked at Nancy for a moment, and then said, "Okay, I won't. Thanks for stopping."

"You can't mean that, but I'll write." She closed the door and Lily put her feet under the sheet. There were no sounds, and after a while she fell asleep. She awoke to a rhythmic knocking. She thought at first of the door, but remembered that Nancy had closed it firmly. Then she realized that the blows were against the wall beside her head. She tried to visualize the other room. It would be the bed, and they would be making love. She picked up her clock and turned it to catch light from the street. It was just after midnight. She had been asleep, although deeply, for only an hour. The knocking stopped and started again, and it was irregular enough to render sleep unlikely for the time being. She smoothed her sheet and blanket and slid farther into the bed. Even after her eyes had adjusted, the room was dark: the streetlight was ten yards down, and there was no moon. Nancy and Kevin's rhythmic banging was actually rather comforting, she thought. She lay quietly for a moment, and then sat up and turned on the light. She felt for her book under the bed. The banging stopped and did not start again, and Lily reached for the light switch, but as her hand touched it, Nancy cried out. She took her hand back and opened her book, and Nancy cried out again. Lily thought of the upstairs neighbor, whom she hadn't heard all evening, and hoped he wasn't in yet. The bed in the next room gave one hard bang against the wall, and Nancy cried out again. Lily grew annoyed at her lack of consideration, and then, inexplicably, alarmed. She put her feet on the floor. Once she had done that, she was afraid to do anything else. It was suddenly obvious to her that the cries had been cries of fear rather than of passion, and Lily was afraid to go out, afraid of what she might see in the next room. She thought of Nancy's comments about Kevin's strength, and of Nancy's carelessness about Kevin's feelings. She opened the door. Lights were on everywhere, shocking her, and the noise of some kind of tussle came from their bedroom. Lily crept around the door and peeked in. Kevin had his back to her and was poised with one knee on the bed. All the bedcovers were torn off the bed, and Nancy, who had just broken free, was backed against the window. She looked at Lily for a long second and then turned her head so that Lily could see that her hair had been jaggedly cut off. One side was almost to her shoulder, but the other side stopped at her earlobe. The skein of hair lay on the mattress. Lily recognized it now. Seeing Nancy's gaze travel past him, Kevin set down a pair of scissors, Lily's very own shears, that had been sitting on the shelf above the sewing machine. Lily said, "My God! What have you been doing?"

Looking for the first time at the hair on the bed, Nancy began to cry. Kevin bent down and retrieved his gym shorts from under the bed and stepped into them. He said to Lily rather than Nancy, "I'm going outside. I guess my shoes are in the living room."

Nancy sat on the bed beside the hair, looking at it. It was reddish and glossy, with the life of a healthy wild animal, an otter or a mink. Lily wished Nancy would say that she had been thinking of having it cut anyway, but she knew Nancy hadn't been. She thought of saying herself that Nancy could always grow it back, but that, too, was unlikely. Hair like that probably wouldn't grow again on a thirty-year-old head. Lily picked up the shears and put them back on the shelf above her sewing table and said, "You were making love?"

The door slammed. Nancy said, "Yes, actually. I wanted to. We decided to split up, earlier, outside," She looked at Lily. "And then when I got in bed I felt happy and free, and I just thought it would be nice."

"And Kevin?"

"He seemed fine! Relieved, even. We were lying there and he was holding me."

"I can't believe you —"

At once Nancy glared at her. "You can't? Why are you so judgmental? This whole day has been one long trial, with you the judge and me the defendant! What do you know, anyway? You've never even lived with anyone! You had this sterile thing with Kenneth Diamond that was more about editing manuscripts than screwing and then you tell my husband that I'm not in love with him anymore! Of course he was enraged. You did it! You hate tension, you hate conflict, so you cut it off, ended it. We could have gone on for years like this, and it wouldn't have been that bad!"

"I didn't say I knew anything. I never said I knew anything."

Nancy put her face in her hands and then looked up and said in a low voice, "What do I look like?"

"Terrible right now — it's very uneven. A good hairdresser can shape it, though. There's a lot of hair left." Nancy reached for her robe and put it on; she picked up the hair, held it for a moment, and then, with her usual practicality, still attractive, always attractive, dropped it into the wastebasket. She glanced around the room and said, "Well, let's clean up before he gets back, okay? And can you take me to the airport tomorrow?"

Lily nodded. They began to pick things up and put them gingerly away. When they had finished the bedroom, they turned out the light in there and began on the living room. It was difficult, Lily thought, to call it quits and go to bed. Kevin did not return. After a long silence Nancy said, "I don't suppose any of us are going to be friends after this." Lily shrugged, but really she didn't suppose so either. Nancy reached up and felt the ends of her hair, and said, "Ten years ago he wouldn't have done this to me."

Had it really been ten years that they'd all known each other? Lily looked around her apartment, virginal again, and she was frightened by it. She felt a sudden longing for Kevin so strong that it approached desire, not for Kevin as he was but for Kevin as he looked — self-confident, muscular, smart. Her throat closed over, as if she were about to cry. Across the room Nancy picked up one of her hairbrushes with a sigh — and she was, after all, uninjured, unmarked. Lily smiled and said, "Ten years ago he might have killed you."

SHARON SHEEHE STARK

The Johnstown Polka

(FROM WEST BRANCH)

FRANCINE COMES TO the doorway of the room where her husband is watching *Lie Detector* and rolling socks from the dark load.

"Let the holey ones set," she says. "I'll darn them later."

Ray does a clownish double-take. "Hey, don't *you* look snazzy!"

She is *not* snazzy and knows it. She'd drawn a quick red mouth and combed her hair, is all. She belongs to a group called the Friendly City Singers and tonight they are scheduled up at the rest home again. Good-natured to start with, Ray has been especially helpful since the wiremill shut down. Tonight when he's finished sorting the laundry, and once the kids are rough-housed and bedded down, he'll putz around with the fire company radio set. Francine is glad he signed on with the Jack-Be-Quicks. Other jobless guys keep busy with drinking or barking at their wives all day. "What are you staring at, hon?" asks Ray with a small, wavery smile.

"Nothing," she says. She would never mention the bubble of dullness that routinely drops between her and the faces of her family. She has to look hard then; they could just as well be vaguely familiar strangers she's hard put to place. Brenda and Karen were seven and five when she lost them and their father in the last flood. Her first husband's name was Frank. Frank and Francine, as if they'd been cut from the heart of the same gentle saint. They'd occupied the right half of a double on Saylor Street. Now this whole wave of new people: big Ray Tomachk with his flat nose and sweet, sleepy expressions. Two more daughters born of pregnancies so easy her body feels unused. The left half of a double on West McBride. She watches as four-year-old Dawn Marie claps Tara under the empty green plastic laundry basket. Tara, who is two, sparks and twinkles like a jarred lightning bug. Francine does not have bad dreams about these children. In their dimness and distance, they seem safe enough to her.

Out front her friend Cookie Cannini honks once. Francine dawdles several seconds longer in the archway. The subject on *Lie Detector* is about to have his polygraph read. "It embarrasses me," says Ray, "when F. Lee Bailey has to tell someone they're lying." Francine has a sudden clear picture of herself, haunting her own life, a ghost hanging around to spy on the folks who moved in. She hurries off seconds before the moment of truth.

She is about to open Cookie's car door when she looks back to see Ray bearing down on her, one kid ram-rod style under each arm. "You forgot to kiss us chickens goodbye," he is calling, in a voice close to tears.

Last year, at the firehouse Superbowl party, Cookie, trying to recruit Francine for the Friendly City Singers, delivered a little canned speech about "spreading the notes of hope and cheer among the less fortunate." "Less fortunate than me?" Francine said too loudly. "Why, I'd have to run a national hard-luck contest to find the poor buggers." They both went into hysterics, throwing the entire bar into embarrassed silence.

"I'm not crazy about performing up at the home," Cookie says now. "I mean no amount of songs about sunshine is liable to snap somebody out of being old."

"But don't people in the cheerin'-up business have to expect some hopeless cases?" Francine winks to show she's teasing.

"Hey, know that real *real* old one that spits in the the flower-pots? She watches you like a hawk, Francine. With them little beady eyes."

"Her and me, we got to gabbing some last time. She's a corker all right. Her name is Libby Quigg. Wears a badge that says Oldest Living Survivor. City Council had it made up just for her." Francine neglects to mention how much she is looking forward to seeing the old woman again.

"Oldest Living Survivor of what?"

"The eighteen ninety-nine flood. Didn't I tell you that?"

"Anymore you never tell me nothing, Francine."

It is February, the haggard month. The night is whitish and gummy. For the first time Francine notices how stingily lit downtown has become. She watches two delicate baubles of light pass one another on the shadowy hulk of Westmont Hill. All her life the quaint old cable cars, long obsolete, have been going up and down, up and down, keeping a kind of plodding rhythm nobody in Johnstown seemed willing to surrender. "You ever ride up the incline, Cook?"

"Nope, not a once in thirty-six years. Isn't that something?"

"New Yorkers probably don't go up on the Statue of Liberty either."

"His Nibs says it's the longest incline plane in the world." Cookie's pet name for her husband Carl is "His Nibs."

"Not the longest, the *steepest*. Hard to believe anybody born and raised in town would bollix up their facts regarding the incline."

"Well, pardon me, Francine Irene!"

Time has tuned their friendship so that it produces not the occasional large, crashing spat but rashes of itchy, picky eruptions. The two women go back a long way: as Cookie is fond of saying, they've been watching each other's perms grow out since grade school. And Francine has kept the acne pits from the years they were both broken out, both round-faced nobodies at Bishop Sweeney High. They wore their school jumpers on the long side and rarely tried to get away with knee socks or colored blouses. To describe the nondescript the yearbook staff resorted to such words as *quiet, pious* and *gentle*. The only activity listed under their pictures was Glee Club 3, 4.

At the rest home the Friendly City Singers set up in a stained and sagging lounge so overheated it smells like the presser room at the cleaners. Nobody would dare open a window because old people would gutter and die like candles in a draft. As a rule the singers do the sunshine songs plus "You Light Up My Life," "Singing in the Rain" and a medley of showtunes. Tonight it is from *Fiddler on the Roof,* about as close as you can get to a disaster musical.

She searches among faces which range from sound asleep,
through indifferent, through hostile, to almost aggressively vi-
vacious. She spots Libby Quigg in a folding chair against the
wall wearing rose-colored waffle-knit polyester pants and a
flower barrette. Flanked by two stout aides, she looks under
guard, as if she were some museum's very best piece. In the
middle of *Sunrise, Sunset,* their eyes meet and Libby Quigg
winks, making Francine feel the two of them are in cahoots.
Oddly pleased and discomfited at the same time, she glances
uncertainly toward Cookie, who flattens her final note into a
broad, companionable smile.

"You have lipstick on your tooth," Francine whispers.

Cookie swipes a wrist across her bridgework and then Aggie
Wojnoroski bounds out with the accordion, plants her feet far
apart and strikes up the lead-in to the *Johnstown Polka.* It is
something of a sign-off number and they can always get a handful of live-wires to do a few stomping turns around the room,
accompanied by a lot of clapping and whooping and some occasional grumbling about old fools.

Afterwards the home always provides light refreshments. Tonight there is a beverage and butter cookies on a Ping-Pong
table spread with a birthday cloth and matching paper napkins.
Francine takes two Lorna Doones and ladles purple Kool-Aid
for herself, then fills several other cups held out to her. One is
attached to Libby Quigg. "Don't yis know no snappy numbers?"
she asks.

Francine smiles. Next to the withered creature, she sees herself as benignly huge, floating, a balloon Petunia Pig. "Anybody's got a request, they can drop it in the suggestion box we
pass around." It has not escaped her how deftly Libby Quigg is
stuffing her pockets with free cookies.

The old woman squints, studying Francine. "Where do you
live anyways?"

"A little piece from here. Down closer to town."

She pokes Francine in the forearm and leans close. "We got
take-out here," she whispers.

"I don't see no lunch counter. Take-out what?"

"Only item we got. Oldtimers like me."

Francine stares down and Libby Quigg adds confidentially,

"As you say, Missy, ain't no picnic lookin' at them gummers all day." Then before Francine can reply, she whistles through two fingers and one of the heavy-set aides hustles over, buxom, open-faced, ruddily cheerful.

"Riley, this here lady's askin' after that there new program."

Riley thinks. "Oh, you mean our Foster Grandpersons' program. Well, now I can't imagine which of our many deserving residents we're talking about here," she teases, securing the sliding barrette.

Francine looks hard at the old woman, all bone and blue veins, bituminous eyes bright, her proud badge festooned with a faded blue ribbon: she might be first prize in an antique doll contest, the kind of doll too fragile to touch. "You'd let her go off with just — anybody?"

"Mercy, no. Not just anybody. Interested parties have to be screened and approved by our director."

"Just so's you're clean and keep a Christian tongue in your mouth."

"Libby," says Riley, "You're a piece of work."

As one of the heavy losers in what they now call Flood '77 Francine was, for a short time, famous. Lately, people shyly compliment her on how she's "come to terms" and call her a trooper. But what they perceive as tranquillity, Francine experiences as a sort of unpleasant limpness, her heart a slack muscle, as if after having delivered an outsized grief, it never quite snapped back and stubbornly holds, if not sorrow itself, then the soft shape of it. Fearing the worst always made the best moments better, pulled them snug and taut. Now that the worst has happened the world is at least a size too big, and she is loose in her skin, at-large in time.

Oddly enough — and Ray says it's the Slovenian peasant in her — the one thing she is afraid of is starving. Against this possibility, she is fortunate to have a part-time job, four mornings a week, at Kloiber's lingerie department. "Have you Kloibered today?" reads the Easy Grade billboard. The store smells of redskin peanuts and something faintly fishy Francine has convinced herself is a chemical they add to merchandise so you know it's cheap.

After a slow start the morning begins. Two elevators discharge a flutter of noisy women with smudged foreheads. Ash Wednesday services at St. John's has just let out. The women surround the tables where winter clearance items lie in soft, vaguely disreputable piles; they rummage without pushiness or hurry for there is plenty left this year. In mantillas and rayon babushkas they chat and laugh, hold pajama tops against the bosoms of strangers shaped similarly to mothers and daughters, making Francine recall almost happily why the town is called The Friendly City. This morning the voices carry a bright overlay of excitement. "What's going on?" Francine asks someone when she hears the name, Morley Safer, bobbing up out of the conversations again and again.

"Why, the *Sixty Minutes* crew is down setting up in the park. Mr. Safer wants us to stop down after bit, to get interviewed. And me dressed like a big bum!" The woman is wearing a black satin jacket that says Cambria County All Stars — 168 pounder. "My Stanley's wrastling coat. I sure wasn't planning on bumping into nobody famous."

Two women approach the check-out. One of them dumps an armload of large pink underpants on the counter, taps Francine delicately on the elbow. "Beg pardon, Miss, but isn't Gene Kelly a Johnstown boy?"

Francine says, "I always heard he comes from Pittsburgh, ma'am."

"I told you, Floss. That was his sister run the dance studio on Main Street." The second woman wears a tarnished pin spelling *Polski Power*.

"Well, Bea, then that leaves us with Carroll Baker and Johnny Weismueller."

"Strickly speaking," Francine interjects, "Weismueller's more from Windber — better check them pants for flaws, ma'am."

The soiled foreheads call to mind something Francine heard back in grade school, that removing the ashes was the same as wiping off the Savior's kiss. Thus warned, she kept adding coal ashes from the school boiler room. Now she doesn't go to church at all except maybe from time to time when Cookie gets it into her head to run down to St. Basil's for the guitar Mass. Lately Ray's been studying with a nice Jehovah's Witness couple

who started coming around about the time of the heaviest lay-
offs. They are living in the Last Days, Ray insists. The hard
times will give way to something called the New System. "This
is not your basic heaven thing," he is careful to point out. Then
he tries to explain how Francine can look forward to reunion
with *all* her loved ones in a place that sounds suspiciously to her
like the same old planet, the same old grubby milltown. "Now
what kind of goofball would sign up for a deal like that?" she'd
said, confusing him so he could not reply. But from some dim
fifties classroom inside her a hand shot up and a child's voice,
small but rushingly hopeful cried, *Me! Oh, me. Oh, I will!*

When the worst of the mid-morning rush is past and the
customers have started downstairs to pursue stardom in the
park, Francine sets aside a flannel nightgown reduced to $3.49
because she can picture Libby Quigg in it.

Francine is doing her food shopping in the supermarket section
of Kloiber Brothers where she has a choice of using her em-
ployee discount or double coupons. Tara rides in the cart while
Dawn Marie skips alongside. Earlier, out front, she caught a
glimpse of the morning's headlines in the window of the newspaper machine: IT'S OFFICIAL — JOHNSTOWN HOME OF NATION'S
HIGHEST UNEMPLOYMENT. The letters were inky and boastful and
made her very hungry.

It amazes her now to see what she's heaped into the cart
without thinking. Italian-cut veal, fresh scallops, grapes, persim-
mons, three kinds of Pop Tarts . . . and Tara tossing on top,
with joyful abandon, a half dozen Ring-Ding Juniors. Francine
lifts her out of the seat. She tries to stand her upright next to
Dawn Marie, at which point the child goes off like some hair-
trigger, fiendishly shrill alarm. She draws up her legs, making
herself a dead weight, as heavy as two small girls, three, four;
Francine feels she could snap from the weight of so many
youngsters hanging from her branches, and still they do not
reach the ground.

Weepy and confused, she phones Ray and he gets a neighbor
to run him over to Kloiber's. He takes the baby to the drugstore
for a Slurpy while Francine and Dawn Marie return everything
to the shelves but what she came for plus an econo-pak of

chicken legs on special. The Muzak system, which has been piping a seamless ribbon of old smoothies that makes her feel, annoyingly, like skating in the aisles, stops short, pauses and starts pumping out the *tompa, tompa, tompa* of the *Johnstown Polka*. Dawn Marie whirls around the cart in a dance that resembles someone stamping out small grass fires.

That night, Francine is kept awake by the thump of words and music in her head. *Let's play the Johnstown Polka, for the city with a will. Let's play the Johnstown Polka, the city that flood waters couldn't kill.* To keep the beat it is necessary to rush the words "flood waters" together. When Francine was a girl she always thought the song went, "the city that *Bud Walters* couldn't kill."

Back then, the last thing people worried over was another trial by water. Like smallpox and polio, floods were considered a threat of some dim and savage past, magnanimously vanquished by none other than FDR. After the flood in '36, it was Roosevelt that put the Army engineers to work on the river, and when they were through, he dedicated the handsome floodwalls himself. Francine always pictured a frail, fatherly figure scribing a benediction over darkish waters, while somewhere in the depths of the city set in a hole in the mountains skulked a gent named Bud Walters, wearing shiny brown waders and hatching plots.

"The floods were all different!" she says aloud, at 3:05 A.M., her voice glittery with discovery and indignation.

Ray comes noisily unstuck from sleep. "Wha' happened?"

"Those dumb old walls didn't mean a thing, Ray." She says this as if pointing up some hypocrisy he had personally to answer for. "Except for thirty-six the rivers never even got a chance to rise. In eighteen eighty-nine it was a busted dam wrecked up the place. In *my* flood it rained like crazy, water poured off the hills and the town filled up like a cup of filthy tea."

His large hand paws her breast in an ungainly measure of love and helplessness. Sometimes it's hard to remember this bear of a man is Cookie's little brother. "Let's move," he says thickly. "Want to go someplace where it's nice year round?"

A sudden vision of this proposed peaceable kingdom makes her unexpectedly queasy. "No!" she snaps, thinking at the same

time how she would never have left Frank Suttmiller either,
bullyish and mean-tempered as he got occasionally. Once he
whipped a safety razor at her, chipping her collar bone. It was
the toughknuckled stuff that held you. What the yearbook staff
said about Francine was, "She'll gently steal your heart away."
All that meant was nobody knew she was alive.

Sunday night. Rain drumming on the flat roof of the Jack-
Be-Quick firehouse. Ray has drawn bartending duty this weekend and Francine sits next to Cookie at the nearly deserted bar.
Francine's second wedding reception was held here and the first
one took place in a similar firehall out in Holsopple. The wed-
dings slosh together in a slather of French dressing, baked ziti
and spilt beer. Both times a rowdy bunch drove her and the
groom thrice around the block in the back of a screaming red
pumper. It is possible to believe she died in '77 and came back
as the same person. Of course she didn't marry Ray in white.
She wore instead something buff-colored borrowed from
Cookie. It was cut in a princess line with a bolero jacket, a little
slack across the bust.

Francine dips a pretzel in mustard and sits back, sipping Iron
City draft and waiting for *60 Minutes* to start. For some reason
it does not seem surprising to her that the show opens with a
profile shot of Miss Libby Quigg in a high-backed rocker.
Cookie is beside herself. "Look, it's that flood lady!" she cries.

"Trick photography," says His Nibs, explaining how it so happens you can see right through Miss Quigg's body to the dark
background shapes of smokestacks and mountains. The voice-
over identifies her briefly, calling her a living testimonial to
some high-sounding notion Francine doesn't quite follow. Then
polka music kicks in, the focus solidifies and Safer steps into
the picture, extends a courtly hand and asks Miss Quigg to
dance.

Cookie says, "I bet they had to cut out the part where she
spits in the fern." Francine has to laugh, especially when she
thinks how she'd just today arranged with the rest home director to take the spitting fool for one overnight. Why Francine
wants to do this she can't imagine.

Some people Francine does not know come on now relating

what Ray calls "heart-rendering tales." Then she sees the woman in the black satin jacket, looking sheepish as the camera zooms in on the sharp white wrestling figure over her breast. In the middle of a sentence she stops short, crossing her arms determinedly high. "Hey," she says almost crossly, "we have to live in our lives. Same as you, mister." Francine looks close but cannot tell if the ash smudge is still there.

There follows a sequence featuring Mayor Popp, hatless and fitlooking, as he strolls with Safer in a wind that makes a noise like bronchitis in the mike. "Darnedest thing, Morley," he says, letting on like the two of them are old friends. "The economic picture around here might look a little hairy, but son of a gun, that old crime rate keeps coming down. Johnstown's a darn safe place to live."

A swell of pride makes Francine feel bloated and foolish, so she says, "Son of a gun, Morley, Kloiber's Santa Claus got busted for shoplifting."

"Shhh," says Cookie. "Isn't that Ziggy and Joan Yuhas?"

The segment ends with Safer riding up on the incline, scarf whipping, his clean blade of commercial baritone paring them down to a moral, "this tough little Pennsylvania town the rest of us would do well to remember next time we're tempted to grumble about the weather or the price of bridge mix."

"Well, I think that was real nice," someone says at the break. "What the heck is bridge mix?" The next story is about a ring of frozen food hijackers working out of Shreveport.

"Oh, before I forget . . ." Cookie digs in her handbag. "I picked up these refund forms for you at the Shop 'N Save. A Bird's Eye Orientals and a Head & Shoulders."

"I don't have dandruff," says Francine, and Cookie looks crestfallen. Cookie likes to think they're twins. They should both have dandruff. Once she said, "Isn't Laverne and Shirley you and me all over again?"

Francine can't see this. They'd never pulled harebrained or scary stunts. The worst thing she remembers is the time they wrote "wash me" on the convent station wagon. In terms of Lucy and Ethel, they were more like Ethel and Ethel.

"I cut out some coupons for you," she says, "but didn't I go and forget them."

His Nibs never sits with the women but stands up by the TV
with Ray. The two of them crack-up over something, then Ray
comes down toward the women carrying the joke in his mouth.
It's for her, Francine. He will feed her fun and laughter and
drown out the sound of the rain.

So prim and subdued is Libby Quigg at supper that Francine
imagines the home has a policy of drugging its clients so they
don't act up when they're out. The children steal glances, grow
bolder. At last Libby Quigg looks up from her plate, fixing
Dawn Marie fiercely. "See here, Missy, once I was young as your
mum and not half so plain." When Francine passes the tossed
salad, she snaps, "I'd sooner have slaw." She takes three help-
ings of strawberry junket. Her greed and bad manners throw
the children into raptures of glee.

At bedtime, when she demands a Mr. Bubble bath, Ray helps
get her in and out of the tub, trying hard not to peek. Miss
Quigg's flesh looks like it's been steeping in brine for years; her
breasts melt away in drips and squiggles. Then Francine dresses
her in the Kloiber's nightgown and paints the horny yellow
fingernails with rainbow sparkles.

Later, sleeping next to Ray on the sofa bed, she dreams that
she is walking down the aisle of a trolley as it approaches her
street. Unaccountably, the contents of her pocketbook begin to
fall on the floor. As quickly as she can recover things — a button, a spatula, a chalkware chicken — others drop out. She pur-
sues marbles and jawbreakers under the seats. The process is
endless, impossible. Looking out the window, she sees that it is
not her stop after all. She has never seen this neighborhood
before.

Francine wakes all knotted up and her heart hurts. The
dream lingers, lays in her hollows, but as soon as she can grope
free of it, she rises and puts on her slippers and climbs the
narrow staircase to see if the old woman is still breathing.

"I figgered you'd show up." The brassy tones spinning out of
the dark startle Francine. She has never had a secret lover, but
meeting a man might be like this, touchy, dangerous, her skin
prickling. She cannot speak what she wants, doesn't know why
she's come.

"I knowed from the first who you are. I seen your pitcher in the paper."

"You did?" Francine is obliquely disappointed. She'd imagined a special telepathy between them, some rare communion of victims across time. She'd almost forgot about the article, how the reporter held her hand as she talked and the soft sound of the tape recorder munching on her pain.

"Tell me again the part where your hubby says, 'The house is about to shift, Toots.' "

Nobody says *Toots* anymore. Nobody asks her these things. Who would have the nerve? "You mean when we were all up setting on the bed?"

"I believe that's the part. Yep."

"What can I say, Miss Libby? We had the kids between us. We were listening to the rain, hoping the water wouldn't rise no more — it was already past the stair landing. Just after Frank said that, there was a horrible crunching sound and we had to just set there and watch the bathroom split apart. And then the bedroom. 'Ride with it,' he says and then everything was flying and me trying to grab hold of everybody at once. *Don't let go!* one of my girls yelled above the racket. For a second, you know, it was just like we was at the tippy top of the Hershey Park Coaster." Her lips go dry; her mouth sticks, stops.

Libby Quigg huffs impatiently. "Then what?"

"Then something whacked me across the head and back and well, I hardly remember — from being stunned and all."

The old woman pops up in bed. Her voice is like gristle. "You let go of them youngsters, that's what."

Francine tries to ignore the remark. "The coroner came to see me in the hospital. 'Your husband have a missing fingertip?" he wanted to know. 'Your children wear underpants with stars on them?' " Moonlight pushing under the drawn shades sets the nail sparkles aglitter. "Still and all," says Libby Quigg, "As floods go, yours don't amount to beans."

Francine's voice is calm as deepest cold. "No," says she. "It wasn't near so bad as eighty-nine."

"Wanna hear about a *real* flood?"

Francine sits down on the edge of the bed, demurely, innocently, head bowed. As if her heart weren't thundering like ten hearts, as if she had nothing to fear from these details, nothing to gain.

Libby Quigg pinches Francine's thigh. "As you say, Missy, when I'm dang good and ready, mebbe I'll tell you." Then she squeezes creepy eyelids shut and starts to snore.

Francine feels like a fool. "Faker!" she says huskily. "I was plannin' on taking you up the incline next week. But why should I do anything for some old meanie who isn't even no relation of mine."

Libby Quigg opens one eye. "Can I at least have a churry pop to take home with me?" And Francine says, "We'll see."

Several days later Riley telephones to remind Francine she promised — *promised* — Libby Quigg a trip up the incline. Francine can hear the old woman's voice prompting in the background. Shoot, she thinks, but isn't Libby the pisser. Bullheaded, bossy, a little tetched to boot. A scrap on the sleeve of the living. And it's starting to look like Francine is stuck with her. "Riley," she says, "That old lady gets a heck of a kick out of herself."

It has not occurred to Francine to ask if the rushing air might be too much for Libby Quigg. She cannot conceive of harm in air, air flapping around you like a light coat. But the incline plane operator tries to lead Miss Quigg toward the rear of the car, which is more sheltered. His arm moves easily around the small, sloped shoulders, a natural gesture, thinks Francine, in a city of oldsters. It is rare anymore that new people move into town. Most residents have been here for years and now the generations pile up, on the same street, in the same house. Grandmothers are a prized lot, kept out of the cold, in pink sweaters. "Back up a bit, Mom," the boy is saying gently.

By way of reply, Libby Quigg tightens a two-fisted grip on the metal tailgate. The car starts to climb, and Francine imagines herself and Libby as passengers at the windy railing of *Love Boat*, fog boiling around them, glazed salmon and whole lobsters waiting below deck. She wishes she'd thought to bring a small snack.

Pulleys tug them higher and higher. The town spreads out, low-slung and numb-looking under graphite skies. Churches everywhere, craning out of the valley, tucked into the hills and

ridges, the tandem spires of St. Joe's and St. John's. Down by
the stadium, the metallic wishbone formed by three frozen rivers. It shocks her now to see how unbothered the skies are, just
a couple sickly-yellow plumes when years ago you were hard-
pressed to find any sky at all through coils of smoke and fumes.
And if you stood on Prospect Hill when they opened the blast
furnaces you would witness the heavens turn all the gorgeous
shades of Hell. And practically everyone she knows has a relative who'd fallen into a vat of molten steel and been rolled,
pulled, or molded into something useful.

At the top it is already snowing. "Down, please," she says,
politely, just as if she were in Kloiber's elevator. The smooth
descent makes her stomach rise and when she looks down she
cannot find where the land falls away beneath them. "Oh, it *is*
steep," she says to nobody, for Libby Quigg has thrust her head
out and is trying to spit against the airstream.

The old woman refuses to disembark at the base station.
"*No*sir!" she says.

"Well, all right," Francine says uncertainly. "One more time."

By their second descent snow is coming in furious funnels.
The tumultuous air makes Francine feel upended and a little
dizzy. Seeing the terminal approach, Libby Quigg says, "One
more time. You *promised!*"

"Stop saying that! I should know what I promised."

"Tell you about the Big Flood, hope to die!"

"But I'm cold, aren't you?" The word *cold* cracks her voice
into an ugly whine. But fearing the old woman's gift for guff,
sighing, Francine shells out another dollar. Then she draws
Libby Quigg back from the open air. "At least talk where I can
hear you good."

"Okay, okay. Can I borry a hanky first?" Francine shoves a
crumpled tissue into her hand. When Libby Quigg is finished
blowing her nose, she stabs a sudden finger at the heart of town.
"We lived down there," she says. "One-oh-two Jackson. I was
hiding in the attic when my papa called. Course I didn't pay
him no mind. That was my way back then."

"*Then?*" says Francine under her breath. "That's a laugh!"

"My papa called and called and 'fore long I saw him out my
window with Mama and Brother running to beat the band

across the back yards." She pitters her chest, out of breath herself.

"Way-el," she continues, "Just about the same time I hear a turrible, *turrible* sound, like a train roarin' up from Franklin. At first sight it didn't look like nothing but a big wall of dust — later, folks would call it the 'devil mist' — mebbe fifty foot tall at the middle." She makes a careless gesture into the distance and Francine catches herself squinting hard, as if she might make out such a wonder looming high above the bleary rooftops. "How old were you then?" she asks.

"Near seven. And clever for my age!" She gives an abrupt nod. "Now, as you say, anything got in the path of that wave was a goner. Why, St. John's steeple busted off like a icicle. When it comes closer I could see — not water, no you couldn't see no water t'all — just this mountain of stuff, coal cars, rooftops, chimneys, dead cows, church pews. It was such a stupefyin' sight I almost forgot to be askeared, till it hit. Why, that there fine house rockered back and forth just like a tooth bein' yanked." She pauses importantly, jabs a finger in Francine's ribs. "Think of it, Missy! Then all of a sudden them walls split and the floorboards broke upward, all jagged and horrible. I was a falling . . ."

As in a dream of falling, Francine feels her body jerk. Instinctively, she reaches out to grab the old woman's elbow, and when she does Libby Quigg clamps her mouth shut and draws an imaginary zipper across her lips.

Francine says, "You got money to get back if I don't pay the fare?"

Libby Quigg thinks this over. "Oh, all right," she says. "Anyways, next thing I'm hightailin' it across town on a mattress. I yelled to a young fella tryin' to keep his balance on top of a B & O caboose, but he just went his merry way. Solly, the ice man, and his family sweeps by on a big wood floor. My, my, but they was busy beavers, packin' all their belongin's in a little Saratoga trunk. Next second the whole bunch got crushed under that there caboose. A half-nekked fella come by on a pitched roof. He waved and I waved and then he was gone."

Almost absently Francine tucks a few strands of fine hair into Libby Quigg's hat. The old woman squirms against her pleasure. "Pay attention now," she says sternly. "I led an excitin' life up till now."

"I'm not going nowhere, Miss Libby."

"Way-el, soon I was floating along real calm on a cellar door I hooked up with a way back. But just when I started lookin' for a place to drop anchor, so to speak, the current slammed into the mountainside and there I was, a shootin' back the way I come."

Francine gapes incredulously. She shakes her head. Then it comes to her that this is the part toward which she's been steering from the very start. It's the question she has to ask even though somehow she has known the answer since the first time she laid eyes on Libby Quigg. Francine straightens her shoulders and unravels a long breath. "And the family — your papa and them. They — did they — everybody made it to high ground?"

"The dickens they did. They was carried all the way down the crick to the Loyalhanna. And Mama — why, they didn't find Mama t'all. People up on Benschoff Hill took me in and brung me up proper."

There is an instant of perfect white quiet before Francine is taken with craziness. A red hot rush rope-burns her spine; the base of her brain is burning. She clenches and unclenches her fist and then her fingers fly out and take a fearsome grip on Libby Quigg. She digs her nails, presses so hard the tension trembles the old shoulders. Black and canny, Libby's eyes blaze back at her. Francine is wild to speak it. Speak what? The words that say rage and pain and forever are swept like minnows, like grains of sand — like children — into the mouth of God. Everything in Francine's world is either too large or too small. "I . . . ," she starts. "G-god . . ."

"Well, spit it out," says Libby Quigg.

"You!" she says finally, fiercely. "Shame on you! You make that flood sound like the circus come to town, like you was just havin' yourself a ball."

The old woman sniffs and shoves out her lower lip. "So what if I was?" she says coyly. "What if I was?" Daring Francine to make something of it.

With a sudden jerk Francine hitches Libby close to her side, tugs her front and around until they are both belly against the tailgate. "Hey!" squeals Libby in protest. Francine makes another fist and holds it under her mouth like a microphone. She's about as far she's ever been from quiet and pious and gentle. "Hey!" she hollers into raging white space. "Mind your own business, mister!" Libby giggles into her sleeve. Staring down at her, Francine blinks and blinks, breathing very fast and very hard.

They are heading down now for the last time. The *very* last time, Francine has informed the very old child. Watery supper hour lights show through the cold curtain. "Hungry?" she asks. Libby says, "Yup." The car is plunging, rocking into the wind. Libby's hand is cold and smooth as mother-of-pearl. Houses with lighted porches rush up at them and Francine leans out looking hard for one house, half a house, set deep in a teacup town filling fast with snow.

JOY WILLIAMS

The Skater

(FROM ESQUIRE)

ANNIE AND Tom and Molly are looking at boarding schools. Molly is the applicant, fourteen years old. Annie and Tom are the mom and dad. This is how they are referred to by the admissions directors. "Now if Mom and Dad would just make themselves comfortable while we steal Molly away for a moment . . ." Molly is stolen away and Tom and Annie drink coffee. There are brown donuts on a plate. Colored slides are slapped upon a screen showing children earnestly learning and growing and caring through the seasons. These things have been captured. Rather, it's clear that's what they're getting at. The children's faces blur in Tom's mind. And all those autumn leaves. All those laboratories and playing fields and bell towers.

It is winter and there is snow on the ground. They have flown in from California and rented a car. Their plan is to see seven New England boarding schools in five days. Icicles hang from the admissions building. Tom gazes at them. They are lovely and refractive. They are formed and then they vanish. Tom looks away.

Annie is sitting on the other side of the room, puzzling over a mathematics problem. There are sheets of problems all over the waiting room. The sheets are to keep parents and kids on their toes as they wait. Annie's foot is bent fiercely beneath her as though broken. The cold, algebraic problems are presented in little stories. Five times as many girls as boys are taking music lessons or trees are growing at different rates or ladies in a bridge club are lying about their age. The characters and situa-

tions are invented only to be exiled to measurement. Watching
Annie search for solutions makes Tom's heart ache. He remembers a class he took once himself, almost twenty years ago, a
class in myth. In mythical stories, it seems, there were two ways
to disaster. One of the ways was to answer an unanswerable
question. The other was to fail to answer an answerable question.

   Down a corridor there are several shut doors and behind one
is Molly. Molly is their living child. Tom and Annie's other child,
Martha, has been dead a year. Martha was one year older than
Molly. Now Molly is her age. Martha choked to death in her
room on a piece of bread. It was early in the morning and she
was getting ready for school. The radio was playing and two
disc jockeys called the Breakfast Flakes chattered away between
songs.

The weather is bad, the roads are slippery. From the back seat,
Molly says, "He asked what my favorite ice cream was and I
said, 'Quarterback Crunch.' Then he asked who was President
of the United States when the school was founded and I said,
'No one.' Wasn't that good?"
   "I hate trick questions," Annie says.
   "Did you like the school?" Tom asks.
   "Yeah," Molly says.
   "What did you like best about it?"
   "I liked the way our guide, you know, Peter, just walked right
across the street that goes through the campus and the cars just
stopped. You and Mom were kind of hanging back, looking
both ways and all, but Peter and I just trucked right across."
   Molly was chewing gum that smelled like oranges.
   "Peter was cute," Molly says.

Tom and Annie and Molly are at the Motel Lenore. Snow ac-
cumulates beyond the room's walls. There is a small round table
in the room and they sit around it. Molly drinks cranberry juice
from a box and Tom and Annie drink Scotch. They are nowhere. The brochure that the school sent them states that the
school is located thirty-five miles from Boston. Nowhere! They
are all exhausted and merely sit there, regarding their bever-

ages. The television set is chained to the wall. This is indicative, Tom thinks, of considerable suspicion on the part of the management. There was also a four-dollar deposit on the room key. The management, when Tom checked in, was in the person of a child about Molly's age, a boy eating from a bag of potato chips and doing his homework.

"There's a kind of light that glows in the bottom of the water in an atomic reactor that exists nowhere else, do you know that?" the boy said to Tom.

"Is that right?" Tom said.

"Yeah," the boy said, and marked the book he was reading with his pencil. "I think that's right."

The motel room is darkly paneled and there is a picture of a moose between the two beds. The moose is knee-deep in a lake and he has raised his head to some sound, the sound of a hunter approaching, one would imagine. Water drips from his muzzle. The wood he gazes at are dark. Annie looks at the picture. The moose is preposterous and doomed. After a few moments, after she has finished her Scotch, Annie realizes she is waiting to hear the sound. She goes into the bathroom and washes her hands and face. The towel is thin. It smells as if it's been line-dried. It was her idea that Molly go away to school. She wants Molly to be free. She doesn't want her to be afraid. She fears that she is making her afraid, as she is afraid. Annie hears Molly and Tom talking in the other room and then she hears Molly laugh. She raises her fingers to the window frame and feels the cold air seeping in. She adjusts the lid to the toilet tank. It shifts slightly. She washes her hands again. She goes into the room and sits on one of the beds.

"What are you laughing about?" she says. She means to be offhand, but her words come out heavily.

"Did you see the size of that girl's radio in the dorm room we visited?" Molly says, laughing. "It was the biggest radio I'd ever seen. I told Daddy there was a real person lying in it, singing." Molly giggles. She pulls her turtleneck sweater up to just below her eyes.

Annie laughs, then she thinks she has laughed at something terrible, the idea of someone lying trapped and singing. She raises her hands to her mouth. She had not seen a radio large

enough to hold anyone. She saw children in classes, in laboratories in some brightly painted basement. The children were
dissecting sheep's eyes. "Every winter term in Biology you've got
to dissect sheep's eyes," their guide said wearily. "The colors are
really nice though." She saw sacks of laundry tumbled down a
stairwell with names stenciled on them. Now she tries not to see
a radio large enough to hold anyone singing.

At night, Tom drives in his dreams. He dreams of ice, of slick
treachery. All night he fiercely holds the wheel and turns in the
direction of the skid.

In the morning when he returns the key, the boy has been
replaced by an old man with liver spots the size of quarters on
his hands. Tom thinks of asking where the boy is, but then
realizes he must be in school learning about eerie, deathly light.
The bills the old man returns to Tom are soft as cloth.

In California, they live in a canyon. Martha's room is there,
facing the canyon. It is not situated with a glimpse of the ocean
like some of the other rooms. It faces a rocky ledge where owls
nest. The canyon is full of small birds and bitter-smelling
shrubs. There are larger animals too who come down in the
night and drink from the pans of water the family puts out.
Each evening they put out large white pans of clear water and
in the morning the pans are muddy and empty. The canyon is
cold. The sun moves quickly through it. When the rocks are
touched by the sun, they steam. All of Martha's things remain in
her room — the radio, the posters and mirrors and books. It is
a "guest" room now, although no one ever refers to it in that
way. They refer to it as "Martha's room." But it has become a
guest room, even though there are never any guests.

The rental car is blue and without distinction. It is a four-door
sedan with automatic transmission and a poor turning circle.
Martha would have been mortified by it. Martha had a boyfriend who, with his brothers, owned a monster truck. The
Super Swamper tires were as tall as Martha, and all the driver
of an ordinary car would see when it passed by was its colorful
undercarriage with its huge shock and suspension coils, its long

orange stabilizers. For hours on a Saturday they would wallow in sloughs and rumble and pitch across stony creek beds, and then they would wash and wax the truck or, as Dwight, the boyfriend, would say, dazzle the hog. The truck's name was Bear. Tom and Annie didn't care for Dwight, and they hated and feared Bear. Martha loved Bear. She wore a red and white peaked cap with MONSTER TRUCK stenciled on it. After Martha died, Molly put the cap on once or twice. She thought it would help her feel closer to Martha but it didn't. The sweatband smelled slightly of shampoo, but it was just a cap.

Tom pulls into the frozen field that is the parking lot for the Northwall School. The admissions office is very cold. The receptionist is wearing an old worn Chesterfield coat and a scarf. Someone is playing a hesitant and plaintive melody on a piano in one of the nearby rooms. They are shown the woodlot, the cafeteria, and the arts department, where people are hammering out their own silver bracelets. They are shown the language department, where a class is doing tarot card readings in French. They pass a room and hear a man's voice say, "Matter is a sort of blindness."

While Molly is being interviewed, Tom and Annie walk to the barn. The girls are beautiful in this school. The boys look a little dull. Two boys run past them, both wearing jeans and denim jackets. Their hair is short and their ears are red. They appear to be pretending that they are in a drama, that they are being filmed. They dart and feint. One stumbles into a building while the other crouches outside, tossing his head and scowling, throwing an imaginary knife from hand to hand.

Annie tries a door to the barn but it is latched from the inside. She walks around the barn in her high heels. The hem of her coat dangles. She wears gloves on her pale hands. Tom walks beside her, his own hands in his pockets. A flock of starlings fly overhead in an oddly tight formation. A hawk flies above them. The hawk will not fall upon them, clenched like this. If one would separate from the flock, then the hawk could fall.

"I don't know about this 'matter is a sort of blindness' place," Tom says. "It's not what I had in mind."

Annie laughs but she's not paying attention. She wants to get into the huge barn. She tugs at another door. Dirt and flakes of rust smear the palms of her gloves. Then suddenly, the wanting leaves her face.

"Martha would like this school, wouldn't she," she says.

"We don't know, Annie," Tom says. "Please don't, Annie."

"I feel that I've lived my whole life in one corner of a room," Annie says. "That's the problem. It's just having always been in this one corner. And now I can't see anything. I don't even know the room, do you see what I'm saying?"

Tom nods but he doesn't see the room. The sadness in him has become his blood, his life flowing in him. There's no room for him.

In the admissions building, Molly sits in a wooden chair facing her interviewer, Miss Plum. Miss Plum teaches composition and cross-country skiing.

"You asked if I believe in *aluminum?*" Molly asks.

"Yes, dear. Uh-huh, I did," Miss Plum says.

"Well, I suppose I'd have to *believe* in it," Molly says.

Annie has a large cardboard file that holds compartmentalized information on the schools they're visiting. The rules and regulations for one school are put together in what is meant to look like an American passport. In the car's back seat, Molly flips through the book annoyed.

"You can't do anything in this place!" she says. "The things on your walls have to be framed and you can only cover sixty percent of the wall space. You can't wear jeans." Molly gasps. "And you have to eat breakfast!" Molly tosses the small book onto the floor, on top of the ice scraper. She gazes glumly out the window at an orchard. She is sick of the cold. She is sick of discussing her "interests." White fields curve by. Her life is out there somewhere, fleeing from her while she is in the back seat of this stupid car. Her life is never going to be hers. She thinks of it raining, back home in the canyon, the rain falling upon the rain. Her legs itch and her scalp itches. She has never been so bored. She thinks that the worst thing she has done so far in her life was to lie in a hot bath one night, smoking a cigarette and saying *I hate God.* That was the very worst thing. It's pathetic. She bangs her knees irritably against the front seat.

"You want to send me far enough away," she says to her parents. "I mean, it's the other side of the dumb continent. Maybe I don't even want to do this," she says.

She looks at the thick sky holding back snow. She doesn't hate God anymore. She doesn't even think about God. Anybody who would let a kid choke on a piece of bread . . .

The next school has chapel four times a week and an indoor hockey rink. In the chapel, two fir trees are held in wooden boxes. Wires attached to the ceiling hold them upright. It is several weeks before Christmas.

"When are you going to decorate them?" Molly asks Shirley, her guide. Shirley is handsome and rather horrible. The soles of her rubber boots are a bright, horrible orange. She looks at Molly.

"We don't decorate the trees in the chapel," she says.

Molly looks at the tree stumps bolted into the wooden boxes. Beads of sap pearl golden on the bark.

"This is a very old chapel," Shirley says. "See those pillars? They look like marble, but they're just pine, painted to look like marble." She isn't being friendly, she's just saying what she knows. They walk out of the chapel, Shirley soundlessly, on her horrible orange soles.

"Do you play hockey?" she asks.

"No," Molly says.

"Why not?"

"I like my teeth," Molly says.

"You *do*," Shirley says in mock amazement. "Just kidding," she says. "I'm going to show you the hockey rink anyway. It's new. It's a big deal."

Molly sees Tom and Annie standing some distance away beneath a large tree draped with many strings of extinguished lights. Her mother's back is to her, but Tom sees her and waves.

Molly follows Shirley into the cold, odd air of the hockey rink. No one is on the ice. The air seems distant, used up. On one wall is a big painting of a boy in a hockey uniform. He is in a graceful easy posture, skating alone on bluish ice, skating toward the viewer, smiling. He isn't wearing a helmet. He has brown hair and wide golden eyes. Molly reads the plaque beneath the painting. His name is Jimmy Watkins and he had died six years before at the age of seventeen. His parents had built the rink and dedicated it to him.

Molly takes a deep breath. "My sister, Martha, knew him," she says.

"Oh yeah?" Shirley says with interest. "Did your sister go here?"

"Yes," Molly says. She frowns a little as she lies. Martha and Jimmy Watkins of course know each other. They know everything but they have secrets too.

The air is not like real air in here. Neither does the cold seem real. She looks at Jimmy Watkins, bigger than life, skating toward them on his black skates. It is not a very good painting. Molly thinks that those who love Jimmy Watkins must be disappointed in it.

"They were very good friends," Molly says.

"How come you didn't tell me before your sister went here?"

Molly shrugs. She feels happy, happier than she has in a long time. She has brought Martha back from the dead and put her in school. She has given her a room, friends, things she must do. It can go on and on. She has given her a kind of life, a place in death. She has freed her.

"Did she date him or what?" Shirley asks.

"It wasn't like that," Molly says. "It was better than that."

She doesn't want to go much further, not with this girl whom she dislikes, but she goes a little further.

"Martha knew Jimmy better than anybody," Molly says.

She thinks of Martha and Jimmy Watkins being together, telling each other secrets. They will like each other. They are seventeen and fourteen, living in the single moment that they have been gone.

Molly is with her parents in the car again on a winding road, going through the mountains. Tonight they will stay in an inn that Annie has read about and tomorrow they will visit the last school. Several large rocks, crusted with dirty ice, have slid upon the road. They are ringed with red cones and traffic moves slowly around them. The late low sun hotly strikes the windshield.

"Bear could handle those rocks," Molly says. "Bear would go right over them."

"Oh, that truck," Annie says.

"That truck is an ecological criminal," Tom says.

"Big Bad Bear," Molly says.

Annie shakes her head and sighs. Bear is innocent. Bear is only a machine, gleaming in a dark garage.

Molly can't see her parents' faces. She can't remember the way they looked when she was a baby. She can't remember what she and Martha last argued about. She wants to ask them about Martha. She wants to ask them if they are sending her so far away so that they can imagine Martha is just far away too. But she knows she will never ask such questions. There are secrets now. The dead have their secrets and the living have their secrets with the dead. This is the way it must be.

Molly has her things. And she sets them up each night in the room she's in. She lays a little scarf upon the bureau first, and then her things upon it. Painted combs for her hair, a little dish for her rings. They are the only guests at the inn. It is an old rambling structure on a lake. In a few days, the owner will be closing it down for the winter. It's too cold for such an old place in the winter, the owner says. He had planned to keep it open for skating on the lake when he first bought it and had even remodeled part of the cellar as a skate room. There is a bar down there, a wooden floor, and shelves of old skates in all sizes. Window glass runs the length of one wall just above ground level and there are spotlights that illuminate a portion of the lake. But winter isn't the season here. The pipes are too old and there are not enough guests.

"Is this the deepest lake in the state?" Annie asks. "I read that somewhere, didn't I?" She has her guidebooks which she examines each night. Everywhere she goes, she buys books.

"No," the inn's owner says. "It's not the deepest, but it's deep. You should take a look at that ice. It's beautiful ice."

He is a young man, balding, hopelessly proud of his ice. He lingers with them, having given them thick towels and new bars of soap. He offers them venison for supper, fresh bread and pie. He offers them his smooth, frozen lake.

"Do you want to skate?" Tom asks his wife and daughter. Molly shakes her head.

"No," Annie says. She takes a bottle of Scotch from her suitcase. "Are there any glasses?" she asks the man.

"I'm sorry," the man says, startled. He seems to blush. "They're all down in the skate room, on the bar." He gives a slight nod and walks away.

Tom goes down into the cellar for the glasses. The skates, their runners bright, are jumbled upon the shelves. The frozen lake glitters in the window. He pushes open the door and steps out onto the ice. Annie, in their room, waits without taking off her coat, without looking at the bottle. Tom takes a few quick steps and then slides. He is wearing a suit and tie, his good shoes. It is a windy night and the trees clatter with the wind and the old inn's sign creaks on its chains. Tom slides across the ice, his hands pushed out, then he holds his hands behind his back, going back and forth in the space where the light is cast. There is no skill without the skates, he knows, and probably no grace without them either, but it is enough to be here under the black sky, cold and light and moving. He wants to be out here. He wants to be out here with Annie.

From a window, Molly sees her father on the ice. After a moment, she sees her mother moving toward him, not skating, but slipping forward, making her way. She sees their heavy awkward shapes embrace.

Molly sees them, already remembering it.

Biographical Notes

RUSSELL BANKS is the author of eight books of fiction. "Sarah Cole: A Type of Love Story," included in his forthcoming book of stories, *Success Stories,* represents his third appearance in the *Best American Short Stories* series. Mr. Banks teaches at Princeton University and in the Graduate Writing Program at New York University.

MICHAEL BISHOP is the author of eleven novels, including the Nebula Award—winning *No Enemy But Time.* He has also published criticism, poetry, and many short stories, some of which have been gathered into two collections. A volume of his science fiction—related nonfiction, entitled *Alien Graffiti,* will appear in 1986. Mr. Bishop lives in Georgia with his wife and two children.

ETHAN CANIN, a former fiction editor of *The Iowa Review,* now lives in Boston, where he is a student at Harvard Medical School. His stories have appeared in *The Atlantic Monthly, Ploughshares, Redbook,* and elsewhere, and he is the recipient of a Henfield Foundation/*Transatlantic Review* Award.

E. L. DOCTOROW was born in New York City and educated at Kenyon College and Columbia University. He is the author of five novels, *Welcome to Hard Times, Big as Life, The Book of Daniel, Ragtime,* and *Loon Lake;* a play, *Drinks Before Dinner;* and a collection of short stories, *Lives of the Poets.* His new novel, *World's Fair,* will be published by Random House in November 1985.

MARGARET EDWARDS was born in Atlanta, Georgia, and educated at Bryn Mawr College and Stanford University. She teaches American poetry, the short story, and writing at the University of Vermont in Burlington.

STARKEY FLYTHE, JR., is currently a South Carolina Fellow in Literature. He was one of the re-founding editors of *The Saturday Evening Post* in 1971, spent three years with the army in Ethiopia, and has also lived and worked in the Midwest and Georgia. An earlier story of his appeared in an *O. Henry Prize Stories* anthology.

H. E. FRANCIS, whose latest collection of stories is *A Disturbance of Gulls*, published by Braziller, is a professor of English at the University of Alabama in Huntsville. His stories have appeared in the *O. Henry, Best American,* and *Pushcart Prize* anthologies, and he won the Iowa School of Letters Award for Short Fiction in 1973. He translates Argentine literature.

BEV JAFEK lives in San Francisco, where she earns her living writing about scientific and technological subjects. Her fiction has appeared in *Missouri Review, Mississippi Review, Columbia Magazine of Poetry and Prose,* and *Bachy,* among other journals, and has won *Columbia*'s Carlos Fuentes Award. She was educated at Reed College and Brandeis University.

JOHN L'HEUREUX's stories have appeared in *The Atlantic Monthly, Harper's, Esquire, The New Yorker,* and a number of times in the *O. Henry Prize Stories* and *Best American Short Stories* anthologies. His most recent collection is *Desires,* published by Holt, Rinehart and Winston, and he is completing a new novel.

PETER MEINKE is the author of two books of poetry, *The Night Train & the Golden Bird* and *Trying to Surprise God.* His short stories have won awards including the Emily Clark Balch Prize and the PEN Syndicated Fiction Award. One story was selected for the 1983 *O. Henry Prize Stories* volume. He is director of the Writing Workshop at Eckerd College in St. Petersburg, Florida.

WRIGHT MORRIS's recent book is *A Cloak of Light,* the third and final volume of his memoirs.

BHARATI MUKHERJEE is the author of two novels, and her first collection of short stories, *Darkness,* will be published in the fall of 1985. She is also co-author, with her husband, Clark Blaise, of a nonfiction book, *Days and Nights in Calcutta,* which will be reissued in paperback in 1986. Ms. Mukherjee has taught at McGill, Emory, Skidmore, and the Writers' Workshop at the University of Iowa.

BETH NUGENT lives in Iowa City, Iowa. She received an M.F.A. from the Iowa Writers' Workshop in 1982, and her work has appeared in *Mademoiselle, North American Review,* and *Editor's Choice,* Volume I.

JOYCE CAROL OATES's most recent novel is *Solstice,* published by Dutton; her new novel, *Marya: A Life,* will appear in February 1986. She lives in Princeton, New Jersey, where she teaches at the university and helps edit *The Ontario Review.*

NORMAN RUSH's stories have appeared in many magazines, including *The New Yorker, Grand Street,* and *The Paris Review.* From 1978 to 1983 he lived in Africa, and *Whites,* a sequence of African stories, is scheduled for publication in 1986 by Knopf. This is Mr. Rush's third appearance in *The Best American Short Stories.*

MARJORIE SANDOR grew up in Los Angeles. She attended the University of California at Davis and the University of Iowa, and now lives in Boston with her husband. "The Gittel" is her first published story.

DEBORAH SEABROOKE grew up in Huntington, New York, and was educated at Cornell University and the University of North Carolina at Greensboro. Her stories have appeared in *Intro, The Greensboro Review,* and *The Virginia Quarterly Review.* She lives in Greensboro with her husband and two young children, and works at a desk built by her father.

JANE SMILEY teaches at Iowa State University. She is the author of three novels and a number of short stories. She is at work on a historical novel about the medieval Norse settlement on the southern tip of Greenland.

SHARON SHEEHE STARK's stories have appeared in *Agni, Kansas Quarterly,* and *Massachusetts Review,* and her first collection, *The Dealer's Yard and Other Stories,* was published by William Morrow in the spring of 1985. Ms. Stark lives outside Lenhartsville, Pennsylvania, and is finishing a new novel.

JOY WILLIAMS lives in Florida. She is the author of two novels, *State of Grace* and *The Changeling,* and a collection of stories, *Taking Care.*

100 Other Distinguished
Short Stories of the Year 1984

SELECTED BY SHANNON RAVENEL

DICKSON, MARGARET
Can Ball. The Antioch Review, Winter.

DIXON, STEPHEN
Wheels. Western Humanities Review, Summer.

DUBUS, ANDRE
Land Where My Fathers Died. Antaeus, Autumn.

DUFF, GERALD
Fire Ants. Ploughshares, Vol. 10, No. 4.

DYBEK, STUART
Hot Ice. Antaeus, Spring.

FLAHERTY, GERALD
The Man Who Saved Himself. Negative Capability, Winter.

GALLANT, MAVIS
Overhead in a Balloon. The New Yorker, July 2.

GARDINER, JOHN ROLFE
Our Janice. The New Yorker, August 27.

GILDNER, GARY
A Week in South Dakota. The Georgia Review, Fall.
Burial. Tendril, Winter.

GIVNER, JOAN
The Lost Sheep. Wascana Review, Vol. 18, No. 2.

GLOVER, DOUGLAS
Red. Playgirl, September.

GREENBERG, ALVIN
The True Story of How My Grandfather Was Smuggled Out of the Old Country in a Pickle Barrel in Order to Escape Military Conscription. Black Ice, No. 1.

GREENE, PHILIP L.
They Got It All. The Literary Review, Winter.

HELLERSTEIN, DAVID
The Spirit of the Grove. The North American Review, September.

HIERS, CHERYL
Sasha Broken Down. The Crescent Review, Spring.

HITCHCOCK, GEORGE
The Day the Kites Went Away. Quarry West, No. 19.

HUDDLE, DAVID
Only the Little Bone. New England Review and Bread Loaf Quarterly, Winter.

HUGHES, LUCINDA
Western Women Are Tough. The Virginia Quarterly Review, Spring.

JANOWITZ, TAMA
Demons. Mississippi Review, Spring.

JOHNSON, CHARLES
Menagerie, A Child's Fable. Indiana Review, Vol. 7, No. 2.

KINCAID, JAMAICA
A Walk to the Jetty. The New Yorker, November 5.

LIPMAN, ELINOR
Best Men. Playgirl, January.

MASON, BOBBIE ANN
Love Life. The New Yorker, October 29.

MATHEWS, ROBIN
His Own Son. Saturday Night, January.
The Strawberry Field. Descant, Winter.

MAXWELL, WILLIAM
My Father's Friends. The New Yorker, January 30.

MILLER, ELLEN VOTAW
There Is a Balm in Gilead. Mississippi Review, Spring.

MILTON, EDITH
Dwyer's Girl. The Kenyon Review, Spring.

TALLENT, ELIZABETH
Grant of Easement. The New Yorker, December 24.

TARGAN, BARRY
Drexel's Garage. Southwest Review, Spring.

TAYLOR, ROBERT, JR.
The Woman in a Ditch. The Chariton Review, Spring.

TELEKY, RICHARD
Goodnight Sweetheart. New England Review and Bread Loaf Quarterly, Summer.

TINSLEY, MOLLY BEST
The Herb Farm. New England Review and Bread Loaf Quarterly, Spring.

TREADWAY, JESSICA
And Give You Peace. The Hudson Review, Autumn.

TUELL, CYNTHIA
Where I Learned How to Do Things. The Seattle Review, Fall.

UPDIKE, JOHN
Poker Night. Esquire, August.
Slippage. The New Yorker, February 20.

WANNER, IRENE
You Are Here. Ploughshares, Vol. 10, Nos. 2 & 3.

WEAVER, GORDON
The Parts of Speech. The Kenyon Review, Summer.
Whiskey, Whiskey, Gin, Gin, Gin. Quarterly West, Fall/Winter.

WEINTRAUB, J.
The Well of English, Defiled. Ascent, Vol. 10, No. 1.

WHATLEY, WALLACE
Something to Lose. The Southern Review, October.

WHISNANT, LUKE
Wallwork. New Mexico Humanities Review, Summer.

WILKINSON, SYLVIA
Chicken Simon. The Chattahoochee Review, Fall.

WILLIAMS, JOY
Gurdjieff in the Sunshine State. Grand Street, Winter.

WILSON, ERIC
The Axe, the Axe, the Axe. The Massachusetts Review, Vol. 24, No. 3.

WOIWODE, LARRY
Evidence. Antaeus, Spring.

Editorial Addresses of American and Canadian Magazines Publishing Short Stories

When available, the annual subscription rate, the average number of stories published per year, and the name of the editor follow the addresses.

Agni Review
P.O. Box 660
Amherst, MA 01004
$8, 10, Sharon Dunn

A.I.D. Review
American Institute of Discussion
P.O. Box 103
Oklahoma City, OK 73101

Akros Review
University of Akron
Akron, OH 44325

Amazing
Dragon Publishing
P.O. Box 110
Lake Geneva, WI 53147
George Scithers

Analog Science Fiction/Science Fact
380 Lexington Avenue
New York, NY 10017
$19.50, 70, Stanley Schmidt

Antaeus
18 West 30th Street
New York, NY 10001
$20 (two years), 15, Daniel Halpern

Antietam Review
33 West Washington Street
Hagerstown, MD 21740
$3, 10, Ellyn Bache

Antioch Review
P.O. Box 148
Yellow Springs, OH 45387
$18, 25, Robert S. Fogarty

Apalachee Quarterly
P.O. Box 20106
Tallahassee, FL 32304
$12, 30, Allen Woodman, Barbara Hanby, Monica Faeth

Aphra
469 62nd Street
Brooklyn, NY 11220

Arizona Quarterly
University of Arizona
Tucson, AZ 85721
$5, 12, Albert F. Gegenheimer

Ascent
English Department
University of Illinois
Urbana, IL 61801
$3, 20, Daniel Curley

Atlantic Monthly
8 Arlington Street
Boston, MA 02116
$9.75, 18, C. Michael Curtis

Aura Literary/Arts Review
117 Campbell Hall
University Station
Birmingham, AL 35294
$6, 10, rotating editorship

Asimov's Science Fiction Magazine
380 Lexington Avenue
New York, NY 10017
$19.50, 65, Shawna McCarthy

Bennington Review
Bennington College
Bennington, VT 05201
$4, varies, Nicholas Delbanco

Black Ice
Black Ice Press
571 Howell Avenue
Cincinnati, OH 45220
20, Dale Shank

Black Warrior Review
P.O. Box 2936
University, AL 35486
$5.50, 12, Kim Thomas

Bloodroot
P.O. Box 891
Grand Forks, ND 58201
$9, 3, Joan Eades, Dan Eades, Linda Ohlsen

Brown Journal of the Arts
Box 1852
Brown University
Providence, RI 02912
rotating editorship

California Quarterly
100 Sproul Hall
University of California
Davis, CA 95616
$10, 4, Elliott L. Gilbert

California Voice
1782 Pacific Avenue
San Francisco, CA 94109

Canadian Fiction
Box 946
Station F
Toronto, Ontario
M4Y 2N9 Canada
$30, 40, Geoffrey Hancock

Capilano Review
Capilano College
2055 Purcell Way
North Vancouver
British Columbia
Canada
$9, 6–10, Dorothy Jantzen

Carolina Quarterly
Greenlaw Hall 066A
University of North Carolina
Chapel Hill, NC 27514
$10, 20, rotating editorship

Chariton Review
Division of Language & Literature
Northeast Missouri State University
Kirksville, MO 63501
$4, 10, Jim Barnes

Chattahoochee Review
DeKalb Community College
2101 Womack Road
Dunwoody, GA 30338
$12.50, 25, Lamar York

Chelsea
P.O. Box 5880
Grand Central Station
New York, NY 10163
$9, 6, Sonia Raiziss

Chicago Review
5700 South Ingleside
Box C
University of Chicago
Chicago, IL 60637
$10, 20, Victor King, Felicia Sonn

Christopher Street
249 West Broadway
New York, NY 10013
$24, 12, Thomas E. Steele

Cimarron Review
208 Life Sciences East
Oklahoma State University
Stillwater, OK 74078
$10, 20, Neil John Hatchett

Clockwatch Review
Driftwood Publications
737 Penbrook Way
Hartland, WI 53029
$6, 5, James Plath

Colorado State Review
360 Eddy Building
Colorado State University
Fort Collins, CO 80523
$5, 10, Wayne Ude

Columbia Magazine of Poetry and
  Prose
404 Dodge Hall
Columbia University
New York, NY 10027
$4.50, varies, rotating editorship

Commentary
165 East 56th Street
New York, NY 10022
$33, 5+, Marion Magid

Confrontation
English Department
C.W. Post College of Long Island
  University
Greenvale, NY 11548
$8, 25, Martin Tucker

Cottonwood Magazine
Box J
Kansas Union
Lawrence, KS 66045
$12, 15, Sharon Oard Warner

Crazyhorse
Department of English
University of Arkansas
Little Rock, AR 72204
$8, 10, David Jauss

Creative Pittsburgh
P.O. Box 7346
Pittsburgh, PA 15213

Crescent Review
P.O. Box 15065
Winston-Salem, NC 27103
$7.50, 24, Bob Shar

Crosscurrents
2200 Glastonbury Road
Westlake Village, CA 91361
$15, 50, Linda Brown Michelson

CutBank
Department of English
University of Montana
Missoula, MT 59801
$6.50, 10, Joyce H. Brosin

December Press
3093 Dato
Highland Park, IL 60035
$12.50, 6, Curt Johnson

Denver Quarterly
University of Denver
Denver, CO 80208
$12, 16, David Milofsky

Descant
P.O. Box 314
Station P
Toronto, Ontario
M5S 2S5 Canada
$18, 20+, Karen Mulhallen

descant
Department of English
Texas Christian University Station
Fort Worth, TX 76129
$6.50, varies, Betsy Colquitt

Ecology Digest
P.O. Box 60961
Sacramento, CA 95860
Max Peters

Epoch
245 Goldwin Smith Hall
Cornell University
Ithaca, NY 14823
$8, 20, C. S. Giscombe

Esquire
2 Park Avenue
New York, NY 10016
$17.94, 10+ (fiction issue), Rust Hills

Event
Kwantlen College
P.O. Box 9030
Surrey, British Columbia
V3T 5H8 Canada
$8, 10, Leona Gem

Expanding Horizons
93-05 68th Avenue
Forest Hills, NY 11375

Fantasy & Science Fiction
Box 56
Cornwall, CT 06753
$17.50, 100, Edward L. Ferman

Fiction
Department of English
City College of New York
New York, NY 10031

Fiction/84 (see Gargoyle)

Fiction International
Department of English
San Diego State University
San Diego, CA 92182
$12, 25, Harold Jaffe, Larry McCaffery

Fiction Monthly
545 Haight Street
Suite 67
San Francisco, CA 94117
free, 20, Stephen Woodhams

Fiction Network
P.O. Box 5651
San Francisco, CA 94101
Jay Schaefer

Fiction-Texas
College of the Mainland
Texas City, TX 77590

Fiddlehead
The Observatory
University of New Brunswick
Fredericton, New Brunswick
E3B 5A3 Canada
$15, 20, Kent Thompson

Florida Review
Department of English
University of Central Florida
Orlando, FL 32816
$6, 16, Pat Rushin

Four Quarters
LaSalle College
20th and Olney Avenues
Philadelphia, PA 19141
$8, 10–12, John Christopher Kleis

From Mt. San Angelo
Virginia Center for the Creative Arts
Sweet Briar, VA 24595
9, William Smart

Gargoyle
Paycock Press
P.O. Box 3567
Washington, D.C. 20007
$10, 25, Richard Peabody, Gretchen Johnsen

Georgia Review
University of Georgia
Athens, GA 30602
$9, 12, Stanley W. Lindberg, Stephen Corey

Good Housekeeping
959 Eighth Avenue
New York, NY 10019
$14.97, 24, Naomi Lewis

Grain
Box 1885
Saskatoon, Saskatchewan
S7K 3S2 Canada
$9, 15, Brenda Riches

Grand Street
50 Riverside Drive
New York, NY 10024
$20, 20, Ben Sonnenberg

Gray's Sporting Journal
42 Bay Road
South Hamilton, MA 01982
$23.50, 8, Edward E. Gray

Great River Review
211 West 7th
Winona, MN 55987
$7, 12, Orval Lund

Greensboro Review
Department of English
University of North Carolina
Greensboro, NC 27412
12, Lee Zacharias

Harper's Magazine
2 Park Avenue
New York, NY 10016
$18, 12, Gerald Marzorati

Harpoon
P.O. Box 2581
Anchorage, AK 99510

Hawaii Review
University of Hawaii
Department of English
1733 Donaghho Road
Honolulu, HI 96822
$6, 12, Holly Yamada

Helicon Nine
P.O. Box 22412
Kansas City, MO 64113
$15, 6, Ann Slegman

Hoboken Terminal
P.O. Box 841
Hoboken, NJ 07030
$6, 15, C. H. Trowbridge, Jack Nestor

Hudson Review
684 Park Avenue
New York, NY 10021
$16, 8, Paula Deitz, Frederick Morgan

Indiana Review
316 North Jordan Avenue
Bloomington, IN 47405
$10, 20, Jim Brock

Iowa Review
EPB 308
University of Iowa
Iowa City, IA 52242
$12, varies, David Hamilton

Issues
Box 1930
Brown University
Providence, RI 02912

James White Literary Review
P.O. Box 3356
Traffic Station
Minneapolis, MN 55403
Phil Wilkie

Jewish Monthly
1640 Rhode Island Avenue NW
Washington, D.C. 20036
$8, 3, Marc Silver

Kansas Quarterly
Department of English
Denison Hall
Kansas State University
Manhattan, KS 66506
$12, 35, Harold Schneider, Ben Nyberg,
  John Rees

Karamu
English Department
Eastern Illinois University
Charleston, IL 61920

Kenyon Review
Kenyon College
Gambier, OH 43022
$15, 15, Philip D. Church, Galbraith M.
  Crump

Ladies' Home Journal
3 Park Avenue
New York, NY 10016
$20, 10, Constance Leisure

Lilith
The Jewish Women's Magazine
250 West 57th Street
New York, NY 10019
$12, 4, Susan Weidman Schneider

Literary Review
Fairleigh Dickinson University
Madison, NJ 07940
$12, 25, Walter Cummins

Little Magazine
Dragon Press
P.O. Box 78
Pleasantville, NY 10570
$16, 5, David Hartwell

Mademoiselle
350 Madison Avenue
New York, NY 10017
$12, 14, Eileen Schnurr

Malahat Review
University of Victoria
Box 1700
Victoria, British Columbia
V8W 2Y2 Canada
$15, 25, Constance Rooke

Massachusetts Review
Memorial Hall
University of Massachusetts
Amherst, MA 01002
*$12, 12, Mary Heath, John Hicks, Fred
    Robinson*

Matrix
Box 510
Lennoxville, Quebec
J1M 1Z7 Canada

McCall's
230 Park Avenue
New York, NY 10169
$9.95, 20, Helen DelMonte

Mendocino Review
18601 North Highwood One
Fort Bragg, CA 95437
$8.95, 40–50, Amanda Avery

Michigan Quarterly Review
3032 Rackham Building
University of Michigan
Ann Arbor, MI 48109
$13, 10, Laurence Goldstein

Mid-American Review
106 Hanna Hall
Department of English
Bowling Green State University
Bowling Green, OH 48109
$6, 12, Robert Early

Minnesota Review
Department of English
Oregon State University
Corvallis, OR 97331
$7, varies, Fred Pfeil

Mississippi Review
Southern Station
Box 5144
Hattiesburg, MI 39406-5144
$10, 25, Frederick Barthelme

Missouri Review
Department of English, 231 A&S
University of Missouri
Columbia, MO 65211
$10, 25, Speer Morgan, Greg Michalson

Mother Jones
1663 Mission Street
San Francisco, CA 94103
$12, 6, Dierdre English, Ruth Henrich

Ms.
199 West 40th Street
New York, NY 10018
$14, 15, Ruth Sullivan

MSS
Department of English
State University of New York
Binghamton, NY 13901
$10, 30, Liz Rosenberg

Nantucket Review
P.O. Box 1234
Nantucket, MA 02254
$6, 15, Richard Burns, Richard Cumbie

National Jewish Monthly
1640 Rhode Island Avenue NW
Washington, D.C. 20036

Nebraska Review
Writers' Workshop
ASH 215
University of Nebraska
Omaha, NE 68182
$5, 6–8, Art Homer, Richard Duggin

Negative Capability
6116 Timberly Road North
Mobile, AL 36609
$12, 14, Sue Walker, Ron Walker

New Directions
W. W. Norton Company
500 Fifth Avenue
New York, NY 10110
*$ to be announced, 12, James Laughlin,
    Peter Glassgold*

New England Review and Bread Loaf
    Quarterly
Box 170
Hanover, NH 03755
*$12, 20, Sydney Lea, Jim Schley, Maura
    High*

New Laurel Review
828 Lesseps Street
New Orleans, LA 71007
$8, 4, Lee Meitzen Grue

New Letters
University of Missouri
5346 Charlotte
Kansas City, MO 64110
$15, 20, David Ray

New Mexico Humanities Review
Box A
New Mexico Tech
Socorro, NM 87801
$8, 15, John Rothfork

New Orleans Review
Loyola University
New Orleans, LA 70118
$20, 15, John Biguenet

New Quarterly
English Language Proficiency
    Programme
The University of Waterloo
Waterloo, Ontario
N2L 3G1 Canada
20, Harold Horwood

New Renaissance
9 Heath Road
Arlington, MA 02174
*$10.50, 11, Louise T. Reynolds, Harry
    Jackel*

The New Yorker
25 West 43rd Street
New York, NY 10036
$32, 100

North American Review
1222 West 27th Street
Cedar Falls, IA 50614
$11, 35+, Robley Wilson, Jr.

Northwest Review
369 PLC
University of Oregon
Eugene, OR 97403
$11, 25, Cecelia Hagen

Ohio Journal
Department of English
Ohio State University
164 West 17th Avenue
Columbus, OH 43210
$5, 4

Ohio Review
Ellis Hall
Ohio University
Athens, OH 45701
$12, 20, Wayne Dodd

Old Hickory Review
P.O. Box 1178
Jackson, TN 38301
$5, 5, Dorothy Stanfill

Omni
909 Third Avenue
New York, NY 10022
$24, 36, Ellen Datlow

Only Prose
54 East 7th Street
New York, NY 10003

Ontario Review
9 Honey Brook Drive
Princeton, NJ 08540
$8, 8, Raymond J. Smith

Paris Review
45-39 171 Place
Flushing, NY 11358
$16, 18, George Plimpton

Partisan Review
121 Bay State Road
Boston, MA 02215
$16, 12, William Phillips

Passages North
William Boniface Fine Arts Center
7th Street & 1st Avenue South
Escanaba, MI 49829
$2, 12, Elinor Benedict

Pequod
536 Hill Street
San Francisco, CA 94114
$9, 4, Mark Rudman

Piedmont Literary Review
The Piedmont Literary Society
P.O. Box 3656
Danville, VA 24543
$10, 8, David Craig

Playboy
919 North Michigan Avenue
Chicago, IL 60611
$22, 20, Alice K. Turner, Teresa Grosch

Playgirl
3420 Ocean Park Boulevard
Suite 3000
Santa Monica, CA 90405
$20, 12, Mary Ellen Strote

Ploughshares
P.O. Box 529
Cambridge, MA 02139
$14, 25, DeWitt Henry

Plum
1121 First Ave #4
Salt Lake City, UT 84103

Poetry East
Star Route 1
Earlysville, VA 22936
$10, 5, Richard Jones

Prairie Schooner
201 Andrews Hall
University of Nebraska
Lincoln, NE 68588
$11, 20, Hugh Luke

Present Tense
165 East 56th Street
New York, NY 10022
$14, 4, Murray Polner

Primavera
Ida Noyes Hall
University of Chicago
1212 East 59th Street
Chicago, IL 60637
$5, 7

Prism International
University of British Columbia
Vancouver, British Columbia
V6T 1W5 Canada
$10, 12, Chris Petty

Quarry West
Porter College
University of California
Santa Cruz, CA 95060

Quarterly West
312 Olpin Union
University of Utah
Salt Lake City, UT 84112
$6.50, 10, Wyn Cooper

RE:AL
Stephen F. Austin State University
Nacogdoches, TX 75962

Reconstructionist
270 West 89th Street
New York, NY 10024
Dr. Jacob J. Staub

Redbook
230 Park Avenue
New York, NY 10017
$11.97, 35, Kathy Sagan

Richmond Quarterly
P.O. Box 12263
Richmond, VA 23241
$10, 20, Jerry Lazarus

River City Review
P.O. Box 34275
Louisville, KY 40232
$5, 12, Sandra Dutton

Rubicon
McGill University
853 rue Sherbrooke ouest
Montreal, Quebec
H3A 2T6 Canada
$8, 10, Peter O'Brien

Salmagundi Magazine
Skidmore College
Saratoga Springs, NY 12866
$10, 2, Robert and Peggy Boyers

San Jose Studies
San Jose State University
San Jose, CA 95192
$12, 3, Fanneil J. Rinn

Saturday Night
70 Bond Street
Suite 500
Toronto, Ontario
M5B 2J3 Canada

Seattle Review
Padelford Hall
GN-30
University of Washington
Seattle, WA 98195
$6, 10, Charles Johnson

Seventeen
850 Third Avenue
New York, NY 10022
$13.95, 12, Bonni Price

Sewanee Review
University of the South
Sewanee, TN 37375
$12, 10, George Core

Shenandoah
Box 722
Lexington, VA 24450
$8, 12, James Boatwright

Shout in the Street
Queens College of the City University
   of New York
63-30 Kissena Boulevard
Flushing, NY 11367

Sidewinder
Division of Arts and Humanities
8001 Palmer Highway
Texas City, TX 77591
$3, 8, Brett Jarrett, Thomas Carter

Sinister Wisdom
P.O. Box 1023
Rockland, ME 04841
$14, varies, Melanie Kaye/Kantrowitz

South Carolina Review
Department of English
Clemson University
Clemson, SC 29631
$5, Richard J. Calhoun, Robert W. Hill

South Dakota Review
University of South Dakota
Vermillion, SD 57069
$10, varies (22 in 1984), John R. Milton

Southern Humanities Review
9088 Haley Center
Auburn University, AL 36849
$9, 8, Dan R. Latimer, Thomas L.
   Wright

Southern Review
Drawer D
University Station
Baton Rouge, LA 70893
$9, 20, Lewis P. Simpson, James Olney

Southwest Review
Southern Methodist University
Dallas, TX 75275
$10, 12–16, Betsey Mc Dougall

Sou'wester
Department of English
Southern Illinois University
Edwardsville, IL 62026
$4, 9, Dickie Spurgeon

St. Andrews Review
St. Andrews Presbyterian College
Laurinsburg, NC 28352
$12, 5, Dr. Robbie Rankin

Stories
14 Beacon Street
Boston, MA 02108
$20, 30, Amy R. Kaufman

Story Quarterly
P.O. Box 1416
Northbrook, IL 60062
$12, 20, Anne Brashler

Tendril
Box 512
Green Harbor, MA 02041
$12, 12, George E. Murphy, Jr.

Texas Review
English Department
Sam Houston State University
Huntsville, TX 77341
$4.20, 10–12, Paul Ruffin

13th Moon
Box 309
Cathedral Station
New York, NY 10025
$13, varies, Marilyn Hacker

Threepenny Review
P.O. Box 9131
Berkeley, CA 94709
$8, 10, Wendy Lesser

TriQuarterly
1735 Benson Avenue
Northwestern University
Evanston, IL 60201
$16, 60, Reginald Gibbons

Twilight Zone Magazine
800 Second Avenue
New York, NY 10017
$11.97, 45, T.E.D. Klein

U.S. Catholic
221 West Madison Street
Chicago, IL 60606

University of Windsor Review
Department of English
University of Windsor
Windsor, Ontario
N9B 3P4 Canada
$10, 10, Alastair McLeod

Vanderbilt Review
911 West Vanderbilt Street
Stephenville, TX 76401

Virginia Quarterly Review
One West Range
Charlottesville, VA 22903
$10, 12, Staige D. Blackford

Wascana Review
English Department
University of Regina
Regina, Saskatchewan
Canada
$5, 8, Joan Givner

Waves
79 Denham Drive
Richmond Hill, Ontario
L4C 6H9 Canada
$8, 20, Marvyne Jenoff

Webster Review
Webster University
Webster Groves, MO 63119
$5, 6, Nancy Schapiro

West Branch
Department of English
Bucknell University
Lewisburg, PA 17837
$5, 10, Karl Patten, Robert Taylor

Western Humanities Review
University of Utah
Salt Lake City, UT 84112
$15, 10, Jack Garlington

Whispers
70 Highland Avenue
Binghamton, NY 13905
$10.95, 30, Stuart D. Schiff

Wind/Literary Review
RFD #1
Box 809K
Pikeville, KY 41501
$6, 18, Quentin R. Howard

Wittenberg Review
Box 1
Wittenberg University
Springfield, OH 45501
$3.50, 3, Candice J. Floyd

Writers Forum
University of Colorado
P.O. Box 7150
Colorado Springs, CO 80933
$8.95, 15, Alexander Blackburn

Yale Review
250 Church Street
1902A Yale Station
New Haven, CT 06520
$14, 12, Mr. Kai Erikson

Yankee
Yankee, Inc.
Dublin, NH 03444
$15, 10, Deborah Navas

10087085
ISBN 0-395-39058-3